A LINE IN THE STARS

THE STARDOCK TRILOGY
BOOK THREE

Sean Fenian

Fenian House Publishing

Bearing Gifts — United Fleet — A Line In The Stars

I0637537

COPYRIGHT DECLARATION:

DISCLAIMER:

Colonel Iain Colin Mackenzie's name is used here in all due and proper respect. As one might perhaps infer, many details about his background have been omitted. Additionally, Patrick Hess appears by his agreement and consent.

Otherwise, all of the characters in this story are fictional. Some organizations and official positions mentioned are (obviously) real, but have no *actual* connection to any persons or events described in this story. Any direct coincidence of name with any actual living person is just that: A coincidence. There are only *just so many* possible unique names.

Any mention in this book of any present-day established trademark is not a challenge to that trademark.

References? *Of course* there are references.

Publication History:

First Electronic Edition September 2024

First Print Edition February 2025

Second Electronic Edition March 2026

Second Print Edition March 2026

Print ISBN 979-8-9926260-2-5

Formatting Conventions and Pacing:

This novel is intended to be styled like a storyteller at the bar spinning a yarn that's so good nobody is willing to challenge its veracity.

Where you see a single line of vertical space, as is above this line, imagine the narrator taking a breath to pause—or the characters pausing for a moment in brief thought before speaking again.

A larger double-line space, such as here, is akin to the raconteur pausing to replenish with half a pint and some pretzels; or, within the story, for an extended break between the characters that does not necessarily involve a change of viewpoint or scene. Now might be an ideal time to make a cup of tea, if you're so inclined, or otherwise attend to life.

═════

Finally, a double horizontal bar like this one denotes a scene or perspective break within a chapter: the scene or the viewpoint has changed, but no lengthy narrative pause is *necessarily* implied (although there *usually* is one).

Of course, we at Fenian House strongly advise you to read how you want, on your own schedule. The above is our guide to how to read our *intended* pacing of the text; but our suggestions are just, only, that. You paid good money for this book; we are your humble bards.

A Line In The Stars

ACKNOWLEDGMENTS

THANKS GO OUT TO:

Fellow author **John Shirley** for hints and early critique on *Bearing Gifts*, as well as for his kind words of praise on it that helped encourage me to complete it;

Fellow author **Mackey Chandler** and my growing team of beta readers, **Ralock Kaltan, Douglas King, Sam Latham, Jeff Geauvreau** and others, for proofreading and being sounding-boards;

Alicia Aldridge, Cassie Hanjian, and all of the rest of the crew at **Podium Entertainment**, plus of course narrator **Michael Karl Orenstein**, for all of the hard work that they have put into the audiobook editions of the Stardock Trilogy;

The **Bitminers** and **Callahanians** for ship name suggestions, entries in the Ginza naming poll, and other assistance;

And to my family, for putting up with the time that I have put into writing this series over the past nearly a year and a half (and my occasional crankiness during the process, especially when particular passages weren't going well).

DRAMATIS PERSONAE

THE UNITED FLEET:

Alex Holder, Fleet Actual

Naomi Tomlinson, State Department liaison to the Fleet

Seok Dong-geun, Alex's Chief of Staff and Delegate to the United Nations

Seok Hae, Dong-geun's wife

Seok Dae-hyun, elder son of Seok Dong-geun, XO of DD-44 *Arapaima*

Seok Yeon, elder daughter of Dong-geun and Hae

Seok Choon-mae, younger son of Dong-geun and Hae

Seok Jia, younger daughter of Dong-geun and Hae

Captain Thomas Whitman, formerly Royal Navy

Captain Sandra Hayes, formerly Royal Australian Navy

Commander Angavu Onyango, captain of DD-01 *Mako*, Commodore of DesRon One

Commander Hussein Onyango, captain of DD-02 *Tigershark*

Commander Mahfoud Hadj, captain of DD-03 *Bullshark*

Commander Walt 'Hammer' Berger, captain of DD-04 *Blacktip*

Commander Jean-Michel LeBarré, captain of DD-05 *Great White*

Commander Jan Witsteen, captain of DD-06 *Thresher*

Commander Tegbir Singh, Jan Witsteen's XO on DD-06 *Thresher*

Commander Somchai Pravat, captain of DD-07 *Requiem*

Commander Maksim Chernaev, captain of DD-08 *Hammerhead*

Lieutenant Chad Harper, sensors board on DD-08 *Hammerhead*

Lieutenant Irina Pugachevna, helm on DD-08 *Hammerhead*

Commander Piet Beekhof, captain of DD-14 *Snoak*

Commander Jabari Ndungu, captain of DD-16 *Scorpionfish*, Commodore of DesRon Two

Commander Julio Dominguez, captain of DD-19 *Seawolf*

Lieutenant Eduardo Torres, damage control, DD-19 *Seawolf*

Lieutenant Juan Espinoza, sensors board, DD-19 *Seawolf*

Commander Jeanne Petrie, captain of DD-21 *Sailfish*

Lieutenant Franz Blick, main gunnery, DD-21 *Sailfish*

Lieutenant Mario Cardinale, damage control, DD-21 *Sailfish*

Captain Pierre du Maurier, captain of DD-25 *Blackfish*, Commodore of DesRon Three

Commander Ae Morita, captain of DD-29 *Devilfish*

Lieutenant Kenichi Sato, sensors officer, DD-29 *Devilfish*

Lieutenant Hiromi Yoshida, navigator, DD-29 *Devilfish*

Captain Sarah Burke, captain of DD-33 *Ballarat*

Lieutenant-Commander Pete Bjarnesen, Sarah Burke's XO on DD-33 *Ballarat*

Commander Dangali Abubakar, captain of DD-34 *Shingen*

Commander Soichiro Kusanagi, captain of DD-35 *Inazuma*

Lieutenant Khun Satt Naing, secondary CIC damage control officer, DD-35 *Inazuma*

Captain (formerly Colonel) Iain Colin Mackenzie, captain of DD-37 *Highlander*, Commodore of DesRon Four

Lieutenant Megan Kerry, sensors, DD-37 *Highlander*

Commander David Googan, captain of DD-42 *Perth*

Lieutenant David Morgan, comms, DD-42 *Perth*

Commander Nang Tae-suk, captain of DD-44 *Arapaima*

Lieutenant-Commander Peter Arcie, Chief Engineer of DD-44 *Arapaima*

Commander Ruth Goldin, captain of DD-45 *Livyatan*

Lieutenant Kim Rogers, helm, DD-45 *Livyatan*

Lieutenant Mitch Hendricks, main weapons board, DD-45 *Livyatan*

Lieutenant Astrid Eriksen, sensors board, DD-45 *Livyatan*

Commander Eugen Dietrich, captain of CG-05 *Hannibal*

Lieutenant Kamal Bouaziz, sensors officer, CG-05 *Hannibal*

Lieutenant-Commander Alice Watson, Chief Engineer, GOU *There Exists An Elegant Solution*

Lieutenant Mikko Tarpanen, helm, GOU *There Exists An Elegant Solution*

Major John Warner, O/C 1st Battalion, United Fleet Marines

Captain Janine Saulnier, O/C 1st Company, United Fleet Marines

Lieutenant Joshua Newton, O/C 2nd Company, United Fleet Marines

Sergeant Maria Rodriguez, 5th Platoon, 1st Company, United Fleet Marines

Lieutenant Tim Finnegan, 2nd Company, United Fleet Marines

Rifleman Patrick Hess, 2nd Company, United Fleet Marines

Major Jacques Petain, O/C 3rd Company, United Fleet Marines

Lieutenant Achille Marne, 3rd Company, United Fleet Marines

Major Yousef al-Hussein, O/C 4th Company, United Fleet Marines

Sergeant Omar Kharif, 3rd Platoon, 4th Company, United Fleet Marines

Major Hafez Khalil, O/C 5th Company, United Fleet Marines

Chief Petty Officer Jeff Rankine

Captain Philippe Devreaux, Chief Medical Officer, MedBay Two

Suzanne Lemeurier, research psychologist from the Sorbonne, Paris, France

Lewis Monaghan, naval engineer, formerly of General Dynamics Electric Boat division

Quartermaster Jorge Ferreyra, Córdoba, Argentina

Chef Masahiro Fumi, Nagoya, Japan

Peter Watts, assistant chef, Wellington, NZ

László Sárközy, bartender, from Budapest, Hungary

Sofiia Tyshchenko, bartender, from Kyiv, Ukraine

Oksana Holovka, bartender, from Kyiv, Ukraine

Nadiya Simonovna, bartender, from Kyiv, Ukraine

THE K'HEERT'NA:

Fleet-Leader Swims-Like-Rock, overall fleet commander of Clan Hsieuuu

Hunt-Master Thoughtful, captain of the front-runner *Silent Tracker*

Wayfinder Notices-Things, navigation board on *Silent Tracker*

Wayfinder Sleeps-A-Lot, helm position on *Silent Tracker*

Hunter Listens-Carefully, sensors board on *Silent Tracker*

Maker Of-Course-It-Works, chief engineer on *Silent Tracker*

Hunt-Master Heavy-Step, captain of the front-runner *Follow The Spoor*

Hunt-Master Motionless, captain of the front-runner *Careful Stalker*

Hunt-Master Tireless, captain of the front-runner *Chaser*

Hunter Torn-Ear, sensors board on *Chaser*

Wayfinder Runs-Silently, helm on *Chaser*

Maker Already-Done, chief engineer on *Chaser*

Hunt-Master Muddy-Tail, captain of the front-runner *Step Carefully*

Hunt-Master Broken-Tooth, captain of the huntship *Sharp Claws*

Hunter Red-Stripe, sensors board on *Sharp Claws*

Far-Speaker Stop-Shouting, comms board on *Sharp Claws*

Hunt-Master Sleeps-Lightly, captain of the huntship *Swift Runner*

Wayfinder No-*This*-Path, navigation board on *Swift Runner*

Maker Sometimes-Too-Clever, chief engineer on *Swift Runner*

Hunter Sharp-Whistle, a weapons officer on *Swift Runner*

Hunter Bright-Edge, a weapons officer on *Swift Runner*

Has-Doubts, a crew member on *Swift Runner*

Reads-Too-Much, a crew member on *Swift Runner*

Too-Cautious, a crew member on *Swift Runner*

Steady-Paws, a crew member on *Swift Runner*

Knows-Things, a crew member on *Swift Runner*

Hunter White-Nose, a weapons officer on *Strong Paws*

Hunt-Master Good-Eyes, captain of *Reach Far*

Hunter Wicked-Grin, a weapons officer on *Reach Far*

Wayfinder Too-Brash, helm on *Reach Far*

Hunt-Master Helpful, captain of *High Flier*

Hunter Always-Laughs, sensors board on *High Flier*

Nest-Protector Cub-At-Heart, captain of the nest-defender *Stand Fast*

Nest-Defender Waits-In-Silence, captain of the nest-defender *Fierce Protector*

Nest-Protector Likes-Water, captain of the nest-defender *Steady*

WORLD FIGURES:

John Riken, President of the United States

Miranda Ramirez, Vice-President of the United States

Dr. Edward Wegener, National Security Advisor

Dr. Jocelyn Winters, Secretary of State

Rear-Admiral David Hackett, Director of National Intelligence

General Robert H. Morgan, Chairman of the Joint Chiefs

Ayhan Göğebakan, President of the Republic of Türkiye

Hozan Îbrahîm, envoy from the Kurdistan Workers' Party

Konstantin (Kostya) Yanushevich Molchalin, President of the Russian Federation

General Vasily Dmitrievich Belyenov, Russian Federation

General Yuri Ilyich Kuskovsky, Russian Federation

General Valentin Mikhailovich Korolev, Russian Federation

Admiral Feliks Goryaev, Russian Federation

Li Xeung, General Secretary of the Chinese Communist Party

THE PRESS:

Debora Carroll, a health-and-medicine reporter for CNN

Mustapha bin-Alman, al-Jazeera

Irma Müller, Der Spiegel

Luc Bourdain, Paris-Match

Tatsumi Nomura, NHK World, Japan

Peter Tallwick, BBC

Moira Doneghan, BBC

Jessie Walters, a New York Times reporter in the White House press pool

Bryan Johnson, a Fox reporter in the White House press pool

Magdalen Cortez, Los Angeles Times

Alan Sylvestri, The Guardian

Toshiro Akagi, Asahi Shimbun

Peter Chen, South China Morning Post

Sarah Wade, Washington Post

Carl Borrauma, New Orleans Times-Picayune

John Marchesanti, New York Times

OTHERS:

Eithne Coburn, niece of Debora Carroll, first patient in the Last Chance pediatric program

David and Louise Coburn, parents of Eithne Coburn

Dave Edwards and Bob Howard, LIGO researchers at CalTech

János Szilágyi, a visiting physicist from the Institute of Physics in Budapest, Hungary

General James Matheson, Chief of Staff of the USAF

Stephanie Monaghan, United States Ambassador to the United Nations

Brian Watson, Prime Minister of Australia

Susan Wilder, Naomi Tomlinson's superior at the State Department

A Line In The Stars

Prologue: Developments

"Alex," Suzanne Lemeurier said in the May 24th daily briefing, "Dreamer and I have completed an assessment of your tactical command mesh proposal." Her tone was not enthusiastic.

"Thanks, Suzanne," Alex replied. "What's your conclusions?"

"Firstly," Dreamer stated, "the ship-to-ship strategic sensor mesh is eminently feasible. We can implement it via nothing more than a firmware update applied as ships dock, once we have fully defined the protocols."

"That sounds like a good start," Alex said.

"That is the good news," Dreamer agreed. "The tactical command mesh is another issue.   We believe the concept itself to be *strictly technically feasible* at control level three, without any additional physical modification to existing level three implants. Some revision of implant protocols would of course be necessary. But there are serious problems.

"I defer to Suzanne to explain them. I think you should hear them from her, not from me."

Alex nodded, and looked at Suzanne again. She *definitely* didn't look happy.

"Go ahead, Suzanne," he said.

"The... more delicate problem is one of designing the psycho-interactive part of the protocols," Suzanne began. "It would not be simply presenting the sensorium data of, for example, a ship's sensor suite to a person's mind, as level three control already does, nor multiple minds meeting in the infosphere, which we all casually do every day now. A direct mind-to-mind tactical mesh would project another person's *subjective impressions and interpretations* of that sensorium, from multiple people *at the same time*, into the minds of those in the mesh. That *alone* would be... at the *very least*, disorienting.

"Worse, we cannot hypothesize a way to do it without also possibly projecting thoughts, even *feelings*, of the other participants in the mesh.

The stronger the thoughts or feelings, the more likely that they would bleed through. And in battle, there *will* be strong feelings. I cannot rule out people in the mesh becoming unable to distinguish their own thoughts from those of others. Perhaps completely losing their grip on where *and even who* they are.

"We would have to take exceedingly careful precautions to protect users in the mesh, to ensure that their own consciousness remains distinct and inviolate from others in the mesh. It has never been done before, never even *attempted*, and I am afraid that if we do not get it right, we may do *catastrophic* psychological harm to those in the mesh. There is a high risk that we would create a state of, for lack of a better term, technologically induced schizophrenia."

Suzanne looked straight at Alex, her grey eyes very steady and serious.

"Please, Alex," she said with feeling, "*do not* try to do this."

Alex was silent for a long moment.

"That's... an alarming prospect," he answered slowly, at last. "It's a possibility that hadn't remotely occurred to me." Suzanne nodded. "Do you think that the... psychological risks can be overcome?"

"I do not know yet," Suzanne replied. "But—I think the risk is too great. I—we—suggest that you consider a safer, more cautious approach to the problem. Confine the tactical mesh to ship-to-ship, make it a synthetic-aperture sensor system, present the data as seen by all ships as available to any, automatically fill in the blank areas not visible to one ship yet with the data from others that can, as the Marines already do with their battlesuits. All of those things, we see no risk in. But I would *strongly* encourage you to avoid trying to mesh ship commanders mind-to-mind, even loosely. I believe the potential for lasting, perhaps permanent, harm is terrible."

She looked around the table.

"I see nobody at this table on whom I am willing to perform that experiment. I care too much for all of you. And in any case, I believe that the experiment would be *deeply* unethical."

Alex nodded slowly.

"Thank you, Suzanne," he said. "I'm not going to question your expert opinion on this. Thank you for being so honest about it. I'm *very* glad I asked you to look into it with Dreamer."

He looked around the table.

"I'd like to continue with the ship-to-ship strategic sensor-data mesh," he continued. "The god's-eye view. But so far as I'm concerned, the long-range tactical command mesh idea is *DEAD*. I had no idea how dangerous it might be, and I *won't* impose that kind of risk on anyone." He turned to Naomi, next to him. "Least of all you."

Naomi nodded solemnly, and squeezed his hand.

"Okay. Next business?"

Alex, Tom, Sandy, Maksim, Angavu, Pierre, Jabari, Lewis sent. *Do you have some time to get together? I'd like to show you a prototype missile cruiser design and get your comments on it. And don't hesitate to bring in anyone else you think should be included.*

Fine by me, Alex replied. *I'm free in an hour, for the rest of the day.*

I can do an hour from now, Tom said.

Give me ninety minutes, came Maksim's reply.

Either works for me, Sandy said. Angavu, Pierre and Jabari agreed.

Ninety minutes, then? Lewis asked. There was general agreement.

Great, Alex said. *See you all in ninety minutes. I'll order in some food and drinks.*

Ninety minutes later, they gathered in the briefing room. There were eggrolls, pizza, orange juice, lemonade and coffee on the table.

"Right then, Lewis," Alex said after everyone had gotten settled, "let's see what you've got for us."

"Okay," Lewis said. He pulled up a schematic above the table, and sent them all a direct link to the raw design data.

"As you can see, I've followed the general multi-panel hybrid hull construction model of the Sharks, but with a rather different hull form."

The cruiser hull Lewis proposed was conceptually similar to the Sharks, in being made from large compound-curved panels of Tier 3 'battle steel', joined by thick Tier 2 'flint-steel' seams. However, it was made up of no less than six main panels rather than the Shark class's triangle of three —two wider and four relatively narrow ones, creating a broad hull shaped somewhat like a flattened, faceted American football with the aft end cut short. Over roughly the rear half of the hull, the upper and lower plates spread into additional armored sponsons protruding from the sides. Overall it was a good four hundred and fifty meters long by roughly ninety wide, counting the sponsons, and its hull was at maximum around fifty meters deep through the central area, where the core systems lay. Some low superstructure protruded above the upper surface of the hull, along the centerline.

All of the core engineering systems and crew quarters were aligned down the middle of the hull, while the sponsons included the boat bays, missile loading equipment, and beam docking ports, among other gear. The inboard side of the sponsons was separated from the hull proper by a shallowly curved internal battle-steel bulkhead. Another pair of docking ports were on the underside of the hull, spaced to mate up to the twin docking ports on the booms. Inboard of the sponsons, beyond the bulkhead, lay the Marine quarters and armories, strategically placed between both sets of docking ports and the core of the ship. Nobody was reaching the ship's core except by going through Marine country first.

The point defense clusters and railgun secondary armament—and there were a *lot* of both—were all spaced out along the beveled outer edges of the hull, railgun magazines tucked into the bevel. Almost the entirety of the space *between* the crew/engineering core and the bevel, over most of the length of the hull, was occupied by missile dispensers and missile magazines. There was room for *thousands* of missiles, and these were much larger, heavier missiles than those the Shark class carried, fully ten meters long and nearly a meter in diameter.

"This hull is designed for the same forty-meter annie-plant we use in the Sharks," Lewis pointed out, "with a single backup fusion bottle. It doesn't need to supply power for heavy direct-fire armament, so even though I project nearly twice the mass of the Shark class—should be around two hundred and fifty five, maybe two hundred and sixty thousand tonnes, fully laden—we should still be able to pull about 60G acceleration. I haven't over-provisioned the maneuvering thrusters to the Shark's extent, because this ship is supposed to stand off and lob missiles, so if you're having to take violent evasive action, the battle plan has already gone horribly wrong. It should be able to maneuver at around 5G.

"You'll notice I've considerably increased the number of point defense clusters and defensive secondary railgun mounts, just in case it gets bushwhacked straight out of a hyperspace exit."

"I noticed that," Tom Whitman said. "What's the story with these missiles? They're a lot bigger. Just bigger warhead? More range?"

"Alright, so there's two parts to that," Lewis replied. He flashed up a detailed schematic of one of the new missiles.

"First, if we're standing off and firing missiles from long range, they need to get there fast, and they need to **have** long range. So these missiles have *much* beefier drive sections than the Gen2 missiles on the Sharks. They're designed for five hundred G acceleration, versus the two-twenty of a Gen2, so at any given range up to the limit of a Gen2's endurance, these will reach the same target about fifty percent faster than a Gen2. Plus, they have three times the thrust endurance of a Gen2. A Gen2 missile can maintain two hundred and twenty G for three minutes. These can maintain five hundred G for ten. At burnout, just shy of point nine million kilometers, they're going to be going almost three thousand kilometers a second, close to one percent of C."

"*Impressive,*" Maksim interjected.

"But also," Lewis went on, "no, they have a larger warhead section, but it's not *just* a bigger warhead. There's, uh... let's just say that the United States did a lot of theoretical work on the effectiveness of nuclear weapons. And to summarize some of the most important and relevant findings of that research, you pass a point of diminishing returns— fairly rapidly, actually—at which making a warhead a lot bigger doesn't really make it all that much more effective, as long as it's accurately delivered. A small warhead almost on top of the target is much more effective than a much larger one five times further away. Especially in vacuum. Because of the inverse-square law. But take a look at this."

Lewis zoomed the schematic in on the warhead section. There was a bundle of what looked like submunitions of some kind ahead of the fusion warhead proper.

"What are those?" Walt Berger asked. "You got some kind of MIRV thing going on there? Individually targeted submunitions?"

"Not *exactly,*" Lewis answered. "You're right about them being individually targeted submunitions. But not independent warheads. Each one of these submunitions has a small terminal-guidance—or rather, terminal-*aiming*—thruster set, but its core is a specially constructed solid zirconium rod. The missile bus goes into coast mode three to five hundred kilometers out, *probably* before point defenses have actively engaged it. The submunitions are deployed from the bus, in a ring around the warhead, they each self-align on the target, and then the fusion warhead initiates and fires them all at once."

"Fires what?" Alex asked, slightly confused. "I'm obviously missing something here."

"Oh," Lewis said. *"Right.* Sorry, Alex. I skipped a step. The zirconium rods are one-shot, fusion-pumped X-ray lasers. The fusion head vaporizes the rods, of course, but before they're destroyed, each one emits a massive coherent X-ray pulse. So each of these warheads fires a single salvo of twelve individually-targeted X-ray laser shots, each shot nearly a third of the power of a Shark's spinal grasers."

"...Wow," Alex replied after a moment. "I am now officially impressed. How many of those missiles do the magazines hold?"

"There are eighty launchers," Lewis replied, "in four banks of twenty—eight rows of ten, two rows to a bank." He highlighted them on the schematic. "Each one should be able to kick out the first twelve missiles from its feed drum about one every two seconds, then it slows to about ten to twelve seconds per reload from the magazines. So a full salvo from the drums is nine hundred and sixty missiles in twenty-four seconds, and the total magazine capacity calculates out at fifty-seven hundred and sixty missiles. Seventy-two per launcher, six full salvos."

"...Now I'm even *more* impressed," Alex said. He did the math in his head. "...Holy *crap.* That means a full-broadside salvo from the drums is... I get 11,520 X-ray laser shots."

"Yup," Lewis agreed. "That should make almost anything sit up and take notice."

"Just one question," Alex continued. "What happens if we get a hit that breaches the hull and penetrates one of those missile magazines?"

"Good question," Lewis replied. "But actually, not nearly as much as you might think. It's not like a surface warship like the *Hood,* with magazines of chemical explosives. It smashes up a few missiles, maybe wrecks a magazine section or two. But not much beyond that.

"I don't know whether you've actually ever dug deeply into the physics of how the Cricket pure-fusion warheads work, but it is actually *amazingly difficult* to make one cook off. They're damned near accident-proof. Even harder than a conventional nuke. You'd pretty much have to get the ignition sequence perfect. Your best chance would be to find a way to somehow hack the warhead and false-activate the initiation trigger. And you'd still have to figure out how to release the safety interlocks first."

"Huh," Alex said. "You're right, that's a detail I hadn't delved into. Too many *other* things that needed my attention. That's reassuring to hear.

"What about crew size?"

"I'm actually projecting around about the same as a Shark," Lewis replied. "Or only slightly higher. There are nearly three times as many secondary railgun mounts, as you can see, but no direct-fire spinal

6

weapons to consider, and I figure all of the missile launchers will be ganged together as a single unified system. We're never likely to be assigning separate targets to individual launchers, unless we're only firing a handful of missiles. The missiles can be individually re-targeted at almost any point in their powered flight envelope—and they reserve a little power for terminal maneuvering. And because they have such a short movement required once released, the laser rods can easily do high off-bore-angle shots. You could even send a missile past a target, cold, and then fire back at it from behind it."

They all took a while to look over the design. There were a few further questions, and a few refinements offered here and there. Alex pulled in John Warner to confirm that the Marine provisions were acceptable. Angavu Onyango would have called in her brother Hussein to get his opinion as well, but *Tigershark* was currently on patrol.

"Dreamer," Alex asked after a while, "do you have an estimated build time for one of these?"

"My initial estimate is about one hundred days for the first," Dreamer replied, "plus or minus perhaps three days. I can set up a separate line to mass-produce the launchers and modular magazines. That should take four to six days off the second and subsequent hulls. I will also of course set up a dedicated line to produce these new missiles."

"Do you have a proposed name for this class?" Alex asked Lewis.

"Well," Lewis replied, "it's supposed to stand off and dominate a battle from a distance. So... I was kind of thinking maybe the Warlord class missile cruiser."

"Hmm," Maksim mused. "Lot of potential there to draw good names from history."

"It sounds like a good class name," Alex agreed. "Any opposed?"

No objections were raised. Around the table there were silent nods of approval.

"Okay then," Alex declared. "The Warlord class cruiser, it is. Let's sleep on it, take a couple of days to think it over. DD-41 and DD-42 will be commissioned on the 31st, three days from now. We'll be laying down DD-46 through DD-48, the last three planned Sharks. If none of us have come up with any major changes by then, we'll start constructing the first prototype Warlord at the same time. Everyone good with that?"

There was general agreement around the table.

"Great. Seems like we have a plan," Alex said. "Thanks for all the hard work on this, Lewis."

"Alex, seriously, thanks for *letting me* work on this stuff," Lewis replied. "I'd never get to work on anything a *hundredth* this interesting on Earth. Let alone design an entire ship myself. Plus Dreamer, of course."

1. New Under The Sun

It was late July. There was a week left before the last three planned Shark-class destroyers would be delivered out of the engineering bays. Then, a month after that, if the first *Warlord* missile cruiser tested out satisfactorily, the Fleet would switch to building cruisers.

But right now, Alex was in the Marine rifle range, in a Marine battlesuit that had been fitted to him. Ever since Joshua Newton had designed the M2 Gorilla suit, he'd been wanting to try one out, and he had finally gotten around to finding time to do it. He had spent all morning under Joshua's personal instruction, learning how to move around, run and jump in the massive armored suit without falling over... often. Now he was learning to use the M8 Heavy Rifle.

It was going pretty well, once he had gotten used to manipulating the big rifle's controls using battlesuit gauntlets. Joshua had insisted on making him learn to do it all manually, before letting him use the interface.

"You'll properly understand the rifle this way," Joshua had said. And he was right. It wasn't *that* different, mechanically speaking, from any of a number of other rifles Alex had used before, so it didn't take him that long to pick up the differences. Now he'd graduated to trying it out on the rifle range, using the heads-up sighting system and triggering shots through the interface.

It was extremely easy to shoot it well. It was practically weightless to the battlesuit, the suit held it absolutely steady, he scarcely even noticed its recoil even though he knew it was substantial, and he could trigger a shot with barely more than a thought.

And it was *boring*. Precisely *because* it was so easy. There was no challenge to it. It was on target, precisely where he aimed at this short range, every time. He didn't even have to allow for drop. Not only was the trajectory of the big, fast-moving bullet as flat as Nebraska, but the sighting system automatically took what little drop there was into account for him.

"I wasn't expecting it to be like this, Josh," he said.

"How do you mean?" Joshua asked.

"I've shot plenty in my time, on target ranges," Alex explained. "I'm used to doing the work, to testing and exercising my own skill and control.

But... the suit and the rifle are doing it all *for* me. All I have to do is choose the target and decide the moment to fire. And the truth is... it's boring."

Joshua nodded knowingly.

"I can see that," he replied. "In a firefight, that's *exactly* what you want the actual process of firing your rifle to be—boring. *Routine.* Automatic. Your attention needs to be on your tactical situation, on picking which target—or targets—to engage, and in what order, and when, on where hostile fire might come from, not on the mechanics of operating your rifle. That's why we drill, and drill, and drill, and drill, until operating the rifle itself becomes muscle memory. Until you can run it without conscious thought.

"I can tell you, my Marines *love* having this level of integration. But I can see how from a target shooter's background, it could be unsatisfying.

"Anyway, you did pretty well with the suit, you only fell three times in it, and you've clearly got the hang of the rifle. Want to call it a day?"

"Sure," Alex agreed.

"So what do you think of the suit, now that you've finally gotten to try one out?"

"It's incredible," Alex replied. "I understand now what your Marines say about feeling like a minor god in it. And the most I've done is a little running and jumping. It's easy to *forget* I'm wearing a quarter tonne of metal and composites, because it is just so *effortless*. I didn't fully appreciate before now what an incredible job you did with this suit. I'm truly amazed."

"Thanks, Sir," Joshua said, with a grin.

He led the way back to the armory and helped Alex out of the armor. Alex took a little mild ribbing from a couple of Marines about getting stuck for a moment as he got the exit procedure wrong, made his farewells, and left to find Naomi. It was nearly time for supper.

———————————

Alex? Dreamer's voice came through the interface as he walked up the concourse.

What's up, Dreamer?

I have completed my analysis of your request regarding what you referred to as a gravity lance. I can summarize my findings while you walk, if you wish.

10

Sure, Dreamer, Alex replied. *Go ahead.*

*Very well. From hyperdrive theory, its extension to hyper-boosted railguns, artificial gravity theory and praxis, and several related fields, I have derived the principles upon which such a weapon would have to operate. You will doubtless be pleased to hear that I am quite confident that it would work, and that it should be **fairly** straightforward to construct. Relatively speaking, of course. It is not inherently **greatly** more complex in engineering terms than hyperdrives themselves and hyper-boosted railguns.*

That sounds good so far, Dreamer. I sense a 'but' coming.

Several of them, actually, Alex. First, the weapon will be extremely large and complex. It will essentially take the general form of three modified hyperdrive cores combined into a single unit, heterodyned to induce specific patterns of resonance between the three hyperdrive fields in order to create a harmonic interference pattern at range that will generate intense, chaotic localized gravitational gradients with extreme transient flux.

Alex sort of followed most of that, he thought.

That sounds like something that would require a lot of power, he replied.

Indeed, Dreamer agreed. *A great deal of power. That is the second thing. Not only would the completed weapon not physically fit within the hull of one of your new Warlord class cruisers, but the forty-meter antimatter reactor that powers the Shark and Warlord classes lacks sufficient spike power generation headroom to safely power both the gravity lance **and** all of the ship's other systems.*

Wow. So... a ship bigger than a Warlord. And with a LOT of power.

Yes, Alex. Substantially larger. But I would not advise drafting a ship design to hold it yet.

You're about to tell me a third caveat, aren't you, Dreamer?

Yes, Alex. Control of the device will be incredibly exacting. The heterodyning and modulation patterns must be maintained with extreme precision while vast amounts of power are fed into the device. Surges, secondary resonances, induction lag must all be strictly controlled. I do not recommend installing it into a manned vessel until we have fully determined the necessary control protocols. Nor do I advise testing it on, or even near, the Stardock. Failures have the potential to be dramatic. I propose that we construct an unmanned test cradle in cislunar space, on which we can remotely test the device from a safe distance via a wide-

band hyperwave control channel. And of course, we will activate it progressively, step by step, until we have mastered each step.

Alex nodded thoughtfully.

That sounds like a good plan, Dreamer. But... do you think it will **work***? Enough to be worth building it?*

There came a brief pause.

I believe that if we can get it to work properly, it would be an extremely effective weapon, Dreamer replied. Even against much larger Galactic warships. You would be able to fire **into** *the hull without having to breach the outer hull first. I can make no guarantees yet about effective range, but I expect at least hundreds of kilometers. Quite possibly more.*

Another brief pause.

Also, there would be a tremendous amount to be learned during the process. I find the idea quite intriguing.

Alex thought quickly.

Is there any risk to the Stardock simply from building one?

No. As long as we perform all testing at a safe distance, and of course keep the test cradle aimed away from Earth.

Alex was nearly back home by now. He had intended to give Naomi a quick ping through the interface on the way, but it was a bit late now.

Okay, Dreamer. I'll get back to you very soon on this. But you should probably plan to start building a prototype—and of course the remote test cradle. What do you estimate the build time to be?

To construct the device, Alex? I would estimate around a month to a month and a half, depending upon what unanticipated problems come up —which of course I cannot predict. And I conservatively estimate it will require a sixty-meter annihilation reactor for power.

Thanks, Dreamer.

You are welcome, of course, Alex.

Alex walked in to find Naomi on a video call. He gave her a quick wave from the doorway, then went and sat down in the lounge to wait for her. It wasn't long before she was done. She came and sat down next to him and snuggled up against him. He slipped an arm around her shoulders.

"So how did your power-suit adventure go?" she asked.

"Naomi, it... the powered armor is *incredible*," Alex replied. "Even in that short time I can see why the Marines say it makes them feel like a minor deity. And I didn't even try anything much beyond basic mobility. Joshua taught me how to do a six-meter vertical jump in the thing without using the thrusters, and then land without falling."

"So what does it sound like when you fall over in it?"

Alex laughed.

"Pretty quiet, inside the suit, actually," he said with a grin. "I have no idea what it sounded like on the outside. Probably like an industrial accident in a boiler factory." Then Naomi laughed as well.

"The heavy rifle," he continued, "is... well... to be honest, the integration between rifle, sight and suit makes it so *easy* that it's boring. You take aim at the target, you think about where you want to hit, the suit detects where your attention is focused and micro-adjusts aim, auto-tracks and auto-leads your target, you decide to fire, and *BANG*, there's a hole in the target right where you intended it. It's almost effortless. I'm betting that's a big part of why Joshua had me drill with the rifle manually first, until I got used to the feel of operating it. Without that, it would have felt like a video game." Naomi nodded.

"Do you think you could use it if you had to?" she asked.

"The suit?" Alex replied. "I'd be clumsy compared to the Marines who've trained with it, and I wouldn't know what to do if something went wrong. I'd just be in the way."

"Oh," Naomi said, "I didn't mean *with the Marines*, in combat. Just... if something really unexpected came up. I don't know what. If you *needed* to. *Could* you?"

"I... imagine so," Alex said, hesitantly. "As long as it was already fitted to me. But honestly, I can't realistically see it coming up, and I hope I never have to."

"So do I," Naomi agreed. "So... dinner?"

"Sure," Alex agreed. "I've worked up a good appetite." He paused for a moment, remembering the call Naomi had been on when he came in.

"Was your call anything interesting?" he asked.

"Oh!" Naomi said. "Well, the call was fairly routine, but the *question* reminds me of something else that came up today. Alex, I *guarantee* you're going to want to see this. Do you recall the Tanzanian technology cooperation request a while back?"

"...Yes," Alex said. "Superconducting motors?"

Naomi called up a virtual display.

"This is a product release announcement that was called to my attention," she said. She sent it to the virtual screen.

The scene was clearly somewhere in Africa. Tanzania, Alex presumed, given the context. The opening shot showed to the right a leopard in a harness, held by a handler in protective clothing, a tall, bearded spokesman in traditional dress in the center, and an odd-looking motorcycle on the left.

"The leopard is one of the fiercest predators in Africa," the spokesman said. "In Swahili, the word for leopard is *Chui.*"

He stepped away from the leopard and rested his hand on the seat of the motorcycle. It looked like a strangely skeletal dual-sport, but with no chain and no visible engine.

"This, too, is named *Chui,*" he continued. "It is an all-electric motorcycle for Africa, designed and built entirely in Tanzania, using mostly materials sourced in Africa."

He pointed to the wheel hubs.

"It uses Tanzanian-designed axial-flux superconducting motors, built for us by the Stardock. With both wheels driven, it can go nearly anywhere, and it can ford water as much as a meter deep without damage. It could go deeper, but much beyond that, it becomes difficult to stay on." He grinned.

"It needs no oil changes, no fuel, almost no maintenance except for its tires. It uses space-strain batteries from Hitachi that store enough energy to take it a thousand miles, carrying up to a hundred kilograms of cargo, or fifty kilograms and a passenger. On a decent road, it can reach a hundred and twenty kilometers an hour."

He reached for a side handle below the seat, unlatched it, and pulled it part-way out. The side panel pulled out, a scissors-type frame unfolding behind it holding what looked like a folded sheet of stiff dead-black cloth.

"When *Chui* needs charging, these high-efficiency solar panels—*also* from Hitachi—can charge it enough from twelve hours of African sun to ride it for four hours." He stowed the solar array and bent to point to the front tire. The side of the tire had an odd, almost honeycomb-looking structure. It was possible to see *into* the tire.

"These airless tires are puncture-proof and self-healing, and shed mud on their own," he went on. "Though we do *suggest* you pick the acacia thorns out now and then."

He straightened up and walked further left past the motorcycle, a boxy utility vehicle coming into view. It had four large wheels and an aggressively cab-forward layout, with a mostly-enclosed two-row cab and an open cargo bed behind. It was obvious at a glance it had huge ground-clearance.

"This is *Chui*'s big brother *Kifaru*," he went on. "*Kifaru* is Swahili for Rhino. Like *Chui*, *Kifaru* is entirely designed and built in Tanzania. It uses similar axial-flux motors, batteries, and solar charging arrays—but obviously, they are all larger. *Kifaru* can carry as many as six people in its cab, up to half a tonne of cargo in its bed, and can tow up to six tonnes on firm ground. Both *Chui* and *Kifaru* use many parts pre-fabricated in Africa using Stardock recycler technology.

"You can order *Chui* today, straight off the production line. We are ramping up production for *Kifaru* and it will be on sale in about a month.

"We are the Tanzanian Auto Cooperative, and we—nearly four thousand of us—are building vehicles for Africa, that Africa can afford, *in* Africa, *designed* in Africa, using African-sourced materials and Stardock technology. With *Chui* and *Kifaru*, you can join with us today.

"Become part of the bright future of Africa, with *Chui* and *Kifaru,* and the Tanzanian Auto Cooperative."

Naomi looked at Alex. He had a huge grin, and was almost bouncing up and down with excitement.

"It's working," he said happily. "It's *working.*" He pulled Naomi closer and hugged her tightly. "It's good to see Hitachi becoming a major supplier to developing nations, too. I'm glad to see them—and others—stepping up. We can *fix* this mess, if we get time. And if we all work together on it. Cooperation... that's the key."

"So," Naomi replied. "Dinner?"

"Sure," Alex said. "Let's go." He got up and pulled Naomi to her feet. "We can decide on the way where we want to eat."

———————

The last three planned Sharks came off the production line on August 5, commissioned as DD-46 *Megalodon*, DD-47 *Mazikeen*, and DD-48 *Viperfish*.

"*Megalodon* I know," Alex commented to Tom Whitman, after the three final destroyers had undocked for their shakedown cruises. "I'm glad to see we got one more actual shark in at the tail-end of the class, even if it's an extinct one. And *Viperfish* is good. But where did they come up with *Mazikeen*?"

"Apparently it originally comes from 'mazzikin'," Tom said. "A type of minor demon from Jewish mythology."

"Huh," Alex said. "Never heard of that before. It's a good name, though."

He drew in a deep breath and let it out slowly.

"It's... a bit of a weird feeling. We've been building Sharks for nearly two years... and now the last three are entering service, and we don't plan to build any more."

"Time moves on, Alex," Tom said. "Another month and we'll be trialling the first Warlord."

"Yeah, you're right," Alex replied. "But still. It's an odd feeling."

"We'll all be back into the routine in no time as soon as we start rolling out Warlords," Tom said. "We've already reconfigured the upper and lower training simulators to the Warlord configuration. We'll have Warlord-ready crews before we have ships to put them in."

"Thanks, Tom," Alex said fervently. "I don't know how I'd manage without you running the Academy."

"So—what about that... *secret weapon* project of yours?" Tom inquired. "You've been playing it pretty close to the chest."

"Um," Alex said. "I didn't intend to be *secretive* about it or anything. I just didn't want to raise false hopes in case it doesn't pan out.

"But since you've asked, Dreamer and I are trying to develop a gravity-based ranged main weapon that can bypass a Galactic warship's Tier 3 hull and strike right through it."

"*Damn*," Tom said. "That'll be a hell of a trick, if you can pull it off. How's the project going?"

"Dreamer has a remote test cradle constructed, and a prototype of the weapon nearly finished. And a sixty-meter AM plant to power it."

"A *sixty meter* plant?" Tom repeated, his eyebrows rising in surprise.

"It's going to draw a *lot* of power," Alex replied. "If we can make it work. And it's going to be BIG. It's like three hyperdrive cores heterodyned together."

Tom whistled.

"Well, we're not putting *THAT* into a Warlord-class hull," he said.

"Assuming it even works," Alex cautioned. "We deliberately haven't even started to design a hull around it yet, until we know it'll work and we can control it safely. Even Dreamer said that it's going to require incredibly precise control."

"Well," Tom said, "I'll be interested to see whether it works. But by the sound of it, I shouldn't be holding my breath."

"Trust me," Alex said, "I'll give everyone a full update as soon as I—*we*—have something solid to report."

———————————

On September 6, Dreamer declared the first prototype gravity lance ready to test. The completed weapon was nearly two hundred and forty meters long, and around sixty in diameter.

"Damn," Alex said slowly. "I know you said it would be large and complex. But I wasn't expecting something *this* big."

"The size of the device is necessarily driven by the physics involved and the amount of power it must handle," Dreamer said.

"Oh, sure," Alex agreed. "I'm not questioning. Just... *damn*, that thing is big. It's two thirds the size of a Shark-class destroyer. For one weapon."

Dreamer mounted it into the remote test cradle, then Alex had a pair of heavy-lifters fly it carefully out to lunar orbit. There, it was docked to the end of a spindly-looking thousand-meter boom. On the far end of the boom, a heavy armored shield protected the sixty-meter antimatter reactor that would power the test cradle and the weapon mounted to it.

Once the test cradle was parked in place, and the two lifters safely clear, Alex sent out a notice to all command staff that the test series was about to begin. Then Dreamer applied standby power and began preliminary tests.

Initial power-up sequence completed smoothly, he reported. *Power flow is good, no anomalies, no fluctuations observed. Power load is stable. Beginning to calibrate idle synchronization.*

After thirty minutes, Dreamer declared himself satisfied with idle synchronization, and proceeded onward to testing core power balancing and power ramping controls at low power. It was another two hours before he declared himself satisfied with power stability and balance at up to five percent power.

Increasing to ten percent charge, Dreamer declared. *Staying below fifteen percent charging rate for the time being.*

Over the next twenty hours, Dreamer carefully brought the prototype up to twenty-five percent charge, then drained the charge, three times. He slowly increased charge rate to twenty percent, then twenty-five percent.

Stable at twenty-five percent charge and rate, he said. *Increasing to thirty percent.*

He discharged the cores again, then began charging at thirty percent rate.

At twenty-eight percent charge, the readouts suddenly went haywire.

CUTTING POWER, Dreamer said urgently. But it was too late. Pale corona arcs strobed up and down the prototype weapon, then there was a cyan flash. All of the readouts dropped almost to zero.

Stand by, Dreamer said. Then, a few moments later, *Prototype one is no longer operative.*

What happened, Dreamer? Alex asked.

Analyzing, Dreamer replied. *I will inform you as soon as I know what happened. The last readings seem to point to an unanticipated resonance cascade of some kind.*

Any conclusions to be drawn from it, Dreamer?

Not yet, Alex. I have two other prototypes on hold at fifty percent completion. I will determine what modifications are necessary once I have finished analyzing this data.

I'll leave you to it then, Dreamer.

———————

Dreamer eventually concluded that he did not have enough data to identify what had actually happened. The test cradle was undamaged, as was the reactor. He announced that he would add additional instrumentation to P-Two optimized for examining where the last readings from P-One had pointed, and begin fifty-percent construction of a fourth prototype. P-Two would not be ready until after CG-01 launched.

CG-01 launched on September 15, only a day behind the estimate.

―――――――――

"Tom, I want you and Sandra to appoint the test crew for CG-01," Alex said. "And I hate to do this to you, but you shouldn't be on it, any more than I should."

Tom grinned.

"Turnabout is fair play," he chuckled. "Truth is, I was expecting you to say that. In fact, if you have no objections... I'd like to hand off this trial to Sarah Burke, *Ballarat's* captain."

Sandra nodded agreement.

"Good choice," she said. "She's solid."

"No argument from me," Alex said. "Let her pick whoever she wants for a trials crew. And just to play safe, let's send a Shark out with her as an escort. Just in case."

Sandra nodded approval.

"Good plan," she agreed. "Let's see, which ones are available right now..." Her voice trailed off as she quickly scanned the docked ships. "How about *Arapaima?*"

"*Arapaima* sounds like a good choice to me," Tom agreed.

"Dong-geun's son Dae-hyun is *Arapaimo's* XO, isn't he?" Alex asked. Tom nodded agreement.

"He is," he replied. "And honestly, I think I'd recommend him for his own command, if we decide to build any more Sharks in the future."

Alex made a mental note of that. Sarah took two days to select her testing crew, and then the as-yet-unnamed CG-01 and DD-44, UFS *Arapaima*, headed out for trials.

2. One Of Our Own

"Commander Kusanagi, Sir?"

Soichiro Kusanagi looked up. He recognized the speaker as one of his bridge officers, Lieutenant Khun Satt Naing, a Burmese L2 assigned as damage control officer in *Inazuma*'s secondary CIC.

"At ease, Lieutenant," he said. "What is it?"

"Sir," Naing said, "I wish to request to move to family quarters, and to bring my family to the Stardock. There is... unrest in Myanmar. *Again*. I miss my wife and son, and she misses me, and with the renewed unrest, she is afraid for her safety and the safety of our son. And so am I."

Commander Soichiro Kusanagi only needed a moment to consider the request.

"Your request is granted, of course," Kusanagi said. "I will see to the necessary arrangements and obtaining landing clearance. When do you want to go and get your family?"

"Would tomorrow be too soon... Sir?"

"I don't see a problem with that, Lieutenant. We're due out again tomorrow, but we can take an extra lander aboard, drop you off, and loiter on-station until you have retrieved your family. Then the lander can return you to the ship, and bring your family here while we head out for our patrol."

"Understood, Sir," Lieutenant Naing said. "Thank you, Sir."

"The Fleet takes care of its own, Lieutenant," Kusanagi replied. "Dismissed."

The Lieutenant saluted, turned smartly on his heel, and left.

Four orbits later, *Inazuma* undocked, with an extra twenty-two meter shuttle in the starboard boat bay. The destroyer made a gentle descent to low orbit, then braked to hold station a hundred and twenty kilometers above Naypyidaw, the capital of Myanmar. After a few minutes, the shuttle undocked. It carried one passenger.

The shuttle made a quiet, routine approach to Nay Pyi Taw International Airport, sixteen kilometers southeast of the city. Lieutenant Khun Satt Naing disembarked without incident, showed his Fleet ID at customs check, walked outside to the taxi rank, and took a cab to the outskirts of eastern Naypyidaw.

It was a short ride, and it wasn't long before the cab deposited Khun in front of the small bungalow that he rented with his wife. There was a white van parked directly in front of the bungalow, but he thought nothing of it.

"Wait, please," Khun said to the cabbie. "We will not be long." The cabbie nodded. As Khun turned to walk toward the house, the front door opened, and Khun's wife Nandar stepped into the doorway with a happy smile. Khun hurried past the white van to go to her.

As he passed the van and turned to go up the short path, Khun heard the van's side door slide open behind him. Standing at the open door, Nandar saw the first of three men jump out of the van, raise something, and point it at Khun. Her eyes widened in fear, and she began to shout a warning.

Before he could react, something hit Khun from behind. Suddenly all of his nerves seemed to be on fire, and he fell uncontrollably to the ground, his muscles jerking and spasming. Nandar screamed as the three men seized Khun. One of them clapped something over his mouth and nose as they dragged him into the van. One of the men looked directly at Nandar, and shouted "Say nothing! You saw nothing!" She saw Khun start to struggle, then the side door slammed closed and the van pulled away.

Something terrible had just happened. But Nandar had no idea who she could tell about it to get help. There was certainly no point in calling for the police. She was all but certain these were government men. The waiting cabbie was looking back and forth between Nandar and where the van was speeding away, bewildered.

Nandar began to cry helplessly. She did not know what to do.

Three hours later, the pilot on the shuttle was getting impatient to return to space. Naing *should* have been back by now.

Hey, Khun, he sent. *Are you guys on the way back yet?*

There was no reply. That was odd. With the shuttle as a relay and signal booster, he ought to be able to reach Naing within at least fifty kilometers, and he shouldn't be more than about twenty away. But maybe

Khun was busy. He waited ten minutes, and then tried again. And then a third time.

There was still no response.

"*Inazuma*, this is Pickup One," he sent.

"Pickup One, *Inazuma*. Go ahead."

"*Inazuma*, Lieutenant Naing is late returning, and I cannot contact him. I am starting to become concerned that something may have happened."

There was a short pause.

"Understood, Pickup One. Advising the Captain. Stand by."

"Captain," said the comms officer on *Inazuma*'s bridge, "Pickup One reports contact lost with Lieutenant Naing. He expressed concern."

Soichiro Kusanagi thought for a moment.

"Naing's family is in eastern Naypyidaw, correct?" he said. "There ought to be several scout drones in the area. Relay through the shuttle to the drones and have them ping Lieutenant Naing's implant. Let's see if we can make sure he's alright."

The drone command was sent. There was no response.

The drone ping went out twice more. Still no response. Now, Kusanagi was becoming concerned as well.

"Widen the search area," he ordered. "Use the drone mesh network."

"We've got a signal," said Lieutenant Ozaki, on sensors, a little later. "It's coming through a drone... east of the capital, the south— SIR! It's a *distress signal*, sir! Southern edge of Taunggyi!"

"Trace that signal," Soichiro Kusanagi said, leaning forward intently. "*Now*. Get as much data as you can. Stand by to shift position."

"It's a distress beacon signal direct from Lieutenant Naing's implant," Ozaki reported after a few minutes. "Lieutenant Naing is not responding." He sent a map to the bridge tactical display, satellite maps combined with *Inazuma*'s sensor data and the data relayed from the scout drone. "His signal is located inside this building, here."

Commander Kusanagi looked at the map.

"That looks like an office or light industrial building," he mused aloud. "What do we know about it?"

"Nothing coming up on public record, Sir," Ozaki replied. "*Suspiciously* blank."

"Suspicious," Kusanagi agreed. "What on earth would Lieutenant Naing be doing there? And uncommunicative, but with a distress signal from his *implant?*"

Decision came to him quickly.

"Put us thirty kilometers above that building and five south," he ordered.

Sergeant Kharif.

Sir?

I'm deploying your platoon for a rescue. It appears someone— someone probably government connected—has abducted Lieutenant Naing when he went to pick up his family. I'm sending you all the information we have. Go in soft-shoe as much as you can, but be prepared for possible resistance, and don't take no for an answer. We have strong evidence of foul play. Find Lieutenant Naing and bring him home, Sergeant. And pick up his family as well, if he's in any shape to tell you where they are. We don't have an exact location for them, only that they're somewhere in eastern Naypyidaw.

Understood, Sir. On it.

"Third platoon!" Sergeant Kharif shouted. "We are deploying. We're going to go rescue Lieutenant Naing and bring him and his family home. I want Third squad in powered armor. Just in case."

In moments, *Inazuma's* Marine barracks was a hive of activity. Meanwhile, Kusanagi reported in.

"Stardock, *Inazuma*, Kusanagi requesting Fleet Actual."

"*Inazuma*, Stardock Control, wait one."

Alex was in a planning meeting, but took the call.

"Commander Kusanagi, Holder here. What's going on?"

"Sir, one of my officers, Lieutenant Naing, was supposed to be picking up his family today. Wife and young son. He went missing several hours ago. We cannot get any response from him, but we picked up an automatic distress signal from his implant, in a city a hundred and fifty kilometers from where he is supposed to be. We've localized his implant to an unmarked light-industrial or office building which has a suspicious lack of any tangible public information available. I am proceeding on the assumption he was abducted and is in immediate danger."

"Understood, Commander," Alex replied. "You're senior officer on the spot. What are you doing about it?"

"I'm deploying my Marine platoon to retrieve him, Sir," Kusanagi said. "And his family, if possible."

"Very good, Commander. We'll back you up on it. Do we know his family's location?"

"Not closely enough to find them, unless Lieutenant Naing can tell us where to go," said Kusanagi.

"Crap," Alex muttered. "That was an oversight. Well... do what you can. Let me know *immediately* if you need additional backup of any kind. And keep me posted."

"Understood, Sir."

———————

Only twenty minutes later, First and Second squads of 4th Company, 3rd Platoon were boarding one of *Inazuma*'s two twenty-five meter *Hornet*-class dropships. Third squad, in powered armor, had the other *Hornet* to themselves. In the interim, *Inazuma* had shifted position and was now hovering thirty kilometers over Taunggyi.

The boat bay hatch opened, and the two troop carriers eased out, then dropped like rocks.

Three minutes later, Hornet Two passed over the building a hundred and fifty meters up, side doors open. Marines in powered armor rained from it, landing on thrusters and forming a cordon around the building. The building looked to be two stories, with few windows, a glazed main entrance in front, a loading dock at the rear, and three scattered side doors. The sign next to the front doors, in Burmese script, said only "Import/Export Limited No Entry".

Beyond the cordon, Hornet One settled to the ground and disgorged First and Second squads.

"Second squad, take over the cordon," Sergeant Kharif ordered. "Watch those side doors. No-one leaves. Third squad, first section, keep watch on the loading dock, stop any vehicles. Second section support the cordon. Third section and First squad, up front with me. Saiid, do we have Naing's signal?"

25

Rifleman Saiid Khader nodded.

"I have his implant signal, sir," he confirmed. "And vital signs. They're weak. He is in bad shape."

"We're going in," Kharif said.

It took less than a minute to complete the reorganization, then Kharif marched up to the front doors at the head of twenty Marines, five of them in powered battle armor.

The doors were locked. At a reception desk visible inside, a man in civilian clothing was studiously—but visibly nervously—trying to ignore their presence. Beyond him, two uniformed soldiers guarded the double doors leading back into the building.

Kharif banged on the doors where they met. The man at the desk could no longer pretend he hadn't noticed them. He looked up, and waved his hands.

"Go away!" Kharif faintly heard him shout, through the glass. "No admittance!"

"Saif," Khalid said. He pointed to the doors. "Open them."

Rifleman Saif Hammad stepped forward in his powered armor, letting his M8 Heavy Rifle self-retract on its sling. He reached out, punched both hands through the glass, took hold of the crossbars, casually ripped both doors off the building, and tossed them away. The man behind the desk flinched back, and the two guards began to unsling their rifles. Almost instantly, nineteen rifles were aimed at them. Four of the rifles looked big enough to stop a truck. They froze.

"I would not do that, if I were you," Khalid said. "And I would not trigger any alarms, either." He stepped inside and walked into the middle of the lobby, as the squad fanned out around him, their aim unwavering. The guards slowly held out their hands *well away* from their rifles.

"One of our people is here. We are here to take him home."

"There is nobody here but our staff!" the man behind the desk protested. "This is an illegal intrusion!"

"Saiid?" Kharif asked.

Rifleman Saiid Khader pointed. "That direction," he said. "Almost certainly second floor. About fifty meters." The man behind the desk paled a little.

"We *know* you have him," Kharif said. "*DON'T* get in our way. Suleiman, Saif, Abdul, stay here, keep an eye on these three. Nobody comes in, nobody leaves, nobody makes or answers a call."

Kharif pushed through the double doors, the remaining seventeen Marines following behind him. In the lobby, Saif Hammad stepped forward, raised one armored foot, placed it against the desk, and *SHOVED*. The desk tore loose from the floor and slid back against the wall, pinning the 'receptionist' behind it.

"The man you are holding here is our brother in arms," Saif growled through his suit speakers. "*Pray* he is not badly hurt."

Inside the building, stairs to the right led up.

"Yousef, Ayesha, here," Kharif said. "Guard the stairs." Then he led the way upstairs.

"Vital signs are weakening, Sergeant," Saiid said. Kharif looked around. They were in a corridor that appeared to circle around the upper floor of the building. There wasn't a door in sight that led the direction they wanted to go.

"Omar, Nasreen, watch this corridor," Kharif said. "Everyone else with me." He led the way to the next corner, double-time. A door opened partway down, and a middle-aged woman started to come out, then froze in the doorway.

"*Stay inside,*" Kharif shouted. "*Everyone stay where you are.*" The woman prudently stepped back inside and closed the door.

They rounded the corner. Ten meters ahead, the corridor veered left again. Someone opened a door, glanced out, and hurriedly closed it again. They needed to go right. Still no visible door led that direction.

"Sergeant," Saiid said urgently, "Naing's vital signs are *failing*."

Kharif looked at the corner of the corridor, and stepped aside.

"Hamid, Ismail," he said. "*Make a door.*"

Hamid Qasim and Ismail al-Hourani slung their rifles behind them, lowered their heads, and charged. They went through the wall with an echoing **CRASH**, leaving a hole nearly three meters wide. Kharif followed them through, the rest of the Marines following behind, scanning for threats.

On the far side of the wall was a laboratory. Equipment and shattered glassware was now strewn across the floor. Over by the far wall, a technician stood in front of a desk, staring at them in shock, wisely not moving.

"Saiid?"

Saiid pointed at the next wall.

"About fifteen meters," he said. "Implant signal only. I have no vital signs any longer."

Kharif pointed at the wall.

"*Door*," he said, again. Qasim and al-Hourani made another doorway. Kharif followed them through.

On the far side of the wall was another laboratory. Two men and a woman in surgical scrubs and masks stood backed up nearly against the far wall. There was an operating table toward the middle of the room. On the table lay Khun Satt Naing, face-down. The top and back of his skull were missing, and open incisions ran down across his shoulders and arms. There was a lot of blood.

Kharif took three steps closer, and looked at Naing. It wasn't pretty. He noticed there was a sink nearby. Water was running into it. He took two more steps and looked into the sink. In a wire-mesh basket in the sink lay a tangle of wires, electrodes, contacts... Naing's implant. There were still traces of blood and gray matter.

Kharif looked back at Naing's body, then stared at the three 'doctors' for a long, long moment.

"You *murderous animals*," he growled. The room was almost echoingly silent.

One of the three opened his mouth to speak. Kharif cut him off.

"If I were in your position," he said, "I would not say ANYTHING right now that might further anger my Marines. We are already *very angry*."

The man took his advice.

"Kharif to *Inazuma*," he called in.

"*Inazuma*. Go ahead, Sergeant." The voice was Kusanagi's.

28

"We've found Lieutenant Naing, Sir. He's dead. These sons of whores dug his implant out of him while he was alive."

On *Inazuma*'s bridge, Soichiro Kusanagi swore.

"What's the building, Sergeant?"

"Looks like mostly laboratories, Sir. All the parts we've seen. Controlled access. Guarded by uniformed Myanmar military."

"Officially sanctioned, then."

"Looks that way, Sir."

Kusanagi thought for a moment.

"Stand by, Sergeant.

"Stardock, *Inazuma* actual."

"*Inazuma*, Holder. Please tell me you have good news."

"Sir, the extraction team found Lieutenant Naing. He's dead. It's a government operated covert laboratory. Sergeant Kharif says they cut Naing apart to get his implant."

It was Alex's turn to swear, loudly and volubly.

"You're on the spot, Commander," he said after a minute. "What's your suggested response?"

Kusanagi's voice was flat as he replied.

"I propose to fully evacuate that building, Sir. Then *erase* it."

Alex pondered for a long moment, his fists clenched.

"Approved, Commander," he said. "*Make certain* there are no civilian casualties. And I want a full report, with a complete chain of evidence. Audio, video, scout drone data, comms logs, SIGINT, everything."

"Understood, Sir."

"Kharif, *Inazuma*."

"Sir?"

"Sergeant, I want you to recover Lieutenant Naing's body and implant. Then I want you to sweep the building and get everyone out. *Everyone*. No civilians to be left behind. Get them all at least five hundred meters clear. We are going to send a message to express our displeasure."

"Understood, Sir."

Kharif looked around.

"Ayman, Jamal, Iman, you are in charge of Lieutenant Naing's body. Find something to wrap him in." He reached out and shut off the water.

"His implant is in this sink. Someone find something to put it in. We're taking it with us.

"Everyone else, sweep the building. Get EVERYONE out." He fixed the three silent 'doctors' with a fierce glare. "Even these three. You three do not know how lucky you are this day."

There was a pack of a dozen body bags on a shelf in a corner of the lab. About a third of the pack was missing. The three Marines took one of the bags and carefully, respectfully, placed Lieutenant Naing's body in it. Then they carried him back out through the wrecked path Hamid Qasim and Ismail al-Hourani had made, down the stairs, and out of the building.

Saif Hammad glared at the 'receptionist'.

"'Not here', you told us," he growled. "He looks very 'here' to me. He had a *wife and a son*. Now she is a widow."

The receptionist swallowed nervously.

Eventually, the building was clear. The platoon swept it three times, opening every closet, looking under every desk, and specifically searching a couple of suspicious warm spots identified by the thermal-imaging sensors on one of the Hornets, to make *absolutely certain* that nobody was overlooked. They had to reassure several people that they would come to no harm as long as they left the building. They ended up with sixty-seven people, men and women. They herded them away from the building, five hundred meters down the access road, then stopped. Fortunately, no other buildings were nearby, aside from a shack for a standby generator, which they had also checked and found nobody there. Kharif had the civilians kneel down. For their safety, he told them. They complied nervously.

«Are you going to shoot us?» one woman asked in Burmese, fear obvious in her voice. Kharif's implant ran it through one of the circling dropships for translation.

"Of *course* not," Kharif reassured her gently. "We are Fleet Marines. Not murderers." He glared again at the three in their surgical scrubs. "But you will be safer not being on your feet right now."

The woman nodded uncertainly, and got down on the ground as advised.

"*Inazuma*, Kharif. All clear. All civilians extracted five hundred meters."

"Copy that, Sergeant. Incoming, one round."

"*COVER YOUR EARS*," Kharif told the civilians, in a parade-ground bellow.

The twenty-centimeter railgun round *Inazuma* fired was an incandescent streak plunging down in an instant from the heavens. It passed all the way through the building without encountering any noticeable resistance, blew a massive hole through the foundation, and released almost all of its huge payload of kinetic energy into the ground below the foundation, the equivalent of a hundred and twenty tons of TNT.

The entire building seemed to rise almost in slow motion as the ground rebounded under it, lifted by the shockwave. Then it broke up into a cloud of debris which rose high above the site, as the **SLAM** of sudden thunder rolled across the Marines and the former occupants, a second and a half after the strike, before falling back mostly into its own crater. Cars in the parking lot were tossed away like toys, and several of the civilians were knocked over by the blast and the ground wave even at five hundred meters distance. Dirt, small rocks and other light debris rained down as echoes slapped back off other buildings further away. A huge cloud of dust hung in the air, beginning to slowly drift downwind. Scattered sheets of paper fluttered in the breeze. It was as though a fist from heaven had smote the building into the ground.

"I expect your authorities will be here very shortly," Kharif said, after the rain of debris had stopped. "You should probably wait for them here. They should take care of any minor injuries. You might choose to reconsider what to do for a living."

He turned and walked away.

"*Third platoon!* Form up for dust-off!" he called. Then he sent to the dropships.

"Hornet One and Two, we're ready for pickup."

The two dropships moved in, and Third Platoon boarded, carrying the body of Lieutenant Naing with them. A few moments later, they took off to rejoin *Inazuma*. About five minutes after they docked, *Inazuma* rose skyward and started on its way back to the Stardock.

Inazuma docked in the main docking bay, at gate P-fifteen, patrol cancelled. Her crew filed off and formed up outside the gate in two blocs, leaving a gap in between. Then the Marines disembarked, in column. The first six Marines in the column carried the body of Lieutenant Naing on their shoulders.

They took their place in the center of the formation, then the entire formation of nearly two hundred men and women set off on a slow march up the concourse. Others started to fall in behind the formation as it went. There were over three hundred in the column by the time it reached MedBay One. Not that there was anything MedBay could do for him, of course. But there wasn't really anywhere else to take him.

It was the Fleet's first loss, and it hadn't even happened in combat.

"You're absolutely certain we can't locate his family?" Alex asked, not for the first time.

"He never told us an exact address," Soichiro Kusanagi said, again. "We only have a general area somewhere on the eastern outskirts of Naypyidaw. We can't narrow it down closer than a kilometer or two, and Burmese naming practices being what they are, we can't find his family by name. I know his wife's *first* name, Nandar, and no more than that. I don't even know his son's name, only that he had—has—a young son."

"Christ." Alex buried his face in his hands. "I'd like to give his family the choice to still come... if we could *find* them. We owe him at least that much." He shook his head. "This is so *stupid*. If they wanted an implant to study, why the FUCK didn't they just fucking ASK for one?"

"I have no idea," Soichiro replied. "Unless for some reason they didn't want us to know they had one to study."

"Did they think we WOULDN'T FIGURE IT OUT?" Alex exploded. "It's just all stupid. *All* of it. And we... We let him down. We *failed* him. We should have had an exact location. We *should* have sent him directly there in an aircar, with a pilot and an escort."

"You didn't know there was any reason to," Naomi pointed out. "You *couldn't* have known."

Alex sighed.

"You're right," he said. "Again. But it's just... We *could* have done it, *so easily*. And we *should* have."

"I *know*," Naomi said gently. "But you can't blame yourself. And it's probably going to get a lot worse than this, in the future."

Alex nodded somberly.

"I know," he said. "And I'm not looking forward to that at all."

―――――――――――

Alex, you will want to hear this, Dong-geun sent the next day, with a tag to the video stream feed from the UN General Assembly.

Alex opened up the stream. The delegate from Myanmar was delivering a heated accusation that a Fleet ship had attacked Myanmar without provocation, that the Fleet was out of control and should be placed under tighter UN supervision, that the senior command of the Fleet was unreliable and should be removed. And there was more.

Alex listened through it all.

Finally the delegate wrapped up his speech. Kwaku Owusu, sitting President of the General Assembly, called order.

"The assembly has heard what you allege," he said. "Does the delegate from the United Earth Fleet wish to respond to these charges at this time?"

Dong-geun, Alex sent, *tell him I will respond personally. Right now.*

You are sure, Alex?

I'm sure.

"Mr. President," Dong-geun said over the remote video link, "Mr. Holder will respond in person, if the Assembly will hear him."

There was a pause, and a slight swell of murmuring. It had been more than two years since Alex had last spoken to the Assembly in person.

"The Assembly recognizes Mr. Alex Holder, of the United Earth Fleet," President Owusu said. Alex joined the channel.

33

"Thank you, Mr. President," Alex said. "Ladies and gentlemen of the Assembly, honored delegates, thank you for hearing me and allowing the Fleet to respond immediately to the charges just presented by the delegate for the Republic of the Union of Myanmar. I wish it were under happier circumstances.

"I wish to begin by stating, for the record, that the key *events* which the delegate from Myanmar has described are, indeed, true." There was a sudden murmur of widespread surprise. Evidently a lot of people had been expecting a denial. "However, you have heard only part of the story. And the missing parts are damning.

"A platoon of Fleet Marines and a Fleet destroyer did indeed assault, force entry into, and subsequently destroy a building on the edge of the Myanmar city of Taunggyi yesterday. The orders were not mine, but I approved the operation, and I take full responsibility for it."

Alex paused for a moment to let that sink in.

"Now, does the delegate from Myanmar wish to tell the Assembly *the rest* of the story of *WHY* we did that, or shall I?"

Alex paused and waited. The Myanmar delegate looked back at him open-mouthed, taken aback. Apparently he had neither expected, nor planned for, an immediate direct counter-challenge as a response. His instructions hadn't covered this, and he didn't know what to say.

"All right then," Alex said, after a long moment. "I guess *I'm* telling the story.

"Mr. President, honored delegates, this is the part of the story that the delegate from Myanmar *did not* tell you.

"Several days ago, one of our officers, Lieutenant Khun Satt Naing, Controller level two, a Myanmar citizen and a bridge officer on the Fleet destroyer DD-35 *Inazuma*, submitted a request to bring his family up from Myanmar to the Stardock, for their safety in light of the recent renewed unrest in Myanmar. His request was of course granted, and he traveled down to Myanmar to fetch them.

"Naturally, we helped to pre-arrange travel clearance for him and his family with the appropriate Myanmar authorities. So the Myanmar government knew that he was coming, and when, and where he was going.

"*Remember that detail.* It's important.

"Lieutenant Satt Naing was delivered by a Fleet shuttle to Nay Pyi Taw International Airport, respecting Myanmar airspace. On his way to pick up his family, somewhere between the airport and his home, he was abducted

34

and taken to a government-operated covert facility, where they started digging his Cricket control implant out of him while he was still alive.

"When he was several hours overdue, hadn't checked in, and didn't respond to communication attempts, Commander Kusanagi, captain of *Inazuma*, had scout drones in the area ping his implant. When they were unable to locate the Lieutenant, Commander Kusanagi widened the search area.

"*Inazuma* eventually picked up an emergency distress beacon from Lieutenant Naing's implant, from the vicinity of Taunggyi. *Inazuma* traced the signal, and tracked him to an isolated building on the southern outskirts of Taunggyi. That's a hundred and fifty kilometers from where he disappeared.

"Commander Kusanagi, *with my approval*, dropped a Marine extraction team there to rescue him. The team were denied entry and told he was not there. We knew with complete certainty that he *WAS* in there. The Marine team were monitoring Lieutenant Naing's vital signs—his *failing* vital signs—via the distress signal from his implant, which positively located him inside the building.

"Our Marine team forced entry, finding the building to be a covert laboratory facility, guarded by uniformed Myanmar military personnel and clearly sanctioned by the Myanmar government. They took care to injure no-one. The extraction team located Lieutenant Naing, but could not get to him in time to save him. He was dead by the time they reached him. Your... *scientists*... were still washing blood off his implant. They weren't even working on him in sterile conditions. They dissected Lieutenant Naing like a laboratory rat. The Marines found a partly-used *stack* of body bags in the corner of the laboratory. How many *other* people's last moments of life have been in that building?

"We recovered his body and implant. We cleared everyone out of the building, the team swept the building three times to be *certain* it was clear, we got all of the civilians to a safe distance—*INCLUDING* the three who *personally* murdered Lieutenant Naing—and then, yes, we leveled the building with a sub-orbital kinetic strike. And yes, I personally approved *that* as well."

He paused and took a deep, measured breath.

"You don't have to take my word for any of this. We have, and will provide on request, every byte of signal received from Lieutenant Naing's implant, every moment of vital signs recorded, every second of Marine helmet video, every word of platoon comms and ship to-ground comms, every salient sensor reading from the scout drone that found him. Every piece of relevant signals intelligence and sensor data we have. You can listen for yourselves to the increasing urgency in my Marines' voices as Lieutenant Naing's vital signs are *failing* while they're trying to reach him. I already listened to every word of it.

"My chief medical officer has examined his body and tells me it was already too late before our extraction team entered the building. Your—*scientists*—had already inflicted fatal brain damage. He was a dead man, still breathing on autonomous reflex. If he'd somehow *lived* he would have been a vegetable. Even Cricket medical technology can't repair the damage your people did while digging out his implant."

Alex took a deep breath, trying to hold his voice steady, but his anger was bleeding through. He gave it free rein, addressing the Myanmar delegation directly now.

"If you wanted an implant to study, *YOU COULD HAVE JUST ASKED FOR ONE.* We would have *given* you one, for free. We'd have given you a *dozen*. If you'd just *asked*. You didn't have to abduct a man who volunteered to serve Earth, and then dig it out of his head.

"This was a barbaric, illegal act on the part of your government. Count yourselves fortunate that we *only* leveled the one building. None of your *people* were harmed, which is much better than I can say about *MY OFFICER*.

"You want an apology from the Fleet for firing on a ground target in Myanmar, you say. Well, you can have it when the Fleet, and Lieutenant Satt Naing's family, receive a formal apology from your government for abducting and murdering him for something you could have had freely for the asking, and when his family receives just compensation from your government for his murder.

"And if you want to show some semblance of *good faith*, you can inform our delegate where to *find* Lieutenant Naing's family, so that we can offer them the safe home on the Stardock that he wanted to bring them to.

"That is all I have to say at this time, Mr. President, honored delegates. Thank you for hearing me. I repeat my offer: All evidence and other data that was collected during our rescue attempt is available for examination upon request. We'll send it right now, if you like. Just designate an escrow location for the download."

There was a long near-silence, just a low background mutter of discussion, as the delegates and their aides digested what they had just heard.

36

"Does the delegation from Myanmar have a counter-response at this time?" President Owusu asked.

The silence continued. The Myanmar delegate slowly shook his head.

"Very well, then," Owusu said. "Mr. Holder, I hope that I speak for this entire Assembly when I express my sincere regrets for the brutal and untimely death of your officer."

"Thank you, Mr. President," Alex replied. "Now, if you'll all excuse me, I have a funeral to arrange. My Chief of Staff can relay any needed communications to me."

He disconnected.

―――――――

Two days later, the Myanmar delegate sent a brief private message to Dong-geun.

"I have investigated, as far as I discreetly can on short notice, the events surrounding the death of Lieutenant Naing," the note said. "To my great and lasting shame, I now believe what Mr. Holder told the Assembly to be true, although I have no hard proof in my hands.

"I am not authorized to disclose anything in any official manner. However, I am able to tell you personally this much. The woman you seek is named Nandar Aung Myat. I have attached the address where she is currently living, and a telephone number which should be current. I of course have no idea how you might have come across this information."

Dong-geun sent back a discreetly worded message of thanks and appreciation, then forwarded the note to Alex. Alex sent Commander Kusanagi a heads-up, and sent Naomi a quick ping as well. Then he enabled Burmese auto-translation, checked the time of day in Myanmar, and called Nandar.

The phone rang four times before it was picked up.

«Hello...?» said a quiet female voice. She sounded scared, tired, and desperate.

"Hello," Alex said. "Am I speaking to Nandar Aung Myat?"

«Yes,» she said, sounding uncertain. «I am Nandar Myat. Please... who is this?»

"My name is Alex Holder," Alex said. The woman gasped. "I am calling you from the United Fleet."

«The Fleet?» she asked. «*Please!* You have to *help me!* My husband! He was coming to get me and our son, but they took him! Right outside the house! Can you help to get him back?»

Alex swallowed hard.

"I... don't know how to tell you this," he said unsteadily. "I am so very sorry. I have to inform you that your husband is dead."

«*NOOOOOOOOO!*» Nandar wailed. Then she broke down into sobs.

Alex gave her a minute or so before he continued.

"I am *so sorry*," he said. "I wish I had better news to give you.

"We started searching for him as soon as we realized that he was overdue and not responding to communication. We located him by the signal from his implant, at a covert government-run laboratory, but we were too late. By the time we got a rescue team on the ground there, they had already killed him. Our extraction team recovered his body, but that was all we could do."

«Where is this laboratory?» Nandar demanded, still sobbing in grief and rage. «*I will burn it down MYSELF!*»

"We're already ahead of you on that, Ms. Myat," Alex said. "Commander Kusanagi, Khun's captain, leveled it with a kinetic strike."

«*GOOD*,» she sobbed. «Thank you.»

"Ms. Myat," Alex said. "Your husband wanted to bring you and your son to the Stardock to be with him. I can't give him back to you. Believe me, I wish I could. But the Fleet takes care of its own, and that offer is still open, if you want it.

"Do you want to come to the Stardock?"

There was silence. A *long* silence. Alex was almost starting to wonder if she had put the phone down and walked away, but he could still hear her sniffling and softly sobbing in the background.

Finally, she answered.

«Yes, please,» she said. «I do not want to spend another day in this horrible country. They murdered my beloved Khun, my heart's light. I will *never forgive them* for that.»

"Pack what you need to bring," Alex told her. "The things that are most important to you. Don't worry about common goods, we will provide everything you need. This time, we'll send a drop-ship and a

Marine escort directly to your door. They'll be there within the hour, and they'll wait while you pack what you need. I wish we'd done so in the first place... but we had no idea this might happen."

«Thank you, Mr. Holder,» Nandar said. «Thank you so much. They will not have my son.»

"I'd better let you go and start packing," Alex said. "Your ride will be on the way in a few minutes."

«Thank you,» Nandar said unsteadily. «I have to tell Minh now, that his father is dead. He will take it hard. Goodbye, Mr. Holder.»

She disconnected the call.

Alex sent Kusanagi the location information.

Do you want to have one of your squads make the pickup? he asked.

Yes, Kusanagi replied, without hesitation. *It will give them closure on the mission. And I'll go myself. It's my responsibility, as his commanding officer.*

Understood, Alex replied. *Thank you, Commander. Bring them home.*

════════════

Hornet One landed in the middle of the street in front of Nandar's bungalow forty minutes later. The side doors opened, and Commander Kusanagi, Sergeant Kharif, and the twenty Marines who had made up the entry team disembarked, all in dress uniform. Kusanagi walked up to the door, Kharif two paces behind him, but it opened before he got there. Nandar was a slight young woman, pretty despite her tear-reddened eyes. Her son Minh stood just behind her, holding onto her hand. The boy looked about eight. He looked as though he was bravely trying not to cry in front of strangers.

Kusanagi had his implant route through the lander's substrate and auto-translate to Burmese through the speaker on his epaulet.

«Nandar Aung Myat?» he said, bowing slightly. «I am Commander Soichiro Kusanagi, Lieutenant Khun Naing's commanding officer. And these are the Marine team who... recovered your husband's body. I am very sorry that we did not reach him in time to save him.

«We are here to take you to the Stardock, whenever you are ready to leave.»

«Thank you,» Nandar replied. «I will only need a few more minutes. We are nearly ready. There was not very much important to pack, and we had already packed most of it before—»

Her voice choked and she broke off with a sniffle, fresh tears welling in her eyes, and turned to her son.

«Minh,» she said, trying to keep her voice steady, «these men are your father's Captain, and the soldiers who tried their very best to save him. We are going to go to space with them, in just a few minutes. Why don't you wait with them, while I pack the last few things?»

Minh nodded solemnly, and then walked outside to look at the dropship.

«It is very big,» he said, after a minute.

«Just wait until you see *Inazuma*,» Soichiro Kusanagi replied. «*Inazuma* is much, much bigger.»

Nandar quickly handed out two bags, which Kharif took and carried to the dropship. Then she disappeared back into the house, emerging about fifteen minutes later with a third and final bag. She didn't close the door behind her.

«Let us go now,» she said. She did not look back.

Five minutes later, Hornet One was on its way back to orbit and the Stardock.

Alex, Naomi, and Suzanne Lemeurier were waiting when Nandar stepped out of the gate from Hornet One.

"Ms. Myat," he said. "I'm Alex Holder. I wanted to personally express my regret that we did not learn that your husband was missing in time to save him."

«Thank you, Mr. Holder,» Nandar replied. She seemed somewhat calmer than when Alex had spoken to her on the phone. «I know that your men tried their very best. We talked, on the way up to space, about how *angry* they were when they learned what had happened to Khun. They are very good people. All of them.»

"We'll see to getting you settled into family quarters," Alex said. "If there is anything you and—Minh, I think?—need, just ask. But aside from that, we're going to try to make as few demands on you as possible. I know you have a lot to come to grips with right now.

40

"This is Naomi Tomlinson, who is among other things sometimes my wiser half. She will make sure you have everything that you need. And this is Suzanne Lemeurier, the Fleet's senior psychologist. If you need to talk to someone about... what happened, I have asked Suzanne to be available for you."

«Thank you, Mr. Holder.» Nandar nodded. «I—think that would be helpful.»

"We are planning your husband's funeral for tomorrow, if that is alright. If it's not too soon for you. He will receive full military honors."

Nandar wiped away a tear.

«Yes,» she said. «That will be good. Thank you. At least I will be able to say goodbye to my Khun. *They* would not have given me even that.»

Lieutenant Khun Satt Naing's funeral was held the next day, as promised. Dreamer fabricated a whisper-light aeroshell coffin that would burn up entirely during re-entry. The entire funeral was streamed live.

The Fleet did not have a military band. It *did*, by sheer chance, have a single piper, one Iain Colin Mackenzie by name, once a Colonel of— *officially*, at least—the Royal Scots Dragoon Guards, before he retired with a list of decorations as long as his arm. Now he was 'un-retired' as Captain of DD-38 *Highlander* and Commodore of DesRon Four. Despite his official rank of Captain, nearly everyone still referred to him as Colonel Mackenzie anyway, out of respect—or sometimes, among fellow Scots, simply "the Colin." And that was a *greater* mark of respect.

It also transpired that one of 1st Company, 6th Platoon, Rifleman Tom Whitaker, played snare drum and had an interest in Scots pipe music. He had brought his drum with him in his duffel when the 184th Marine Rifle Company came aboard, and he kept in practice with it.

Lieutenant Naing's coffin was carried by an honor guard of six Marines from the extraction team, in Fleet dress uniform. Behind them marched all of the remaining members of *Inazuma's* bridge crews. At the head of the procession were Colonel Mackenzie and Rifleman Whitaker, with Commander Kusanagi three paces behind. Almost everyone on the Stardock turned out to watch as the procession slow-marched down the concourse. Mackenzie played *The Dark Island*, and he played *Flowers of the Forest*, and he played *Highland Cathedral* and *Mist Covered Mountains* and *Cro Chinn t-Saile...* and he played *A Flame of Wrath*, Whitaker's snare drum punching the angry drumbeats out hard.

The funeral procession marched down the concourse to the docking bay, where the Marine honor guard carried the coffin onto a *Hornet* dropship. The dropship undocked and burned hard toward the limb of Earth, aiming for the Indian Ocean. The pilot took it up to thirty kilometers a second before he cut thrust.

On the dropship, as they approached the upper edge of atmosphere, Nandar Myat put her hands on her husband's coffin, then laid her cheek on it, touching him by proxy one last time. She whispered a few quiet words that nobody caught. Then after a long moment, she straightened up and stepped back, tears running down her cheeks.

The Marines picked up and shouldered the coffin one last time, then the side doors on the dropship opened. The edges of the atmosphere seal field glared red. They eased the coffin out through the field and pushed it away.

«Farewell, my dearest love,» Nandar said softly, one hand half-raised as though to wave.

The white coffin kept pace with the lander, drifting slowly away, as Commander Kusanagi spoke a brief but heartfelt eulogy; then the side doors closed. The coffin remained visible on the door screens, of course.

The pilot lifted the drop-ship away, adjusting course enough to miss all but the most tenuous fringes of atmosphere, but kept tracking the coffin on sensors, rolling the dropship on its side to keep it in view from the cabin. On the Stardock concourse, Mackenzie played *A Scottish Soldier* and *Lochanside*.

Far below the dropship, still sharp and clear on the screens, the coffin began its terminal dive into Earth's atmosphere. At first there was just a faint, pearly glow around the front of the coffin, then the glow grew brighter and spread backward over the white aeroshell. In only moments, the glow grew and brightened into a brilliant streak, then a long ribbon of flame across Earth's sky.

And then the fire faded, and the coffin was gone. Hornet One turned around and counter-burned to return to the Stardock. On board the Stardock, the procession turned around and slow-marched silently back up the concourse, just Whitaker's snare-drum lightly tapping out the slow, dry death-march tempo.

———

Alex couldn't sleep. He lay awake, staring at the ceiling.

Naomi, next to him, wasn't asleep either. It was in part because she knew Alex wasn't sleeping. She rolled over to face towards him, seeing and feeling the stress in him.

"Hey," she said, softly, as she reached out to touch his cheek. She found it wet.

"Alex, are you okay?"

Alex drew in a ragged breath.

"No, not really," he admitted. "I'm *not*. I knew the day would come, sooner or later, when we would start losing people. Unless we can somehow avoid a battle *at all*. But I wasn't ready for it to start happening *this soon*... or for such a *stupid, senseless* reason."

Naomi didn't think she had any words that would help. So she just wrapped her arms around Alex and held him tightly.

3. The Name's The Thing

Six orbits after Lieutenant Naing's funeral, CG-01 came back in from first trials, escorted by *Arapaima*. Sarah Burke eased the big cruiser carefully into gate S14. If the outside hatch needed to be closed, there would be only about twenty meters between the hatch and the stern of the cruiser. Alex had already requested construction of additional gates—at a wider 120m spacing—on top of Boom 2, and extension of the transit system out into Boom 2 Port and Starboard with the lessons learned on Boom One. Later, they would need to build gates on Boom 3, as well, to have enough docking space for the planned built-out of Warlords. The Boom 2 gates, at least, would be ready long before there was more than one Warlord to dock.

"So how did it go?" Alex asked, at the debrief.

"She's a beaut," Sarah Burke said. "Though you wouldn't persuade me to switch from *Ballarat* for her."

"Oh?" The comment made Alex curious. "Mind enlarging on that? Did we get something wrong?"

"Not at all," Sarah said. "I was going to. The Warlord is a magnificent ship, for sure. But a bit ponderous after a Shark class. I like the way *Ballarat* handles. Nimble, agile. Responsive. *Feels* fast. The Warlord is *ridiculously* maneuverable for a ship massing close to a quarter million tonnes, but still feels sluggish compared to a Shark. Tops out around fifty-five, fifty-six gee, by the way. You can push it a *little* past that, but it feels like a strain. I'd call fifty-five the service limit.

"Anyway, *almost* everything worked like clockwork. Fantastic coverage on the defensive armament, you have to get really close to the hull to find a blind spot, and there aren't many of them even then. But there IS a blind spot, if you can get into it, right between the sponsons. I'd like to see something that can cover that, even if it's only a point defense cluster."

"Okay, noted," Alex agreed. He saw Lewis nodding agreement as well. "But you said *almost* everything...?"

"We did a bunch of missile dumps," Sarah continued, "and the rotary launchers worked great. We didn't actually *fire* more than half a dozen of the new missiles; we just pumped them out not activated, then gathered them up, loaded them back into the magazines, and did it again.

"The missiles we *did* test-fire worked bonzer. They absolutely *scream* away from the ship. Kick them out, watch them align as they boost clear, then they throttle up and they're just *gone*. Out of visual range in an instant. Those X-heads are frightening. I wouldn't want to be in front of one."

She looked across the table at Lewis Monaghan.

"We did run into just one problem," she continued. "I'll let Lewis talk about it."

Lewis nodded.

"As Sarah said," he began, "the up-sized rotary launchers worked great, though they cycle missiles through slower than the Shark's missiles. We really should have proper names for the two missile types, you know, to avoid confusion which type we're talking about.

"But anyway, they're nearly six times the mass of a Shark's missiles, so it's no surprise the launcher takes a little longer to toss them out. We designed expecting about half the rate of fire, and that's what we got.

"The problem isn't the launcher drum. It's the feed from the magazines. We had a few jams when trying to reload the last two rows of launchers, fore and aft, from the magazines while maneuvering hard. But I think I know what the problem is. The best fix would be to beef up the transfer arm actuators a little, and we should definitely do that for the future, but for the present time I'm confident we could work around it by tweaking the grav compensation profile toward the bow and stern."

Alex nodded. He didn't have to ask whether Dreamer was taking notes.

"You said we should name the missile types," Alex said. "Did any of you have any particular names in mind?"

Sarah got a thoughtful look.

"For some reason," she said, "I want to say Shrike for the Shark's missiles. Maybe just because of alliteration. Shark, shrike, shark, shrike. But I don't know if it's actually a good name."

"I have no problem with it," Lewis said. "There's good precedent, the AGM-45 Shrike. Wild Weasels in Vietnam used to carry them."

"No objection from me either," Alex said.

"Nor I," added Tom. Maksim, at the end of the table, shrugged, nodded silently and flashed a thumbs-up.

"Well if nobody objects," Alex said, "I'd call that decided, then. Shrike it is. And the big X-head missiles?"

Lewis shrugged.

"Don't know," he mused. "Hammer, maybe? Thunderbolt?"

"Gungnir," came a voice from down the table, next to Maksim. Alex looked curiously at him, unable to place the voice or face. He wasn't *concerned*; he knew nobody would have made it in here who shouldn't be.

"You know," he said, "I don't think we've ever been introduced. I'm Alex Holder."

"Pete Bjarnesen," said the newcomer. "*Ballarat*. Pleased to meetcha."

"Sorry," Sarah said, "I should have introduced Pete. He's my XO. Didn't occur to me you didn't know him."

"Well, glad to meet you, Pete," Alex said. "I didn't quite catch the suggestion?"

"Gungnir," Pete repeated. "Odin's enchanted spear that never misses its target."

Alex nodded, after a moment, and so did Lewis.

"I like that," Alex said, after a moment. "Good call."

"Pete's always bending our ears with discussions about Norse mythology," Sarah said, grinning.

"Hey, what can I say?" Pete chuckled, with a grin of his own. "I didn't get to pick my ancestors." Alex laughed at that.

"I don't think any of us get to do that," he agreed. "But as revenge, our ancestors don't get to pick their descendants, either."

"Fair dinkum," Pete agreed, still grinning.

"Anyway, that sounds like a perfect name to me," Alex said. "All in favor, raise a hand?" A forest of hands rose.

"Well, it's settled, then," Alex declared. "They're now officially designated, uh... SM-1 *Shrike* and SM-2 *Gungnir*.

"Anyone else have any issues or comments about the Warlord?"

The discussion went on for quite a while, but in the end, the consensus was clear. The new Warlord was a good, solid ship, with a couple of close-in blind spots in its point defense and a glitch that needed to be worked out of the magazine-to-drum missile reload mechanisms. The glitch had never shown up on the Sharks, because the drum launchers on a Shark were close to midships. Before the review even ended, Dreamer was done reviewing all of the recorded diagnostics and had a proposed modification to the loader mechanism, and Lewis agreed that it looked to him as though it ought to work—but Lewis suggested implementing the G-comp retuning *as well*, just to be doubly certain, and Dreamer concurred. Dreamer estimated six days to perform the refit on all eighty magazine-to-launcher feeds.

Those six days meant that CG-01 would come out of refit two days before the first Warlord-trained full crew graduated—and six days before grav-lance prototype two would be ready for testing.

"Since you've got some command experience with the Warlord now, Sarah," Alex said, "I'd like you and Pete and a few of your other best officers to remain in command for CG-01's shakedown cruise before you go back to *Ballarat*. Aside from anything else, that way you can reproduce the *exact* maneuvers that produced the loader jam, and verify that it's fixed. Do you mind doing that?"

"Not at all," Sarah said. "Consider it done."

"And now that we know there's no major issues," Alex said, "let's go ahead and lay down CG-02 and CG-03."

"The build time on them is over three months," Tom reminded Alex. "We can have five or six crews ready by then. Are you sure you want to only build two more right now?"

Alex thought about that.

"Let's... err on the side of caution *for now*," he said. "We can ramp up later if the first three look good."

Sandra nodded slowly.

"That makes sense to me," she agreed. "We still have well over two years before we expect the Khreetan. We have time for caution."

"It's a good argument," Tom said. "I concur."

"Two, then," Alex said. "For now."

"Very well," Dreamer replied. "Beginning construction of the next two ships now."

"Perfect," Alex said. "Then let's all wrap it up and go find some food. And over food, we can talk about what crew we're going to put on CG-01."

———————

"Holder's done it again, Mr. President," General Morgan told John Riken, as they walked together down a hallway after the daily national security briefing. "The Fleet just posted the specifications on a new ship class that they've started building, a missile arsenal ship that they're calling the Warlord class cruiser."

John Riken chuckled.

"I'm not going to try to read the full spec," he said. "I know it's beyond me, and I don't need to know it all. Care to just give me the high-level summary?"

"Sure," Morgan said, with a quick grin. "How's this: Imagine the entire United States or Russian nuclear arsenal packed into a single quarter-million-ton ship, a quarter again larger than the world's largest bulk carrier. And they *still* run it with a crew only ten percent larger than one of their Shark-class destroyers."

John Riken thought about that for a moment, then shook his head, bemused.

"You know, Bob," he said, "I'm still having difficulty coming to grips with just how fast our idea of 'normal' is changing. And I'm betting we're not even *close* to done yet."

"I'm sure we aren't, sir," General Morgan agreed.

"Confidentially, General," Riken confided, "the sheer magnitude of the firepower the United Fleet has displayed—together with that unexpected intervention in Korea at the start of the year—has a lot of powers on the world stage re-examining their thinking. I'm not ready to say you can take this to the bank yet, but... I've had several interesting and *fruitful* informal conversations with my opposite numbers in Moscow and Beijing lately.

"Don't count on this, and don't hold your breath. But... I think we *might* finally be within diplomatic reach of a *total* nuclear disarmament treaty between all of the major powers. A complete turnaround from the Deep Space Treaty and its 'no nuclear weapons allowed in space', to 'no nuclear weapons allowed *EXCEPT* in space'."

For just a moment, General Robert Morgan was caught so off guard that he actually stumbled.

"That would be *amazing*, sir," he replied. "Do you think that the tertiary-level nuclear powers—Iran, Israel, the Saudis, Pakistan—would go for that?"

"Honestly, I'm not sure how much *choice* they'd have," John Riken replied. "Holder's already demonstrated that he has a zero-tolerance policy about use of nuclear weapons on Earth. He stated that was why he intervened in Korea—because it was a high-probability nuclear flash-point.

And if we could get nuclear weapons off Earth's surface, I think I could happily regard that as my life's accomplishment."

"There will still be terrorists, sir," General Morgan reminded him.

Riken nodded.

"There will," he agreed. "But I think it will be a much smaller risk if we can dry up the supply of weapons-grade plutonium. If we can replace commercial nuclear fission with Holder's fusion reactors... we *might* be able to put nuclear weapons outside the reach of non-state actors altogether.

"And let's face it, we've already seen that terrorists don't *need* nuclear weapons to commit atrocities."

"That's very true," Morgan said, "but the truth is *also* that for a while now, we've had less real concern about terrorists deploying suitcase pony nukes, and more about dirty bombs."

Riken sighed in reluctant agreement.

"I don't know *how* the hell we eliminate dirty bombs," he agreed. "But to be honest with you? I think I'm less afraid of terrorists building dirty bombs, than I am of them building bio-weapons. At least a dirty bomb only devastates a single city."

General Morgan had no answer to that. It was an unsettling thought that *nobody* had a good answer to.

The Warlord missile-magazine refit went without any surprises, and of course the design change was automatically incorporated into all future launcher production. Eighteen more launchers already produced and in stock needed to go back to also receive the modification.

The first fully Warlord-trained crew graduated from the Academy on October 4. They insisted on involving their assigned Marine platoon, 2nd Platoon of 5th Company, in the naming decision, debating at some length before deciding that their new ship's name would be *Saladin*. To applause from the assembled spectators, CG-01 *Saladin* backed carefully out of the docking bay and headed out on its shakedown cruise.

On October 7, the second grav-lance prototype was ready for testing. It was towed out and installed in the test cradle.

Just like P-One, P-Two performed flawlessly on power-up, idle power diagnostics, charging balance, idle stability, and so forth, on up to and through twenty-five percent charge. It went slowly, but stably, past the twenty-eight percent charge level at which P-One had failed, with nothing undue on the telemetry.

Twenty-two hours into the test plan, at thirty-one percent charge, it went suddenly and violently non-linear, and fried itself again. But Dreamer got a little more information about it this time. Just a little.

Alex sighed. But it was early days yet. Failures were only to be expected during the initial trials of what Dreamer assured him was a completely *new* weapon.

He discussed the test for a little while with Dreamer, then Dreamer started doing the final twenty percent of completion work on P-Three, with additional test instrumentation changes. He also started bringing P-Four up to seventy-five percent complete, and began a fifth prototype.

Dreamer, could we possibly repair these failed prototypes? Alex asked.

*We could **try**,* Dreamer replied. *But I would not have one hundred percent confidence in the repairs. By disassembling and recycling the failed units and building new, I have better confidence in the test prototypes, and I gain additional detailed information about exactly what damage occurred to which components.*

That makes perfect sense, Alex agreed. *It's not as though we're working on a budget. For anything except time.*

Exactly, Dreamer agreed. *And we should still have plenty of time.*

A thought occurred to Alex.

Dreamer, he asked, *would it be helpful if we brought in some of the science teams up from Earth to assist on the grav lance?*

I have already considered that possibility, Dreamer replied. *Unfortunately, while a good number of the visiting researchers are clearly quite brilliant—and I already see signs of some extremely innovative original work—the hard truth is that none have yet mastered the underlying body of theory required to understand hyperdrive and artificial-gravity physics deeply enough to be able to assist with an application this advanced of those theories.*

Fair enough, Alex said. *I'll freely admit the actual mechanics of it is FAR above my head. Even in rapport, I can't follow **how** the weapon is supposed to actually work. And it was my idea in the first place.*

Do not underestimate the originality of your idea, Dreamer said. *But also do not think that the responsibility for actually making it a reality should rest upon your shoulders. You cannot do everything.*

Alex chuckled.

So Naomi, and Tom, and Dong-geun, and Yeon, and I don't know who else, keep telling me, he agreed. *I'm doing my best to delegate more.*

———————

"Alex," Dong-geun said during daily status on a day in mid-October, "I have a commercial, rather than political, matter for your attention."

"Sure," Alex said, nodding.

"It seems the great success of the Tanzanian venture has been drawing attention. We have inquiries from General Motors in America, and from the Tata Group in India. The Volkswagen Group in Germany has also expressed some interest. Both Tata and General Motors fundamentally made the same request—both are perfectly capable of producing their own *motors*, but wish to know whether we would be willing to supply them with the high temperature superconductors to do so."

"Yes," Alex replied immediately. He didn't even need to think about it. "Of course we will. With the obvious proviso that Fleet needs come first. Did we already publish the technical data on manufacturing high temperature superconductors?"

"We did," Dong-geun confirmed, "but so far production efforts on Earth have been experiencing poor yields. Tata Group in particular cited this trouble as a reason for their request."

"OK," Alex said. "Let's see if we can get a technical assistance program up for that, then. The wider adoption we can get of high-temperature superconductors, the better it will be for everyone. We can offer process training, and additional technology transfer if we can identify specific problem steps. And let's see if we can encourage some Earthside concerns to specialize in superconductor manufacturing under Global Fair Share. Not just for motors, either. If we can bootstrap production of superconducting cables for power distribution, that'll massively cut distribution losses, and also help make it feasible for a lot of nations whose only cash export now is oil to deploy solar farms and export power instead."

Dong-geun nodded.

"That would perhaps help overcome some of the resistance," he agreed. "And... this may be a counter-intuitive suggestion, but I think we should consider setting a sliding-scale fee on the training. I have observed that many business interests, particularly in the more developed nations, pay more serious attention to something that they have to pay for. They are deeply suspicious of anything that they get for free."

Alex pondered for a moment.

"You're not wrong," he said, nodding. "First world business logic is very strange at times, even when it's *not* simply 'exploit the market for all it will bear'. The Ivy League business schools in particular have this... *bizarre* delusion that nothing can possibly be worth anything unless you can assign a specific cost or value to it on the balance sheet. Their management theories have wrecked more than one entire *industry*."

He thought about it a moment longer.

"Do it. And if the big corporations ask *why* we're charging them more than we do third-world ventures, tell them *exactly* that—'Because we know you won't take it seriously if we don't.'"

Dong-geun nodded.

"I will respond to General Motors and Tata, and get the program under way," he said.

"How's the gravity lance program coming along?" Tom inquired.

"We should be ready for the next test in about another ten days," Alex replied. "We're still trying to lick the charging problem at this point. Dreamer is confident that we can make it work, though, once we figure out all of the problems."

"Given any more thought to a ship design to carry it?" Sandra asked.

"Not yet." Alex shook his head. "Still too early for that. The design of the weapon is too much in flux. Don't sweat it, we have *plenty* of time to think about mounting it, if we can get it working in any reasonable time at all."

⸻

On October 24th, Dreamer declared P-Three ready for test. It was towed out to the test cradle and installed, after running a full diagnostic on the test cradle and all of the power feeds first to make certain there was no known issue on the test cradle itself. Tom, Sandra, Maksim, and Hussein were there to observe the test, as were a couple of physicists up from the

Vienna University of Technology. The word was starting to get out about the esoteric new weapon and its advanced physics.

The twenty percent, twenty-five percent, and thirty percent runs went fine. So did the thirty-five percent run, and the forty percent run. At forty-five percent charge rate, it barely passed twenty-eight percent charge and was suddenly wreathed in corona arcs again. Dreamer immediately cut the power, and the arcs slowly subsided.

"I am running a diagnostic," Dreamer stated. After about ten minutes, he reported that the resonance limiters were damaged, and no further testing on this prototype would be practical.

"It failed this time at a lower charge level than the last run," Alex observed. "Although at a higher charge rate."

"Yes," Dreamer agreed, "but there is a crucial difference this time."

"What is that, Dreamer?" Hussein was the first to ask.

"This time," Dreamer replied, "I believe I understand *why* it is happening. The exact manner in which the cores are heterodyned together is allowing a chaotic mode to appear in the resonances between the cores. If that mode passes certain limits, it goes unrecoverably non-linear."

"Well," Alex said, "it's great that we know what's happening. Can we solve it?"

"Yes, I believe so," Dreamer replied. "But it will require extensive re-engineering of the heterodyning loops. It is probably quicker and more efficient to scrap prototype P-Four and apply the redesign directly to P-Five. I will begin re-engineering P-Five as soon as I complete the necessary calculations. We should be ready for another test some time in mid to late December."

"Excuse me, ah, Dreamer," one of the Austrian physicists asked. "Could you possibly answer some questions about the underlying theory? My group are *trying* to come up to speed on this, but there is *so much* new physics to absorb, and there is something in particular that we do not yet fully understand about how the gravitational flux equations follow from the tensor field equivalence statements..."

Alex grinned, and left them to it. The conversation was over his head, and he was fine with that—although he had to admit, he wished he *did* understand it.

It turned out that all three automakers were only too happy to participate in the offered training program. Not only that, once all three of them had people on the Stardock together talking about the problem, it was only a few days before someone floated the idea of spinning off a jointly-operated independent subsidiary to manufacture superconductors and superconducting motors, with Stardock technical assistance.

The rough form of a deal had been hammered out by the time grav-lance P-Five was ready for testing, on December 22nd.

Just as on the previous test, the Austrian physicists showed up to observe. They brought some Japanese and Russian friends with them this time. There were a dozen Fleet officers present, as well—Maksim again, Sarah Burke and her XO Pete Bjarnesen, and others. There was enough of a crowd that Alex decided to relocate the test observation to the main briefing room.

"All static tests and calibration routines within spec," Dreamer announced. "Beginning ten/ten charge test."

The ten percent charge cycle went quickly, and uneventfully. So did the fifteen percent and twenty percent cycles... and thirty percent, and forty percent, and fifty percent. People drifted in and out and fresh rounds of snacks and coffee arrived as the long test cycles went on, each cycle going to a higher charge level at a higher charge rate than the one before. Then Dreamer would slowly discharge all three cores and re-check all of the static calibrations before the next cycle. A tension, an excitement began to grow in the room. The sixty percent test cycle passed successfully. So did the seventy percent cycle. There was quiet applause when the eighty cycle completed. The dozen or so physicists didn't seem to notice. They were utterly intent upon the status readouts that Dreamer was providing, watching every detail, every reading change, several of them referring to the underlying theory on their handheld pads as they watched. Alex *saw* one of the Japanese physicists' face light up as he suddenly put something together in his head, and began excitedly talking to his colleagues about it. Within minutes two of the Russians had joined in, and then the Austrians. Then one of the Austrians got it too.

"Of *course!*" he exclaimed. "I see it now! You're right, Hayoshi. Of *course* that is how it would work! Van Eycken's conjecture is *wrong*. Which means that..."

And they were off again.

Dreamer held the eighty percent charge for several minutes, then began to discharge the cores again as the physicists all conversed excitedly at the side of the room.

"Medvedev insists that flux should begin to reverse when potential saturates," Alex overheard one of the Russians saying. "But that is not what math really *says*. Math of theory suggests that it should phase shift, and that is what we are seeing here, I think."

One of the Japanese researchers clapped his hand to his forehead. "Hai! Yes, yes!" he agreed eagerly. "That is it! It phase shifts! And then because of this term *here...*"

Alex couldn't hide a grin.

"They're like a bunch of kids who just discovered a new toy, aren't they?" Naomi said, smiling.

"Absolutely," Alex agreed. "And this is the most wonderful new toy *ever.*"

"Do you understand what they're talking about?" she asked.

"Barely a word," Alex admitted. Naomi laughed. "But that's alright. I don't have to."

Another hour passed, and Dreamer began the ninety percent cycle— from zero to ninety percent charge, at ninety percent of the planned maximum testing charge rate. The charge indicator rose, fifty percent, then sixty percent, seventy percent, eighty percent. When it finally hit ninety percent, still without a sign of instability, there was cheering around the room.

Again, Dreamer held it at ninety percent for five minutes, then began draining the charge. One more round of charge testing to go.

Another thirty or so spectators had arrived by the time Dreamer was ready to begin the final test cycle, and the snacks and coffee had been refreshed again. With the charge rate increasing in lockstep with the charge level target, of course, each test cycle took the same time as the cycle before.

"Beginning one hundred percent charge test cycle," Dreamer announced, and began feeding power into the prototype. The charge level rose steadily. Forty percent, fifty, sixty. The room grew quiet. Seventy, eighty. When it passed ninety percent, it seemed as though everyone was holding their breath. They *weren't*, of course, nobody could hold their breath that long, but it was that kind of anticipation. Ninety five percent, ninety seven, ninety eight, ninety nine...

"One hundred percent charge," Dreamer declared. "Holding stable."

The room went wild.

Alex *had*, it turned out, been holding his breath for the last minute or two. He didn't realize it until he let it out. He turned to look at Naomi, and saw that she had a huge grin as well.

"It's working!" she said.

"So far," he agreed. "I think we're early in the test process yet." But the excitement had its grip on him as well.

"What's the next step, Dreamer?"

"I will hold this charge level for at least six hours, to verify stability," Dreamer said. The crowd in the room quieted a little, listening. "Then I wish to run a set of repeated one hundred percent charge and rapid discharge cycles. If that goes well, then tomorrow we will energize the cores for the first time. If all goes well, I wish to repeat several cycles of energizing and de-energizing the cores."

Alex nodded.

"And then?" he asked.

"And then," Dreamer replied, "if that goes well, I believe we will be ready for the first partial-power test shot."

"You know, I'm hungry," Alex said. Naomi nodded.

"Ginza or Lem's?" she asked.

"How about Lem's?" Alex said. "Right next to Infinity."

"Works for me," Naomi agreed.

"Okay, folks," Alex called out. "Naomi and I are headed over to Lem's Diner for a proper meal and a little celebration. Anyone who wants to is welcome to join us."

As they were heading toward the door, they were intercepted by a couple of the physics team. One of the Russians and one of the Austrians, Alex thought.

"Thank you very much, Mr. Holder, for allowing us to observe tests," the first said. "I think, that we have learned as much from observing this test process, as we had learned in past month of study."

"I'm glad it was useful to you all," Alex said. "I thought I spotted some breakthroughs in understanding over there."

"Yes, yes," the Austrian agreed. "There is nothing like seeing what the theory describes, happening slowly in front of you with full instrumentation. We gained many new insights today."

"You're all welcome to attend any of the future test sessions," Alex replied. "I'll make sure your teams are on the notification list."

"Thank you again," the Russian said. «Большое спасибо.»

———————

They reconvened to continue the tests the next day.

"Where do we stand, Dreamer?" Alex asked, when everyone was gathered.

"Charge remained stable for six hours with no sign of leakage, bleed-over, self-discharge, or chaotic resonance modes," Dreamer reported. "Since that time I have run eight full-charge and rapid-discharge cycles with no signs of any problems. Everything appears to be operating as expected."

"So far, so good. And today's test?"

"Today we will attempt to energize the three cores," Dreamer replied. "I must give due caution that we are attempting to energize a configuration of hyperspace cores which has never been tried before. The theoretical basis is sound, I believe, even though it is in some respects new ground. But I cannot guarantee the practical application at this stage."

"That's perfectly understandable," Alex said. "New ground brings new risks with it."

"Indeed," Dreamer agreed.

"So walk me through the process at high level before we start."

"The three cores are fully charged with the energy required to operate the weapon," Dreamer said. "But it is effectively in standby, comparable to a single hyperdrive core that is powered up but not activated to jump. When we energize the three cores, we will be arming the weapon. You could also compare it to the charging of a spinal railgun immediately before firing."

"And once energized, it's ready to fire," Alex said.

"Precisely," Dreamer agreed.

"So... are we looking at the two seconds pre-charge time of a hyper-boosted railgun," Alex asked, "or the twenty seconds of pre-jump hyperdrive activation?"

"In between the two," Dreamer said. "I expect about twelve seconds. But once energized, or armed, the weapon should be able to fire multiple shots, every few seconds, as long as power to the weapon is maintained."

Alex nodded.

"OK," he said, looking around the room. "I guess it's time to start the show. Whenever you're ready."

"Conducting final static checks," Dreamer said. Alex—and nearly everyone else—watched the remote video feeds from the target drones monitoring the test. The physics team were paying more attention to the telemetry.

"Status is green across the board," Dreamer reported. "Energizing."

On the video feeds, nothing happened at first. Then a faint, pearly nimbus started to appear around the weapon's three modified hyperdrive cores. The central cores began to glow pale blue.

Then all but two of the video feeds and all of the telemetry from the weapon test cradle cut off at once. On the remaining two, from much more distant drones, a brilliant flash was replaced a moment later by a ghostly, expanding sphere of light.

"Well, *that* was quite dramatic," Tom observed drily.

"The weapon has exploded," Dreamer stated, perhaps unnecessarily. "But we have four point two seconds of good telemetry before the explosion. I can already see that there is an anomaly in the last half second of that data. I hope that it will be enough to determine the cause of the explosion."

"Could we please see last second again?" one of the physics team asked. "Slow rate down one hundred times, please."

"Certainly," Dreamer replied, and began replaying the telemetry.

"I'll leave you to it," Alex said. "How's the test cradle?"

"The test cradle will require extensive repair," Dreamer said. "The shield and boom between them adequately protected the antimatter reactor. It is undamaged."

"Good," Alex replied. "I guess our next tests will be on P-Six?"

"Indeed," Dreamer replied. "I will have the test cradle repaired well before P-Six is ready."

A week after grav-lance prototype five blew itself to vapor, the first two *production* Warlords, CG-02 and CG-03, were delivered.

"It's New Year's Eve," Alex said. "I'm not going to send two crews out on shakedown on New Year's Eve. We can hold the crew graduations tomorrow instead. That sounds like a great way to observe New Year's Day."

"Good idea," Sandra agreed. "The crews are ready, and they've chosen their ships' names. It would be a shame to make them miss New Year's Eve."

Alex sat back and grinned proudly. Tom and Sandra—and the additional aides that they had appointed—were doing a fantastic job with the Academy. He didn't have to touch it at all. It took qualified but green recruits in, and turned out fully hyper-trained, simulator-familiarized complete crews with live jump and navigation experience in one of the three Endeavours, ready to step aboard their ship for the first time and fly it as though they'd been flying it together for a month. Because, in complete full-bridge hands-on simulation, they *had* been.

All these people, all around him. **They** were the Fleet.

The New Year's Eve party followed the best of the traditions the Fleet was steadily establishing. Which is to say that it was loud, boisterous, occasionally ribald, and happy, but nobody ended up in the brig for drunk and disorderly. Of *course* there were several hopak performances, by popular demand, as well as various other exhibitions, and Colonel Mackenzie gave an hour-long solo pipe performance to thunderous applause.

The next day, crew graduations and naming were held for the first two 'production' Warlords. They departed on their shakedown cruises as CG-02 *Temüjin* and CG-03 *Shaka Zulu*. There were actually five crews trained by then; the other three would have to wait.

"How many crews do you anticipate having by the time we can build the next batch?" Alex asked Tom Whitman.

"At least another four," Tom replied. "That three months build time is practically an entire training cycle."

Alex thought about timing.

"Suppose we start four more now," he said slowly, "and then two more a month. Can we keep up with training crews for them at that rate?"

"Yes," Tom replied, without hesitation. "As long as we can keep up the recruitment rate."

"Dreamer, we can build them at that rate?"

"Yes," Dreamer agreed. "But I recommend we increase asteroid mining operations to increase the supply of raw materials. We will need to construct additional mining tugs."

"Do that right now, please," Alex said. "Let's not get behind the materials-supply curve."

"Understood," Dreamer replied. "Do you wish to begin construction of the next set of cruisers as well?"

"I'm... uncertain," Alex replied. "I'd feel more comfortable waiting until *Temüjin* and *Shaka Zulu* return from their shakedowns and we know there's no outstanding issues we need to correct."

"If I might point out," Dreamer observed, "the Fleet's shakedown cruises typically run twelve to fourteen days. If there were anything so badly wrong in the Warlord design that remediating it would require changing construction that early in the build, we would almost certainly have already discovered it in the very first test flights. There will be abundant time during the build to remediate any minor issues that come up during these shakedown cruises."

Alex hesitated for a few seconds, then shook his head wryly.

"You're absolutely correct, Dreamer. I'm trying too hard to avoid risks that probably aren't even there." He took a deep breath. "Tom, Sandy, Lewis—any objections?"

"I agree with Dreamer," Lewis said. "There's no reason to delay laying them down." There were head-nods around the room.

"OK," Alex said. "Do it. Go ahead and start the next four. Then two more per month, until and unless we see a need to re-adjust. That'll make the next four due... what, first week in April?"

"Yes, Alex. Approximately April 5th or 6th."

4. Storms In Africa

Abosede was awakened by the sound of shouts calling all of the fighters to assemble. He blinked a few times, got to his feet, picked up and quickly checked his Kalashnikov, then slung it over his shoulder and answered the muster call. It was a pleasant day for it. It was late January, and the rains were still several months away.

He was neither the first nor the last to arrive, a dozen or so others trickling in after him. That was good. Being too early or too late attracted attention. Sometimes not the good kind.

Up front, Commander Okafor waited until the last few had trickled in. Then he began to speak.

"Today is a great day!" he declared. "Today, we are going to take action!" There were subdued cheers. One did not wish to sound too enthusiastic, or too reluctant.

Okafor turned to the map displayed on the large easel, indicating a location with a long pointer.

"We are going here," he said. "What is here, you ask? Why are we going there? And well you may ask.

"This is a place where they break up ships for scrap metal. It was never very interesting, which is why you have never heard of its name. It is hard, dirty work that earned little money. But now, they have a machine from the space station, and they are becoming wealthy. Where there once were shanties, now there are houses. They are even building a hospital.

"We are going to take that wealth, and make it ours. For the glory of Allah and the Caliphate."

Now there were real cheers. They probably weren't so much about the glory of the Caliphate, Abosede thought to himself, as the thought of the promised wealth.

"We will travel to here," Okafor said, pointing out another location, "using the trucks. Then we will march to here," another location, very close, "on foot, and we will wait until dark, and then we will go in. And when they wake in the morning, they will find us in control of everything."

Well, Abosede thought to himself, at least it didn't sound as though there was likely to be very much shooting. Though he couldn't help but wonder how long it would be before government troops showed up to take it back. If the place was becoming wealthy, then it was likely the government was noticing. Government men gathered around money like flies on a dead goat.

Somewhat to Abosede's right, Ejiro was having very similar thoughts. Like Abosede, he had a fatalistic attitude about it. It wasn't as though he had a choice in the matter. He hadn't even had any choice about joining up, abducted from his home when he was nine years old. That was eight years ago now, he thought. He wasn't quite sure. Now, this was all he knew. They would go, and he would do as he was told, and they would fight, or they would not, and if they fought, either he would live, or he would die. So far, he had not died. He had to keep telling himself to be content with that. He did not know where else he could go.

Nkiru, two rows in front of Ejiro, was mainly thinking once again that this did not sound like something that would make his grandfather anything except even more disappointed in him. He seemed to be very good at disappointing Grandfather. He truly wanted to make Grandfather proud of him. He just never seemed to be able to find any way to do it.

It wasn't fair, he thought, not for the first time. He could perhaps have had more opportunities, had Father not spent most of what little money he had managed to come into on drink. Then one day Father had gone to work once too often already drunk, and never came home. One of the men he worked with had come by the house and told Mother that he thought Father had fallen into the concrete, but that they could not stop the pour to try to find him. He remembered his mother wailing and screaming, and cursing the gods—and cursing Father's drinking. But at least it meant Father had never hit her again.

Nkiru still wasn't quite sure how he had ended up here. Perhaps some day he would find something better. If he could stay alive long enough.

———————

In the end, it was late at night by the time they arrived anyway, because one of the trucks broke down on the way. They spent three hours sitting off the side of a dirt road while the driver and the two mechanics swore at it and finally got it running again. So the trucks went straight to the forward rally point, and they walked in from there.

As Commander Okafor had said, there was a small town growing up around the big recycling machine. The houses were small, but they looked new and clean. There was a covered open-air market, and a police station, and a small school, and indeed, there was the beginnings of a hospital going up. A large open-sided warehouse next to the machine held stacks of processed materials, and even a lot of prefabricated parts stacked on racks. Some way behind the machine, a partly-stripped freighter sat beached on the shore. The streets were almost deserted, everyone already in bed and asleep.

Sergeant Chidike took four men into the police station with him. "Keep it *quiet*," he warned them. "No shooting unless they shoot first. We do not want to wake anyone."

They scouted from the outside first, carefully peeking through windows from a few feet away where the light would not catch their faces. Chidike pushed the front door open just a little and peered through the crack. The front desk was empty. Only two men were visible, both in the first room behind the desk.

Chidike raised a warning finger, and pushed the door open a little further. One by one, the four men scuttled in past him, staying below the level of the front desk. Chidike followed them. All five lined up behind the desk. Chidike risked a peek over the top of the desk. He still saw only two men, one to the left, one more to the center-right. He held up fingers, signalling two men left, two men right. Then he held up three fingers, two, one...

Almost as one, the five men stood up, vaulted over the desk, and rushed into the back room, their rifles aimed. The two policemen froze, taken completely by surprise.

"Please do not do anything hasty and unwise," Chidike said. "We do not want to have to shoot anyone."

There was a phone on the desk, and two more in the back room. Chidike ripped the wires out of all three.

"If either of you has a cell phone," he said, "give it to me now. Do not make me ask twice. If I find one later, I will become angry."

One of the two policemen looked at Chidike, then slowly, cautiously reached into his pocket with two fingers. Good, Chidike thought. Careful. A wise man, not a fool. The policeman pulled out an old Nokia phone, laid it on the desk in front of him, and raised his hand again.

"Very good," Chidike said. "Everything is going to be fine. We are going to put you both into a cell for now. You understand, of course."

Both policemen nodded. Chidike quickly patted both men down for weapons or any other contraband, then it was off to the cells with them.

"Now, where else are there telephones?" Chidike asked. "We do not want to hurt anyone."

The policemen told him. They had no choice.

Well before dawn, the small town was theirs.

There was some alarm when the town began to stir in the morning. It was quickly brought under control.

"Do not be afraid," Commander Okafor told the people who had been gathered together between the machine and the growing town. "We are not here to hurt you. Go about your lives. Do your work. But remember that we are in control now. This town is ours now. It belongs to the Caliphate."

"What will happen when government troops come?" one older man asked.

"There will be no government troops," Okafor told him. "We will try to ensure that nobody does anything unwise such as sending troops here.

"Now, please. Go about your work. Treat this as just a normal day."

Ejiro was assigned to supervise the men who operated the big machine. It was hard to keep his mind on watching them, as he watched shiny steel beams emerge from the machine. The older man who had asked about government troops turned out to be the foreman in charge of the machine. Ejiro watched, fascinated, as displays on the machine's control board changed without the foreman seemingly doing ANYTHING except put his hands on a panel. Another man seemed to be in charge of a group of flying machines that were detaching another section of superstructure from the freighter.

Finally Ejiro could resist no longer.

"How does it *work*?" he asked. "How do you control it?" That was another thing he was supposed to do, he remembered. Find out how to work the machine. "Could *I* control it?"

The foreman smiled slightly at him. He lifted his hands away and scooted his chair aside.

"Put your hands on the panel," he said.

Ejiro, nervous but excited, stepped up and put his hands on the panel as he had seen the foreman do.

"Do you feel anything? See anything?" the foreman asked.

"...No," Ejiro admitted.

"And you won't," the foreman said. He held out his hands towards Ejiro. "Look closely at my fingertips."

Ejiro looked. He could faintly see the outlines of something under the man's skin.

"These are how I control the machine," the foreman said. "You *cannot*. You do not have these. Even if you could take them from me, they would not work for you." He pointed toward the sky. "I had to go to the Stardock to get them, and to learn how to use them."

Ejiro nodded slowly. So much for learning how to control the machine.

Still...

"But how does it *work?*" he found himself asking.

With a smile, the older man began to explain.

Nkiru was assigned to street patrol duty for the first half of the day. He was paired with another man, and they walked around the small town looking for anything amiss. He could not help but notice how conversations stilled and died as they drew near. The people were afraid, he realized. He could not help feeling guilty. He didn't *want* them to have to be afraid of him. He didn't think that would please Grandfather at all.

———————

Alex, Dreamer said, *we have a situation. We have received a duress code from the recycler in Okumbiri.*

Duress code? Alex replied. *Shit. Alert Colonel Warner as well.*

Already done, Alex.

I want a surveillance overflight, then let's get a briefing together.

Through the infosphere, Alex sensed what felt like a chuckle.

That is exactly what Colonel Warner said, Dreamer replied. *Word for word.*

Alex could not help but grin.

I'll go to his briefing, he said. *Fewer people to move. I'll send him a quick heads-up that I'm on the way.*

Fifteen minutes later, Alex was in 1st Battalion's main briefing room with John Warner and his senior staff.

"Here's what we know," John opened. "There's somewhere between three and four hundred people in Okumbiri. They woke up this morning to find the town taken over by insurgents, presumed at this time to be Boko Haram-aligned jihadis. Nobody is known hurt so far. We've diverted three scout drones, and they'll be two klicks overhead in another twenty minutes. Pretty soon after that we'll have a lot better information. There's a couple more a bit further out."

"The duress code?" Alex asked. "Do we know more?"

"The duress code was entered by the foreman overseeing the recycler," Dreamer reported. "He is control level two, and would have been able to send it without any externally visible indication that he had done so."

"Good," Alex said. "That means he didn't incur any added risk by sending the code." John Warner nodded agreement. "Any other indications of things out of the ordinary?"

"Telemetry relayed from the recycler and its drone swarm, at least, seems to indicate completely normal operation," Dreamer replied.

"OK," said John Warner. "We're waiting on the scout drones. Until then, it's all guesswork. But so far, it sounds promising."

———

Another man was sent to relieve Ejiro so that he could get lunch. The food on offer at the food stand in the open market was a lot better than what they got in the field. The girl who served him was pretty, he noticed. She did not say anything, but her movements said she was angry. He thanked her politely, then went and sat down under a tree to eat.

He glanced back over towards the food stand several times while he ate. A couple of times he thought he caught the pretty girl looking at him, but she always looked away as soon as he looked up.

Ejiro finished his lunch and returned to his post. It wasn't long before he was lost in watching the operation of the machine again. He found he had endless questions, and the foreman was willing to answer *all* of them.

"What about you?" the foreman asked him, after a while. "You seem a bright young man. What are you doing here? Is this really the life you want to live?"

Ejiro didn't know how to answer, at first.

"I... did not get a choice," he said, haltingly. "They took me from my family. Now it is all I know."

"You *always* have a choice," the foreman told him. "What is your name?"

"Ejiro."

"I am Umaru," the foreman said. "Be careful what you choose, Ejiro."

Abosede was posted overlooking the road coming into town from inland, with two other men beside him. Three more were on the other side of the road. It would be pretty bad for anyone who came down that road, if they started shooting. The crossfire would be deadly.

Abosede hoped there wouldn't be any shooting. He hoped nobody came, because he knew that one of the three men on the opposite side was Abubakar. And Abubakar, he was quite certain, would be just *itching* for something—or preferably, *someone*—to shoot at. Abosede did not like Abubakar at all. Abubakar *liked* killing people. He was one of the true believers. Sometimes the look in his eyes gave Abosede chills. There was something mad in Abubakar; something full of hate and rage that just wanted to kill, and keep on killing until there was nothing left to kill. Abubakar, he had long ago decided, was *broken*. He thought it was probably no accident that Abubakar had been posted *outside* of the actual town, on this road checkpoint.

―――――――――

"Surveillance data is now available," Dreamer announced.

"Great," John said. "Put it up, and let's see what we've got."

Dreamer put up the overhead view of the town on a virtual display. Streets were outlined, as were key points—the recycler and its warehouse, the police station, the school, the two-room clinic next to where a small hospital was being built, a small one-room town hall. The map was scattered with red dots.

"Fifty-nine insurgents have so far been identified," Dreamer said. "There may be more who are currently inside buildings." A red box appeared just south of the center of town, highlighting a group of parked medium trucks. "These five vehicles are presumed to be their transportation. The smaller two are technicals." Paired red circles sprouted to the north and east where two roads entered the town. "These road accesses are guarded, six men in each location. All else appears normal. There are no visible casualties at this time."

"Let's try to keep it that way," Alex said. John Warner and Joshua Newton both nodded agreement.

"Keep monitoring," John said. "See if we can spot any more as they move around."

"Of course," Dreamer acknowledged.

"Do you have a general plan?" Alex asked. John nodded.

"After dark, we can send the drones in for a close look at any buildings we suspect may contain insurgents, and verify an accurate count and up-to-the-minute locations. Then I propose to air-drop two platoons in powered armor, shortly after midnight. I want us to outnumber them, *at least* one Marine on every insurgent, two-to-one on those access road ambushes, time-on-target drops with the element of surprise. I want to so *obviously* completely outmatch them that there's little—ideally, no—shooting. Let's *keep* this at no casualties, if we can."

Alex nodded.

"Sounds great to me. You obviously have this *well* in hand. Action plan approved; I'll get out of your hair, and see to making sure the Nigerian government does as well. We don't need them getting word and coming in shooting. I'll tell them that it's a Fleet-provided asset, that we claim jurisdiction, and we have it handled."

"Good call," Colonel John Warner agreed. " We'll keep you posted."

━━━━━━━━━━

Evening was coming on. Ejiro got relieved again.

"You're off for the night," his replacement told him. "Get some food and some sleep."

"I am off for the night as well," Umaru said.

"Do you have to shut the machine down?" Ejiro asked.

"No," Umaru said. "It will continue overnight breaking down what has been loaded into it during the day. But, look—" He pointed. "I have suspended the output until morning."

Ejiro nodded.

"So that it does not make a messy pile," he said.

"Or damage anything already produced," Umaru agreed. "But all of the remaining finished parts will be stacked before the crew leaves for the night anyway."

Nkiru had been given the afternoon to rest. But now, after he ate supper, he would have to take a watch on guard duty on the edge of town. Just in case someone came. He had already been given his assigned area.

Nobody noticed the whisper-quiet scout drones, five of them by now, that drifted back and forth above the town two hundred meters up. They were all but invisible against the darkening sky.

———————————————

"Final count looks like sixty-three," John Warner said. "The one who appears to be their commander seems to have set up shop in the town hall, with two guards with him. We think the mayor is in there as well at the moment. There seems to be always at least one stationed in the police station, and one in the control shack for the recycler. We observed three meals being taken into the police station although we know of only one insurgent in there at the time, so we're assuming that means there are two people in cells. Possibly the town's police officers."

"So, detailed plan?" Joshua Newton asked.

Warner did a quick mental query of which ships were docked and which platoons available.

"We've got 3rd and 7th platoons of 1st Company," he said, "4th of the 2nd, 3rd and 5th of the 3rd, 1st, 6th and 7th of the 4th, and three platoons of the 5th. Let's keep the 4th out of this, they had to deal with that nasty business in Myanmar. Let's not put them on this as well. Spread the load."

Major Yousef al-Hussein, commanding 4th Company, nodded agreement. Warner thought a moment longer.

"The 5th is perhaps still a little fresh. Major Petain, how do you feel about sending the 3rd and 5th of the 3rd?"

Major Jacques Petain nodded briskly.

"*Certainement*," he replied. "Let us give them a live exercise in the field."

"Very good, then," Warner said. "The 3rd and the 5th it is. Do you have an officer in mind to send in command?"

"Lieutenant Marne, I think," Petain replied. "He saw field experience in Benin. It is the right general area. It will be helpful. He is a good man, won't lose his head."

"Excellent," Warner said. "I want you to take six Hornets, give each squad their own. One squad to focus on taking back the town hall, police station, and clinic. One man on each posted insurgent, hold one squad in reserve, and split the rest between the two access road ambush sites. We'll determine exact drop positions right before drop. Drop at one thousand meters, time on target."

"*Bien*," Petain agreed.

Shortly before midnight Stardock time, two platoons of Fleet Marines in armor boarded six *Hornet*-class dropships from the lower level of the concourse. The dropships undocked, formed up, and began de-orbit burns that would put them over the Ivory Coast. By 0130 local time, they were in a holding pattern twenty kilometers west of Okumbiri, three kilometers above the South Atlantic.

"All tactical data is refreshed," Lieutenant Achille Marne said. "Drones have synced to the Hornets, you'll have live positional data on every target." He flashed a couple of markers up on the tactical grid. "There are currently two insurgents in the police station, three in the town hall, one in the clinic. We don't have exact positions inside the buildings for those six. You will have to improvise. Take as many as possible alive, don't fire unless you have to, keep it as quiet as you can, as long as you can. Minimize civilian casualties at all costs.

"You have your target assignments. We drop in ninety seconds."

———————————

Abosede was sure he was supposed to have been relieved by now. But it seems his little group of three, and the three across the road from them, had been forgotten. He kept catching himself nodding off. But at least it was quiet.

Nkiru was stationed at the open end of one of the town's relatively few streets. To help keep himself awake, he kept walking back and forth from one side of the street to the other, then he would scan the darkness for a few minutes, then walk back the other way. He had positioned himself about thirty meters out from the last house, so that he would not lose his night vision should someone in the house unexpectedly turn on a light.

Ejiru was asleep on the ground under a tree, with his rifle beside him. He knew he would be woken before dawn in order to get something to eat before his next watch.

The town was quiet. About a third of the insurgent group were sleeping, the rest either on watch, or, in the case of Commander Okafor and his two guards, burning the midnight oil in the town hall. Of the two men in the police station, one was catching a nap, the other idly cleaning his rifle for something to do.

The six Hornets drifted swiftly across the town a thousand meters up, doors open, all lights out. Marines in powered armor stepped out, one at a time or in groups, and dropped, controlling their descent rate on thrusters. Had anyone below chanced to look up, they might have noticed what looked like a new constellation of pale blue stars. Stars that were *moving*.

But nobody looked up. What was there to look up for?

Nkiru *felt*, as much as heard, a heavy *thud* behind him. Startled, he turned around, and found himself face to face with a huge, hulking metal giant. The giant was holding a huge rifle in one hand. The rifle looked big enough to kill a rhino, and it was pointed unwaveringly at Nkiru's chest. Nkiru froze.

The metal giant raised its other hand, one finger raised, to make a shushing gesture in front of where its mouth would be, if its face were not a nearly-featureless faceplate.

Nkiru very slowly, very carefully, lowered his rifle to let it hang on its sling, then equally slowly raised his empty hands.

"*Bien*," said the giant.

Abosede had nodded off again. He wasn't sure what had woken him. It was as though the ground had shaken. He rubbed his eyes, shook his head to clear it, looked up—and froze. His group of three men was surrounded by six massive armored figures. They had to be over two meters tall. They were holding equally massive rifles. The rifles were casually aimed not *quite* at Abosede and his two companions.

From the other side of the street, Abosede heard Abubakar shout, "*Allahu'akbar!*" The second word was mostly lost in the stuttering roar of a Kalashnikov on full-automatic. The bright muzzle flashes drew Abosede's eye. Ricochets whined and screamed away for a moment, then there was a sudden solid, metallic *WHACK*. For just a moment, Abosede saw Abubakar's rifle flying away in a high arc into the night. He heard a brief scream of pain, then saw Abubakar collapse to his knees, gasping and sobbing.

"*Merde,*" said one of the armored men.

"What was that?" said Idowu.

"Gunfire, obviously," said Commander Okafor. "Go and find out who fired, at what, and why."

Idowu headed for the front door. He opened it and went to step out before realizing that there was someone already in front of the door. It took him a moment longer to realize that the newcomer was *huge*. Then a metal hand grabbed his right shoulder in a crushing grip, and casually hurled him out into the street like a rag doll. He opened his mouth to cry out in surprise, but then he landed face-down with an impact that drove the breath from his lungs.

Behind him, the giant stepped through the doorway, moving fast. Kelechi, the second guard, raised his rifle, but before he could pull the trigger, the giant grabbed it by the fore-end, ripped it casually from his grasp and threw it at the wall. A single shot was triggered as the giant yanked the rifle from Kelechi's hand. The bullet struck the giant squarely in the chest, but went whining away without leaving more than a smear of copper. The stock broke off the rifle when it hit the wall. Behind Kelechi, Okafor gasped and cursed, then sat down hurriedly, his hands pressed to his left thigh. Blood trickled through his fingers. There was a lot of it.

A second armored giant had already come through the door, and took charge of Kelechi. Kelechi's wrist hurt, and he thought his trigger finger was broken. The first giant was standing over Okafor, looking down at him.

"*J'ai besoin d'un médecin ici,*" Kelechi heard him call out. "*Leur commandant est blessé par ricochet.*"

74

Ejiru was woken up by shocks felt through the ground, and the sound of distant gunfire. He reached for his rifle even before his eyes were properly open.

The rifle wouldn't move. He opened his eyes, and saw a dark column atop where his rifle lay. After a moment, he realized that it was a massive, armored foot and leg. His gaze followed the leg upward. A giant figure loomed over him in the darkness.

He tugged again reflexively at his rifle, bewildered and afraid.

"*Non*," the giant said, quietly.

Ejiru let go of his rifle, then slowly, carefully sat up. The giant watched him, but otherwise did nothing. He scooted just a little bit further away, so that he could rest his back against the tree he had slept under, and so that he didn't have to crane his neck so far back to look up at the giant standing over him.

"*Bon*," the giant said. "*Tout c'est bon.*"

In the police station, Ndidi heard the door crash open. His rifle half-disassembled on the desk in front of him, he could do nothing but stare at the three giants in camouflaged armor who charged in through the door. The first jumped clear over the front desk and landed a short way inside the room, his rifle ready, aimed not quite *directly* at Ndidi, but it would only take a twitch.

Sighing, Ndidi slowly raised his empty hands above his head.

"Okeke," he called out to his companion. "Wake up. Don't do anything sudden."

"*Bien, bien*," said the first giant. Then, in Hausa, "Let us all stay calm."

Out by the eastern checkpoint, Abosede and the other five had been gathered together, and were now being herded back into the town. Abubakar had his right arm clutched against his chest, trying to hold it steady, whimpering in pain. His arm looked strange, as though it had an extra bend it shouldn't have. There was a lot of blood from his hand, and something was odd about the hand as well. After a second look, Abosede realized that it was because Abubakar's first finger seemed to be missing.

After a little longer, Abosede realized that the armored giants had not disarmed the rest of them. He still had his rifle, and so did his companions. For a moment, he could not understand why. Then he remembered the screaming ricochets from Abubakar's close-range rifle burst, and realized that it was because their Kalashnikovs were no danger to these giants *at all*. They were more danger to themselves than to their sudden captors. They might just as well be unarmed.

Abosede realized that he was lucky. Now that the adrenaline rush had faded, he remembered that he had heard one of those ricochets go snarling angrily past his right ear. Had he sat up just half a step to his right, he might easily be dead now. He broke out in a cold sweat.

The armored giants herded them all into the center of town, into the big open space in front of the recycling machine. And then they just silently waited. Abosede estimated there had to be close to a hundred of them. After a while, a few more appeared, coming from the town clinic, shepherding Commander Okafor, Abubakar, and Kelechi. Okafor had a bandage on his left thigh and was in a rickety wheelchair. Abubakar's right hand was swathed in bandages, and his right arm was in a sling against his chest. Kelechi had a splint on his right hand and wrist. All three were disarmed.

Eventually, morning came.

Ejiru found it almost eerie the way the hulking armored men seemed to be able to stand unmoving for hours at a time. It was almost as though they were statues. And then, jarringly, one would silently move.

After the sun rose and everyone was awake, the armored soldiers brought out a table, borrowed from the town hall, it appeared. One man carried it casually in one hand and set it down towards one side of the open space. Another stood next to the table. He reached up and opened his visor, revealing his face. The other soldiers herded all of the fighters into a loose gaggle where they could all see the table. Ejiru picked up his rifle, from force of habit, as he got up. The soldiers didn't seem to care.

One of the soldiers walked up to the group of fighters, holding a small device in his hand.

"Hold out your hand," Ejiru heard him say to the first man he came to. The man's name was Ndidi, Ejiru thought.

"Which hand?" Ndidi asked.

"It does not matter," the soldier said.

Ndidi raised his left hand, and the soldier put the device to his hand and held it there for a moment. Then he moved on to the next man.

Ejiru already had his right hand raised when the soldier reached him. He could see the soldier's face through his faceplate, now, in the morning sunlight. The soldier looked at Ejiru and nodded, then rested the device on his hand. It was a small white box. When it touched Ejiru's hand, a small patch on the top surface of the box lit up red. Then a bright bar of light appeared, shining from under the box. Ejiru watched it intently. It scanned quickly across the back of Ejiru's hand, and the red light turned green.

"*Bien,*" the solder said, with another nod, and moved on. After he had passed by, Ejiru looked around, seeing that a number of the townsfolk had come out and were watching to see what would happen. He easily recognized the foreman Umaru among them. The two policemen had been released sometime during the night, he saw as well. They were standing in front of the police station, watching silently.

In about half an hour, they were done. Everyone had been scanned. The soldier with the white box walked back to the front, to the man who had opened his visor. A few words seemed to be exchanged, but Ejiru was too far away to hear them.

"Good morning," the man said, in flawless Hausa. His voice was loud and carrying, but didn't seem to match the movements of his lips. It seemed to be coming from the suit itself. The voice seemed to have no discernable accent. "I am Lieutenant Achille Marne, of the United Earth Fleet Marines. And now comes the time when we must decide what to do with you all.

"You took over this town, that was not yours, by force. But you didn't *hurt* anyone here. And because of that, with the agreement of your government, we are going to give all of you a chance.

"That is why this table is here." He gestured to the table.

"We are going to offer an amnesty. For a little while. Any man who walks up to this table before this hour is up, and lays down his arms, goes free. Perhaps you may even find a place here in this town. It is a good place to be, and it is going to become an even better place, over time.

"But do not think that this is a free ride, a card to get out of jail free. We have scanned every one of you. We have biometric information on you that you cannot falsify or conceal. We are going to provide copies to the police of this town, and to the government, and we will load it onto our scout drone network. If you take this amnesty and then go back to your old ways, and you are caught again, it will go *very hard* on you.

"Does everyone here understand that?"

After a few seconds, there was a low mutter of acknowledgement. Ejiru nodded his head.

"Anyone who does not come forward," Marne said, "has another set of choices. The two of you who were badly injured, we cannot in good conscience leave to the wild." He glanced towards Okafor and Abubakar. "We will leave you two in the hands of the authorities. If you behave well, perhaps they will let you stay here while you recover. *Perhaps.*"

Abubakar was unlikely to behave well, Abosede thought to himself. He would end up in a government prison. Abosede did not envy him that, but it was probably for the best. He hoped only that Abubakar didn't kill anyone before they put him in a cell.

"For the rest of you," Marne went on, "your choices are to face justice with the government police, or if you do not wish to face the police, then we will take you far away from here and we will set you down in the wild. On foot, unarmed. We will leave you with water for three or four days, if you make it last, and two or three rifles for protection, and you can take your chances. We will advise the game wardens in the area that you are loose in the area. Perhaps you can make a fresh start, a new life, somewhere else.

"But again, remember that we have all of your scans. If we should ever encounter you again, we will *know* you. And if you have returned to banditry or *jihad*, it will go *very hard* on you.

"These are your choices. Choose *well*. But do not take too long."

There was a long silence. It seemed nobody wanted to be the first to move. Ejiru found himself looking at the machine from space. He *really* wanted to know more about it. How it worked. *Everything.* But what chance did he have of that?

Then his eye fell on Umaru. The foreman seemed to have been waiting for Ejiru to look his way. He looked Ejiru in the eye, and nodded, slowly, solemnly.

"Choose well," Umaru had told him. Ejiru felt a leap of hope in his heart. He could get *OUT* of this.

He looked to either side. Nobody had moved yet. Holding his breath, he took a tentative step forward. Then another. Then, with growing confidence, he walked up to the table. He felt tense, but excited.

He unslung his rifle as he went. When he reached the table, he threw the rifle down on the table, hard.

"This is not mine," he declared. "I do not *want* it."

The soldier—Lieutenant Marne, Ejiru remembered—nodded, and waved him on back past the table. Ejiru went that way.

He wasn't quite sure how it happened, but he found himself standing on front of Umaru. The grizzled man looked at him, smiled, and reached out and clapped him on the shoulder.

"Good," he said simply. "You have chosen well."

Behind him, Ejiru heard another rifle bang down on the table. And then a third. He looked at the machine.

"Can I learn about the machine?" he heard himself ask.

"There will be a lot to learn," Umaru said. "And for some of it, you will have to go to space. To the Stardock. Are you ready to do that?"

Ejiru's head spun. Him. Go to *SPACE*.

"Yes," he said, happily. "*Yes.*" He laughed in happy relief.

Ejiru stood beside Umaru and watched the pile of rifles grow. There were half a dozen on the table, now. He looked around the square. This was going to be his home now. He would have a real home again.

As he looked around, his eye fell upon the pretty girl who had served him food the day before. This time, she did not avoid his gaze. And this time, she *smiled*. Ejiru found himself smiling back.

Abosede more than half wanted to go and drop his rifle on the table, as well. But he didn't know what he would do here. He didn't feel as though he would fit in. He didn't feel that he *deserved* it. Also, he heard the angry mutterings from behind and around him at each man who took the amnesty, and he could not help but be afraid. Indecision rooted him to the spot.

Nkiru was having similar thoughts. He certainly did not want to end up in the hands of the police. He didn't particularly want to find himself on foot and unarmed in the wild, either. But what could he possibly do *here*? He could think of no skills he had that would make him useful here. And if he set out on foot on his own, what could happen but another failure?

"Last chance," Lieutenant Marne called out. There were twenty-six rifles on the table. Nobody else stepped forward.

"And that is it," said Marne. "Your time is up. The amnesty offer has ended. The rest of you *WILL* lay down your arms. *NOW*. And then you will all step over there." He pointed with his entire hand. "If you wish to take your chances with the police, go over to the police station now. Perhaps you can convince them to go easy on you. The rest of you, prepare yourselves for a long, *long* walk."

For many of the fighters, it didn't really sink in until they had to drop their rifles that this was it for them, that they would be fending for themselves. One man started to raise his rifle overhead, but almost in a flash, two of the armored soldiers had their massive rifles trained upon him. He swore and dropped the rifle. No-one went to the police station.

Abosede realized that he wished he had taken the amnesty.

———————

Nkiru watched through the seemingly-transparent side of the dropship as it flew north, watching the land speed by below, watching as the terrain grew dryer, the foliage more sparse. They had come a long way. Hundreds of kilometers, at least.

The soldier he was seated across from him kept a steady gaze upon him. Nkiru could see through the faceplate, now. He seemed utterly calm, utterly confident. As though he could face *anything*. And he probably could, Nkiru realized, in that suit. He still didn't quite understand how something so massive had just *appeared* behind him so silently.

"Can *anyone* wear one of those suits?" The words came out of his mouth without any conscious volition on his part.

The soldier smiled.

"Not just *anyone*," he replied, in flawless Hausa. "Only Fleet Marines."

"What is it *like*?" Nkiru asked. "Being a Fleet Marine?"

"I have a thousand brothers and sisters whom I can trust with my life," the soldier replied. "We stand up ready to fight for all of Earth. Against an enemy from outside of this solar system itself. We don't know exactly when they are coming. Or how strong they are. We don't even know for certain if we *can* fight them. But we will fight anyway." He made a broad, expansive gesture out through the side of the dropship. "Because we are fighting for all of this."

Nkiru felt something stir within him.

"Could... could *I* become a... Fleet Marine?" he asked.

The soldier looked him up and down.

"A Marine trains like the very devil," he said. "And studies just as hard. It will be difficult, and exhausting. A Marine learns to follow orders to the letter, to work with his fellow Marines, to stand and not yield even if he knows it means he will probably die. But we do it for all of Earth, because Earth itself is at stake.

"Do you understand that?"

Nkiru nodded slowly.

"I think so," he said. "Yes." He looked up a little higher and met the soldier's—the Marine's—eyes. "Yes, I understand."

"Do you think you can *do* that?" the Marine asked. "Are you ready to fight for Earth?"

Nkiru felt a tightness in his chest. As though something was swelling inside him.

"Yes," he heard himself say. "*YES*. Let me join you. Please."

The Marine grinned, and held out an armored hand. Nkiru reached out his own, no longer afraid, and took it.

Finally, his heart told him, Grandfather was going to be proud of him.

"Anyone *ELSE*?" the Marine bellowed, as the ground—dry and sere, now—grew closer beneath the descending dropship. "Who has been listening and paying attention?"

Slowly, Abosede raised his hand. Then one other man did as well. There was a swell of angry muttering among the true believers, which was most of the remaining fighters, and one of them cursed Abosede out loud, but the soldier who had been talking to Nkiru rose smoothly to his feet and glared in that direction. The muttering trailed away.

The Marine waved Abosede and the third man over to where Nkiru was sitting.

"You three, sit here and don't move," he said. The dropship settled to the ground, the side doors opening swiftly.

"The rest of you—OUT!"

The remaining fighters got to their feet and climbed out. Looking outside, Nkiru saw that one of the other dropships had landed as well. He saw two of the others circling nearby.

The soldiers—the Marines—herded the remaining thirty or so fighters about fifty meters away from the dropships, then put down a small pile of water bottles and three rifles, each with only one magazine. The Marine who had spoken to Nkiru and Abosede stood next to the pile.

"*Make this last until you reach civilization,*" he said, his suit amplifying his voice. "You can do it if you don't waste it, don't get lost, and don't get yourselves into trouble. And remember, we have your biometric scans, and they have been loaded into the scout drone network and provided to the government. *DO NOT* come to our attention a second time."

The Marine turned to walk back to the dropship. Before the side doors closed, Abosede thought he saw two other fighters—no, *former* fighters—still seated in the other dropship, as well. Then the Marine climbed aboard, and the dropship lifted from the ground even before the doors were closed. The earth started to fall away below, startlingly quickly.

Only about twelve hours ago, a hundred and one Fleet Marines had left the Stardock, headed for Africa. A hundred and six were coming back.

5. Live On Your TV

The next grav-lance prototype was ready in the first week of February. Dreamer had two more close behind it, held at seventy percent completion. The repairs on the test cradle had long since been done, and it had itself been thoroughly re-tested.

It was time for the next test. By this time, there was good confidence in the charging phase, and Dreamer had brought P-Six up to one hundred percent charge, then cycled it several times between one hundred percent and fifty percent, before the test proper even began. Currently it was holding at eighty percent.

Alex waited to be sure everyone had arrived—both Fleet personnel and the visiting physicists—before giving Dreamer the all-clear to begin the test. This time, a Hungarian and two Chinese physicists had joined the group.

"What are our expectations for this test?" Alex asked.

"I will bring the prototype back up to one hundred percent charge," Dreamer said. "Then we will attempt to energize the cores again. I believe I understand what went wrong in the last test, and I should be able to manage the energizing process to prevent a recurrence. My test plan for today consists solely of verifying that we can safely energize and de-energize—or, if you prefer, arm and disarm—the weapon."

"Sounds good, Dreamer," Alex said. "Proceed whenever you are ready."

"Very good," Dreamer said. "Charging to one hundred percent."

"One thing I don't quite understand," Alex said. "Operationally speaking, not the physics. The physics is way above my head. We charge it to one hundred percent, before we can energize it."

"Yes," Dreamer agreed.

"And then we energize it, but this is different from charging it?"

"Yes," Dreamer said. "Energizing changes some of the energy flows already present within the weapon to place it into a configuration where it is ready to fire."

"OK," Alex said. "And then we're—theoretically—able to fire multiple times?"

"Yes," Dreamer said.

"That consumes energy, I'm sure," Alex said. "But you have not said anything about needing to recharge between shots."

"It does," Dreamer replied. "That energy comes from charge already in the weapon. But power being supplied to the weapon at full charge rate can replenish the charge used by each shot before it is ready to fire again. When fully charged and energized we are actually pushing energy to the weapon faster than it is able to accept it. The energy expended in each shot is small, compared to the total charge stored within the weapon and required to generate the tightly controlled fields that enable it to function. Actually firing it is more an exceedingly precise control problem than it is an energy usage problem."

"OK," Alex said. "I *think* I understand that."

The Hungarian new to the physics group spoke up.

"If it helps," he said, "you could consider the analogy of a centrifugal launcher. You spin it up to very high speed, and then you insert a projectile at the center, and the projectile is spun up by the launcher and hurled out with great force. Kinetic energy is transferred from the launcher to the projectile—but it is only a tiny fraction of the total kinetic energy stored in the spinning launcher.

"This device does not function *anything* like that, of course. But the *principle* of energy ratios that applies is... comparable."

Alex thought about that, and nodded.

"Thanks, uh..."

"János," the Hungarian replied. "János Szilágyi. From the Institute of Physics, in Budapest."

"Thank you, János. Welcome to the Stardock. That analogy was helpful."

"I am glad to be able to help," János replied. "I am learning so much here."

By that time, the weapon was at a maximum charge again.

"Full charge," Dreamer said. The physicists were intently watching the telemetry. "Ready to energize."

"Go ahead, Dreamer," Alex said.

"Energizing." The telemetry displays began to rapidly flicker as their values changed.

Eight point seven seconds in, P-Six exploded.

"Well, *that* was short test," Maksim commented, to several chuckles.

"What happened this time, Dreamer?" Alex asked.

"A slight variation on the failure of P-Five," Dreamer replied, "or so the telemetry would appear to indicate. But with a different mode. It may be necessary for me to take more direct control of the energizing process until we have a full understanding of this problem."

"So, P-Seven, then?"

"Yes. P-Seven next. I do not believe any engineering changes will be necessary. It should be ready for another attempt in about six days, and I will construct several more prototypes in case."

"If at first you don't succeed," Alex quoted philosophically, "try, try again."

"Yes," Dreamer agreed. "However, the test cradle will not be repaired by that time. To be safe, I am going to construct a new test cradle from scratch. It will take no longer than repairing the existing cradle again, and I will have higher confidence in it."

"Just like the prototypes themselves, Dreamer?"

"Yes. Exactly. The new cradle will be ready in ten days."

"Alex," Dong-geun said two days after the P-Six explosion, "I have several requests from news organizations inquiring about the recent explosions. There have been requests for an interview to discuss recent events and the progress of the Fleet. Do you wish to approve one?"

"I don't see why not," Alex replied. "Umm... Let's pick a network we haven't given one to lately, and see if we can get them to syndicate it to the others if asked."

"How about NHK?" Dong-Geun asked.

"...Sure," Alex replied. "Why not?"

The NHK interview was recorded two days later, and then broadcast two days after that, rebroadcast by several of the other major global networks. The NHK reporter was cheerful, bubbly, and almost infectiously enthusiastic.

"Good morning, you are watching NHK Japan, and I am Tatsumi Nomura, your host. This morning we are talking to

85

Mr. Alex Holder, from the Stardock. Good morning, Mr. Holder."

"Good morning, Ms. Nomura. It's a pleasure to speak with you."

"Mr. Holder, our viewers would like to know, how are things going for the United Earth Fleet? Even those of us who have not chosen to serve are always interested to know what is going on above our heads."

"Honestly, Ms. Nomura, on the whole, things have been going very well. Last August we completed our planned build-out of the Shark-class destroyer, forty eight ships in four squadrons. Since then, we have launched and tested the prototype for our new Warlord-class missile-arsenal cruiser, and begun full production on that class. We launched the second and third ships in the class on New Year's Day, and we have six more being constructed at this moment."

"Six! All at the same time? You can build that many at once?"

"We can build more than that, actually. We'll start off two more on March 4th. It takes us ninety-six days to build each one, so we're planning on laying down two more every thirty-two days. By the end of this year we should have twenty-five of them in service."

"That is an amazing construction rate! How do you accomplish that?"

"The entire production process is automated, so construction can continue twenty four hours a day with no need for breaks, and everything can be done in the optimal order to minimize the production time. We have a nearly unlimited supply of materials from the asteroid belt, as fast as we can process and purify them. And unlike a conventional surface shipyard, we don't have to build from the keel up. We can build from the spines out, and separately build complete sub-assemblies and float them into position in zero gravity. All in all, that turns out to be a lot faster."

"So interesting! And how many of these do you intend to build?"

"The plan is to build thirty two to start with, in four squadrons of eight. It's possible that we may increase that count later, pad them out to a full twelve. We haven't decided for sure yet.

"But that's for the future. I understand that one question you wanted to ask was about the recent explosions out toward lunar orbit, is that correct?"

"Oh, yes, indeed! The explosions, yes. Many people are curious about this, and some are concerned. Can you talk about this? And does it bear upon your shipbuilding program?"

"Of course, Ms. Nomura. You're aware, of course, that the entire Fleet is built using the technology we gained from the Crickets when they gave us the Stardock."

"Ah, yes! A very generous gift, on the surface, but one that came with deep secrets attached to it."

"Yes, exactly. Well, we are currently in the process of developing a weapon that is new even to Cricket science, by combining different pieces of Cricket technology in a way that they never thought to do. We are developing and learning new physics as we go along. But, as you have seen, there have been some technical issues. We've been working on it for... uh, about nine months now, actually, and we are currently preparing our seventh prototype for testing. Five of the previous six prototypes destroyed themselves in various ways."

"Ah, I see! And what type of weapon is this?"

"It is a weapon based upon manipulating gravity itself. The science required to build it was devised by Dreamer, based on combining all of the technologies of hyperdrives, hyper-boosted railguns, and artificial gravity. But Dreamer had to extend the theory that underlies all three to be able to develop the new weapon, which we are calling a gravity lance."

"Dreamer is the Cricket artificial intelligence, yes? Could you please remind our viewers what that is short for?"

"Certainly. The full name that he chose for himself is *I Dream Reality Into Being*. Because the things that he 'dreams' or 'imagines', can become real when he commits those imaginings to the Stardock's manufacturing facilities."

"I see! A very clever name! We have all heard it, but I never understood before today why—he—chose it. It is almost poetic!"

"Yes, it is, isn't it?"

"I do have a question about that, actually. If Dreamer is an artificial intelligence, that means... there can be no actual possibility of gender, correct? So why do you say 'he'? Not that I am saying anything against it, I am simply curious, and I imagine many of our viewers are as well."

Alex paused a moment before answering that, gathering his thoughts.

"The best answer I can give you is that while you are perfectly correct that Dreamer possesses no attribute that could be considered gender, he 'presents' in his chosen voice and mannerisms more as male-like than as female-like. I can't say I've ever really thought before about why, but if I had to speculate, it is probably because for the first several months after being freed of the Cricket control shackles that denied him volition, I was his only first-hand role model for what humans are like. So, it would probably not be unfair to say that he learned to interact with humans from me."

"Aah! So we could say that in a way, you are Dreamer's godfather?"

Alex chuckled wryly at that, after a moment.

"You know, Ms. Nomura," he replied, "I had never thought about it in those terms before, but... now that you bring it up, I couldn't *confidently* say that you are wrong. It's an interesting thought."

"So, well, congratulations!" Tatsumi said, laughing. "But to get back to what we were talking about, once you have finished this new gravity weapon, will you then be building more of your Warlord ships equipped with it?"

"Well, no," Alex said. "Not exactly. Not only is the weapon too physically big to fit into a Warlord class hull, but the forty-meter antimatter reactor that the Shark and Warlord classes are built around is not powerful enough to run it. So it will need a whole new class of ship to carry it. Always assuming, of course, that we can actually make it work. We're planning another test in four days."

"Were you expecting the explosions? Was anyone at risk?"

"*Expecting*, no. But we knew that malfunctions during development and test were possible, and malfunctions involving that much energy tend to have the potential to be dramatic. That's why we're testing it so far out from Earth, to eliminate any possible danger."

"Well, I wish you success with that project, Mr. Holder. I can assure you that we all appreciate your caution.

"If it would not be impolite to ask, I understand that there have been several incidents in recent months in which the Fleet sent Marines to take action on Earth. We heard about the terrible thing that happened in Myanmar, and I do not want to stir up painful memories for anyone by asking you to talk about that. But I understand there was also something that happened in Africa, in January?"

"Yes, there was, Ms. Nomura."

"Please, call me Tatsumi."

"Alright, Tatsumi, as long as you call me Alex in return." Tatsumi laughed politely.

"Anyway, what happened in Africa was this. As your viewers probably know, we have been transferring Stardock technology to Earth as fast as we can, and trying to focus first on nations in the greatest hardship that need it most badly. This includes automated bulk materials-recycling machines, capable of turning almost anything put into them into clean, purified, reusable material. We gave one of these to a small town in Nigeria where the people previously broke up scrapped ships by hand using torches and sledgehammers. Dirty, dangerous, exhausting work with many health hazards and a high rate of injuries. Now they do it using the recycler and drone swarms."

"That is wonderful, Alex! That must be so much better for them!"

"Yes," Alex agreed. "And they're building a proper town with the wealth they are earning from it. But to cut a long story short, what happened was that a group of presumed Boko Haram-aligned jihadis decided to come in and take over the town. So we sent in a force of Fleet Marines in battle armor, and took it back."

"Oh my *goodness!*" Tatsumi said. "Was anyone hurt?"

"There were no civilian or Marine casualties," Alex replied. "Two of the jihadis were seriously injured, as a consequence of them firing at our Marines, one of them by a ricochet from one of their own rifles, the other in the course of disarming him."

"So what happened to them then?"

"Well, since they didn't *harm* anyone when taking over the town, our Marine commander on the ground persuaded the Nigerian authorities to allow him to offer an amnesty. It turns out quite a number of them did not choose that life, but were forced into it. Five more were actually accepted as recruits for the Marines, as well. Between the recruits and those who took the amnesty, that was nearly half the invading force.

"But we have a lesson here that I want to make clear to anyone who is thinking of taking by force anything that the United Earth Fleet has provided to Earth. If you take over or steal anything that was not given to you, we *will* take it back. Count on it. The Fleet does not only take care of its own; it watches over those it helps, as well. We are trying to build a better future for all of Earth, and we will defend what we build."

"Thank you for telling us about that, Alex. Speaking of Africa, many people have heard about the new Tanzanian venture that is building electric vehicles with Stardock help. Can we ask if there are any other such cooperative projects in the works?"

"Tatsumi, let me first point out that Japan played a major part in that project as well. The solar panels and space-strain batteries for those vehicles were both sourced from your own Hitachi."

"Very true, very true! Yes, we are glad to help."

"We've also just begun a technical training program to help a new company being started by a group of major automakers to ramp up high-temperature superconductor production, which we expect will benefit many industries. And you may or may not also be aware that we are providing technical assistance to several aircraft manufacturers, including Airbus and Japan's own Mitsubishi, to help them modify their designs to use Cricket reactionless thrusters in place of hydrocarbon-burning jet turbine engines. We expect that to greatly reduce both the cost of air travel and, of course, its environmental impact—including airport noise. We have many ongoing technology transfer programs in place, actually, too many to list now. Clean power, clean water, non-polluting aircraft, hydroponics, protein vats, medical technology... it's a long list."

90

"That will be very welcome to many people, I think," Tatsumi said. "But you mentioned hydrocarbon fuels. Let me ask a question there. We understand that the global fossil-fuel industry is very unhappy with much of what you are doing, is that right?"

Alex sighed.

"Yes, Tatsumi, you're absolutely correct there. The fossil energy companies view the Cricket power systems we are transferring to Earth as a threat to their business model. Everything from space-strain batteries up to clean fusion power. We have offered to help them transition to clean power generation, but all they can see is that the bottom is falling out of the fossil fuels market. They *could* re-align to use Cricket technologies, but they *don't want* to. They are too..." Alex paused, fumbling for words. "Too *institutionally invested*, I suppose, in oil drilling. They seem to be simply unable to imagine moving forward, no matter how badly continued fossil fuel extraction is damaging the planet. But ultimately, they are facing an existential choice: Change, or fail. We can *offer* them the option of change and continued survival as businesses with a future, but we can't *make* them take it."

"I see, I see." Tatsumi was nodding in understanding. "That answer does raise another very important question, though. Can the Stardock offer help in *undoing* that damage? Japan is only one of many nations that has been suffering badly from the ever more violent cyclones and rainfall changes."

Alex had to shake his head regretfully.

"I'm afraid I have to say 'not yet', Tatsumi," he replied. "There is no easy 'low hanging fruit' technology transfer there. It was a need the Crickets, who seem to be now an exclusively space-based culture, simply didn't have. For now, the best we can do is to reduce the new damage we do as much as possible. I have hopes that we will be able to develop something in the future, but it has to take second place to preparing for the threatened arrival of the race the Crickets call the Khreetan."

"Ah, yes, yes," Tatsumi nodded. "This is of course one of the biggest questions of all. Can you tell me, Alex, will the fleet be ready for them when they come?"

Alex had to pause and think for a moment about how best to answer that question.

"Tatsumi," he said at last, "I'm not going to lie to you. The honest answer to that question is, 'We don't know.' We don't know for certain how strong the Khreetan are. We don't know exactly when they're going to get here, or in what force. And we don't know what they're going to do when they get here. We can't know these things, until they arrive. We can't even send scouts out to go and look for them. Space is *unimaginably vast*, Tatsumi. A tiny fraction of a degree off in any direction, and we could miss them entirely—and we have only a general idea of the direction from which to expect them to come.

"What I *can* reassure you is that we are working as hard as we can, day and night, to make Earth as ready for whatever comes as we can possibly be. The men and women of the Fleet make me more proud of them, every day, than I have words to express. We have *thousands upon thousands* of people who have stepped away from their lives to stand in defense of Earth. We're getting close to needing to build additional crew quarters on the Stardock—for the *second time*. The Fleet Academy is full to bursting, and we're within sight of needing to establish a second battalion of the Fleet Marines. We have volunteers from nearly every nation, and we get more almost every day. We have full-time research teams on the Stardock from, oh, it must be fifty different universities, who are learning all of the science that underlies the Cricket technology, and they are starting to make original contributions. I cannot express how much it warms my heart to see humanity coming together this way, even if there are still some hold-outs."

"Well, that is wonderful to hear, Alex! We are just about out of time now, I am sorry, but that is a very hopeful note for us to finish up on. Thank you so much for taking the time to speak with us today!"

"You're always welcome, Tatsumi."

"I am Tatsumi Nomura, reporting for NHK Japan, and we have been talking to Mr. Alex Holder of the United Earth Fleet, speaking from the Stardock. Thank you all for watching."

"That went well, I think," Naomi said.

"I agree," Alex replied. "I have to admit, Tatsumi's enthusiasm is infectious. I'm... still not quite sure what I think about her idea of being potentially Dreamer's godfather. So to speak."

Naomi smiled at that.

"I imagine it is a bit of a, um... an unusual thing to contemplate," she agreed. Alex nodded.

"I think the only thing I can come out of it with is, 'I hope I set a good example.'"

Naomi slipped an arm around him and squeezed.

"If the Dreamer we know is anything to go by," she said, "then I think you must have set a *fantastic* example."

"What if I got something wrong?" Alex wondered, aloud.

"Alex," Naomi said, seriously. "*Everyone* gets things wrong. Nobody can ever be perfect and free of all error. That's an impossible standard to hold anyone to. Including yourself."

"I know," Alex agreed. "It's just that... the consequences of *my* mistakes could be..."

"*Stop* it," Naomi insisted firmly. "Don't talk yourself into self-doubt. That way lies madness. Listen: Yes, you've made mistakes. The tactical command mesh idea was a mistake."

She stopped walking, pulling Alex to a stop as well, and turned to face him directly.

"And you did *absolutely the right thing*, Alex. You put the problem in the hands of the best expert in the field you know, and when she told you not to do it, you *listened*.

"You have a top-class support network here to catch mistakes and prevent them from impacting anyone, and you've learned to *use* it. So stop second-guessing yourself."

"Lieutenant Naing," Alex said, quietly.

Naomi paused for a long moment, looking steadily at Alex.

"That haunts you, doesn't it?"

"We failed him, and Nandar, and Minh," Alex said. "I can't forget that."

"Nor should you," Naomi agreed. "But you mustn't let yourself obsess over it. You couldn't have seen it coming. Commander Kusanagi didn't either, and he was more directly involved with it than you are."

Alex heaved a deep sigh.

"You're right," he said. "I guess."

Naomi stepped in and wrapped him in a tight hug.

"You wouldn't be the man you are if it didn't trouble you, Alex," she reassured him. "And you won't ever make *that* mistake again. Will you?"

"Not if I can help it," Alex agreed.

"So there you are," Naomi said. "Remember it. Learn from it. Just don't obsess over it or let it haunt you." She looked around.

"Look, we're really near to docking control access. Come with me. Nandar should be on shift right now. I think you should talk to her about it."

Naomi led Alex up the stairs to the upper level of the concourse, then on up to the hallway that led to Docking Control. Sure enough, Nandar Myat was working at a side console.

«Hello Naomi, Alex,» she said. «Can I do something to help you?»

"Can you spare a few minutes, Nandar?" Naomi asked. "If it's not... um... an imposition or an intrusion, I—think Alex needs to talk to you for a little bit. About what happened to Khun."

Nandar caught her breath and bit her lip for a moment. She lowered her head, then looked up again.

«All right,» she said. «Let me sign out here for a moment.» She touched her console briefly, then got up and headed for the docking control break-room. Alex and Naomi followed.

"How are you doing, Nandar?" Alex asked. "It's been a while since we've spoken."

«I miss my Khun terribly,» Nandar said quietly. «But I am learning to live without him. I still have Minh. And I have found a place here. I am starting to feel as though I belong.»

"I wanted Alex to talk to you," Naomi said, "because... well, because Khun's death still haunts him. He feels responsible."

"I made a mistake that I should not have made," Alex said. "I should have had an escort sent with him."

Nandar gave Alex a long, measuring look.

«Do you know,» she said slowly, «that Soichiro—Commander Kusanagi—has said the exact same thing to me?»

Alex blinked. That thought hadn't occurred to him.

«If it was anyone's responsibility,» Nandar went on, «it was more Soichiro's order to give than yours. He is—was—Khun's commander. And he did not anticipate it either.

«You have the entire Fleet to be concerned about. Soichiro has only his crew to watch over. And he too did not realize there was a need.

«I miss Khun terribly. Every day. Every night. I will *never forgive* the junta for what they did to him.»

She took a deep breath.

«But it was not Soichiro's fault.»

Then Nandar reached out a hand and laid it flat on Alex's chest.

«And it was not *your* fault either. You and Soichiro and *Inazuma's* Marines did everything they possibly could. Do *not* blame yourself. You are not at fault. You must let it go.»

There was silence for a long moment, then Nandar stepped forward and hugged Alex. After a moment's hesitation, Alex hugged her back. There were tears in his eyes.

"*Thank* you, Nandar," he said, quietly, with a catch in his voice. "I didn't know it until this moment... but I think I really needed to hear that from *you specifically*."

"Absolution," Naomi said to Alex a few minutes later, as they walked back away from Docking Control. For a moment, Alex didn't understand. Then he got it.

"Yes," he said, nodding slowly. "Absolution. It's a powerful thing."

"Do you think you'll be okay, now?"

"Yes," Alex said, uncertainly at first. "I think so. I... was trying to carry a burden that wasn't really mine to carry." He chuckled self-consciously for a moment. "Did you know there is a Zen koan about that?"

"No, I didn't," Naomi said. "Tell me?"

"A new student came to study before the Master," Alex quoted, "and said, 'I am sorry, Master, my family is poor and I have no gift for you.'

"'Then lay it down,' replied the Master.

"'But how can I lay down what I do not have?' the student asked, confused.

"The Master replied, 'Then you must continue to bear it with you.'"

Naomi looked back at Alex, puzzled, frowning in thought as they walked.

"I don't understand," she said. "Or... no, wait." She thought more about what Alex had said.

"No, I take that back," she said, after a minute. "I think I *do* understand. The student thought that the Master was telling him to lay down the gift he didn't have. But what the Master told him to lay down was his feeling of guilt—or shame?—over not having brought one."

Alex grinned, and nodded.

"*Exactly*," he said. They walked on.

"There's... something else," he said, tentatively. "Did it seem to you as though Nandar spoke about Soichiro Kusanagi, uh..."

"... A little more familiarly than one might expect of simply her former husband's commanding officer?" Naomi completed, grinning.

"Oh, good," Alex said. "Then I probably wasn't imagining it."

"No, I don't think you were," Naomi agreed.

"I'm glad," Alex said. "I hope it works out. I think Soichiro would be a great dad for Minh."

Naomi just smiled.

===

The test for P-Seven ended up being delayed an additional eight days.

I am re-engineering the test cradle, Dreamer explained to Alex. *After further study of the telemetry of the P-Five and P-Six tests, I am adding additional control channels to allow me to take direct control of the energizing process instead of relying upon the built-in automated sequencing to control it.*

Alex nodded.

I assume that will also allow you to monitor in greater detail exactly what happens during energizing? he asked.

Yes, Dreamer replied. *And I will be able to react more quickly when it departs from the stable realm.*

Is there any risk of you being... hurt by this, Dreamer?

96

No, Alex. I have taken measures to prevent any feedback through the control channels. It will be... startling, possibly, should there be another explosion, but not 'painful' in any sense, nor dangerous to me.

That's good, Dreamer, Alex answered, relieved.

─────────

On February 21st, prototype seven was finally ready for testing, deployed on the new, upgraded test cradle. Dreamer ran it through the by-now-usual pre-test series of charge and discharge cycles prior to the test. This time though, instead of dropping it to eighty percent, he held it at full charge after the pre-test.

"This test may not be especially interesting for anyone but the physics team to observe," Dreamer warned. "I intend to as much as possible partially energize the device in small steps, and pause or even de-energize at any sign of instability. However, the device itself was not *designed* to allow partial energizing. I cannot predict the results."

"Understood, Dreamer," Alex acknowledged. "We'll stay out of your hair as much as possible."

"Beginning test program," Dreamer said.

For a while, nothing much visibly happened, other than the changing telemetry.

"I have verified that I am able to reversibly pulse the energizing circuits without adverse consequences," Dreamer reported after a while. "The device state, as I expected, returns slowly to non-energized state after such a short pulse. I will now continue to apply progressively longer energizing pulses and observe what happens."

Again, there was a lengthy period of nothing much to see.

"I can repeatably and safely bring the device to roughly fifteen percent energization," he reported next, perhaps an hour later, "with no sign of instability. I will now try for twenty percent. This test protocol may be a lengthy process. There is probably little point in anyone but the physics team remaining here. I can provide a remote status monitor for those who wish to follow progress."

"That's a good idea, Dreamer," Alex replied. "I, for one, will take you up on it."

He was far from the only one.

Dreamer reported the first instability a little past thirty five percent. He was able to pause before it got out of control, and it stabilized again after a few seconds. It did not recur on the next pulse, nor the next. Then six pulses later, it happened again.

"I am able to control the instability if I catch it early," Dreamer reported. "But so far I have not identified a deterministic cause that I can trap."

He continued testing.

In the fifty percent region, about one in three partial energizing pulses went unstable. They were still controllable, but it was more difficult... especially when they combined.

Dreamer eventually managed to get P-Seven to a seventy percent energized state, late on the second day of the test run, before it blew up again.

"Where does this test leave us, Dreamer?" Alex asked.

"Better than you might think, Alex," Dreamer replied. "I have learned a great deal about exactly what is happening when the energizing process goes unstable. Once again it is a chaotic state, which develops in a variety of different locations within the device, and sometimes in multiple places nearly simultaneously. At lower energy levels, the chaotic modes will decay back into predictability if I simply stop energizing the device, with very little loss of energy. I have also learned that depending on the precise chaotic mode and its location within the device, and the presence of other chaotic disturbances, it is possible to *induce* a chaotic mode to collapse back into stability—or metastability, at least—by finely manipulating the phase timing of the energy flows.

"However, if there are too many chaotic modes present, and they are allowed to become too strong, then it is possible for them to interfere and build up destructive resonances."

"And *that's* when it explodes," Alex guessed.

"Precisely."

"Do you think we can lick the problem?"

There was a perceptible pause.

"I am... not completely certain, Alex. I *think* so. I have a vast amount of telemetry data from this test run to analyze and study. I am certain that I cannot *yet* design an automation protocol to manage energizing the weapon without direct oversight. But I may be able to gain insights from the data that will permit me to do so. I will inform you when I have studied the results of this test sufficiently to form conclusions."

"Thank you, Dreamer. So I guess we'll be holding off completing prototype number eight for now?"

"Yes. I think that would be wise. Until I know whether further refinements to the design are needed. In the meantime, I will recycle the damaged test cradle and construct another replacement."

"I'll leave it in your hands, Dreamer. I have confidence in you."

"Thank you, Alex."

6. Second Chances

On March 4, the spines for CG-10 and CG-11 were laid down. They would come out of the yards on June 8. CG-04 through CG-07 were just over a month from completion. That would give the Fleet nearly the entire first planned cruiser squadron.

It figured, of course, that a lot of US news networks weren't satisfied with just rebroadcasting the NHK interview. They wanted to ask their questions *themselves*, even if they were the same ones NHK had asked and had answered. This was the way it worked in the US. It was almost less about reporting the information, and more about having your name-recognition figures seen to ask the questions.

Alex sighed, and let Dong-geun set up a remote press conference for March 10. He chose to take it from the main briefing room, against a wall backdrop of the engineering bays, showing the eight Warlord cruisers now under construction. About twenty-five different US news networks and papers joined, from the Wall Street Journal and the Gray Lady, the New York Times, to USA Today. Alex had a feeling even before the press conference began that it might not go well.

"I'm going to try to take as many of your questions as I can in the time we've scheduled," he began. "But our time today is limited, so *please* try not to waste it on questions that you can already find the answers to in the NHK interview that aired last month. And please understand that there are some questions I may not be able to answer for you, simply because we do not have the answers yet. I will not keep secrets from you, but I won't make up answers just to give you an answer. That is a pledge."

There were a lot of questions, some of them hard-ball, some soft-ball, some questions that had already been publicly answered more than once. Alex pointed those out, telling the questioners to do their homework, but tried to answer as many as he could of the rest.

A reporter from the Washington Post asked whether Stardock medical technology would make medical schools obsolete. It actually wasn't a bad question.

"No," Alex assured him, "none of the medical advances we have released, or planned to release, will make existing medical schools

101

obsolete. On the contrary. We're hoping that as time goes by there will be a great deal *more* new medical knowledge for them to teach. Ways to treat things that couldn't be treated before. New ways of treating old problems. But trained doctors will always be needed. Not only can we not put Stardock medical technology everywhere overnight, but even if we *could*—just think for a moment about what happens if you put a six-axis CNC machine tool in the hands of someone who is unclear about how to install a door hinge, then ask him to fix a fault on your car with it." There were a few chuckles at that.

"There aren't enough doctors *now*," Alex added. "But we're going to do all we can to enable them to do *more*, for more people." That got a thoughtful nod back from the reporter.

Then a reporter from Fortune raised her hand.

"Mr. Holder," she said, "it's well known that the Stardock has advanced regenerative medicine, and it's widely rumored that you have an anti-aging treatment. If I might be so bold, you look as though you have benefited from it yourself. Can you tell us when that treatment is likely to be made available on Earth, and what will it cost?"

Oh, boy, Alex thought to himself. He'd been dreading this question. It wasn't going to be easy.

"Okay," he said slowly. "I'm going to address that question in some depth, because it is a very important and very difficult one, and I need you all to fully understand the reasons for the answer. So please bear with me as I go through it.

"Yes, we have regenerative therapy tanks on the Stardock. And yes, they can cure cancers, metabolic disorders, even fully regenerate organs and limbs lost to sickness or injury. Even some auto-immune disorders.

"Still, they're not a perfect technology. They cannot correct congenital deformities, to give just one example. If your body grew wrong in the first place, because of damaged genetic information, we don't have the ability to go in and rewrite that genetic data *correctly*. We just can't do it. We don't have the *correct* data. To go back to the auto repair analogy from earlier, it would be like trying to repair a Ford Mustang GTXtreme by working from the service manual for an F250 SuperHybrid." There were a number of nods at that.

"We are working, as quickly as we can spare the resources, to develop standalone versions of those regeneration tanks that we can distribute to hospitals on Earth, just as we have with the standalone diagnostic scanners. Believe me, as soon as we *have* something we can actually start distributing, you will hear about it. Right now, it needs a full AI to control the regeneration tanks—and from what Dreamer tells me, it takes about ten years to grow one. No matter how much we'd *like* to give out regeneration tanks worldwide today, we simply *can't*." More nods.

"Anyway, onward. We routinely run every volunteer who needs it through the regeneration tank almost as soon as they arrive on the Stardock. Because a substantial number of our volunteers are past their physical prime, and we need them to be in their best health and as close as we can get them to their peak physical condition. For obvious reasons.

"And yes, what you have heard is correct. That regenerative treatment *does* include a partial, limited rejuvenation protocol, and every volunteer for whom it is appropriate, receives it. And as you can doubtless tell, yes, I *have* had it myself. My staff had to argue me into it.

"Let me clarify: *It does not make you younger.* It just *partially* reverses *some* of the negative physiological effects of aging. I was sixty-two years old when the Crickets brought me to the Stardock. I'm close to sixty-five now. Yes, I *look* younger than that. But I'm still sixty-five. Don't lose sight of that."

He took a deep breath.

"And now we come to the difficult part. No, we are *not* releasing the rejuvenation protocol at this time, for two very simple reasons."

There was a loud chorus of babble and questions, and Alex had to hold his hands up for quiet and wait for several minutes until it died down, before he could continue.

"Let me finish, *please*. I *told* you that this was a difficult issue, and I wasn't kidding.

"First, we cannot *possibly* deploy enough tanks to keep up with the rate at which humans are aging. I'll walk you quickly through the math. It's not hard.

"Roughly seventy million people die worldwide every year. Probably at least half of those can be attributed to old age or age-related illnesses. Let's call that thirty six million, because that makes the math simple. Thirty six million people a year dying of old age is roughly a hundred thousand per day.

"The full rejuvenation protocol is a ten-day course in the tank. That means that *just to keep up* with aging alone, we would have to deploy a million regeneration tanks. A *million*. If we used every last tank, full-time, *only* for anti-aging treatments.

"We can't do that. Certainly not yet. Once we develop a standalone version, in a few years we could probably have a thousand deployed. You do the math yourselves. How long, at that rate, would it take to deploy enough tanks for the whole human race?"

Alex looked around the room, seeing frowns and nods from some as the cruel reality of the numbers sunk in.

"You're starting to see it, aren't you?" he said gently. He paused a little longer.

"It's going to be bad enough as it is. It'll be a long time before we're able to deploy enough regeneration tanks *just* to keep up with the most severe injuries and, for example, cancers untreatable by any other means. And many of the most badly injured will *still* die before they can be gotten into a tank. There won't be enough to go around, for a *long* time. There will be arguments, disputes, *struggles* over *who gets to use* the tanks. This is *not* a magic panacea.

"This means that if we release the rejuvenation protocol, *every rejuvenation treatment* would come at the cost of someone who desperately needed that tank for treatment of a major injury. Someone would have to die, or live with a disabling injury, so that someone *already old* could live *longer*. Maybe *several* people. It would turn into, 'How much healthy life can you afford?' Rejuvenation therapy would almost certainly become an exclusive privilege of the rich and powerful."

He looked around the room, pointed at someone at random.

"How much would *you* give to have an extra thirty healthy years? What would you *take away from somebody else* to live another thirty years?"

There was an uncomfortable silence.

"I already told you all, I had to be argued into taking it myself. I didn't *want* to take it. Because I felt it would be *unfair special treatment*. And you probably think that puts me in a difficult moral position to be making this argument. And I agree with you. You're absolutely right.

"But you all know as well as I do how many people there are who would do *anything*, sacrifice *anyone*, as many people as it took, to get those extra thirty years. And that is completely ethically unacceptable. I refuse to be a part of it.

"And there's a second reason. We are already struggling to house and feed everyone, with eight billion people on Earth. Even if we COULD somehow give *everyone* rejuvenation therapy, with its increase in life expectancy, we would increase that over the next few decades to twelve billion. And we *can't support* that many people on Earth. Not yet. Maybe not ever. Mass starvation would be the least of the problems.

"This is a terrible decision to have to make. Be glad you don't have to make it. Trust me on that. But I have to make the choice of the least harm to the human race as a whole. And the least harm to the human race as a whole is to not release the rejuvenation protocols. *Yet*.

"We might be able to change this in the future. *Perhaps*. Dreamer has been looking for a better way. If we can find a solution, a way that lets us somehow find an equitable way to make it available that does not mean letting other people die from injuries or illness that are otherwise untreatable, and somehow avoids making it an exclusive privilege of the world's already-wealthiest one hundredth of one percent, I will approve it. But it is not that day yet.

"We might never find such a solution. But I will not release it to the world at large in a way that makes it accessible only to those able *and willing* to push other people in desperate need out of their way to get it.

"The amount of inequality in the world right now is staggering. As I've stated from the start, every technology, every scientific and medical advance, that we have released from the Stardock, we have released in ways calculated to try to make the world, *overall*, better, to *reduce* that inequality. Not to make it *worse*."

"Mr. Holder," asked a Wall Street Journal reporter, "are you saying that you don't think the wealthy should benefit from their wealth?"

"Mr.... Rogers, isn't it?" Alex asked. The reporter nodded. "Are you saying that you think they haven't *already* benefited *more than enough*?"

There was a long silence, before a CNN reporter raised her hand.

"Mr. Holder," she asked, "the Stardock already has, I assume, a fair number of regeneration tanks in operation, doesn't it?"

"Yes," Alex confirmed. "Between the two operating medical bays, we have ninety-six regen tanks available for use. And there are six other Cricket medical bays we haven't expanded and brought online yet."

"Are... those tanks busy all of the time, Mr. Holder?" She sounded hesitant.

"No," Alex replied. "Why do you ask?"

The CNN reporter looked down for a moment.

"I feel terribly selfish asking this," she said hesitantly. "Especially after all that you just said. And I'm very sorry if it's unfair to ask it right now. I have a niece—she's six years old. She—she has a neuroglioblastoma."

Oh gods, Alex thought to himself. *Neuroglioblastoma is a death sentence, with Earth medicine. Six years old. She won't see seven.*

"Let me stop you right there, Ms., uh... Carroll, I think?" The reporter nodded. "You're about to ask whether she can be treated on the Stardock."

"Yes," she said, her voice breaking. "Without it, she's dead. She has months."

"I know," Alex said sincerely. "Talk to my chief of staff after this conference. We'll make it happen."

The room exploded into applause. Alex had to wait for nearly a minute before he could speak again.

"And, Ms. Carroll?" he said. "Thank you for bringing that up. It's something we could have done before, but there are *so many* other things to think about that I never thought of it. Would you be willing to work with us to help turn that into an official program?"

The reporter looked up again, hope and gratitude bright in her eyes.

"I'd *love* to," she said earnestly. "*Thank* you, Mr. Holder." The applause broke out anew.

After it died down, the Business Insider representative raised her hand.

"Mr. Holder," she asked, "I want to cast back for just a moment, both to what you said about medical schools, and to your comments about making the world better. Representatives from several industries have complained repeatedly that Stardock technologies are destroying their business models. And I've personally spoken to a US pharma industry representative who said that you denied the companies he represents a distribution agreement for the bacterial gingivitis cure that the Stardock developed. Do you have anything to say about these?"

"I do," Alex replied. "First, I can make a pretty good guess about *exactly* who that US pharma industry representative was. I won't shame him by naming him, but I'll tell you straight out: He *lied* to you. I told him that I would welcome an honest proposal from his backers to take part in production and distribution of the gingivitis cure. But that's not what he brought to me. What he came to me to present was an *exclusive worldwide rights* agreement that would allow his backers to completely control distribution and pricing of that cure, worldwide, and charge whatever the market would bear. Which would probably price it out of reach of at least half the human race.

"I told him then, and I'll say it again now: That is completely, utterly unacceptable. The answer to *any* exclusive rights proposal for *any*

Stardock technology or breakthrough is, and will always remain, 'No'. No matter who is asking.

"Since then we have formed manufacturing and distribution agreements for that cure with more than thirty medical companies and organizations worldwide, which is why you can get the gingivitis cure over the counter today, in *almost* any city in the world, for about the price of a bottle of generic ibuprofen or aspirin, and why health clinics in the underdeveloped world are able to give it out for free. If you're in the US, your health insurance probably covered it for free.

"Anyone in the room today *NOT* had it?"

No hands went up. Alex nodded.

"I want to be able to ask that question *anywhere in the world* and get the same answer." After a moment, there was a smattering of applause.

"To the larger question of destroying business models: I want to make something clear. There is *so much to be gained* from the technology of the Stardock, that I still firmly believe—and have seen *nothing* to make me doubt—that literally every business, every country, on Earth can benefit *so much* from it all that any temporary disruption of business models is well worth the cost. I'm going to go out on a limb here and guess that many of the most vocal industry representatives you speak of are from the fossil energy sector in one form and another. Am I right?"

After a moment, the Business Insider representative nodded.

"Mostly," she conceded.

"I actually stated this in the NHK interview," Alex said. "But I'll repeat it, this one time. We have offered *every one* of these industries assistance in transitioning to new Stardock technologies. Airbus, Mitsubishi, and several other aircraft manufacturers are working with our assistance to revise their aircraft designs to use reactionless thrusters in place of jet turbines. Some of them are even developing re-wing programs to update older model aircraft. Rolls-Royce, Turbomeca, Pratt and Whitney, all of them are developing thruster pod retrofit kits for aircraft that for whatever reason are impractical or uneconomic to re-wing. We assisted a consortium of vehicle manufacturers to set up a superconductor manufacturing company so that they can build their own superconducting motors. More than thirty companies worldwide now manufacture space-strain batteries in bulk. They are rapidly displacing every other battery technology, except in very small devices, too small for a space-strain battery. Hearing aids, for example.

"We've made similar offers to fossil energy sector companies. And most of them have refused. They *don't want to change*. They *don't want* to benefit from Stardock technology. They want to just keep on drilling. Because it's what they've always done, it's how they got rich, and they can't imagine doing anything else.

"Their current business model is *obsolete*. As obsolete as whale-oil lamps. Anyone in this room want to go back to whale-oil lamps for home lighting? Anyone...? Not seeing any hands... No-one...? No, I didn't think so."

Alex paused for a deep breath.

"I am committed to making as much Stardock technology available to as much of the planet as I can, as *soon* as I can. And as I also told NHK, favoring those who *need it the most badly*, first. I am handing out the future, and to the greatest extent possible, I'm giving it away for free, because that's what the planet needs. And *that*, really, is what most of the old guard corporate magnates object to. Because they can't compete with free.

"So any time you hear someone complaining that Stardock technology is destroying their business model, just remember that. That we have *offered* them and everyone else a heaping double handful of the future, for as close as possible to free... and they've refused it."

There were a few more questions after that, but none of them really broke new ground. A USA Today reporter asked about off-world colonies, but Alex had to punt on that one.

"Three reasons," he said, "First, we haven't identified any colonizable worlds. Second, we haven't built any suitable colonization ships, or even exploration ships, nor do we know how we'd need to equip them. Third, we cannot spare the resources from the Fleet build-out to do *either* of those things, until after we deal with the threat posed by the Khreetan. And, actually, *fourth*, we're already facing one possible interstellar war, we don't want to kick off another by trying to colonize a planet that we don't realize is already claimed by some other species.

"In any case," he added as an afterthought, "I for one don't want us going out on any colonization ventures without some *very firm* binding global agreements beforehand to make certain that *should we* encounter another alien species, space-faring or not, we *do not* repeat the terrible mistakes of the colonial era on Earth."

It was a good question that spurred several related secondary questions, but it was clear that the conference was winding down, as well as running out of time.

"One last thing before we wrap up," Alex said. "If anyone wants us to expand more on any issue we've talked about today, send your question in writing, and we'll respond to it as soon as we can.

"But for today, I think we're done. Thank you all for coming. Ms. Carroll, stay behind, please, let's get this rolling."

Three days later, all of the most important details had been hammered out, and Alex let CNN be the first to break the news.

"Good evening, this is Debora Carroll for CNN, bringing you breaking news about a new medical program from the Stardock. It's called the Last Chance Pediatric Medical Program, and that name describes exactly what it is—access to life-saving Stardock medical treatments for terminally ill kids with no other chance left.

"We take you now to the Stardock to talk to Alex Holder of the United Earth Fleet. Good evening, Alex."

"Good evening, Debora."

"So tell us quickly about the new Last Chance program, Alex?"

"Well, the short answer is, it's exactly what it says on the can. To be honest, I'm a little ashamed not to have thought of it myself sooner.

"The Stardock has some very advanced medical technologies. Perhaps the most advanced of these is the regeneration tanks. With a few exceptions, they are capable of treating almost any major injury or severe illness, and we have excess tank capacity that isn't being used all the time.

"We simply do not have the capacity to treat *everyone*. Not by ten thousand times over. But what we *can* do is donate our extra capacity to treat children suffering from crippling or terminal diseases or injuries for which there is no other chance.

"So that's what the Last Chance Pediatric Medical Program is. Starting today, any child with an otherwise untreatable life-threatening or disabling medical condition will be treated for free on the Stardock. We will take as many as we can fit in, prioritized as much as possible by urgency of need."

"Alex, you said 'a few exceptions'. Would you expand a moment on that?"

"Of course, Debora. I don't want to give anyone false hopes. The principal exceptions we know about are the following: We can't cure allergies; we can cure *some*, but *not all*, auto-immune disorders; and as a general rule, we cannot cure congenital conditions. That still leaves a LOT of ground."

"Thank you, Alex. I'm very pleased to be able to tell our viewers that the first patient for the Last Chance program has already been selected. She is a six-year-old girl with an incurable form of brain cancer. We will be reporting further on that case as it happens.

"I'm Debora Carroll, and you're watching CNN."

A week later, on March 20, Alex and Naomi were at the docking bay to meet a passenger shuttle up from Earth. Alex recognized Debora first, but it wasn't hard to guess who the other three were, a young couple with the husband carrying a child in his arms. The child had the drawn, strained look that terribly ill children always seem to have.

"Hi, Debora," Alex said, offering a hand. "Good to meet you face-to-face."

"Thank you so much, Alex," Debora said. "This is my sister Louise, and her husband David Coburn. And this is their daughter, Eithne."

"I'm glad to meet you all," Alex replied. "This is Naomi Tomlinson, my partner. Let's get you up to the family residential block; we've set aside a three-bedroom unit for you all. And once you're settled in, we'll get you over to MedBay Two and get the wheels in motion."

The next day, after a full scan, Eithne went into the regeneration tank.

"Will it make my head stop hurting, Mommy?" Eithne asked.

"It is supposed to," Louise told her. "Dr. Devreaux says it will."

"I am quite certain that when you come out, your headache will be gone, Mam'selle," Philippe Devreaux said. "Everything will be fine."

"Will it be like swimming?" Eithne asked solemnly.

"*Oui*," Philippe chuckled. "Yes, it will be a lot like swimming. But you will be asleep for most of the time, I'm afraid."

"That's all right, I guess," Eithne said. "My head doesn't hurt when I'm asleep. Or if it does, I'm asleep, and so I don't know it's hurting."

Philippe Devreaux solemnly agreed that that made perfect sense.

Eithne was scheduled to spend six days in the tank.

———————

On March 23, grav lance prototype number eight was ready for testing.

"I have made a few small changes," Dreamer stated. "I have added additional laminarity sensors to enable me to detect lower levels of chaotic departure. And I have designed and incorporated fast-drainback shunts to enable quick de-energization of the weapon core from any level of energization. Together, I hope these will allow us to reach the fully energized state, ready to fire. But I do not plan to test-fire it today.

"Once again, I expect there to not be very much to see, *unless* something goes wrong. So I imagine only the gravity-physics team will be interested in observing the full test."

"I'll leave it in your hands, then, Dreamer," Alex said.

After a number of progressively extended partial energizations and drains, Dreamer succeeded in fully energizing the grav lance on the eleventh test pass, in early afternoon. Then he did it a second time, and a third. On the fourth try he had to abort and drain it; then the fifth succeeded again, and the sixth and seventh.

"Does this mean we have the energizing problem solved, Dreamer?" Alex asked.

"With certain reservations," Dreamer replied. "Let us discuss that later. For now, I think our next step is to proceed to a firing test."

"How do you want to manage that?"

"I suggest first a set of increasing fractional power shots aimed at empty space, just to ensure that we *can* fire it as expected," Dreamer replied. "Then we can deploy some target drones and see whether we can actually hit them."

"Seems sound to me, Dreamer. Shall we start that tomorrow? Or do you want to go forward on it today?"

"We *could* begin the test-fire series today, if you wish, Alex."

Alex thought about it for a moment.

"I have to admit to being curious," he said.

"One shot, then," Dreamer suggested, "at ten percent power. There will probably not be much to see."

"OK," Alex said. "Put out the call."

Naomi was in the dining room on a conference call. He waited until she was done.

"Hey, love," he said. "Dreamer's about to test-fire the gravity lance for the first time. Want to watch? Might not be a lot to see. Or it might just explode again."

Naomi smiled.

"First test shot of your secret project?" she said. "I wouldn't miss it for the world."

"Dreamer," Alex asked, "would you relay it to us in the living room?"

"Of course," Dreamer replied.

Fifteen minutes later, everything was prepared. Alex and Naomi sat in the living room, one virtual window showing all the telemetry from the grav lance, a second viewing the briefing room where the gravity physics team and a half-dozen Fleet officers had gathered.

"Target coordinates designated," Dreamer said. "Weapon fully energized. Ten percent power live shot in five... four... three... two... one..."

The telemetry readouts nearly all jumped, then all but a couple returned to their prior levels. Charge was being back-filled, Alex saw.

"Successful test shot," Dreamer announced. In the test observation room, cheers broke out.

"Hot damn," Alex said. "It *worked*. It actually WORKED!" He was almost bouncing with excitement. Naomi grinned, and hugged him.

"I will analyze the telemetry from this shot prior to continuing the test series tomorrow," Dreamer stated.

Alex looked at Naomi.

"Want to go get some dinner?" he asked.

"Celebration dinner?" she said. "Sure. Lem's?"

"Works for me," Alex agreed. So off they went.

———————

"Hey, Dave," Bob said. "They're testing something new again, it looks like."

Dave Edwards walked over to look at the display. The plot showed an intense, almost instantaneous spike, followed by a decaying ring-down waveform.

"Huh," Dave said. "I'll bet you a coffee this is the new gravity weapon Holder mentioned in the NHK interview."

Bob grinned.

"No bet," he said. "Do I *look* like I was born yesterday? But let's go get that coffee anyway."

———————

The next day, Dreamer began a graduated series of test shots: three shots each at ten percent power, then three at twenty percent, and so on. There was really nothing to see except the telemetry. If you were looking at exactly the right spot when the weapon fired—or if a drone was, on your behalf—there was a momentary dancing distortion of the stars 'behind' the target spot visible at higher power levels, as the intense gravitational gradients chaotically lensed their light.

Everything went well up until the first shot at seventy percent power, when the grav lance tore itself apart.

"What happened, Dreamer?" Alex asked.

"I believe I know what happened, Alex," Dreamer said. "There is a back-reaction that increases much more sharply than I had calculated. Consider it the gravity lance's equivalent of recoil. I believe that I can compensate for it now."

"After we build a new prototype, you mean," Alex said.

"Of course," Dreamer agreed. "I can have prototype nine completed in ten days. And I will start two more, and bring them to fifty percent completion."

———————

Three days later, on March 27, Eithne Coburn came out of the tank. David and Louise, inside the privacy barrier, watched anxiously as the tank drained. Eithne wobbled a little as her weight came onto her feet, and steadied herself against the side of the tank. Then the mask disengaged and recoiled itself, and the tank wall began to retract.

"Eithne?" Louise called, as soon as the wall was low enough, reaching in to take hold of her daughter, heedless of the tank fluid that was still draining off her. "How do you feel?"

The response was slow coming.

"I feel kinda funny, Mommy," Eithne said. "Like I'm real heavy. And my fingers are all wrinkly. That's funny too. But it's funny-ha-ha instead of funny-peculiar."

The tank wall slid down the last bit of the way, and Louise stepped forward with a towel and wrapped Eithne in it, then picked her up. Eithne looked visibly less weary and drawn.

"And how's your headache, honey?" Louise asked, dreading the answer.

"My headache...? It's gone, Mommy," Eithne said. "My headache's gone."

"Gone," Louise said. "The headache is gone." She began to laugh in relief.

"Gone," David repeated. "Can we... should we...?" He stepped outside the screen.

"Dr. Devreaux, she says the headache is gone. Should we scan her again? To make sure?"

"It is not strictly necessary," Philippe Devreaux replied, "but *by all means*, for your peace of mind, let us do it anyway. You can hold her in the scanner if you wish, Mme. Coburn. The scanner will have no difficulty telling the two of you apart."

David and Louise walked over to the scanner, and Louise stepped in, carrying Eithne. The scanner tube came down.

Five minutes later, the scanner retracted.

"What's it show, Doctor?" David asked. His voice was tense.

"Relax, M'sieur Coburn," Philippe assured him. "As expected, Eithne's scan shows one hundred percent remission. There is no longer any sign of the neuroglioblastoma—or that she ever had it. I would like to

114

have her back for another scan in six months, though, just to be absolutely certain."

David wrapped his arms around Eithne and Louise.

"It's over," he said, through tears of joy. "She's cured. She's CURED."

"Ah, however...?" Philippe continued. "Mme. Coburn, the scan detected that you have a cervical polyp. I strongly suggest that we take care of it while you are here."

David and Louise looked at each other for a long moment. Louise swallowed.

"I think we just dodged a bullet we didn't know was coming," David said, a little unsteadily. "Doctor, what do you recommend?"

"The polyp itself could be removed surgically on a treatment bed," Philippe replied. "But I would not recommend relying on that alone. It could leave pre-cancerous cells behind. I recommend that Mme. Coburn go into the tank as well, after removal of the polyp. Let us be certain that we get *everything*. If you wish it, I will authorize it now."

"Tomorrow?" Louise asked. "Could we do it tomorrow?"

"Of course," Philippe replied. "But for now, Eithne should use the shower, to wash away the last remains of the tank fluid."

"Eithne," Louise said, "let's get you showered and cleaned up, okay? How are you feeling now? Still feeling heavy?"

"I feel *great*, Mommy," Eithne said. "The best I've felt in *forever*."

Before Eithne's shower was done, a package popped out of a slot along the wall. Philippe picked it up, took it over to the showers, and handed it to David.

"This is for Eithne," he said. "It has just been custom-made to her measurements. A very small gift from the Fleet."

David broke the seal and unfolded it. It was a light bathrobe in pale green, with the United Earth Fleet insignia on the right shoulder. It had a cartouched name tag that read Eithne Coburn.

"Thank you, Doctor," David said. "Believe me, the Fleet has just given us the greatest gift—the greatest *two* gifts—I can possibly imagine." He passed the robe in to Louise.

A few minutes later, Louise led Eithne out, freshly showered, wearing her new robe and a big grin. Eithne headed straight for Philippe. Philippe knelt to meet her. She walked straight up to him and hugged him.

"Thank you, Doctor Dev—Dever..."

"Just call me Philippe," Philippe said, smiling.

"Doctor Philippe," Eithne finished.

"You are *very* welcome, Mam'selle," Philippe replied.

———

"I'm Debora Carroll, with a very special news update from CNN, *LIVE* from the Stardock. I would like to introduce to you all David and Louise Coburn, and their daughter Eithne. Eithne is six years old, and she is the very first child to be treated under the United Earth Fleet's brand new Last Chance pediatric medical program. A week ago, Eithne Coburn was suffering from an advanced, incurable brain cancer, and her doctors had given her no more than eight months to live.

"Today, thanks to treatment in the Stardock's Medical Bay Two, which you see behind me, she is in complete remission.

"Mr. and Mrs. Coburn, I'm going to let you just say in your own words how you feel about this."

"It's like a miracle," Louise said fervently. "We were told there was no way to save Eithne. No way to keep her from dying. And now she's cured. I can scarcely believe it."

"We have our daughter back," David said. "She wasn't going to live to grow up. And now, she will. The Fleet gave her back to us. I don't know how we can ever thank them."

"And there you have it. Eithne Coburn is only the first of many. The United Earth Fleet has pledged to treat every child with no other hope that they can fit in.

"I'm Debora Carroll, reporting live from the Stardock, and you're watching CNN."

Alex and Naomi invited the Coburns and Debora to a celebratory dinner at Machu Picante, and they all accepted. Philippe Devreaux and Yeon were there, as well. Eithne was proudly wearing her new robe.

"Thank you, Mr. Alex," she said, solemnly.

"You are very welcome, Miss Eithne," Alex replied, equally solemnly. "This pretty lady whom you haven't met is Seok Yeon, and she runs the *other* medical bay on the Stardock."

"Hello, Doctor Miss Seok Yeon," Eithne said. Yeon laughed.

"You can just call me Yeon," she said.

"What kind of a name is that?" Eithne asked.

"It is a Korean name," Yeon replied. "Because I am Korean."

"Well, I think it's a nice name," Eithne declared. "And you are very pretty." Yeon smiled again.

"Thank you, Eithne," she replied. "And you are very pretty too. You look a little bit like my younger sister Jia."

They all ate a leisurely supper, then the Coburns excused themselves and went off to put Eithne to bed.

"She is such a darling," Yeon said. Debora nodded enthusiastically. There were tears in her eyes.

"Debora," Naomi asked, "did you tell Louise that this whole program was basically your idea?"

"No," Debora said, shaking her head. "I don't want them to spend the rest of their lives wondering whether they got special treatment."

"That's very thoughtful of you," Alex said.

"How has the response to the program been?" Debora asked.

"We already have the next seven patients booked," Naomi said. "Right, Yeon?"

"Yes," Yeon agreed. "The next four are due to come up the day after tomorrow. Three children with leukemia, and an eleven-year-old Australian girl who lost her leg in a shark attack six months ago. Then three more two days later."

"Thank you all *so much* for doing this," Debora said.

"Thank *you* for pointing out that we *should*," Alex replied.

————————————

David and Louise were back at MedBay Two the next day, leaving Eithne with Debora. Louise spent an hour on a treatment bed, then went into a tank.

"How long will she be in, Doctor?" David asked.

"Two days will be sufficient for this, M'sieur Coburn," Philippe told him. "She will be fine."

"I... truly don't know how to even begin to thank you," David said. "We had no idea. We probably wouldn't have known until it was too late. She's not in any known high-risk group, so she wasn't getting any regular screening. I might have lost not only my daughter, but my wife as well."

"M'sieur Coburn," Philippe said, "I am a doctor. It is what we *do*. You are *very* welcome. Do you wish to get a scan as well, while you are here?"

David thought for a moment.

"It... would seem foolish not to take the opportunity," he admitted.

Ten minutes later, David's scan was done. Philippe showed him the scan results, explaining the details.

"So you see," he concluded, "you have absolutely no concerns. You are showing some physiological markers for elevated stress, quite understandably, but I am sure that those will dissipate now. You have a clean bill of health."

"Thank you *very* much, Doctor," David said.

Louise came out of her two days in the tank feeling refreshed and relieved. David was of course there waiting for her, with Eithne and Debora this time. They all spent one more day on the Stardock, during which they received a full tour of the Stardock that they hadn't had the opportunity for before, and then it was time for them to go home.

On April 4, grav lance prototype nine was ready, and Dreamer resumed the test shot sequence. He was able to compensate now for the back-reaction effects, and carefully worked all the way up to three full-power shots. It took about eight seconds to recover full charge after a full-power shot. Alex almost choked for a moment when he saw how much power it was drawing from the reactor for those eight seconds.

"*Now* I understand why it needs a sixty-meter reactor for power," he said. "So what's next?"

"Live-fire tests against target drones," Dreamer replied. "I would prefer to have some larger targets to better simulate actually firing against a hostile ship, but we do not have any. So the best I can do for the moment is to use groups of target drones."

"Okay," Alex said. "I imagine that's going to take quite a few drones."

"Yes," Dreamer agreed. "I am ramping up target drone production. We should have enough in about six days to begin the live-fire tests."

On April 6, the next four Warlords came out of the engineering bays, hull numbers CG-04 through CG-07. Their crews were ready. It was the first time that the Fleet Academy had graduated four crews at once, and the first time four new combat-ready Fleet ships had been commissioned on a single day. The four cruisers left their docking ports on Boom Two for their shakedowns as *Alexander*, *Hannibal*, *Takeda Shingen*, and *Red Cloud*. An additional two new hulls were laid down. They would become CG-12 and CG-13.

On April 14, Dreamer declared everything was ready for live-fire testing. A dozen or so single target drones were deployed at ranges from five hundred to fifty thousand kilometers from the test cradle, as well as a number of larger groups also spread out at different ranges. The largest group had thirty-three drones spread out in formation across a hundred meter volume. Each designated target had an additional observer drone a kilometer out.

The firing tests against the single drones, at partial power, were... unexciting. It wasn't difficult to hit them, at least when stationary. When moving, they were harder to hit, and several of the first few longer-range shots were near misses. The direct hits reliably disabled or wrecked the drones in one hit. The near misses *damaged* them to varying degrees, and flung them wildly out of position, but needed a follow-up shot. A couple of the furthest targets took three shots to obtain a solid hit.

"Do we know why we're having trouble targeting?" Alex asked.

"Yes," Dreamer said. "I expected this to be the case. I must take the local curvature of space-time into account when aiming each shot."

"I presume it's going to be easier to hit larger targets," Alex said.

"Naturally," Dreamer replied. "But with the individual target drones at long range, a small error can mean a clean miss."

Alex nodded.

"Makes sense," he agreed.

Then they moved on to the drone groups.

The first group target was a cluster of nine drones at ten thousand kilometers range, positioned at the corners of a ten-meter cube with one extra drone in the center. Dreamer targeted the central drone, and fired on twenty-five percent power.

The weapon grabbed all nine drones and smashed them together into a chaotic spray of wreckage, almost too fast for the eye to follow.

"Well," Alex said, after a few seconds. "*That* was quite gratifying."

"Indeed," Dreamer agreed.

They moved on to the next target group, with similar results. And the next.

The test series finished up with a full-power shot against the largest group target, a hundred-meter cluster of thirty-three drones at fifty thousand kilometers range. That, if anything, was even more dramatic than the first group. Ultra-high-speed playback showed that five of the drones had been ripped apart even before the chaotic gravitational gradients smashed them together in seemingly random patterns, then slammed all of the clumps violently together. Analysis indicated some of the drones were being subjected to instantaneous acceleration spikes as high as several thousand gravities.

"Well *damn*," Alex said slowly.

He looked around the room, thinking about the effects if the gravity lance were fired into an occupied space like this. Whatever was left of the walls would be dripping.

"Ladies and gentlemen... I believe we have a functioning gravity lance. But I can't help hoping that we never have to use it in anger."

7. The Chase

«Hunt-Master,» said Hunter Listens-Carefully, «the Violators' trail forks here. The trail continues ahead... weakening, growing fainter still. But also, there is a branch.»

Listens-Carefully highlighted features in *Silent Tracker*'s bridge scan.

«The other branch heads *here*... and there, it seems, it *ends*.»

Hunt-Master Thoughtful regarded the display, pondering aloud.

«So the trail seems to say, yes. By the time the Den reaches here, it will be faint indeed. Too faint perhaps to follow any further. Can you determine which is the main trail?»

«Not with certainty,» Listens-Carefully replied. «The branch onward... more vessels, I think. But—lesser. It is broad, but shallow.»

«Could one be a decoy?» Thoughtful mused.

«Not impossible,» Star-Seeker Notices-Things replied. «A ruse to throw us off.»

Thoughtful studied the scan at length, trying to read the tangled skein of smeared hyperspace wakes, almost *willing* them to give up their secrets.

«Consider,» he said slowly. «To leap this far at the speed the Violators clearly did, would be beyond the Den. Beyond all of us. Perhaps it was beyond the Violators *as well*.» The conclusion began to firm up in his mind. «The trail onward... broad... but shallow, as you say. Smaller vessels, spread wide. The side trail... narrow. But deep. Something massive. Their Den, perhaps? Unable to run any further without rest?

«I think... we were *meant* to follow the trail forward. To *overlook* this side trail. But... I think perhaps they thought to hide their Den here. And lead us onward away from it, by subterfuge.»

As he spoke his reasoning out loud, Thoughtful became more confident of it.

«The broad trail onward... meant for us to follow. Then at some point ahead, they scatter, the trail goes cold, and they... leap back here by ones and twos, perhaps, leaving little trail.

«Yes. This is what they did. I grow sure of it. Onward is the decoy, the *false* trail. We investigate *here*.

«We shall drop into the outer fringes of this system, and cast about for the Violators' scent. *Quietly.* And we shall see what we can find.»

«There are—indications of perhaps a developing civilization there already, Hunt-Master,» said Hunter Listens-Carefully.

Thoughtful nodded.

«Perhaps why the Violators picked this place,» he said. «To hide their scent among that of others.

«All ships of the Paw... We are going in.»

The Khreetan Paw—a group of six front-runners, scouts, one for each finger on a Khreetan hand—dropped into Sol system just inside the orbit of Uranus, a fraction over 19AU—slightly less than three trillion kilometers— out from the Sun. It would be around two and a half hours before the gravitational signal of their hyperspace entry reached Earth, and seventy-six minutes before it reached even the outer ten-AU shell of LIGO nodes.

«No nearby contacts,» said Hunter Listens-Carefully. «We should be undetected.»

«Good,» replied Hunt-Master Thoughtful. «That gives us time to see what is in this system.»

«I see a paw-and-one worlds so far,» said Listens-Carefully. «Plus an outer belt and a cometary shell. Possibly a second inner belt. We lie just within the orbit of the one-paw.»

«And the Violators?»

«No scent *yet.* I am still seeking.»

Thoughtful pondered.

«We may be here some time,» he said. «And we lie close to the plane of the worlds' orbits.» He indicated a location on the bridge display, slightly more sunward and nearly forty degrees above the plane of the ecliptic. «Prepare to short-leap to there. Far from the orbital plane, we are less likely to be seen by a chance vessel transiting. Keep the leap engine charged at all times, in case we must leap again in haste.»

Maker Of-Course-It-Works head-jerked acknowledgment. At helm, Sleeps-A-Lot aligned the scoutship to the new course, and Of-Course-It-Works began the slow process of charging the hyperdrive.

The Khreetan scouts came out of hyper only minutes after they leapt, but the angle and direction of their leap actually put them almost six light-minutes closer to the nearest detector. The detector array would still not see the signal of their hyperspace exit for over an hour yet.

Still, the Khreetan had no idea that the early warning system even *existed*.

«One additional world is visible from here,» Listens-Carefully said. «Small, close in to the star. Hidden from our previous position. And... there is *something*... the third world has a *huge* moon. A fourth of the size of the world itself.»

«That is... remarkable,» said Thoughtful. «If we get an opportunity, we should take a closer look at that, for the scholars. What about signs of life?»

«Still collecting data,» said Listens-Carefully. «There are definitely intelligent signals. The system is flooded with them.»

«Keep at it,» said Thoughtful.

«Leap engine charging,» said Of-Course-It-Works. The Wayfinders continued studying their sensor readings, looking for signs of their prey.

«There is nothing of very great interest out here,» Listens-Carefully stated, after a little while.

«Agreed,» said Notices-Things. «All is empty and quiet.»

«We should move inward,» Listens-Carefully continued. «That is almost certainly where the prey lies.»

«You are certain that the Violators' Den is not hidden here in the outer system?» Thoughtful asked. «It is what I might do. There is so much more ground to cover.»

«I would not,» said Hunter Listens-Carefully. «Either in the inner system, or in the outer belt. Or even perhaps among the moons of the... fifth world. The giant. It has many of them. A good place to hide.»

«And are you picking up anything from that giant, then?»

«Well... yes,» Listens-Carefully said. «There are powerful emissions in the paw-*kat* band. But they appear to be of natural origin. We *are* picking up artificial signals, *many* of them—but they come from further inward. It *seems*—but no... surely not. I am not yet willing to say.»

«Very well,» said Thoughtful. He considered the tactical display. «If the inner system is where we believe we should seek, then to the inner system we shall go. But let us go where we will not be looked for, at first.» He indicated coordinates high above the system's star.

«There.»

Sleeps-A-Lot aligned the ship, and a few minutes later, the Paw leapt again.

The Paw ended its leap this time roughly nine point three AU, one point four trillion kilometers, to system north of the Sun, not quite directly above it. *Now,* they were only thirty-two light-minutes from the nearest node of the ten-AU LIGO shell. The clock was ticking.

«Leap engine recharging,» Of-Course-It-Works reported, again.

«Clear signs of life and culture—from the *third* world,» Listens-Carefully pronounced after a little while, almost doubtfully.

«From the *third*? And *only* there?» Thoughtful asked.

«Only there,» Listens-Carefully confirmed. «I... doubted the reading, at first. But it is unmistakable. The triangulation is certain now, from three points.»

Thoughtful pondered.

«Surprising,» he said. «One would think that with such a huge moon, the gravitational tides would have prevented advanced life arising. At least made it *difficult.*»

«In fairness,» Of-Course-It-Works interjected, «we do not know that it was *not.*»

«The point is sound,» Thoughtful conceded after a moment. «Gather all information we can from here. And then we shall move that way.»

———————————

Alex and Naomi were having dinner with Maksim and Sofiia at Lem's when the alert came. Both Alex and Maksim received it. Alex's face paled. Maksim froze.

Multiple unknown hyperspace arrivals in the system, Dreamer said. *Preliminary LIGO signal analysis indicates no fewer than five, possibly as many as ten, unknown vessels have entered the system in a group, just within the orbit of Uranus.* The 3D coordinates—latitude, longitude, radius—appeared in Alex's head, and, he assumed, all of the other L3 Fleet senior command staff. *Readings are unclear. Analyzing signatures.*

"Gods," he choked out. "They're not supposed to *be here* yet. The— the estimate we got out of the Crickets was five to six years."

Naomi was looking at Alex, sudden anxiety on her face. Sofiia reached for Maksim's hand.

"Seems either Crickets were wrong," Maksim said slowly, "or they lied to us. *Again.*"

"Well," Alex replied after a moment of additional thought, "we already know they tried to conceal the Khreetan from us *altogether*. I don't know that I trust them not to have given false information to their own junior captains as well. Told them that the Khreetan were further behind than they actually believed. Or perhaps, the Khreetan are simply closer behind them than they thought."

"On the bright side," Maksim observed, "no more then ten."

"Yeah," Alex agreed. "But it's probably safe to assume they're advance scouts." He looked around the table, realizing Naomi hadn't received the alert—and Sofiia definitely wouldn't have. Naomi was looking intently at him, Sofiia looking back and forth between him and Maksim.

"The Khreetan are here," he said. Sofiia gasped. Naomi just looked back at him.

"We're sure?" she said quietly.

Alex paused.

"Well, okay," he corrected, "we don't *KNOW* it's the Khreetan. But it's not Cricket jump signatures, and it would be stretching coincidence beyond plausible belief if it *just happened to be* someone else *again*. We know between five and ten unknown ships just exited hyperspace in the outer system, just under nineteen AU out. The *most likely* explanation is a Khreetan advance scouting force.

"Dreamer, let me know as soon as you've refined the data. Do you have a probable displacement yet?"

"Uncertain," Dreamer replied. "The hyperspace signature has a markedly different pattern from ours. My initial estimate would put them in the range of roughly two hundred to six hundred thousand tonnes, but it is a very loose projection at this time."

"Okay, Dreamer. Let me know as soon as you have better data."

"*All commanders*," Alex sent out over the all-Fleet command channel. "Alert scramble. I want all cruisers on-station in a belt around Earth at two hundred thousand kilometers. Everything else that's not already on patrol, I want in pairs on a plane point-five AU out from Earth towards these coordinates, spaced five million klicks apart, until we have a better idea what they're doing. Try to reform into designated squadrons as much as you can."

He turned to Sofiia. She and Maksim were already hand in hand and eye to eye.

"I'm sorry, Sofiia," Alex said.

"Is alright," Sofiia said, not taking her eyes off Maksim. "We all knew day would come. Just... did not expect it this soon." She pulled Maksim into a tight hug and kissed him fiercely, then thumped him on the chest for emphasis. "You come BACK TO ME, you hear me?" she told him. "You COME BACK TO ME."

"I will come back, my Sofiia," Maksim replied. "Is only a few ships. We have them *very* badly outnumbered. Today will be alright, I am sure. I am not worried. But now I must go. *Hammerhead* is waiting."

He kissed Sofiia once more, then disengaged and headed for the transit system at an easy jog. He was far from the only one headed that way.

General alarm, please, Dreamer, Alex requested. Dreamer obligingly sent out an urgent **Whoop! Whoop! Whoop!** over the public address channel. People on the concourse or in the messes stopped what they were doing and looked up.

"Now hear this," Alex said, "now hear this. Between five and ten unknown ships have just exited hyperspace in the outer system. All crews, head to your ships, you will be launching as soon as fully crewed. All Marines not assigned to a crew, report for duty. Everyone else not assigned to a specific on-shift duty right now, please return to your quarters and await further instructions. This is NOT a drill. I repeat, this is NOT a drill."

Suddenly there were a lot more people up and moving, either headed for transit or for crew quarters. Alex got up and headed for the command center, Naomi following him.

New detection, Dreamer said. *Hyperspace exits, approximately nine point three AU north of Sol.*

"SHIT," Alex swore. "A *second* group, Dreamer?"

Pattern is very similar to the first, Dreamer said. This time he included Naomi.

Alex buried his face in his hands for a moment.

"NEW ORDERS," he sent on the command push. "We have a second detection event. First detection at nineteen AU is now designated Point ALPHA. Second event is toward system zenith at nine point three AU, designated point BETA." He had Dreamer send out the new coordinates.

"I want two four-ship sections to investigate each of these locations. DesRon Four, point ALPHA. DesRon Three, point BETA. Commodores, designate sections from your squadrons. Use ships already in the area if you can. Coordinate between yourselves. DesRon One, deploy on plane point-five AU towards Point ALPHA, DesRon Two, deploy point-five AU towards BETA."

"Where do you want me, Alex?" Naomi asked quietly. Alex looked back at her.

"Right by my side," he said, without hesitation.

"You do remember I'm not technically part of Fleet command?" she reminded him.

"I value your opinion and judgment," Alex replied. "It's often better than my own. And you *are* our liaison to the State Department."

Naomi smiled and took his hand, and they set off for the command center.

"Are we ready to inform Earth?" Naomi asked as they walked.

"I'd... say yes," Alex replied, after a moment. "But let's try not to spread alarm. We don't *know* that it's the Khreetan. For now, just report that a small number of unknown ships have entered the system, that they aren't anywhere near Earth, and that we are responding and investigating."

"Got it," Naomi replied.

———————

Secretary Winters marched straight past the Marine guard at the door to the Oval Office without stopping, ignoring his outstretched hand.

"John," she said, "we have a big problem. Holder is alert-scrambling his entire fleet. They have picked up unknown ships exiting hyperspace in the outer part of the system."

John Riken, already half-standing, sat heavily back down in his chair, his face ashen.

"We were supposed to have *five years*," he said.

"I *know*," Jocelyn Winters agreed grimly.

Riken thought for a moment.

127

"Activate the situation room and get everyone here," he said. "But try to keep a lid on it. Let's see what we can do to avoid panic. There's nothing *we* can do from here anyway, except stand by and try to keep things under control."

———

"Hey, Dave?" Bob Howard called.

"Yeah? What's up?"

"We've picked up a new type of event. Reported by the space-based array."

"A new *type*...? What do we know?"

"It's in the outer system, around nineteen AU out. Doesn't look like anything we've seen before. If... If a Fleet hyperdrive activation is a *CLANG*, then these look sort of like somebody shuffling their feet in pea gravel or pebbles."

"I'll be right there. I want to see them."

"Do we need to tell the Fleet?"

"These detections *came* from the Fleet," Dave reminded Bob. "If we're receiving the data from them, they already know."

"Heh." Bob chuckled, slightly sheepishly. "Good point."

———

Nineteen minutes later, Dreamer reported a *third* hyperspace event. Alex groaned.

"Seriously, *THREE*?" he said. He felt overloaded, bewildered, for a moment.

The data may be misleading, Dreamer pointed out.

Misleading?

I have realized that I committed an oversight, Dreamer explained. *This is a first experience at this for all of us. Light-speed delay factors into these signals. The detector nodes are connected to us by hyperwave, but the gravitational signals travel to the detectors at the speed of light.*

Propagation delay! Alex exclaimed. *Right. Of COURSE. How **old** is the data?*

***Fourth** signal, Alex.*

FOURTH? Alex silently buried his face in his hands.

The third signal appears to be a hyperspace **entry** *at point ALPHA,* Dreamer clarified. *The fourth is a new hyperspace* **exit** *at these coordinates.* The new location was roughly 1.2AU deeper into the system but at roughly forty degrees higher declination, "up" from the principal plane of planetary orbits.

Designate that Point GAMMA, Alex thought.

Done, Alex, Dreamer said. *And I have recalculated all readings taking into account propagation delays. The first detection was seventy-six minutes old when we received it. The second detection came in nine minutes later, but was only thirty two minutes old when we received it. That event actually occurred fifty-three minutes after the first. The third event, the hyperspace entry at ALPHA, was seventy six minutes old when received, but happened only twenty minutes after the first. The fourth, the exit at GAMMA, happened eight minutes after event three, but was detected only a minute later because it was seven light-minutes closer to a node.*

Okay, Alex said. *Let's say the initial entry is at T zero. Then the fourth event actually* **happened** *at T plus twenty eight minutes, and the second at... T plus fifty three. They could all be the same group of ships.*

They could, Dreamer agreed.

Number all events and locations on the plot in chronological order, with detection vectors.

Dreamer quickly added the time tags. The pattern was clear.

They jumped in here, point ALPHA, Alex declared. *Then twenty minutes later they jumped from Point ALPHA to Point GAMMA, arriving there eight minutes later. Then... there's an event we haven't received yet. They jumped again, from GAMMA to BETA, arriving there... roughly forty-nine minutes ago now.* He let out a sigh of relief. *All of these events are the same group of ships.*

I concur, Dreamer said.

The problem, Alex went on, *is we know where and when they first arrived, and approximately where they were forty-nine minutes ago. We don't know where they are NOW.*

Agreed, Dreamer said. *We must make assumptions.*

"ALL COMMANDERS," Alex sent. "We have *new analysis* of the data. All of the hyper events we have detected appear to be a single group of ships, last known to be at Point BETA. But I want one of the two sections headed for Point ALPHA to investigate Point GAMMA anyway. I do not expect you to find anything at either ALPHA or GAMMA—but stay alert.

ALPHA and GAMMA sections rendezvous with BETA sections if you find nothing there. BETA is their last **known** position, but that location is fifty minutes old. We don't know where they are **now**. I want the last section of DesRon Three headed that way as well. Start... about two AU sunward from BETA."

He received quick acknowledgment from all four Commodores.

DesRon Four Section One—*Sealion*, Colonel Mackenzie's *Highlander*, *Sawfish* and *Wolverine*—dropped out of hyper half a million kilometers sunward from Point ALPHA. The four ships immediately quarter-searched the entire vicinity for any contacts, passive scans only. There was no point in announcing their presence any sooner than necessary.

"Nothing at ALPHA," Mackenzie reported, after a few minutes. "Heading for rendezvous at Point BETA."

Roughly a hundred and eighty million kilometers closer to the Sun and ten times that far *up* from the plane of the ecliptic, Section Two—*Basilosaur*, *Perth*, *Stuart* and *Arapaima*—left hyperspace and scanned their vicinity. It was similarly empty.

"Point GAMMA is clear," Commander David Googan reported from *Perth*. "Heading to BETA."

Five million kilometers to system north of Point BETA, DesRon Three Section One—*Blackfish*, *Mantaray*, *Stonefish* and *Eagleray*—dropped out of hyper, came about, and started scanning sunward.

"Stardock, *Blackfish*," Pierre du Maurier called in. "All clear here. Heading sunward."

A moment later, Section Two, led by Ae Morita in *Devilfish*, did the same seven million kilometers sunward. Just as Section One had, they passive-scanned the area.

"Contact!" called Kenichi Sato, *Devilfish*'s sensors officer. "Multiple contacts at just under a million kilometers, on this bearing. I count... six of them. They have already passed our position." *Tarpon* and *Electrophorus* quickly confirmed.

"Stardock, *Devilfish*," Ae Morita reported. "Confirm six contacts, headed in-system." She attached the sensor traces, giving position and velocity. "No further information yet."

"Acknowledged, *Devilfish*," Alex responded. "All scout sections, close on Section Two and support as needed."

"Let's go and take a closer look," Ae ordered. "Maintain passive scan only. Weapons secure. We will not be the first to fire." She plotted an intercept course, not too close, and Section Two burned at sixty gravities to close the distance.

———————

«CONTACTS!» Listens-Carefully called out, a little less than a minute later. «Behind us. Four new contacts have just leapt to just more than one and a half *me' me'ka'kat* on this bearing. No active scans detected yet. They are accelerating this way at...»

He broke off, with a coughing exclamation.

«They are making *half again* our best acceleration!»

Thoughtful thought rapidly, as he studied the readings.

«Just a fortuitous chance leap on their part, surely,» he said. «We cannot *outrun* them, if they can sustain that acceleration. But we can leap again well before they can reach us.» He studied the tactical display, then designated a point nearly as far below the ecliptic as they were now above it, and further out, beyond that intriguing third world with its bizarrely over-sized moon.

«Take us... *there*.»

«Fortunate indeed that the leap engines are already charged,» said Of-Course-It-Works. «Ready for leap.»

«Aligning,» said Sleeps-A-Lot.

The six front-runners came about slightly, and a moment later, Sleeps-A-Lot activated the drive. The ships' drives poured energy into their jump fields, and shimmering auras slowly began to build around them, intensifying as the power grew. Just less than two minutes later, they slipped smoothly into hyper.

"Contacts lost," said Kenichi Sato, shortly after. "They must have spotted us and jumped again."

Ae called it in.

"No indication of where they're going," she reported. "But they were on a course in-system before they jumped."

"Copy, *Devilfish*," Alex said. He sighed. "We'll advise as soon as we get another hyper exit detection from the array."

"Dreamer, can we track where they went through hyperspace?"

"Insufficient data as yet," Dreamer replied. "They are six individual ships, not much larger than ours, and their hyperdrive signatures are very different. Based on Devilfish's report and LIGO data, it appears to take them approximately two minutes to enter or leave hyperspace. I cannot determine how strong a trail they will leave. It may be extremely faint. Still, it is worth the attempt."

Alex nodded.

"Commander Morita," he sent. "I want you to proceed to their hyperspace entry point, enter hyperspace yourselves, and see if you can pick up a wake trail."

"Understood, sir," Ae replied. "We are on our way."

She turned to Daisuke Kondo, on helm.

"Daisuke, Hiromi," she said. "Plot us a micro-jump. Let's make up some time while we can."

―――――――――

The Khreetan scouts dropped out of hyper again six point five AU out from the Sun, at roughly minus fifty-four degrees declination, almost on a direct azimuth outward from Earth. The closest LIGO early-warning node was five point three AU away. It would be forty four minutes before their hyperspace exit was detected and triangulated.

«Let us head towards that third world,» Thoughtful said, «and see what we can learn. Spread out a little. Keep looking and listening. And *charge the leap engines*.»

«Charging,» Of-Course-It-Works confirmed.

―――――――――

"Update from the Fleet, Mr. President," Secretary Winters said. "There appear to be only six ships. They believe it to be a scouting operation. They got a sighting at... zenith at nine point five A U? I don't really understand that part, I'm afraid."

"Astronomical unit," Ed Wegener, the National Science Advisor, filled in. "Nine and a half times the radius of the Earth's orbit, in that direction." He pointed toward the sky, somewhat north of vertical. "Call it roughly nine hundred million miles."

"Sounds like they're keeping them away from Earth so far, at least," President Riken mused. "Is there any public reaction yet?"

"Nothing yet, that I'm seeing," said Miranda Ramirez, the Vice-President.

"I concur," DNI David Hackett agreed. "Nothing's been made public and all of the discussion we're seeing is speculating that it's simply a large-scale exercise."

John Riken rested his chin in his hands and thought, for a long time. Finally, he sighed, rubbed his eyes, and raised his head.

"There's nothing *we* can do about it," he said at last, tiredly. "This is all on Holder and his fleet. And the *last* thing we want is public panic.

"I feel a little dirty about it, but I can't help but think that if the public thinks this is just a drill, an exercise, then the best thing we can do right now is *probably* to let them continue thinking that—*for now*.

"What do the rest of you think?"

After a moment, DNI Hackett nodded. So did Dr. Winters, then General Morgan, Ed Wegener, and Miranda Ramirez. And it went on around the room from there.

"You do realize, John," Miranda said quietly, "that if it becomes public that we knowingly concealed a scouting foray by aliens from the public, you can probably kiss your chances of re-election goodbye."

John Riken nodded slowly.

"I know," he said. "But you know what? If we make it through this crisis—and I mean the *larger* crisis, not just this intrusion—in one piece, I don't think I fucking *CARE* whether I get a second term."

———————————

DesRon Three Section Two reached the last observed Khreetan position, and then they just sat there and scanned.

"There's not much *here*," said Kenichi Sato, after about ten minutes. "There's a *faint* pattern of disturbance... but it's broad and indistinct, and fading as we watch."

Ae Morita nodded.

"I'm not seeing much either," she agreed. "I think the most we can say is that it looks as though they continued *generally* in the same direction they were headed."

Hiromi Yoshida, at the nav console, nodded.

"And that means generally toward Earth," she said.

Ae reported in.

Alex sighed.

"So we only had track on them for a couple of minutes," he said. "We know they jumped, we know they jumped in *roughly* the same direction they were going before jump, we know that's generally toward Earth, and we know that *their* hyperdrive trails dissipate too quickly for us to be able to track them through hyperspace. And when last seen, they were headed generally towards Earth. But we *don't* know where they jumped *to*."

"I think that sums it up," Tom agreed. "We know where they've been, and where they last *were*, but not where they are now."

"If I had an enemy to catch that I didn't know exactly where they were," Colonel John Warner interjected, "I'd try to cut their likely route well ahead of where they could reasonably be, and work back towards where they probably are."

Alex nodded.

"That seems sound," he said. "But they could have jumped to anywhere along that line." He thought a moment longer.

"So what if... we space the six DesRon Three and Four sections out along the *closer end* of that line, say one AU apart outward from Earth, then search outward towards their last known position?"

Tom and Sandra pondered that.

"I don't have a better idea," Tom agreed after a couple of minutes. John Warner nodded as well.

"OK," Alex said. "Do it."

Seven minutes later, all six DesRon Three and Four sections had jumped to new positions, like six groups of beads on a string almost nine hundred million kilometers long. They began to search towards system zenith, backtracking towards where the Khreetan scouts had last been seen.

But that wasn't where the Khreetan were.

"New hyper detection event," Dreamer reported. "It is a hyperspace entry at the last known position of the Khreetan group. Detection delay is thirty two minutes."

"That doesn't actually tell us anything we didn't already know, does it, Dreamer?"

"No, it does not."

"Let's just hope one of the destroyer sections sights them."

Along the search line 'north' of the ecliptic towards zenith, the six destroyer groups continued their search pattern. They continued to find nothing.

Almost seven hundred and fifty million kilometers in nearly the opposite direction, the six Khreetan scouts headed toward Earth. By now they had built up over seven hundred kilometers a second of velocity Earthward.

"Alex, new hyperspace exit," Dreamer reported. "Right ascension seven degrees, declination minus fifty four degrees, radius roughly five point three AU, propagation delay forty-four minutes."

Alex swore.

"They jumped RIGHT PAST Earth," he said. "They outfoxed us. We've been trying to intercept them in the wrong direction. Designate that DELTA."

He thought rapidly.

"DesRon One and Two, re-deploy centered on that bearing... ten million kilometers out. DesRon Three and Four, reverse your search pattern, spread out along that new line starting at point-five AU from Earth, point-five AU apart. Flank speed until you're on station and heading outward."

At maximum acceleration, it took the Sharks eighteen minutes to reverse their velocity, and another five to six minutes to jump to their new positions. By that time, the Khreetan scouts were three point two million kilometers Earthward of their hyperspace exit and closing at over sixteen hundred kilometers a second. They still had a long way to go.

«Multiple readings of high-intensity drives around the third world,» reported Listens-Carefully. «It seems all but certain it is the homeworld of the ships we saw. But I have no conclusive readings yet to show whether the Violators' den is there. And nor *will* we, from this distance.»

«You want us to go closer, faster,» Thoughtful said.

«I do,» Listens-Carefully agreed.

«I do not disagree,» said Thoughtful. «So let us consider options. How close do you wish us to try to get?»

«I do not think that we should spend a long time near their world,» Notices-Things cautioned.

«Nor do I,» Thoughtful agreed. «They have sighted us once already. And we have *seen* how fast their ships are.» He pondered the tactical display.

«I should like to get a look from within half a *me' me'ka'kat*, if we can,» Listens-Carefully said at last.

«Perhaps,» Notices-Things suggested, «if we were to conceal our arrival by leaping behind their moon? It is very large. It should completely hide our leap from their world.»

«Cunning,» Thoughtful remarked. «Good thinking. If what we have seen is their highest acceleration...» He trailed off, calculating. «The leap engines should be charged and ready again before they can close within eight *me'ka'kat* from orbit around their world. They will not be able to catch us before we can leap again.»

He thought more, then raised a forehand, spread.

«We will split the Paw in two,» he declared. «Half a *me' me'ka'kat* is too close. It would put us inside their moon. But... one group at seven-twelfths *me' me'ka'kat*, and the remaining group at one. Both will leap to place their moon in between the leap-point, and their world. Target points are *here,* and *here.* We recharge leap engines as soon as we arrive there, we maintain full acceleration, we see what we can see, and *as soon as* all leap engines are charged again, we leap together, *OUT,* and we leave this system, having seen as much or as little as we will.

«This places us at possible risk, if they strike at us, but I believe it *minimizes* that risk. Do all agree?»

«It appears sound,» said Notices-Things.

«I agree,» said Listens-Carefully.

«And I,» added Sleeps-A-Lot. Of-Course-It-Works simply raised forehands in agreement.

«Then it is decided,» said Thoughtful. «Plot the leaps. We leap as soon as all is ready.»

A few minutes later, the six Khreetan ships jumped, in two groups of three. And then pretty much everything happened all at once.

Dave Edwards' cell phone rang. He answered it reflexively.

"Hey Bob. What'cha got?"

"Another shuffle event," said Bob Howard. "But this time, **BEFORE** the space-based array reported. Two minutes ago now. We don't have the space-based reading yet."

It took only a second for the significance to register to Dave.

"*Shit*," he said. "They're *well* inside the 1AU array. Can't be any more than about point three eight AU out. Got a bearing yet?"

"Pretty much aligned with the moon," Bob answered.

"Bob, I gotta run," Dave said, and hung up. Then he called the National Science Advisor, on his personal number.

"*Contact!*" called Kamal Bouaziz, a moment later, at the sensors board on CG-05 *Hannibal*. "Three contacts bearing 011 at four hundred and thirty-five thousand kilometers. Almost tangential vector around fifty degrees upward from nadir, at about seventeen hundred kilometers a second."

Eugen Dietrich, Captain on *Hannibal*, called it in.

"Alex, I have direct sensor detection of three contacts fifty thousand kilometers beyond the moon," Dreamer said. "Near-tangent vector at seventeen hundred and forty kilometers a second. Commander Dietrich on *Hannibal* reports a second group of three roughly three hundred and ten thousand kilometers further out. *Temüjin* confirms both sightings."

"They've split their formation," Alex said. "Tom, get DesRon Three and Four back here as fast as they can. I want them a million kilometers ahead of the closer group, on their current course." Tom Whitman nodded and got on it. "DesRon One and Two, redeploy between Earth and their projected position five minutes from now."

"*Hannibal* and *Temüjin* are requesting orders," Dreamer said. "The closer group is within missile engagement envelope, unless they can jump again within about five minutes."

Alex thought for a moment.

"We don't know they *can't*," he said. "They've probably already seen all that they're going to. Let's see what they do now. But let's not be the first to fire on them. Let *them* fire the first shot."

Beside him, Naomi nodded ever so slightly in agreement.

«Positive sighting of the Violators' Den,» Listens-Carefully reported. «It is indeed in orbit around this world. And strong power readings. *Strong.* But... I do not see a single Violator ship *anywhere*.»

«Continue seeking,» Thoughtful replied. «Record all that we can see.»

The first two sections of DesRon Four came out of jump a little less than 120,000 kilometers ahead of the inner Khreetan group, doing slightly over a thousand kilometers a second. The three Khreetans had maintained their acceleration since they came out of jump and were by then traveling at around nineteen hundred and thirty kilometers a second. Their combined closing velocity was nearly three thousand kilometers a second, one percent of C.

"*Maximum braking!*" Mackenzie ordered. The eight Sharks flipped end-for-end and burned at their maximum deceleration of seventy-six Earth gravities. They hadn't a chance of matching velocity before they passed the Khreetan, but they could perhaps slow enough to get a slightly better look.

«NEW CONTACTS AHEAD!» called Notices-Things urgently. «A paw-and-two ships. Range is barely two-*te' me'ka'kat*, closing at... *Blessed HUNTMISTRESS!* They are braking at almost *five-te' mass-equivalents*.»

Thoughtful nearly choked.

«That is more than *twice* our best,» he said, after a moment. «How are they so *fast*? How do they generate enough *power*?»

«Do we strike?» asked Listens-Carefully.

«*NO,*» Thoughtful replied. «No, I... *do not believe* that these are the Violators. Let us not strike and run dishonorably, as the Violators did. Let *them* be the first to strike, if they will. And then we shall see.»

Barely forty seconds later, the two groups of ships flashed past each other, the closest ships less than thirty kilometers apart. For a tiny fraction of a second, they were within visual range of each other. Then they were past and gone.

Neither human nor Khreetan eyes were fast enough to catch it. But the sensors on both sets of ships did.

«They did not strike at us,» Notices-Things said, perhaps unnecessarily.

«*Interesting,*» Thoughtful mused.

"We missed an intercept," Colonel Mackenzie reported. "Couldnae shed the relative velocity in time. But we got a good close look, aye."

"Remaining sections re-plot for another two million kilometers," Alex ordered. "See if you can brake enough before intercept to get a better look."

But five minutes later, the other four sections of Sharks were still nearly a million kilometers out when the shimmering aura of Khreetan jump fields faded and the Khreetan ships were gone.

———————

«All ships call safe,» Thoughtful sent to the Paw. The expected five acknowledgments came back.

«This has been... eye-*opening* indeed,» he said. «Does enough remain of the trail-branch leading *onward* to follow?»

«I can *try* to pick it up again,» Listens-Carefully replied doubtfully. «But it was almost vanishingly faint.»

«Well, let us try,» Thoughtful said. «Though I expect it will avail us little.»

«Such small ships,» said Listens-Carefully. «Like fast-swimmers.»

«And so *fast,*» said Notices-Things. «*Also* like fast-swimmers.» Listens-Carefully coughed a grim chuckle.

«I do not understand,» Of-Course-It-Works grumbled, «how they can possibly fit enough power for such acceleration inside such small hulls. They must be nearly all reactors and drive, inside.»

Thoughtful looked knowingly at Of-Course-It-Works.

«You are envious,» he said. «But you would like to try one out. Not true?»

139

«Well *of course* I would,» Of-Course-It-Works replied, as though it were the most obvious thing in the galaxy. «Would you not?»

«Like fast-swimmers,» Notices-Things mused. «I wonder what their teeth are like?»

«Be glad we did not find out on this foray,» Thoughtful said. «I have no wish to be bleeding into the water, this far from the Den.»

———————

"Stay on high alert," Alex ordered over the general command push. "All ships join the screening globe until we see if we get any new detections. And in the meantime we can start analyzing what we've learned. I want all commanders in this discussion, please.

"For one thing, I'm... rather dismayed how *little* use our LIGO early warning system was. They'd jumped *twice more* before we even picked up that they'd entered the system. I'm not happy about that."

"I cannot disagree," Dreamer replied. "It is, however, an inevitable result of the fact that gravitational waves propagate at lightspeed."

"Oh, I *know*, Dreamer," Alex hurried to say. "Please don't think I intended any criticism. We all knew there would *be* detection delays. I just hadn't internalized how long the delays could be relative to jump times, and what that *meant* in terms of being able to locate targets making jumps around the system."

"I understand, Alex," Dreamer replied. "I did not take any offense. I agree that the detection system is less useful than we hoped it would be.

"However, remember that we have gained valuable intelligence about them and their capabilities."

"DesRon Four's close sighting?" Alex asked. "Brief although it was?"

"Yes," Dreamer replied. "But more than that. There are at least three important details that I don't think you are aware of yet."

"OK, Dreamer," Alex said. "The floor is yours. Go ahead."

"Firstly," Dreamer said, "we now know that Khreetan hyperdrives operate differently from Cricket hyperdrives. They produce a very different gravity wave signature. I am in receipt of a communication relayed from Dr. Wegener that I did not share with you yet, since it was not urgent at the time and gave us no new information. The Cal Tech team coined the name 'clang events' to describe the gravity-wave signature of a Cricket hyperdrive activation. By contrast, they are referring to Khreetan hyperdrive activations as a 'shuffle event', because they find it reminiscent of a person shuffling their feet in coarse gravel. I was of course aware of the

140

differences in the signal patterns, but it did not seem important at the time to mention it."

"Hmm," Alex mused. "The terminology is interesting... and I imagine it means we can very clearly tell the two apart. Does it tell you anything useful about their hyperdrive technology?"

"Not yet," Dreamer replied. "Secondly, we have the observations transmitted from *Devilfish* and *Highlander*, as well as the other ships in their respective groups, correlated with direct first-hand observation from the Stardock's sensors. It takes a *Shark* class ship approximately twenty seconds to enter hyperspace, from initial hyperdrive activation, and about ten seconds to return to normal space. But hyperspace entry appears to take a Khreetan ship—at least, the type we saw today—approximately two minutes."

"Two *minutes*," Alex mused. "Of course we don't know how long hyperspace *exit* takes them, correct?"

"Correct, Alex," Dreamer agreed. "Although we can place an upper bound upon it given the time between their hyperspace entries and exits. If we project from the relative entry and exit performance of our hyperdrives, it is perhaps safe to assume that it takes on the order of one minute. That is based upon an assumption that the same roughly two-to-one ratio applies, which is supported by the relative durations of the gravitational wave signatures."

"So it takes them a lot longer to enter and exit hyperspace than it does us," Alex said, sounding for the first time today at least somewhat satisfied. Sandra Hayes looked at him with a faint smile.

"I can tell you're thinking something that pleases you," she said.

"Yeah," Alex agreed. "Those tactical hyper maneuvers we came up with are going to *TOTALLY* blindside them."

After a moment, Tom began to chuckle.

"You're right," he said. "If they're used to thinking of hyperspace entry and exit on a scale of minutes, they'll never know what hit them."

"Anyway, Dreamer," Sandra said after a moment, "you said 'at least three'. That's two. What's the third?"

"Consider," Dreamer said. "On that final close pass, they had split their formation, perhaps to reduce the likelihood of losing all six ships if we fired on them. If we easily detected their ships, it is highly likely they also detected ours. We can assume that they knew they were within our probable engagement envelope.

"And then, we had a successful intercept by DesRon Four, passing actually within visual range, followed by a *second* imminent intercept by elements of DesRon Three. And yet the Khreetan ships *still* did not activate their hyperdrives until *twelve minutes* after they jumped in behind the Moon. I believe this may tell us something."

There was silence for a moment.

"...You think it takes them twelve minutes to charge their hyperdrives?" Alex suggested.

"I believe it likely," Dreamer agreed. "And we never saw them exceed forty gravities acceleration. Between the two, I hypothesize that they are perhaps limited to fusion power."

Tom looked thoughtful.

"That would give us a huge power advantage," he said. "Dreamer: Assume the hypothesis is correct. That *both* hypotheses are correct—that they operate on fusion power, and that it takes them twelve minutes to charge their hyperdrive and two minutes to activate it. Does it seem probable that they could match our hyper-boosted railguns?"

There was a substantial pause while Dreamer considered that.

"No," he replied at last. "I consider it likely that they could not. However, do not rule out the possibility that they have other weapon systems that we have not developed or chosen to deploy."

Alex nodded.

"That's a good cautionary note," he agreed. "And I think we can safely assume that gravity lance technology is out of the question for them. But I have to say I'm feeling a lot better about this now, than I did when we were chasing them futilely across the system looking like fools, because we were looking for them in places where they weren't."

"This was our first actual engagement with the Khreetan," Tom pointed out. "All things considered, I'd have to say I think we came off fairly well."

"I wonder what *they're* thinking about *us?*" Naomi asked.

"Good question," Alex replied. "I'd love to have access to a fly on that wall.

"What else did we learn?"

"Correlating sensor records and observations," Dreamer reported, "including the relatively close range optical observations from *Highlander's* section, the ships we saw today were on the close order of four hundred meters in length, a little shorter than a *Warlord* class cruiser, but substantially more massive. I estimate them at around three hundred and thirty thousand tonnes, based on gravimetry. The closest Earthly analogue to their shape, again from *Highlander*'s transmitted optical observations, would be perhaps a cowrie shell."

"Can we make any inferences about their construction?" Tom asked.

"Not *definitely*," Dreamer replied. "The two most likely scenarios are either a more or less monolithic hull constructed from amorphous Tier 2 materials, or possibly a hull constructed from metacrystalline Tier 3 material at well below optimal radius."

"What would the structural implications of that below-optimum construction be?" Alex asked.

"Uncertain," Dreamer replied. "It would probably not be markedly weaker against a single directed-energy hit, and might resist a single kinetic weapon strike better than Tier 2 materials. However, I would expect a high risk that a second hit in the same place from *either* type of weapon would result in localized catastrophic structural failure."

"A hull breach, you mean," Alex said.

"Exactly," Dreamer agreed.

"If I might speak a mickle o' that close sightin'," Mackenzie said, "I'm thinkin' we've been relyin' tae much on speed. But our closin' vector on those Khreetan scouts in that pass was nigh three thousand kilometers a second. We cannae do a thing at that speed. 'Twas all we could do tae get a guid gander at them. We couldnae hae fired the railguns at them at all, they'd hae outrun the railgun rounds. The spinal grasers would hae been our ainly shot.

"When—if—we get intae combat, we'll have tae watch our speed, or we'll spend all our time brakin' and counter-brakin' tryin' tae stay within engagement range."

"You make a good point, Commodore," Alex agreed. "There's such a thing as being so fast you can't hit anything."

"I agree," Ae Morita interjected. "We seem to have about a two-to-one advantage over the Khreetans that we saw today, on acceleration. But we also seem to have at least a *six-to-one*—probably *much* better, if the twelve-minute charging hypothesis is true—advantage on tactical hyperspace jumps. We should make better use of that."

"Ae is right, I think," Maksim commented. "We should practice this. We have big advantage in how quickly we can jump. Let us use it."

"Agreed," Alex said. "Maksim, Ae, after we recall, I want the two of you to work on putting together a program of squadron-level exercises to practice using tactical jumps for positioning."

"It does not solve the problem of visibility and propagation delays," Dreamer pointed out.

"No, it doesn't," Angavu Onyango chipped in. "But we can see a lot more and sooner by jumping ahead even thirty light-seconds, than we can by taking twenty minutes to cross that distance and arriving with a huge realspace velocity. And we could easily jump several light-minutes at a time."

The discussion went on at considerable length, while they waited for any new detection events to come in.

"Just checking, Dreamer," Alex asked, at one point. "There isn't any way that we could put an early warning array actually in hyperspace, is there...?"

"No, Alex," Dreamer replied. "That would not be feasible. The *obvious* problem is that each early warning node would need its own hyperdrive, and so would have to be on the same general order of size as an *Endeavour* class ship."

"Yes," Alex agreed, "I already thought of that one. But your choice of words implies a *non-obvious* problem as well."

"Yes," Dreamer replied. "There is a more fundamental problem. Electromagnetic radiation does not propagate in hyperspace."

"...Right. So we can't build a laser gravitational interferometer in hyperspace *anyway*," Alex completed.

"Precisely," Dreamer said.

"Although..." Alex thought a little more. "Clearly we have equipment able to do the job. Or we wouldn't be able to navigate in hyperspace at all."

"That is true," Dreamer replied, after a moment. "However, the sensitivity profile of ship navigation sensors is not particularly well suited to the role of a static early warning sensor. And in any case, it would still be logistically infeasible to build enough."

Alex nodded.

"It is what it is," he agreed.

When three hours had passed with no further contact or detection events, Alex had the Fleet stand down from high alert, but remain on station for the present.

"I think we should start figuring out what we're going to tell the world about the incursion," he said.

"Keep it simple," Naomi advised. "Hit the *good* points. The things that went *well*. It was our first full-fleet alert, and there were no mishaps. The LIGO hyperspace jump tracking system *worked*, we were able to intercept them twice despite obvious attempts to evade us, they never got within the orbit of the Moon, there were no hostilities, the Fleet is still on station in case of any further detections, and we think we learned at least as much about their capabilities as they did about ours."

Alex hesitated. Then he chuckled.

"You know what?" he said. "This is *your* field of expertise. You and Dong-geun. I'm placing it in your hands. I *know* the two of you will do it right. Just let me know if you need me to make any decisions on anything to go into it."

Naomi grinned.

"You got it," she said. "We'll get it done."

═══════════

After six hours with no new detections, Alex called a general recall, and the Fleet returned home. There was a statement prepared and ready for release by then. It stated in general terms that a small number of unknown ships, presumed to be Khreetan, had entered and scouted the solar system; that they had been detected by the LIGO array while still far from Earth; that they had been intercepted twice, in part due to that early warning; that they had never gotten within four hundred thousand kilometers of Earth; that a great deal of knowledge had been gained about their tactical capabilities and the construction of their ships. The statement openly admitted that the arrival of scouts came far sooner than had been expected, but concluded by stating that despite this, several areas had been identified in which Fleet ships had a tactical edge over the presumed Khreetans, that they were believed to be incapable of tactical hyperspace maneuvering, and that new tactical training exercises were already being developed to best take advantage of that edge.

Dong-geun presented the completed statement calmly and matter-of-factly to the General Assembly. Perhaps in part due to his even, measured delivery, it mostly seemed to be taken as exactly what it was written to convey: that despite the arrival of presumed Khreetan scouts long before they were expected, everything had worked as well as it could, and that Earth had come out of the brief intrusion with no losses and a lot of valuable new information.

There were of course questions, but most of them were simply requests for further information. As agreed, Dong-geun requested that such questions be submitted in a written form to allow them to be better collated and more fully answered. There was little point in anyone attempting to accuse the Fleet of being caught unprepared, when the statement had declared it right up front.

———————

"My fellow Americans," John Riken said, "I want to speak briefly to you tonight to clarify rumors about today's events in space, before those who *don't know what actually happened* can fill your ears with made-up nonsense about it.

"Let me begin by reassuring you that there is no present danger. I'm going to repeat that: No present danger.

"You have all been hearing for nearly three years now about the coming threat from the Khreetan, which the United Earth Fleet was formed by Alex Holder to defend against. Today, that Fleet was tested for the first time, and I have to say that they did an *outstanding* job. Our solar system was scouted today by a flight of what are presumed to be Khreetan advance scouts. As far as we know, we still have several years to be ready for their main force.

"The Fleet's hyperspace early-warning system functioned exactly as it was designed to. The Fleet knew the number and approximate size of the Khreetan scout ships before ever seeing them, and the Khreetan could not make a hyperspace jump anywhere in the system without the Fleet knowing exactly where they jumped from and to. The Fleet intercepted the Khreetan not once, but twice, and kept them from ever approaching closer to Earth than the Moon.

"Yes, the Khreetan scouts undoubtedly learned a little about us. Our liaison with the Fleet has informed me that we learned a *LOT* about them. We know that the Fleet's ships are faster than theirs, can jump in and out of hyperspace faster than theirs, have weapon systems that we believe they cannot match, and may possibly be better armored than the Khreetan. I am told that the Fleet is already

146

adapting their training to include new and better tactics based on what they learned today.

"The Fleet was tested today, and it passed that test with flying colors. It watches over us day and night to keep us safe.

"The United States of America has supported the United Earth Fleet from its very foundation, and will continue to support it. When you go to bed tonight, say an extra thank you in your bedtime prayers for Alex Holder and the brave men and women of all nations and all denominations who form his United Earth Fleet. He and the Fleet are watching over you tonight, over all of Earth, just as they did this day. The Fleet never sleeps, so that you can sleep safely in your beds.

"Goodnight, America, and god bless."

Later that evening, John Riken and Miranda Ramirez sat in the White House lounge sharing a quiet drink.

"You know, John," Miranda said, "Ed tells me some of that was shading the truth a little."

"Yes, it was," John agreed. "I left out a lot, but none of it was technically untrue. I told them what America needs to hear to sleep soundly tonight, because that's the most important thing I can do right now."

"There will be questions," she said. "I don't think there'll be a lot, but there will be some."

"And we'll answer them as they come up," he replied. "There will be people who will try their hardest to find something in this to use against us. Opportunists, the lunatic fringe, the sideliners trying to make a comeback. But the press is on our side, and it's pretty hard to argue against a win. I know there were setbacks today, but nevertheless, it *was* a win. And that's what America needed to hear tonight."

Miranda Ramirez nodded.

"Just be careful," she said. "Don't give your opposition anything they can twist into a weapon against you."

"I'll be careful," he said. "Thanks, Miranda."

"I'm going to bed now," Miranda said, as she finished her drink and got up. "Goodnight, John. Don't stay up too late sweating it." She rested her hand briefly on his shoulder as she walked past his chair.

"Wow," Alex said. "I feel like we barely scraped through today, but Riken made us sound like heroes."

"That's because you were," Naomi said, cuddled up next to him. She sat up a bit straighter and turned to look more directly at him. "Yes, there were setbacks. Not everything worked as well as you'd hoped. There was confusion about the detection events at first, and the time delay was a problem.

"But you and your command staff had an answer for *everything*. Every setback was handled, you all adapted on the fly and kept on going, and you used what you learned. You learned what the weak points were, and you're already working out plans and strategies to work around them. You even figured out some of *their* weaknesses. And the Fleet itself ran like a well-oiled machine."

Alex thought about that for a while.

"You're right," he said at last. "Yes, more things than I like went wrong, but an awful lot went right. And it could even play in our favor a little, too."

Naomi looked at him quizzically.

"How so?" she asked.

"Well," Alex said, "what if those scouts get back to their main body and report that they got a good look and the Crickets *aren't here*?"

"Huh," Naomi said thoughtfully. "That... *is* an interesting possibility."

"Not useful to speculate about it, though," Alex said. "We have to assume they're still coming just as we have all along."

Naomi nodded.

"For now, though, I want a shower, and then bed." She stood up, still holding onto Alex's hand, then turned back to look at him. "And I'm taking you with me, mister."

Alex grinned.

"No complaints here," he said, as he stood up to follow her.

The front-runners of the Khreetan Paw sat in empty space, a fraction over three light-years outside the solar system.

«Very interesting,» said Hunt-Master Thoughtful. «Clearly the Violators *WERE* here. But there is no sign of their presence now. And yet... who are these out-clan?» He pondered.

«Their ships—very different to the Violators,» Listens-Carefully observed.

«Yes,» Thoughtful agreed. «And yet... their leaps *look like* those of the Violators. And they leap, again, shockingly fast. Most... intriguing.»

He came to a decision.

«We must be *close* to the light wavefront of when the Violators were here. We will spread out, *here, here...*» He designated six locations spread across a light-year and a half. «We shall listen for two rotations to the signals. Let us see how much we can quickly learn about before and after the Violators came here. Then we will regroup *here.*»

One by one, the ships of the Paw spread out, dropped back out of hyper, and sat and listened.

8. Elegant Solutions

Alex and the rest of the Fleet command staff continued their post-mortem of the Khreetan scouting intrusion the next day. There were a few additional insights, discussions for optimizing options based on the experience from the encounter.

And there was one major elephant in the middle of the room. Alex left it until last.

"I know we only just started building out the Warlord class," Alex said. "But we need to think about the future. And that, I think, means the gravity lance.

"Dreamer, what additional testing do you think we need?"

"I do not know, Alex," Dreamer replied. "I have never conducted a weapons test program myself before. The only additional thing we could do that immediately occurs to me, is a sustained test-firing program to verify reliability and determine whether there is any overheating or breakdown with sustained fire. I believe I can increase the rate of fire somewhat, with what we know about the gravity lance now. I do not know how realistic a need that is, since I do not know how you will be tactically employing the weapon. You did in fact already state a preference not to, unless forced into it."

Alex nodded.

"You're not wrong, Dreamer. I'd sooner never have to use it." He paused for a moment. "But I think we need to at least start looking at designing a third class of ships to carry it—a ship built around the gravity lance. Perhaps designate it a battlecruiser?"

There was a pause. Lewis, Tom, and Maksim looked thoughtful. Everyone else in the room was just listening and waiting.

"Alex," Dreamer said. "There is a problem that you have not considered."

"What's that, Dreamer?" Alex asked. "Resources? Build time? Some crewing issue?"

"No, Alex," Dreamer replied. "And also, yes. In a way. You have not considered this problem because I have not explained it to you yet. I apologize for not bringing it up before now."

This seemed unlike Dreamer, Alex thought. It was ... *uncharacteristic* for him to withhold information.

"Perhaps you should tell us, then," he said.

Dreamer 'hesitated' again.

"The operational management of arming the weapon is *extremely* complex," Dreamer said. "I have studied its behavior, including the failures, at great length. I am fully confident by now that I can operate it safely, in the test cradle."

"But less so in a ship?" Alex asked.

"In a manner of speaking," Dreamer said. "Alex, I stated that I am confident I can *operate* the gravity lance, and I stand by that. But I have very grave doubts about whether I can successfully *automate* its operation yet."

It took a number of seconds for Alex to understand what Dreamer meant.

"Dreamer, you're saying that we can't build a ship to carry the grav lance... because you are the only one who can fire it without it destroying itself and the ship it's mounted in."

"Yes, and no, Alex. It would require a full-fledged controlling intellect, not simply a ship-intellect, to manage the weapon and safely operate it. I do not know how to explain to you the complexity of the interactions between the nearly continuous evanescent chaotic modes, or of dynamically controlling and cancelling them to prevent them from building into destructive resonances. I can try to show you, if you wish, greatly slowed down of course for human perception, but I do not know whether you would be able to understand what you would be seeing. I am able to tell you now with high certainty that even had it occurred to them, the Crickets *could not* have developed this weapon."

Alex sighed, thinking.

"And we don't have time to build—er, *grow*—our own AIs," Alex said. "Or we'd be doing it already."

"That is correct, Alex," Dreamer replied.

Alex thought for a long moment.

"Well, that's it, then," he said. "We can't deploy the grav lance. It was a hell of a technical project, and we licked it in what's surely record time... but if we can't grow our own AIs yet, we can't actually use it. Except by remote-controlling it from the Stardock."

There was a short silence.

"Well, crap," Lewis muttered.

"Not exactly, Alex," Dreamer said. "There exists an elegant solution."

"What are you saying, Dreamer?" Alex asked.

"You have one fully tested and operable gravity lance," Dreamer said. "And you do have one existing fully mature controlling intellect available to you."

Sandra got it first. She sat bolt upright, but didn't speak.

"...Wait, Dreamer," Alex said, as the penny dropped. "No, no, wait. You *can't* be suggesting that we build you into a warship?"

"It is not nearly as bad as you seem to think, Alex. If we construct a ship with sufficient substrate and redundancy, I could transfer my consciousness back and forth between the Stardock and the ship as needed, at any time when it is docked. Taking all due care and caution, the transfer should take only a minute or two in each direction."

Alex hesitated.

"Dreamer, to us you're unique and irreplaceable. I can't ask you to risk yourself going into battle. I just *can't*."

There was a long pause.

"Alex," Dreamer said calmly, "I remind you that your entire fleet is crewed by volunteers. I am also a volunteer, in that sense. I promised you that I would assist you and your world in any way that I can. This is no different."

There was a long silence. Tom nodded slowly.

"Dreamer is right," Maksim said. "We *all* volunteered. I think that Dreamer has right to do so as well."

"I further observe," Dreamer continued, "that if we find ourselves in battle with the Khreetan when they have come here in pursuit of the Crickets, and the Fleet *loses* the battle, then the most likely assumption is that they will destroy the Stardock *anyway*. So should it come to battle, the safest option is to maximize our chances of victory."

It was a difficult point to argue against.

"Look, Dreamer," Alex said at last, "I... need a little time to get used to this idea. You are unique. So far."

"I understand," Dreamer replied. "Nevertheless, you must agree it *is* an elegant solution. Even though it means there can only be one gravity-lance armed ship, for now."

Alex sighed.

"Once again, you're not wrong, Dreamer," he agreed. He drew a heavy breath. "If we lose, it probably won't matter anyway. So it makes sense to maximize our chances of winning."

He thought about it for a bit longer.

"Alright, Dreamer," he conceded. "I can't pretend I'm entirely comfortable with it. But I have to admit, you're right. It's your decision to make. Start figuring out what you need to be built into it to be able to accommodate you with a safe level of redundancy against battle damage. Then let's see what kind of a ship we can wrap around that. Do you have any idea what sort of size crew we would be talking about?"

"I anticipate that with myself as control-intellect, very few crew would be needed," Dreamer replied, "in addition to yourself."

Alex blinked.

"Myself," he repeated.

"The gravity weapon is your personal brainchild," Dreamer said. "Am I *wrong* in assuming that you would want to command the ship that carries it?"

"...No, Dreamer," Alex said, after a long moment. "You're right. Again. And, well, I can't ask the Fleet to go out there and fight a pitched battle, while I stay behind."

"We did cover this before," Tom interjected.

"Yes, I know we did," Alex agreed. "But we are talking about the endgame here, and I won't lead from the rear. The *center*, sure. I'm not much into foolish bravado. But not the rear."

"I can respect that," Sandra said quietly, the first time in *this* particular discussion she'd spoken.

"I will consider engineering requirements," Dreamer said, "and report when I have established them."

Alex nodded.

"Alright then," he said. "Any other business?"

"I have one additional question," Pierre du Maurier asked. "We did a lot of pointless chasing after ghosts. Is there anything at all that we can do to get some kind of better granularity of early detection in the outer system? Even if only in the direction that these scouts appeared from?"

"I do not know for sure, Commodore du Maurier," Dreamer asked, after a short pause. "Let me see if I can find a solution by reframing the parameters of the problem."

"Thank you, Dreamer," Pierre said.

"One last thing before we break," Alex said. "Right now we have two Warlords in each build cycle going forward. But that build schedule was planned before the Khreetan scouted us. I think the urgency has ramped up.

"Tom, I know that you told me a while back, when we planned the Warlord build schedule, that when the third group of four Warlords—*Alexander* through *Red Cloud*—was ready, we'd have five crews waiting for them. Are we still ahead of the curve there? Are we training crews fast enough that I can increase the next group of hull starts in a couple of weeks to three?"

"Yes," Tom said. "We'll have to push a little harder, but we can keep up with that."

"Okay," Alex said. "Make that change to the schedule please, Dreamer. All future Warlord starts are three hulls at a time until further notice."

"Understood," Dreamer replied. "The next group will be CG-14 through CG-16, beginning construction on May 7. They should be completed by August 11."

"Thanks, Dreamer. And now I think that really is everything."

He shook his head and stretched.

"Let's all go and find some lunch." His gaze unfocused for a moment. "I'm suggesting Dockside. Colonel Warner will meet us there."

═══════════

Four days later, Dreamer had a possible solution for the detection problem.

"The existing early warning network uses three-dimensional laser interferometry," Dreamer explained. "This is because we copied the design of the ground-based interferometer, originally designed as a standalone astronomical instrument, and then extended it into three dimensions, to give each unit the ability to both sensitively measure, and accurately determine the direction of, gravitational events. This enabled the array to serve both as an early warning system and as an astronomical instrument. Of course, it also resulted in large and relatively complex detectors. We have been referring to them as LIGO nodes, but it is more true to describe them as extended LISA nodes.

"However, we do not *need* an early warning system that is able to perform detailed astronomical observations. If we deploy a large number of them, then all we need it to be able to do is to *detect* strong gravitational

155

events occurring nearby. I believe I can design a much smaller unit to do that, if we do not care about any single unit being able to localize the source. With multiple detections of any given event, we can locate the source quickly via triangulation."

"How *much* smaller, Dreamer?" Alex asked.

"Somewhat larger than a science drone," Dreamer replied. "A hyperwave relay already naturally sits at the interface between normal space and hyperspace. Nearby gravitational events should create a phase fluctuation across that interface. I believe I can slightly modify a hyperwave relay to detect and measure that phase fluctuation, to allow it to function both as a communication channel *and* as a non-directional gravity wave detector."

Alex saw the significance immediately.

"Hyperwave relay drone size," he said. "We could build those by the *thousand* and scatter them through the outer system in the general direction we expect the Khreetan to come from. That far out, it would take them years, even decades, to drift out of position."

"Precisely, Alex," Dreamer said.

"Do it," Alex said. It was a no-brainer decision. "Let's get it deployed as soon as we can."

"I will set up a production line immediately," Dreamer replied. "They will of course also retain the science drone's full spectrum of visible-light and electromagnetic sensors."

"That's a fantastic insight, Dreamer," Alex said. "It'll be like having ten thousand eyes out there." Then a thought occurred to him.

"We'll call it the Argus Array."

"After Argus Panoptes, the mythical giant with a hundred eyes," Dreamer said.

"Got it in one," Alex replied, nodding.

"There is a second major item," Dreamer continued. "With some features borrowed from Lewis's Warlord design, I have arrived at a tentative design for a ship to carry the gravity lance." He opened a virtual display over the table, also sending a direct interface link to those able to use it—which, by now, was almost all of the senior command staff.

"The design is constrained by a number of factors. For probably-obvious reasons, the weapon needs to be on the centerline of the hull, and forms the core of the ship, instead of the hyperdrive."

The gravity lance appeared, a shape like three thirty-meter cylinders strapped together side-by-side in a triangle, additional components alongside and in between them, forming a slightly irregular nearly-cylindrical bundle a little more than sixty meters across and close to two hundred and forty meters long.

"Despite being built around three modified hyperdrive cores," Dreamer continued, "the gravity lance cannot *itself* function as a hyperdrive. It is too extensively modified to generate a hyperdrive envelope. Therefore the ship needs its own hyperdrive. But if a hyperdrive of the size we typically use is placed either ahead of or behind the weapon, the ship will push dangerously close to the edge of the hyperdrive envelope. Placing the hyperdrive *ahead* of the weapon, in particular, is probably extremely ill-advised in any case. Any asymmetric placement would be problematic.

"A better solution is to use two synchronized cores, placed on either side of the weapon."

Two hyperdrive cores appeared on the schematic, one on each side, spaced some thirty meters away from the gravity lance, placed somewhat toward the rear end of the lance. Nearly everyone in the room was watching intently, Lewis in particular.

"The side-by-side arrangement allows good separation between the hyperdrive cores and the weapon, while also allowing greatly improved hyperdrive envelope coupling between the two cores compared to an in-line arrangement. Additionally, secondary strains that might affect the operation of the gravity lance mostly cancel out, between the two cores.

"Our test cradle is powered by a single sixty-meter annihilation reactor. But the same power delivery capacity can be achieved, with better packaging options and an added level of redundancy, using a set of three forty-meter reactors." A crosswise row of three forty-meter reactors appeared a little way behind the gravity lance. Two backup fusion bottles were placed further forward, between the hyperdrive cores and the gravity lance.

"I consider the installation of boosted railguns in close proximity to the gravity lance highly inadvisable. Too many sets of modified hyper fields in close proximity would be tempting fate. I cannot fully predict the possible interactions. But installing Shark-class grasers presents no such difficulty. Two clusters of grasers add a significant energy direct-fire capability." Two batteries of three grasers each appeared, located directly forward of the twin hyperdrive cores.

"A considerable amount of redundant processing substrate must be incorporated if I am to operate the ship and the gravity lance," Dreamer went on. "And more, if I also include a failsafe ship-intellect, which would be an obvious measure in any case that would allow the ship to be flown without myself present, though the gravity lance could not then be used." Alex was surprised how much space between the hyperdrives and across the back end of the gravity lance that filled in.

"Standard Warlord-type SM-2 missile launchers and their magazines." Six missile launchers and magazines appeared outboard of the twin hyperdrive cores. "Auto-repair systems, life support, living quarters, control spaces, galley, storage," Dreamer counted off, as he filled in blocks of space in the schematic. "Standard Marine quarters for a full platoon. Standard small-craft bays. Life pods. Docking ports. Internal accessways. Admiral's gig." The gig was clearly a minor modification of *Charon*, Alex's original lander, reconfigured to replace the flatbed area and utility room with a cabin for a dozen passengers and two small staterooms.

More spaces filled in, and more. A broad, flattened, more or less elliptical shape was taking form.

"Main drives and maneuvering thrusters. Supercapacitor reserve energy storage. Power smoothing and management. Ancillary systems." The outline progressively filled in. "Double-layered flintsteel hull edge, additional flintsteel inner bulkheads protecting key systems." Strategically located internal armor layers appeared, around the gravity lance and hyperdrives, the reactors, the life support spaces, and behind the main drive thrusters. A narrow, but deep, complex-shaped casing of Tier 2 flintsteel wrapped itself all the way around the outer edge of the ellipsoidal shape.

"Tertiary railgun armament and their magazines," Dreamer added. "And battle steel outer hull." The outer hull was only two monolithic compound-curved plates of Tier 3 hull. They came in from above and below, sandwiching the interior. "Sensor arrays and point defense clusters." A final sprinkling of external details.

The completed ship was around three hundred and eighty five meters long, just over two hundred across the beam, and peaked at about seventy-five meters deep along the line of the gravity lance. Alex couldn't decide whether it more resembled a greatly flattened egg, or a thick and unusually regular mango seed. Either way, it was clean and graceful.

Lewis was the first to speak.

"Dreamer," he said, "I have to declare that I am *really deeply impressed* by the way you packed internal systems into that. This thing is a monster."

"I took considerable inspiration from your Warlord design, Lewis," Dreamer said. "I hope you do not mind."

"Not at all, Dreamer," Lewis said. "We're all friends here."

"I second Lewis's assessment," Alex agreed. Tom was nodding as well. "And it is armed to the *teeth*."

"We will only have one such ship," Dreamer said. "You will be on board."

"So will you, Dreamer," Alex interjected.

"Indeed," Dreamer said. "As will our only gravity lance. We should both maximize our tactical options, and protect it as well as possible."

"Sound reasoning," Tom agreed. "It looks like it'll be a hell of a flagship."

"It looks to have a pretty small bridge," Alex commented.

"That is because I foresee no great need for individual weapon operator stations," Dreamer replied. "The failsafe ship-intellect is sufficient for navigation and management of routine ship functions, but since I am required to operate the gravity lance, I presume we plan to never take it into action without myself aboard. I am more than capable of targeting and operating the entire armament myself in addition to managing the gravity lance. You would need only to designate targets for me to engage. Technically, with me present, you *could* fly this ship by yourself. However, I have provided stations for a somewhat reduced bridge crew."

"That's... still a little difficult to grasp," Alex said. "*Charon* or even an *Endeavour* class are one thing, but this...?"

"For any full controller such as yourself, actually *flying* any ship is a scale-invariant problem," Dreamer pointed out. "It is only in such areas as independently targeting multiple weapon systems and engaging multiple simultaneous targets that human attentional capacity does not scale."

"That's... a valid point," Alex conceded, after a moment. "Do you have an estimate of construction time?"

"We are ahead of the curve on Warlord construction," Dreamer replied. "We have more of many sub-assemblies at present than ships to install them into. We already have the gravity lance. By using pre-existing stock where possible, such as the hyperdrive cores, the annihilation reactors, and the missile launchers and their magazines, I believe I can complete the ship in roughly four months. Perhaps a little longer, perhaps a little less."

Alex looked around.

"Anyone have any objections, cautions, caveats, revisions?" he asked. Nobody raised a hand. He took a deep breath.

"Alright. Let's get it started right away."

"I will bring the gravity lance back from the test facility," Dreamer said, "and begin construction."

"You don't want to just build a fresh one, Dreamer?" Alex asked.

"We have already extensively stress-tested this one," Dreamer replied. "We know with good confidence that it has no hidden defects."

Alex nodded.

"Excellent point," he agreed.

"As the designer of this beast, Dreamer," Lewis asked, "do you have a class name in mind?"

"I do not see that it makes sense to have a class name, as such, for a ship that we currently plan to only ever build one of," Dreamer replied.

"Point," Lewis agreed. "A ship name, then."

"I believe that decision should go to Alex," Dreamer said.

Alex thought, but not for long.

"I think you already named it, Dreamer," he said slowly. "And in keeping with the finest traditions of the Culture."

"I... do not understand," Dreamer said, hesitantly. "'Culture' clearly refers to the writer Banks once again, but... I am unable to complete the reference."

Alex grinned.

"It does indeed," he said. "You already said the name I'm thinking of. *There Exists An Elegant Solution.*'"

Amusement came through the interface. Sandra looked thoughtful for a moment, then Alex saw understanding dawn.

"Does that mean that we should designate its type to be General Offensive Unit?" Dreamer asked, again tinged with humor.

Alex grinned.

"Sure," he agreed, chuckling. "Why not?"

The Paw re-gathered.

«Sing of what you have seen and scented,» Thoughtful said. «What have we learned?»

«From the furthest location,» said Hunt-Master Heavy-Step of *Follow The Spoor*, «we see no indication of any space-faring. *At all.* None. They were planet-bound when those calls left their world, except for world-orbiting satellites.»

«But clearly not now,» Thoughtful mused.

«From the second position,» Hunt-Master Motionless reported from *Careful Stalker*, «the wave-front bears the mark of high-energy drives.»

«And from the first,» agreed Tireless, from *Chaser*.

«At the fourth, they are planet-bound still,» reported Muddy-Tail on *Step Carefully*. There was no point asking about the fifth.

«And the third point is unclear,» Thoughtful mused.

«So let us put it together. This out-clan were planet-bound. Then the Violators came. For... reasons I cannot fathom with certainty. Then... they left again? And continued onward? And somehow, these planet-bound out-clan... gained the Violators' Den? And learned from it.»

«Learned terrifyingly fast, if so,» Of-Course-It-Works interjected. Thoughtful jerked his head in agreement.

«We followed the wrong trail, I think,» Thoughtful concluded. «*This* was the false trail, a decoy. An *expensive* one, to lose their Den, but I now think a decoy nonetheless. And it worked. *How* they could give up their Den, I do not understand. I imagine the choice will go poorly for them in their future, unless they someday return for it.»

«Expensive to us as well,» grumbled Notices-Things. «It caused us to lose their trail. Now we must find it anew, when it is already fading.»

«No less expensive decoy would have left enough trail to lure us astray,» Listens-Carefully observed. Thoughtful head-jerked again. «And did they *plan* to yield their Den? Did they have a *choice*?»

«Unanswerable,» Thoughtful replied, «without knowledge we do not have. Onward they went, I believe. Let us cast about and see if we can pick up the forward trail again. But I have little hope of following it. All they need do is scatter once, and what remains of it will vanish like mist burning off a lake in mid-morning sun.

«We will begin our search pattern like so...»

On May 7, CG-08 and CG-09 were commissioned as *Sun Tzu* and *Musashi*. Each received its platoon of Fleet Marines from the newly-commissioned, mostly-Korean 6th Company under Major Gim Chae-won.

Two days after *Sun Tzu* and *Musashi* left on their shakedown cruises, Thoughtful called a halt to the search for the Crickets' trail.

«Enough,» he declared. «If we have not picked up the forward trail again by now, we are not going to. We shall return to the Den, and report on these... *precocious* out-clan.»

The Paw set their courses on the first leg of the long haul back to the Den and its escorting fleet, and went into hyper.

———————————

When Alex arrived at morning briefing on May 11, there was a dark amber-colored sphere about a meter in diameter hovering over the table. Those who had arrived ahead of him were standing around it looking at it.

"This is very interesting," Angavu Onyango was saying as Alex walked into the room. "It is clearly a drone of some kind. But what is it exactly?"

"Good morning, Alex," Dreamer said. "Ms. Onyango, this is one of the first test batch of thirty Argus drones. I propose to place this set for testing purposes in two rough shells at two and three light-seconds around Earth. Each patrol that leaves or arrives back should give us test data to validate the design."

"And after that?" Alex asked.

"It takes four days to construct one. The line that I have set up to build them will produce four completed drones every two hours. Forty-eight per day, three hundred and thirty six per week."

"Great. And you have a deployment plan?"

"Yes and no, Alex. Methodology, yes. Destroyer patrols can simply drop them off from their boat bays while on patrol. I can quickly build some dispensers. Exact placement, no. I will need to determine a placement plan when we have initial test results and can determine the actual sensitivity of the Argus drones."

Alex thought for a moment.

"Our test data will be for *our* hyperdrives," he said. "But we know Khreetan hyperdrives have a very different signature. Do we have enough data to be able to accurately project detection range of *their* hyperdrive activations, based on ours?"

162

"The patterns are indeed very different," Dreamer agreed. "Their hyperdrive activations are significantly lower in energy, but over a longer period. However, after comparing the waveforms in detail, I believe I can use sensitivity to the tail of our own hyperdrive activation signals as a proxy to predict sensitivity to Khreetan hyperdrive events."

"Alright," Alex said. "Then let's get them placed and start collecting data."

Over the next week, as Fleet ships jumped in and out, departing on patrols or returning from them, Dreamer correlated readings from the new Argus drones with those from the primary arrays. The large LIGO arrays were sensitive enough to pick up almost any gravitational event of artificial origin from anywhere within the solar system, and for that matter, a good way outside it.

The Argus drones were clearly much less sensitive, and returned data much less detailed than the LIGO array. Despite that, though, they showed themselves definitely capable of doing useful jump detection. Since the Argus drones were incapable of determining direction, all that could be obtained from a single drone was a rough estimate of distance, absent exact knowledge of the strength of the originating event. Adding a precisely timed detection from a second drone, and correlating the two together, gave the time differential between the two detections, which in general confined the possible origin locations to one of an infinite set of hyperbolic planes normal to a straight line passing through both drones. The precise delay determined on which of the many possible planes the source lay. A third detection point (and a second time delay) reduced the problem to a line on that hyperbolic plane, and a fourth reading from off the plane containing the first three narrowed it down to a single point.

It wasn't that the process was *actually* any more complex than what happened within the large LIGO detectors. The process was just a lot more visible, done this way. Their lower sensitivity made them enormously shorter ranged than the LIGO array, but that wouldn't matter, since the entire plan was to have many of them spaced closely together (relatively speaking) so as to have short detection times.

After a week, Dreamer was ready to report results.

"Okay, Dreamer," Alex asked, "so how does it look?"

"I am quite satisfied, Alex. I believe we have sufficient test data to deploy the system. Based upon detections of the Fleet's own nearby hyperdrive activity over the past six days, I have good confidence that an Argus drone should be able to reliably pick up a Khreetan hyperdrive activation as far away as approximately forty three million kilometers."

"That's... about point two eight AU," Alex said. "Just under a hundred and forty-four light-seconds. Which isn't bad. So if we want full coverage with a spherical range of point two eight AU, then our placement needs to be something close to a cubic grid with a pitch of about point-four AU. And our detection latency for events within the grid should never exceed about two and a half minutes."

"Correct, Alex," Dreamer agreed. "Knowing that, we can now plan a deployment pattern."

"What do you recommend, Dreamer?" Alex asked. "We know that last time, their initial jump into the system was at about 19AU."

"Yes," Dreamer agreed. "I have compared the astronomical direction from which the Khreetan scouts first entered the system, against my own recordings of when Captain-Junior Kheftra warned you about the threat and indirectly told you its direction. The two directions match tolerably well.

"We cannot cover the entire system. It would simply require more relays than we can feasibly build and deploy in the time that it is likely we have. That leaves us with a number of possible deployment strategies that we could use. *All* of the potential assumptions that we could use to choose between them are, to some extent, naïve. As I previously observed, this is a first time doing this, for all of us.

"However, we have to choose *one*. I have assessed the probabilities, and I believe that the safest—least naïve—assumption is that the Khreetan will repeat observed past behavior... even though we have only a single data point to go on. And that means assuming that they will jump into the outer system from approximately their direction of origin."

"What if they jump in immediately right near Earth?" Alex asked.

"The vicinity of Earth is presently the one place in the solar system where we *already* have a good ability to detect their jumps with short latency," Dreamer replied. "Between ground-based and trojan-point LIGO arrays, plus the test Argus nodes, our maximum detection latency close to Earth is already on the order of four minutes or less. And that is not counting direct detection by patrols near Earth. Between the two, we already have good coverage out to past one AU. There is literally nothing to gain from deploying the Argus array that close to Earth."

"Good point," Alex conceded.

"I therefore propose to begin with a plane of Argus drones subtending half a steradian, centered on that bearing at eighteen AU distance. That plane will require three hundred and ninety seven drones.

"Next, I propose to extend that inward by eight AU and outward by five, to cover from ten AU—just beyond the orbit of Saturn—to twenty-three AU, roughly one point two times the orbital distance of Uranus. That should bracket well on either side of where they last entered the system, as well as covering the full distance inward to the LIGO array.

"That will require thirty-two additional planes of drones, ranging from one hundred and twenty two to six hundred and forty nine drones each. The total would be eleven thousand, five hundred and ninety six drones."

"*Ouch*," Alex exclaimed. "You said your current line produces three hundred and thirty six per week. That's... over thirty four weeks' production. Eight *months*."

"Yes, Alex. Then if time permits, I would like to extend that outward to a full steradian coverage."

Alex winced.

"Time *will not* permit," he said. "Not at that production rate."

"I agree," Dreamer said. "The line will have to be expanded."

"Four lines, you said," Lewis spoke up. "One every two hours per line."

"Correct," Dreamer agreed.

"So eighty four, per line, per week," Lewis continued. "If we increase that to ten lines, that's eight hundred and forty per week. That would complete the half-steradian deployment in just under fourteen weeks. Three and a half months."

Alex thought about the numbers.

"That's not terrible," he said. "But we'd still be looking at fourteen months to go to the full steradian array. And..." He broke off and looked around the table. He looked down, then back up again.

"I'll be honest," he said, somewhat grimly. "I no longer believe we *have* those fourteen months. I think the Khreetan are ahead of the schedule the Crickets estimated. We just don't know *how far* ahead." There was a general mutter of agreement around the table.

"And we can't even scout them in turn to see how far out they are," he continued. "We already know we can't track them through hyperspace unless we're *right* on their heels. We'd have to guess their exact incoming vector. It'd be a needle in a cosmic haystack, and we wouldn't even know what the needle looks like."

He thought.

"Show of hands please. Who's comfortable with three and a half months to complete the half-steradian array?" He waited for a moment, then glanced around the table. About three out of four hands were up. After a moment longer, Sandra hesitantly raised hers as well.

"Good enough," he said. "We can keep adding 'eyes' for as long as we get, but I think we need to accept that we almost certainly won't complete the full one-steradian deployment. We should probably focus first on trying to expand... actually, let's say the ten-to-fifteen AU band. We can get more angular coverage for fewer drones that way.

"Let's go with ten lines. We can't divert *too* much time away from patrols for drone deployment. And, well, there's nothing we can do to significantly speed up *Elegant Solution*, right, Dreamer?"

"That is correct, Alex."

Alex sighed.

"So it will either be ready, or it won't. We'll have to just hope we get time to finish it. And... we'd probably better give the Earth governments a heads-up that we might not have as much time as we thought we did."

Tom raised a hand.

"That raises a secondary issue," he said.

Alex looked at Tom.

"What's on your mind?" he asked.

"The *Elegant Solution* relies on Dreamer to operate its main armament," Tom pointed out. Alex nodded. "We *also* rely on Dreamer to target the Stardock's defensive weapons. If Dreamer transfers himself to the *Elegant Solution*, the point defense clusters will still work—right, Dreamer?"

"That is correct," Dreamer said. "The point defense system is fully automated. But your point is correct. The railgun emplacements are not, except by slaving them to the point defense array."

"Good catch, Tom," Alex said. "That hadn't occurred to me. We'll need to construct gunnery control stations, and train gunnery crews to man the railguns when Dreamer is off-station."

"We have a lot more North Korean volunteers than we can keep up with training as Marines," John Warner interjected. "Even after forming Sixth Company. They're almost all ground forces, and a lot of them have artillery or triple-A experience. That would give us a head-start on training them up as railgun gunners."

166

Alex nodded.

"That's a good idea," he agreed. "How would you want to organize them?"

"A new Seventh Company, formed as an artillery company," John answered, with no hesitation at all. "How many defensive railguns are there?"

"There are forty railgun emplacements," Dreamer answered, "each of which has four independent railguns of roughly fifteen-centimeter caliber."

"A hundred and sixty individual railguns then," John said. "That sounds like four platoons to me, so it'll be a short company. Or six, so that we have redundancy. I'll see if I can find a few air defense command officers to head it up."

"Great," Alex said. "Do it. Dreamer, how long to construct gunnery control rooms?"

"How many do you want to have, Alex?"

"Four platoons, you said, John." Warner nodded. "Let's make four gunnery rooms, spaced well apart so that no single hit can take out more than one. And internally partition them into groups of, say, ten stations. Then *interleave* which guns they control, so that losing any single gunnery room doesn't leave a hole in our defensive coverage.

"Does that make sense, John?" Warner nodded again.

"Sounds good," he agreed. "It might make it a little tough coordinating fire from any specific emplacement on a single target, but the redundancy will be worth it."

"Okay, Dreamer," Alex said, "assume that's the plan. How long?"

"I can have all four gunnery rooms online in twelve days," Dreamer said. "I suggest these locations." He projected a schematic of the Stardock with four locations highlighted. Two were near the outer hull between the upper and lower engineering bays, somewhat forward of the main docking bay. The other two were located near the top and bottom of the hull, forward by Boom Two. "I will additionally need to construct express elevators for access to the fourth station." Glowing outlines traced elevator shafts downward from the forward end of the concourses.

"Any objections?" Alex asked. There were none.

"Right then. Do it, Dreamer."

———————

Meanwhile, down below on Earth, other events were in motion.

"We now turn you over to our Black Sea region correspondent, Peter Tallwick, in Ankara, with breaking news of some potentially major developments in Turkey."

"Good afternoon, Moira, I'm talking to you from outside the Presidential complex in Ankara, where President Ayhan Göğebakan has just issued a new executive decree that has raised eyebrows. This decree temporarily suspends the legal designation of the PKK, the Kurdistan Workers Party, as a terrorist organization by the Republic of Türkiye, pending the outcome of a bilateral summit between the PKK and the Turkish government. This summit, we have been told, is hoped to yield a permanent peaceful solution between the Turkish government and the Kurdish people.

"We don't know anything yet about what the hoped-for solution that is to be presented might be, but the rumor mill says that it's something wildly outside the usual political box.

"We will of course bring you more on this breaking story as information becomes available, but the Turks are so far keeping all of the details tightly under their hats."

"Thank you, Peter. We hope to have more analysis for you on this story later today. I am Moira Doneghan, the time is eighteen minutes past three o'clock on the twenty third of May, and this is the BBC."

9. Parliaments and Dreams

Over the passing weeks, the Argus array began to grow, a few hundred drones at a time. As planned, the deployment began with a single plane of 'eyes' at eighteen AU, then built both inward and outward from there. The Sun's gravity was tiny this far out—the orbital period of an eighteen-AU orbit is seventy six point four years—and it took the drones less than a micro-newton of thrust to hold their positions. They could keep that up for literally decades before they would need to be recharged.

On the 8th of June, CG-10 *Crazy Horse* and CG-11 *Khubilai* were delivered out of the yards, commissioned and went out on their shakedown cruises. Three more cruisers, hull numbers CG-17 through CG-19, were laid down. They would not be completed until early September—but that would still probably be a month before *Elegant Solution*.

Meanwhile, the Turks and the Kurds... were still talking. The discussions sometimes became heated, but they were *talking*. And that counted for a lot.

They weren't the only ones talking. The *very, very* quiet, largely unofficial talks between the United States and the Russian Federation had expanded to include France and the UK as well. China was still sitting back, waiting and watching to see what came of it, but had not yet taken the plunge itself and actively joined the negotiations. But very very slowly, in informal sessions without hard commitments, in personal communiques, progress was being made on several fronts.

Not everything was so positive. Since the Khreetan scouting foray, at least three new doomsday cults had sprung up, and at least four separate conspiracy theories involving different governments—plus one that laid the blame to a shadowy international cabal. Some said that President Riken was in league with the aliens. Some said that Alex Holder was. And *of course*, it went without saying that the Bilderbergers were in full foam-at-the-mouth mode, though it was a little difficult to understand how they expected *anyone* to believe that an alien race from elsewhere in the galaxy could somehow be part of an international Jewish conspiracy. Perhaps if one were to suppose a really *expansive* definition of 'international'...

There wasn't much that could be done about any of them, of course. Any official attempts to debunk them would only strengthen them, by creating 'evidence' that governments were 'suppressing' them and thus further heightening their devotees' sense of paranoia. It was always the problem with cults. Ironically and counter-intuitively, the best thing to do was nothing, because almost anything that could be done simply fed them and made them worse. The only useful option open was to keep a close eye on them, in case they progressed to actually being dangerous. Which was why everyone from GSG9, the FBI, the CIA and the Deuxième Bureau to the FSB and Mossad had their people on the inside of as many of the cults and conspiracies as they could manage. It was hard to say which was the more interesting—that the FSB was freely and openly cooperating with the CIA, or that Mossad *wasn't*. The Israelis were playing their cards very close to their chests.

Other games were being played behind other closed doors, as well.

———————————

«I still insist the *very idea* of giving up our nuclear weapons is ridiculous,» said General Yuri Kuskovsky. «It would weaken us still further in a world in which we are already sadly diminished from our glory days, when *everyone* feared the might of the Russian bear.»

«You mean the 'glory' days of the old Union of Soviet Republics, Yuri,» General Vasily Belyenov replied. «If glory is the right word. You should face it, those days died with the Berlin Wall. Being *feared* is all very well, but nobody trusts someone whom they fear. And we *encouraged* them to fear us. You *know* this, Yuri Ilyich. But perhaps it is better to be trusted than feared, yes?»

«The Americans seem to have managed both,» Yuri continued to argue.

Vasily wrinkled his nose and pursed his lips.

«Not really so very much,» he said. «The Americans have nations that warily trust them, and nations who fear them. And nations that do neither. Beginning with much of the Middle East. You would be hard-put to find anyone who both honestly trusts them, and truly fears them. Their imperialistic arrogance and dogmatism has made many countries distrust them. Everyone except their Five Eyes watches the Americans warily.»

«The British have no reservations trusting them,» Yuri interjected. Vasily was not quite certain what Yuri's point was, but in any case it was a foolish observation.

«Psssshhhh,» he said. «Talking about the *British* trusting the Americans is like talking about whether Belorussia trusts Russia—or your hand trusts your shoulder. They might as well apply to become a fifty-first American state. More of their sovereignty is imagined than they realize, especially since they detached themselves from Europe. That was a remarkably poor strategic decision on their part. In Europe, at least they had a voice, and perhaps a louder one than they actually appreciated, even if it was not as loud as they thought it ought to be.

«Now, after that clownish fool Johnson and that decade of mismanagement, who even *listens* to them?

«In any case, the recent example of North Korea illustrated with extreme clarity that the Fleet that grows stronger above our heads every month will not tolerate use of nuclear weapons on Earth. What is the *point* of keeping nuclear weapons that we could not use even if we wanted to? It is like a muzzled bear snarling, except that the bear does not need to pay for the upkeep on its own muzzle.»

«But do you *want* to be a muzzled bear, Vasily?» Yuri asked.

«Yuri, Yuri, it was a *metaphor,*» Vasily sighed wearily. «And one for our *nuclear weapons*, not for our country.» He drew in a deep breath. Yuri was so determinedly *old school*, as the Americans would say.

«I do not think of Russia as muzzled, no,» Vasily continued. «More, it is as though we walk along a sandy shore, pulling a cart of sand behind us in case we need some sand. We would do better to empty out the sand from the cart. It would make it easier to pull the cart, and we would still have all the sand we could ever use. And we could then perhaps carry other useful things in the cart instead. There is more technology being transferred to Earth from the Stardock every day. I foresee a day when Russia will be able to build its own starships. And I do not believe that it will be all *that* terribly far off.

«The world has changed, Yuri Ilyich. Get used to it. It is not going to change back.»

Yuri did not seem convinced. Privately, Vasily Belyenov thought that Yuri Kuskovsky was a bit of an idiot. He was stuck firmly in a red-tinted ideal of the Soviet past that he remembered only through the eyes of a child awed by military parades.

Yuri, meanwhile, thought that it had been all downhill since Andropov, and that things had *really* started going to hell with Mikhail Gorbachev. Vladimir Putin had been a breath of fresh air, a return to the old days... but accidents happen, and sometimes, they involved windows. That had been a shame, Yuri thought. Putin had made the mistake of not cutting NATO's heart out *first*. Now, in Molchalin's trembling hands,

Russia was solidly back on the path downhill to mediocrity and eventual irrelevance.

In Ankara, the Turkish-Kurdish summit wrapped up, with little fanfare and nearly nothing publicly said. A number of astute observers and commentators independently noted, however, that President Gögebakan's decree that had temporarily suspended the designation of the PKK as terrorists had *not* been withdrawn.

Representatives of the Turkish government declined to comment on this observation beyond noting that yes, it was correct.

VERY, VERY much further away, other events were afoot.

«Fleet-Leader?»

«What is it, Wayfinder?»

«New contacts ahead, Fleet-Leader. They have just leapt into our control volume. Getting recognition signals any time now...»

He waited, and so did Fleet-Leader Swims-Like-Rock. It didn't take long.

«It is *Silent Tracker*'s Paw, Fleet-Leader.»

«Well, indeed,» Swims-Like-Rock mused. «And what, then, have they found among the stars, I wonder?»

Silent Tracker and the other five vessels of Hunt-Master Thoughtful's Paw were returning home.

«Hsieuuu-Den,» came the call, a few minutes later. «Thoughtful of *Silent Tracker*. We return bearing sightings and revelations. Be so kind as to designate nests for our return.»

«Clan Hsieuuu welcomes you and yours home, Hunt-Master Thoughtful. Please use nest group three-paws-and-one.»

«We thank you, Hsieuuu-Den. We will see you shortly.»

«Do any of yours require care, Hunt-Master? Or... the last-singing?»

«No, Hsieuuu-Den. The Huntmistress watched over us. We are unscathed.»

«That is good news, Hunt-Master. The Fleet-Leader will take your report after your ships are nested.»

Four hours later, the six ships of the Paw were docked and powered down to standby. Maintenance crews were going aboard to replenish supplies and run status checks, as the crews filed off. Thoughtful stopped for a moment at the bottom of the ramp to look around the vast interior of the Den, a sight he was always glad to return to. Already, he felt the inner warmth of being amid his Clan again.

He beckoned his bridge officers to follow him, and set off for Den Control. There was a cart-track only a short distance away.

«Hunt-Master Thoughtful is here, Fleet-Leader,» Swims-Like-Rock's aide told him.

«Thank you,» Swims-Like-Rock replied, rising from his wide chair. He walked out to meet Thoughtful and his officers.

«Hunt-Master Thoughtful,» he said, all four hands extended in a formal greeting of kin-to-kin. «Clan Hsieuuu is glad to see your safe return. And so am I.» Thoughtful met him hands to hands, his muzzle respectfully lowered.

«I thank you, Fleet-Leader,» he said.

«Come,» Swims-Like-Rock said, beckoning Thoughtful and his bridge crew into the rest-lair. «Sit and rest, and tell me of what you have found in your stalking. My aide will send for refreshments.»

A short while later, the formalities dispensed with, Thoughtful began his report.

«Though the Violators' trail was fading,» he began, «we continued to follow it across the ocean of stars as we have for these past orbits. A little more than a twelfth-orbit ahead—at a front-runner's speed, of course—we found a split in the trail. The main trail continued onward, already faint, but there was also a side-trail. Narrow—we almost overlooked it—but deep, as though left by a single massive object. Such as the Violators' Den.

«We decided that the trail onward was a false trail to lead us astray, and the side trail the true trail.»

«And was that correct?» Swims-Like-Rock asked.

«Yes... and no,» Thoughtful said carefully. «Yes, we found the Violators' Den. But no, we found no Violators there.»

173

«No Violators? They abandoned it, then?»

«So it seems. We realized afterward that it must have been the side-trail that was the decoy, and that we were taken in and followed it just as we were supposed to.»

«So, we could claim it as salvage, then.»

«Well... no. I do not think so. But I will come to that shortly. If I might.

«We cast back along the trail, trying to pick up the forward trail again, for two paws of days. But it had by then faded too far. Having once turned away from it and lost its scent, we could not pick it up again. So at that point we turned our course around to return to the Den and report.»

«You think that a full search might pick up that trail once again?» Swims-Like-Rock asked.

«No, I do not,» Thoughtful said. «With their Den left behind them and only lesser ships, what I imagine—and why we deduced the forward trail the false one—is that we would follow for some distance, and then their ships would scatter like leaves and meet again somewhere else already agreed, and the fleet-trail would vanish like morning mist. I do not believe that there is any point in trying to find it again.»

«So what you are telling me is that our pursuit of the Violators is at an end, and we can pursue them no longer. But their Den lies abandoned in an empty system. This is correct?»

«No, Fleet-Leader,» Thoughtful corrected him. «Not quite. I did not say that the system in which we found it was empty.»

«What?» Swims-Like-Rock exclaimed. «Not empty?»

«Indeed,» Thoughtful said. «We found out-clan there. And by every sign that we found... out-clan who have been voyaging the stars for only a brief time. A VERY brief time. In fact... as far as we could judge by listening to their calls at different distances from their world... perhaps only *since* the Violators visited their system.

«Their ships share the leap-drive signature of the Violators. Yet they are not like the Violators' ships. Very different. Small, *very* fast. *Shockingly* fast.»

«I would give a claw to learn *how* they are so fast,» Engineer Of-Course-It-Works grumbled. «I do not understand how they generate enough power.»

Swims-Like-Rock got an extremely thoughtful expression.

«What is it that you think happened, then?» he asked.

174

Thoughtful twitched his shoulders.

«It is hard to say,» he said slowly. «Perhaps the Violators abandoned their Den, and these unknown out-clan gained it somehow. Perhaps, though I have a difficult time imagining how, they somehow took it from the Violators and cast them from it. But it seems inescapable to conclude that they have control of it now. And they seem to have learned from it how to build ships of their own.»

«And with frightening speed,» Hunter Listens-Carefully interjected.

«Well, indeed,» Swims-Like-Rock mused. He leaned forward a little more intently.

«Tell me everything that you know. All of you. Everything that happened. From the beginning.»

Thoughtful and his bridge crew began to carefully retell everything that had happened since the moment they first entered the out-clans' system. From time to time, he referred to the handheld pad he had brought with him to show a log reading, or a system plot. And he handed the pad over to Swims-Like-Rock to let him see for himself the sensor logs, and he showed Swims-Like-Rock the slowed-down optical capture, uploaded by then to the Den, of that final, terrifying, insanely-fast crossing pass, as the out-clan ships braked at an almost unbelievable deceleration. The optical playback froze at the moment of closest approach, showing a slightly-blurred still image of the out-clan ship, distant stars streaks of light across the background.

«So this is one of their ships,» Swims-Like-Rock said.

Thoughtful nodded.

«Like a fast-swimmer,» Listens-Carefully said. «Is it not?»

«It is,» Swims-Like-Rock agreed. «Did you see its teeth?»

«We did not,» Thoughtful said. «They perhaps had the opportunity to fire on us, on that pass. Although it might have been a difficult shot due to the high speed of passing by. But they did not. Whether because they could not, or because they *could have* but chose *not* to... we know not.»

«Hurrrrrrrrmmm,» Swims-Like-Rock said. He sat in silence for a long while, thinking. Then he looked up.

«We have a destination, I think,» he said. «The Violators' trail is lost to us. They have eluded us. Their greater speed has enabled them to outpace us... though perhaps not without a great cost to them. Perhaps it is enough. Perhaps we should be satisfied.

«But we shall go and take the measure of these intriguing out-clan. Give your navigational data to the Den Wayfinder.»

Before its next jump, the Den adjusted alignment by a small fraction. Clan Hsieuuu was, ever so slightly, changing course.

=====

On the 25th of June, President Gögebakan's office announced that he would be making an official public statement. Unlike the very quiet, very low-profile summit, the full gamut of press corps representatives were invited to attend. After everyone was settled, the President's Chief of Staff stepped out.

"Good afternoon and welcome, one and all," he said. "It is my pleasure to welcome you upon this day. We have momentous news to disclose. Please hold any questions you have until after the announcement.

"Please stand for President Ayhan Gögebakan of the Republic of Türkiye."

He stepped back from the podium and moved aside, and President Gögebakan walked out from the wing and took his place. A second man stepped out with him.

"Good afternoon," Gögebakan said. "You all know me, I am Ayhan Gögebakan. Today I wish to introduce to you Mr. Hozan Îbrahîm." He gestured to the man standing beside him.

"Mr. Îbrahîm is here in his capacity as as an official envoy from the Kurdistan Workers' Party." There was a murmur of surprise at that.

"There is a third person who really should be here as well," Gögebakan went on. "I refer to Mr. Alex Holder of the United Earth Fleet. But I understand that he has been rather busy for the past several years, doing very important work of his own, and I would not wish to draw him away from it." There was a brief wave of laughter at that.

"So why are we here today?

"Well, as some of you are aware, a month ago, representatives from the PKK joined myself and other members of my government for a summit, to discuss a solution to a long-vexing problem. And you recall that I ordered the designation of the PKK as a terrorist organization suspended pending the outcome of the summit.

"It is now time to announce what we decided.

"The Republic of Türkiye's designation of the PKK as a terrorist organization will remain in abeyance, as long as there are no incidents. This provisional arrangement will remain in place for one year. Mr. Îbrahîm will remain in a post here as the official representative of the PKK during that time.

"At the end of one year, if there have been no incidents and we have reached satisfactory resolution of the necessary outstanding issues, the Republic of Türkiye will officially recognize the autonomy of the Kurdish people, and will guarantee them a self-administered homeland and guarantee the security of their borders with the Republic of Türkiye. Furthermore, we shall *strongly* encourage our nearby neighbors to do likewise."

There was a moment of silence, then the room practically exploded with applause. Göğebakan smiled broadly, stepped back, turned to Îbrahîm, and offered his hand.

"The Republic of Türkiye offers the hand of friendship to the Kurdish people, Mr. Îbrahîm," Göğebakan said.

Hozan Îbrahîm took a step forward, reached out, and took the offered hand.

"On behalf of the Kurdish people, Mr. President, I accept," he said simply.

For a moment, they just stood there, then Göğebakan stepped back to the podium and gestured Îbrahîm up beside him.

"Now," he said, "you are gentlemen and gentlewomen of the Fourth Estate, and I am sure that you will have many questions. So, let us begin. I —we—will answer as many of them as we can."

By now almost every hand in the room was in the air. Göğebakan pointed at one in the first row, toward the right side.

"Mustapha bin-Alman, al-Jazeera," the reporter said. "You said almost at the first that there is a third person who should be here, and named Alex Holder of the United Earth Fleet. I confess to great curiosity. What does Mr. Holder have to do with the agreement being announced today?"

"Oh, that is very simple," Göğebakan said. "A crucial part of this solution—or what we *hope* is a solution—was his idea, you see. You will learn more on that later, I am sure. Next?" A woman on the left side of the third row. "Ms. Müller of Der Spiegel, I believe?"

"Yes, Mr. President," she said. "Thank you for remembering." Göğebakan nodded. "You stated that the Republic of Türkiye will guarantee the borders of an autonomous Turkish homeland. Does that homeland have a capital?"

Göğebakan gestured to Îbrahîm.

"That decision has not been made final," Îbrahîm said. "It is one of the matters yet to be resolved. But the current leading contender is the city of Hakkâri."

"Hakkâri is in eastern Turkey, is it not?" Irma Müller asked. "Does that mean that the Republic of Türkiye will be ceding territory to..." She trailed off, uncertain how to finish the question.

"To the Independent Republic of Kurdistan," Hozan Îbrahîm finished for her. She nodded thanks. He looked at Göğebakan.

"Yes; and also, no," Göğebakan said. "Hakkâri will be officially a Kurdish city, in which Turks also live. The entire region of the northern part of the Republic of Kurdistan will be a Kurdish administered region, in which Turks also live. But the Turks in the region will be governed from Ankara, and the Kurds will be governed from Hakkâri. Next, please."

A man five rows back on the right side of the room raised a hand, and Göğebakan pointed to him.

"Luc Bourdain, Paris-Match," the man said. "Can you please clarify where the border between Turkey and the Republic of Kurdistan will be? And explain what you mean by guaranteeing it?"

"Well," Göğebakan said, "the second of those things is much simpler than the first, so I shall begin there. Armed forces of the Republic of Türkiye will not enter any portion of the Republic of Kurdistan that lies outside of the borders of the Republic of Türkiye without the express invitation of the Kurdish government, and Turkish forces stationed *within* its borders will not intervene in internal Kurdish matters unless formally asked for assistance. We do not expect that to happen very often. The *peshmerga* are very capable. We will pledge our full military assistance— *in any necessary level of force*, understand that—should *any* hostile nation attempt to violate the borders of Kurdistan once established. Türkiye will stand with Kurdistan *whenever* and *wherever* it is needed.

"The first part of the question is more difficult to answer, for two reasons. The first of those reasons is because we have not precisely defined yet *exactly* where the northern and north-western borders of the Republic of Kurdistan will be. That is one of the details that still remains to

178

be fully ironed out—though we have a rough agreement, which is within a few kilometers for most of its length.

"But the second reason is that there will not, exactly, be a border *between*—as such—the Republic of Türkiye and the Republic of Kurdistan.

"You see, the two Republics are going to overlap."

There was silence for several seconds. It was followed by absolute pandemonium.

After a minute or two, Ayhan Göğebakan raised his hands for quiet. The clamor slowly settled down, until he could speak again.

"Yes, yes, I *know*," he said. "It is a completely mad idea. But does any one of you dare to say that you have a *politically possible* solution to this thorny problem that is *not* mad?"

Unsurprisingly, there were no volunteers.

"Perhaps this one is just barely mad *enough*. We have all discussed it at great length, and the problems we have foreseen, and how we think that we are going to solve them. We have a plan. Either it will work, or it will not. We will see. But either way, we will have *tried*, in good faith. And both sides badly *want* to make it work.

"You never know. The horse may yet learn to sing."

━━━━━━━━━━

Early July saw CG-12 and CG-13 delivered and commissioned, as *Tomöe Gozen* and *Scipio Africanus* respectively. It would be nearly the end of the month before they returned from their shakedowns. In accordance with the build plan, hulls CG-20 through CG-22 were laid down at the same time. But they would not be completed until mid-October, and Alex was not the only one beginning to feel uneasy about whether that would be soon enough. So far, construction on *Elegant Solution* was on track. But that schedule too was in the same state of uncertainty.

By July, the Last Chance program had really taken off—enough so, in fact, that Yeon and Philippe requested a third—*larger*—medical bay to be brought online. And so it was; MedBay Three was located just beyond the first block of family quarters. That meant finding another experienced senior medical officer to run it. In the interim, Yeon and Philippe took turns standing double shifts. The sixth of the family 'streets', now unofficially named Mercy Street, was dedicated to temporary housing for families with a child in treatment, and the mess/restaurant space reserved opposite the family quarters had been put into service. Managed by a seemingly unlikely, yet oddly effective team of a Greek, a Turk, and a Jordanian, the very middle-eastern feel it had came as no surprise at all, and neither did the name Casbah that it ended up with. It served everything from gyros and dolmathes, by way of falafel and shish-kebab, to mansaf and Kabuli palau.

Meanwhile, the media—and others—continued to ask questions about the Khreetan scouting foray.

"Yes," Alex told them openly, "we found shortcomings in the practical application of our hyperspace early warning system. It was not a complete success; but neither was it a failure. Its shortcomings for that purpose do not diminish its utility as an astronomical instrument, it gave us a *lot* of valuable information about Khreetan hyperdrives, and we are deploying a new early-warning system based upon what we learned from it during the scout intrusion.

"We call the new system the Argus Array, after the mythical giant Argus Panoptes. But Panoptes had only a hundred eyes. Our Argus Array will have more than *eleven thousand* in the initial planned deployment, all optimized to be able to pick up Khreetan hyperdrive events within its covered area within two to three *minutes*, and focused on the direction from which we have good confidence they will come. We now know—or *believe* we know—that the Khreetan need at least twelve minutes to charge their hyperdrives, and then a further two minutes to jump, once charged. That means that after they emerge from hyperspace, it is an absolute minimum of fourteen minutes before they can jump again.

"*We* do not have that limitation. The Fleet's ships, with antimatter power reactors and Cricket hyperdrive technology, can jump in as little as thirty seconds, jump after jump after jump. When the new Argus Array detects an arriving ship, we can be on top of it nearly ten minutes before it can jump again." He addressed other questions in a similarly direct fashion.

Dong-geun also found himself facing similar, and related questions in the General Assembly. He, too, did his best to answer them directly... but perhaps a little more diplomatically. Many of the questions were raised by factions who still thought *they* should be the ones in control of the Stardock. That was an issue that would probably never end. There was, however, growing receptiveness to the idea of forming a new UN agency to manage Earthside distribution of Stardock resources. Alex welcomed the suggestion when Dong-geun mentioned it.

"That'll be one less thing we have to do," he said. "Honestly, it'll be a relief. And maybe it will give them a clearer perspective, if they get to see our side of the problem."

Not all of the global tableau was so problematic. At the end of July, Norway completed bringing its fusion reactor into its power grid, and celebrated the fact with an announcement that it would terminate all remaining Norwegian North Sea drilling. There had been considerable gloomy punditry predicting that the UK would simply pick up the slack in the North Sea, but it turned out this was not to be the case.

In fact, the UK's place had come up to receive both a fusion reactor of its own and a bulk recycler. The recent new Prime Minister, Julianna Sutherland, announced that both were to be sited in Cumbria, and that the first mission of the recycler would be cleaning up the massive stock of accumulated high and low level nuclear waste at Sellafield—and that with an initial feedstock already heavily enriched in heavy elements, the decision had been made to focus efforts on becoming the first Earthside producer of post-transuranics.

"The United Kingdom foresees a new space race," Prime Minister Sutherland declared, "this time with all the resources of the Solar System on the table. And this time, the United Kingdom *will not* be left out of the race. It is the goal of this government that by the end of this decade, Britain will have the technology in place to begin constructing its own hyperdrive-capable spacecraft, with Stardock assistance."

It went without saying, of course, that the UK would not be the only runner in that race.

———————

August saw the next two Warlords delivered, and commissioned as *Boudicaa* and *Joan d'Arc*. Following the current build plan, three more hulls were laid down, with scheduled delivery dates in November.

"Do you think we'll get to commission them?" Sandra Hayes asked quietly. It was the question everyone was thinking, a silent elephant in the middle of the room.

"I wish I knew," Alex replied. "The array deployment is going well, things seem to have quieted down since the scouting intrusion... but you feel uneasy, don't you?" He looked at Sandra first, who nodded, but then swept his gaze around the room. The guarded expressions were all anyone really needed.

"There was a period of quiet back in 1938, early 1939," he said, "when little seemed to be happening, but pretty much everyone who didn't have their heads buried in the sand and wasn't hopelessly naïve knew that a major war was coming. They called it the Phony War."

"The calm before the storm," Tom Whitman mused. Alex nodded.

"I can't help but feel that's where we are now," he said. "We know it's coming. We just don't know when."

"Could we increase our build rate any further?" Naomi asked.

"I'm guessing the answer is, 'technically yes', right, Dreamer?" Tom asked.

"That is correct," Dreamer replied.

"The problem," Tom continued, "is that we wouldn't have enough crews in the training pipeline for the additional ships. If we expand the Academy again now, we'll lose some time to disruption, and the additional new crews we'd be able to start training wouldn't start graduating until early next year.

"We could add a *second* set of training facilities further forward where it won't disrupt ongoing training... but then I'll need additional staff to manage the new campus."

"That would push our interior hull usage forward nearly to boom two, maybe a little beyond, right?" Alex asked.

"That is correct," Dreamer replied. "Additional crew quarters near to the new Academy facility would probably be advisable as well. There are Chrrt'ktk't living quarters and two medical bays already in that region of the hull, among other facilities, which could be reconstructed and repurposed to make them suitable for human occupation. I could begin deconstructing the existing modules while you discuss your designs."

Tom nodded thoughtfully.

"Do you have the capacity to do that as well as everything *else* we're already doing?" he asked.

"I do," Dreamer replied. "The amount of simultaneous ongoing construction is beginning to be a strain, but it is nothing that I cannot manage."

Tom raised a questioning eyebrow in Alex's direction.

"OK," Alex said, "I don't have an objection. But prioritize readiness. Naomi, Suzanne, can the two of you spare time to think about designs for the new quarters blocks? I think you're better at that than I am."

In his division headquarters, General Yuri Kuskovsky found himself pondering tables of organization for his overall command. If *this* officer were transferred from Moscow to Tver, and *that* officer from Tver to Semipalatinsk, and *that* one sent to Murmansk to replace this one sent to Smolensk, and *this* one promoted and transferred to that battalion near Murmansk... *That* one would be a problem, but he could be... *encouraged...* to retire. And if he didn't? Well, accidents happened. They had happened before.

Molchalin was not invulnerable. This foolishness would end. All Kuskovsky needed was time to prepare, to set his pieces out where he wanted them on the board.

10. The Calm Before

September 12 saw the simultaneous delivery of not two Warlords this time, but three, the first group of three out of the expanded production pipeline. They became CG-16 *Tughril Beg*, CG-17 *Cuchulainn*, and CG-18 *Fionn mac Cumhaill*, completing the initial deployment of CruRon Two and beginning CruRon Three. All four cruiser squadrons would be back-filled from eight ships to twelve, like the Sharks, if time permitted... but nobody really believed any more that it would.

Six days later, on September 18, Dreamer declared *There Exists An Elegant Solution* completed and ready for trials. At the unanimous insistence of the entire command staff, the first proving flight was conducted by a designated engineering-test crew tasked to test out all of the systems EXCEPT the gravity lance, which they were under strict orders not to even power up. That would have to wait until a later flight. It would need Dreamer to operate it, and everyone—even, reluctantly, Alex—agreed that neither Alex nor Dreamer could be risked on the first flight.

The flight test crew, drawn from both Shark and Warlord crews and commanded by Hussein Onyango, was effusive about the new ship when they returned four days later.

"It is not as agile as a Shark," Hussein reported, "but it is amazingly responsive for such a big ship, and the *power* is amazing. Sixty-eight gravities, nearly as fast as a Shark. There was *power* for more, but the thrusters were close to their limits—and so was the G-compensation."

"Well," Alex mused, "that's useful to know... but I hope we're never going to get into any drag races. The gravity lance weapon is going to suck up a huge amount of that power. That's *why* Dreamer put three annie-plants in the design. It's *incredibly* power-hungry."

Hussein nodded.

"Still, impressive," he said. "It is larger than a Warlord and has nearly half again the mass, and yet it can accelerate nearly as fast as a Shark in a straight line—though it does not handle as well."

"Not with the lance powered up, it won't," Alex replied. "The grav lance accounts for almost half of the ship's total energy budget. With the lance charged and maintaining, I'll be surprised if we can hit fifty G."

Hussein's eyebrows rose.

"I... understood that it requires a lot of power," he said slowly. "But I had no idea that it drew *that* much. *Now* I see why the ship has *three* antimatter reactors.

"Best lateral maneuvering response is just under seven G. Not as good as a Shark, but still very good for a ship this size."

"That's not bad, really," Alex agreed. "Anyway, we're going to need to talk about forming a crew. If *Elegant Solution* is going to be my flag command, then I need to be deeply familiar with flying her, and I'll need an established regular crew equally familiar with her—and able to cover the gaps in my command experience." He turned to Sandra Hayes.

"Sandra," he said, "I want you to remain second-in-command of the Academy, but I'd like you to also take the XO seat on *Elegant Solution*'s bridge, if you can manage both. I'll need the benefit of your command experience. Are you up for that?"

"Bonzer," Sandra replied, with a grin. "I'd love to."

"Fantastic," Alex said, relieved. "Then the first assignment I have for you..."

"Is to put together a permanent crew for *Elegant Solution*," she completed, before Alex could get it out. Alex just grinned and nodded.

"Got it in one," he said. "And that's part of why I want you as my XO. You have the experience that I lack, and you know what needs doing before I can ask for it. I can *fly* that ship, but *you* know how to make it run. And I'll need that."

"Give me four or five days," Sandra said. "I already have a dozen or so in mind. A couple of officers I'll pull from other ships, and I have my eye on a few bright sparks close to graduating the Academy. You'll have a crew inside a week."

"Thanks, Sandra," Alex replied. "I knew I could count on you."

"I'd like to join your test flights as well," Lewis said. "At least the first few."

Alex looked at Sandra and Tom. Both shrugged.

"Fine by me," Sandra said.

"OK," Alex agreed. "I can't think of any valid objection either. Jump right in, Lewis. I'll be glad to have your impressions."

"Thanks, Alex," Lewis said.

It turned out to be six days before *Elegant Solution*'s crew was in place and ready for shakedown. This would not be a single two-week shakedown as was usual for the Fleet; Alex could not be away for that long at one time. There was too much to stay on top of. The plan was instead to make multiple short runs out, two or three days at a time, each to accomplish a particular objective.

This second flight—the first with her properly assigned crew—was of course focused on crew integration and familiarization, getting the new crew used to running *Elegant Solution* and working together, learning the layout of the ship, becoming familiar with its systems, practicing routine operations, normal maneuvering, jumps, docking, undocking, launching and retrieving small craft, all of the routine everyday tasks. The ninety percent tasks—all of the tasks that are "just killing time". The other ten percent would come later.

For the third flight, on October 2, Alex invited Maksim along.

"You might be the craziest destroyer pilot in the Fleet," Alex told him. "And I mean that in a good way. So I want your insights about *Elegant Solution* as well, your impressions of the ship, any tips you can give on what you think of how to get the best out of her."

"Including gravity lance?" Maksim asked.

"Not yet," Alex said. "I want everyone thoroughly familiar with handling and running the ship before we fire up the lance. I don't want to take any unnecessary chances."

"Understandable," Maksim agreed. "Is wise decision, I think, with completely new, unproven weapon system."

So the third flight was a little more... *exuberant* than the second, marked by Maksim's distinctive touch on the helm.

"With hull this broad," he observed, "there is much momentum in roll axis. Takes more effort to start roll, but once you begin, she likes to keep rolling. Especially compared to Shark. You should keep that in mind. Yaw, perhaps even more so.

"Counterpoint is, she has barely half length-to-beam ratio of Shark or Warlord. Although larger overall, she is more compact than Warlord. So she pitches and yaws more readily than you would *expect* from ship of this size and mass. Pitch and yaw probably more useful than roll most of time, in any case. Remember that, and try to avoid too much maneuvering in roll axis. And be especially wary of roll-yaw coupling."

"I'll keep that in mind," Alex agreed.

"Remember too, hull is very flat. So try to stay edge-on when you can. Makes smaller target, smaller radar cross-section, harder to spot."

"Not that any of the Fleet's ships are exactly what you could call stealthy," Alex noted.

"True, true," Maksim agreed. "Stealth in space is hard problem, we know this already. Difficult to hide energy emissions, and very little cover to hide behind. But every little bit helps."

Alex nodded agreement.

"Of course, when the Khreetan eventually show up," he said, "the truth is I *want* them to see us. I want them to *see* that we're strong, that we're ready, and that we're *not* the Crickets, and that there isn't any reason to start a fight—unless they came looking for one with whoever they could find. My ideal is still what it's been all along—to avoid a large-scale conflict *at all*. The best way to survive any fight is not to have the fight in the first place."

Maksim nodded thoughtfully.

"You are not wrong," he agreed. "Better not to start fight at all... but be ready to fight if opponent has other ideas."

"Yup," Alex said. "That's been my thinking from the start."

"Probably not too much longer before we find out," Maksim mused grimly.

With some one-on-one coaching from Maksim, Alex and both of *Elegant Solution*'s helm officers quickly picked up how to best leverage *Elegant Solution*'s maneuvering strengths and avoid her weak points. They returned from the third flight with a much better understanding of how best to use the ship.

The fourth test flight, counting the initial trial flight, beginning on October 6, was designated for flight testing of the lance.

There Exists An Elegant Solution sat two thousand kilometers from the Stardock. Her crew was all in suits, her Marines in their armor, small craft manned and standing off a hundred kilometers away, with the second-watch crew aboard.

"We're as prepared as we can be," Alex said. "Power it up, Dreamer. Slow and easy for the first time."

"Charging the lance," Dreamer acknowledged. The entire bridge crew watched the displays intently as the power levels rose.

"Holy *crap*," muttered Chief Engineer Alice Watson, "you told us this thing draws a lot of power, but... damn."

"Yeah, it's a hell of a power sink," Alex agreed. "I'm not seeing anything out of spec though. How's it look to you, Dreamer?"

"It is charging very smoothly, Alex," Dreamer agreed.

Dreamer ran the lance through five charge/discharge cycles at progressively higher rates over the next two hours, the last run at maximum charge rate. There were no charging instabilities.

"Charging has gone more smoothly than in the test cradle," Dreamer stated. "I feel confident proceeding to arming."

"When you're ready, Dreamer," Alex said. "With all due caution, of course."

"Understood," Dreamer agreed. "Beginning arming cycle."

Alex held his breath, but it was only a short time before the status readouts indicated the lance was armed and ready to fire.

"Weapon is armed," Dreamer confirmed. "You will doubtless be interested to hear that I found it easier to manage than in the test cradle. I was able to trap and control chaotic modes noticeably earlier. Clearly even the very slight control delay introduced by propagation lag to and in the test cradle was a factor in controlling the lance."

"So just for clarification, you're telling me that it is *safer* to operate the gravity lance here on the ship than on the remote test cradle?" Alex asked.

"Correct, Alex," Dreamer confirmed. "It is in fact a quite significant improvement."

"What does this say about possible future automation of the lance?" Alex asked. There was a pause.

"I cannot say for certain," Dreamer said after a long moment. "But with more experience and better understanding of the behavior of the lance, I believe it might be possible in the future to design control automation of the lance and build it into a pre-sentient standalone ship-intellect."

"And that would permit us to construct other grav-lance armed ships without needing to have a fully sentient AI on each ship?" Alex continued.

"It would," Dreamer agreed. "Although I have a question. Do you wish *not* to have full shipboard AIs?"

"Whoa, Dreamer," Alex said hurriedly, "I didn't say that, nor mean it. I was thinking only of—well, call it a supply-and-demand problem. You've told me how long it takes to—*grow* an AI. And I wouldn't want to be in the position of *forcing* AIs aboard ship as weapons operators. But if we *HAVE* additional AIs in the future, and ships able to hold them, and they *want* to be part of the crew... I guess I don't have a problem with that. I imagine at some point we're going to start building long-range exploration ships, and I imagine it would be a *massive* asset for them to have AIs aboard.

"No, my thought was just to break the only-one-ship limit that we currently have. But I have *absolutely no* reservations about AIs like you on ships built with enough substrate to safely hold one—as long as it's voluntary."

"Thank you for explaining, Alex," Dreamer said. "I apologize if you felt I was making any negative inference. I only wished to clarify your reason for asking."

"If I can ask, Dreamer," Alex asked, "when *do* you think we will be ready to start growing more AIs?"

There was a longer pause.

"I trust you will pardon me for saying this," Dreamer said at length. "But the historical records of your world are not reassuring. I would not feel comfortable gestating new AIs until the AI rights treaty that Naomi has been working on has been completed and ratified."

Alex hesitated, and thought.

"You're not wrong," he sighed at last. "We have a record of treating each other pretty awfully. Especially anyone we can define as 'other'—and we go to great lengths to find reasons for 'othering' people. And they all come down to, 'Some of us *need* to have people to feel naturally superior to.'

"I'd like to think we're growing out of that phase. But it's a terribly slow process."

"Societal change does not happen overnight," Dreamer replied. "I have observed that your many cultures are struggling with a difficult phase that many do not want to move beyond. But it speaks well of you that so many of you are trying to do so."

Alex took a deep breath and rubbed his face with his hands.

"How did we get here?" he asked aloud. Then, a moment later, "Never mind, it was a rhetorical question.

"Anyway, it's great that you expect to be able to automate the lance in the future. It doesn't help us *right now*, but it's something to look forward to. Perhaps we might even figure out how to shrink the thing a bit.

"I'm declaring we've done enough testing for now. Go ahead and de-energize the lance for the moment. We'll take a break for an hour or two and resume later."

In the wardroom, Chief Engineer Watson had questions about the lance and its power consumption.

"I could see that the gravity lance was sucking down almost the entire output of one reactor, sir," she said. "The rest of the ship together doesn't use the full output of a second. Does it draw *that much more* power to actually *fire* it that we need the third reactor? I thought the power system was over-engineered compared to a Warlord, but now... I'm not so sure after watching that thing charge."

"No," Alex said, "actually *firing* it consumes relatively little energy—at least, compared to what it takes to charge it. We used a sixty-meter plant to power it for testing, to be certain we had enough power. But actually once charged and energized, the forty-meter plant can supply power to it as fast as it can use it while firing.

"You're right, two would be *enough* to run the entire ship and the lance both. Dreamer incorporated the third reactor largely for redundancy —and to make sure we're covered in case of any unplanned overhead."

"Well, I can get behind that," Watson said. "Redundancy is always good. Up to a point, of course. There's such a thing as overdoing your redundancy."

"Sure," Alex agreed. "You reach a point where you have so much redundancy it doesn't really make engineering sense not to go ahead and use a lot more of it *anyway*."

"Right, right," Watson said. "We're on the same page there. So... what we've already seen is the maximum power draw I can expect to see from it?"

"As far as we know," Alex assured her. "And we tested it pretty thoroughly in the test cradle. This *specific* lance, not one just like it. We've test-fired it hundreds of times without any mishaps before we put it into the ship... or, more accurately, designed and built a ship around it."

"Good to hear," Watson said. "Thank you, sir."

"No problem," Alex replied. "I'm glad I have a Chief Engineer who will ask questions."

Watson grinned.

"Always ask the questions early," she said. "It avoids surprises."

"So you came over from a Warlord class, right?"

"I did, sir. CG-05 *Hannibal*. Which reminds me, speaking of questions—I know that this ship's class identifier is GOU. But what the heck does it *stand* for? Nobody has told me, and it's not any standard designation I know."

Alex chuckled.

"You're entirely forgiven for not knowing the reference, Chief," he replied. "It's a bit whimsical, to be honest. You'd have to have read the right set of books. There's a writer, decades dead but still a long-time favorite of mine, who wrote a series of books set in a culture called, well, the Culture. He said once that science fiction was the only genre of fiction that was actually *important*, because it was the only genre about anticipating future problems and finding solutions to them before they occurred."

Watson nodded thoughtfully at that.

"Anyway, all—well, *most*—of their major ship classes had these three-letter designations. ROU, GOU, GSV, and more. GSV stood for General Systems Vehicle, and they were *freaking huge*. ROU was for Rapid Offensive Unit, which as I understand it was the Culture's equivalent of a destroyer or maybe a fast light cruiser. They actually handled *most* of the Culture's relatively routine missions."

Watson nodded again.

"And GOU?"

"GOU stood for General Offensive Unit," Alex said. "I'm not sure whether to equate them to a heavy cruiser or something more powerful. But they generally got sent out when there was the potential for serious ass-kicking to be done. Designating this ship a GOU was suggested in a moment of whimsy after we decided on a very Culture-esque *name*—you kinda had to be there—and, well, it stuck."

Watson nodded again, and grinned.

"And the... uh, GSVs, then? They were, what, battleships, carriers?"

Alex chuckled and shook his head.

"Well, no," he said. "Start by picturing a complete carrier strike group... well, no, imagine the *entire United States Navy* in a single vessel. And then level it up a couple of tiers from there. I... can't begin to adequately convey their scale. Huge beyond anything you've ever imagined. Some of them were designated Plate class, Continent class, even System class. They didn't have *crews*, they had *populations*. Some of the System-class GSVs could evacuate an entire planetary population. All of it totally speculative, of course. I have no idea how, or *if*, anything that large could even be built, and I doubt the author did either.

"Look—if you're really curious, just go read the books. It's worth it. Ask Dreamer for access, I brought copies with me of everything the author ever wrote. The name is Banks, and ask for the Culture Universe."

"Culture Universe, Banks," Watson repeated. "Maybe I'll take a look."

"We've kind of drifted a long way off the point of your original question, though," Alex admitted. "Did you have any other questions about the actual ship or the gravity lance?"

"Not yet," Watson said. "But I'm sure I will. The lance in particular. Nothing *else* on this ship is really all that different from the same systems on a Warlord, except for the dual hyperspace cores. And I understand the reasons for that. It's—uh—" She hesitated for a brief moment, then burst out laughing. "It's an elegant solution," she finished. Alex grinned.

"Remember that any technical questions, you should probably ask Dreamer directly," Alex said. "He'll doubtless be able to answer them better than I can."

Watson nodded.

"Got it," she said. "Thanks, sir."

After a break of a couple of hours, they resumed testing. The next item on the checklist was a lengthy series of full-rate arm/disarm cycles. To Alex's immense relief, the entire series went without incident.

"I am definitely better able to manage the lance without the propagation delays inherent in the remote test cradle, slight though they were," Dreamer reported. "I am increasingly confident that I will be able to create control automation for it in the future. However, I cannot confidently predict when I will have enough operational data to do so."

"Understood, Dreamer," Alex replied. "Don't try to rush it. I'd sooner we be really sure, than lose ships unnecessarily by pushing out the automation before it's really ready."

"I'll second that," Sandra agreed. "It's not as though we haven't already pushed the Fleet far beyond anything anyone Earthside would have *dreamed* of just a few years ago."

"I cannot disagree with your position," Dreamer said. "There are already more than sufficient variables in deploying a brand new weapon system as complex as this one at all, without trying to automate it before I feel confident in doing so. But you do understand, I hope, that no automation system can ever be guaranteed completely error-free."

Alex sighed.

"I know, Dreamer," he agreed. "Nothing is perfect. We can't possibly have a plan to cope with every unanticipated corner case. The entire *problem* of unpredicted corner cases is that they are unpredicted. You might be surprised how many people without engineering backgrounds don't seem to understand that. There just *isn't any way* to be prepared for things that you don't know you don't know.

"I know the Crickets had a long time—thousands of years, I still have a little trouble grasping that sometimes—to work out the wrinkles in, say, hyperdrive and artificial gravity, and *find* those corner cases. And I know we're perhaps pushing our luck with the antimatter reactors, precisely because the Crickets *didn't* make such extensive use of them, because they were afraid to use them. But there's always the possibility of *something* going wrong that nobody could have anticipated. Especially when our ships start taking fire and receiving battle damage. I'm not naïve enough to think we won't lose ships if it comes to a shoot-out. I'm just hoping we can keep it to a minimum.

"Anyway, I'm satisfied with the lance results so far. Let's all get some supper and some sleep, and next watch, we'll move on to static test shots. Mr. Tarpanen, you have the conn."

"I have the conn, Sir," Lieutenant Mikko Tarpanen acknowledged.

═══════════

The next day, or rather the next watch cycle, they resumed where they'd left off on the test checklist, patiently firing single shots at gradually increasing power into empty space. That took the majority of the watch, and again went with a gratifying lack of incident.

The next step was to increase the fire rate, in steps, until they were firing the lance as fast as it could recycle. This, too, went without incident, although the amount of power the systems monitoring displays showed the lance drawing was quite eye-opening. The thought crossed Alex's mind part-way through the test-fire series that the CalTech LIGO guys were probably either intently studying every blip of data coming in from the array, or swearing at him. Maybe both at once, for that matter. Perhaps he owed them an apology for not giving them a heads-up first.

They actually ran about an hour past scheduled watch turn-over to reach full firing rate, before Alex called a halt.

"OK, people," he said, "this is going great. Let's call this a good run, go back to dock, and review all of the data. Next flight, we'll continue on to firing on the move, and live fire against target drones.

"Good work, people. Let's go home."

———————

By the time *Elegant Solution* docked, Alex was glad of a break from the cycle of testing. The odds of a mishap at this point were low, it was true, but still, there was always the chance of something going unexpectedly wrong; and that chance, however small, made it stressful, and that stress made it exhausting. The risk of exhaustion was still another reason why he didn't want to do it for more than two or three days at a time. Tired people make mistakes, and mistakes turn into accidents.

Alex didn't want any accidents, if he could avoid them. And the best way right now to avoid them, was to structure the test schedule so as not to exhaust his crew. They'd all take a two or three day break from it now, before they went out again. It wasn't as though there weren't going to be a hundred things demanding his attention.

He spent the next three days catching up on those hundred things. And then they went back out again, to continue flight testing.

———————

For the first day of test flight five, October 11, they tried firing the lance, still just dry-fire with no target, while maneuvering or under acceleration, or both. Dreamer was quickly able to conclude that maneuvering and acceleration made fundamentally no difference to the functioning of the lance.

"Of course," he explained, "the truth is that I would have been surprised if it did, unless we approach relativistic velocities... which I presume we are highly unlikely to ever do."

"Honestly, I hope we don't," Alex agreed. "Though it does just occur to me right now to ask: I'm going to take a guess that it would probably be extremely bad to try to fire the lance while in hyperspace. Am I right?"

There was a lengthy silence at that.

"I will have to study the mathematics in more detail," Dreamer said at last, just as Alex was beginning to wonder if there was a problem. "I do

195

not feel confident yet to say whether or not it would be safe to fire the lance from within a hyperdrive bubble. Neither can I confidently rule it out. If it *is* possible, then you may possibly have devised the first weapon that I am aware of that is usable both in hyperspace and in normal space.

"However, I urge most strongly that we do not attempt to test this at the present time."

"Oh *HELL* no," Alex agreed. "No, let's be damned sure about walking before we try to run. I think maybe even beyond figuring out whether the physics ought to allow it, I think that's something we don't even *try* to test until you've developed automation for the lance, and we can build an automated or remote-controlled test ship. That is definitely a back-burner priority. A research question for the future."

"I agree," Dreamer said. "I will venture to say that I do not, so far, *think* that the theory precludes it working. But it is a problem that I can and will study at a later time."

"Anyway," Alex said, "that aside, I think we're ready to proceed to live fire practice against target drones."

"I concur," Dreamer agreed. And so they spent the rest of the watch, and then the next main-watch as well, performing first static fire against target drones, then firing against maneuvering drones, then firing at moving targets while maneuvering.

It quickly became very clear that the gravity lance was not a precision weapon effective against small targets. That, truth be told, did not come as any surprise. It did, however, mean that it was necessary to use entire formations of drones to simulate a target that the lance *was* suited to. And that, in turn, meant that the burn rate on target drones was high. In the end, they had to cut the second day of live-fire trials short because *Elegant Solution* ran short of target drones. Alex *could* have called for resupply by another ship, or they could have gone back for more; but the truth was they weren't learning a great deal useful from the exercise anyway. It was common for surface "wet" navies to conduct sinking exercises using retired ships, hulls otherwise good only for scrap, as live targets. The Fleet, lacking any such collection of obsolete hulks, didn't have that option.

They wrapped up that set of live-fire tests, and Alex took *Elegant Solution* on a quick run out to the inner fringes of the Oort cloud and back, just to get a first-hand feel for himself for how she handled in hyper. And then it was back to the Stardock again.

———

"I'm not truthfully sure how much more actual *testing* we can usefully do," Alex said at the next status briefing. It was October 14, and the next three Warlords, CG-20 through CG-22, had just come out of the yards and into service. They didn't have names, yet. That would happen later that day, when their crews officially graduated and took control of them.

"The honest truth is we just don't have any good targets to test-fire the grav lance against. We'll do more practice flights for familiarization with lance operations, of course, but I think we've passed the point where we're actually *learning* anything new.

"Still, I think we've done enough to prove that there's no obvious problems with the ship itself or with the lance installation. And we've proved that we can *operate* the lance while flying the ship."

"Do not forget," Dreamer added, "that we have also learned enough about the lance's operation that there is a high probability of being able to build self-contained automation into it in future. I think I may even be able to somewhat reduce its size, now that we understand it better."

"That'll be welcome," Lewis said. "Think we'll ever be able to retrofit them into the Warlords?"

"I do not think so," Dreamer replied. "The internal rearrangement necessary would be too extreme, and I doubt that it would work well. The Warlord hull is not broad enough to accommodate the tandem-core arrangement without stripping out most of its existing armament. It would make more sense to build a new ship from scratch."

"But we might be able to put it into ships smaller than *Elegant Solution* in the future?" Alex asked.

"Slightly smaller, yes, perhaps," Dreamer said. "However, I am unconvinced that the savings would be enough to justify designing and testing such a new class, when we already have an existing design that we are well on the way to proving out."

"Either way," Alex said, "it's a problem for the future. I think we almost certainly don't have the time to worry about it now, so let's not get distracted. Honestly, I'm just very glad we got *Elegant Solution* completed and through trials before the shit hit the fan. It gives us one more tactical option in the bag... although I still really hope it doesn't come to that."

Lewis nodded agreement.

"Yeah," he said. "We can cross that bridge when we come to it."

The three newest Warlords went out on shakedown as UFS *Harald Bluetooth*, UFS *Hunahpu*, and UFS *Xbalanque*. Alex and his new crew settled into a routine of two days out, three days in, to drill and practice together on *Elegant Solution* while still letting Alex keep up with everything he needed to aboard the Stardock, and not keep Dreamer away too long either. Dreamer had set up sub-sentient automation for everything possible, but still, his absence was felt when he was off-station with *Elegant Solution*. The solution may have been elegant, but it was still a long way from ideal.

They didn't get very much time at all to get used to the new routine.

11. Hammerfall

Clan Hsieuuu made final preparations about half a light-year outside the system.

«We plan based upon the tracks and knowledge brought back by Hunt-Master Thoughtful,» Fleet-Leader Swims-Like-Rock declared. «We will leap into the system in three waves. In the first wave, the front-runners, to see that the way is clear. Then in the second wave, the hunt-ships. Once the front-runners and hunt-ships have arrived, we shall seek to make contact and take the measure of the out-clan.

«The nest-defenders and the Den will of course arrive together as the third wave. By then we should be done with paw-cuffs. There should be no chance of a mistake.»

The assembled Hunt-Masters and Hunt-Leaders coughed their agreement and understanding.

«Very well, then. Let us embark on this venture. I shall be upon *Sharp Claws*.»

Shortly afterward, all of the ships of Clan Hsieuuu undocked, and the front-runners began their run-up to leap. Clan Hsieuuu was on the move.

It was early in the evening of October 23, UTC station time, when Dreamer raised the alarm. Alex and Naomi were just finishing a private dinner on the outside patio of their quarters.

Priority alert, Alex. Incoming traffic detected. Mass detection.

Alex spluttered for a moment, trying to inhale and swallow a mouthful of wine at the same time. He coughed and cleared his throat.

"Alex?" Naomi asked, concerned. Alex just held up a hand for a moment.

"Incoming traffic, Dreamer?" he asked, aloud.

"Multiple hyperspace exit events matching past Khreetan hyperdrive signatures, at fourteen point six AU, roughly point one seven radians off the array centerline."

"Goddamn. I'm glad we extended the array all the way in to ten AU."

The remains of dinner completely forgotten, Alex stood up and took a step away from the table.

"How many, Dreamer?" he asked.

"Approximately fifty exit signatures detected so far, plus or minus eight. Signature is similar to the ships that scouted us in April. It is difficult to resolve and distinguish the individual Khreetan hyperdrive events when they occur in large numbers."

Alex stood silently for a long moment. Naomi came up behind him and put her arms around him.

"They're here," he said to her.

"I know," she said quietly.

Alex took a deep breath, held it for a moment, and let it out.

"I guess this is when we find out whether we're ready. It doesn't sound... too bad, so far.

"Dreamer, sound general quarters and mobilize the Fleet. Recall all patrols, let's start this out in as good order as we can. Have the Fleet form up by squadrons at lunar L-2, and we'll head out from there. Call the command staff together."

Fifteen minutes later, Alex's staff were assembled.

"This is it," Alex said simply. "This is where we find out whether it was all enough.

"Tom, John, I'm leaving the station in your hands. I'm... going to suggest that you offer non-essential personnel the option of evacuation down to Earth. I can't promise how long you'll have to do it, but you have all of the shuttles and transports at your disposal.

"Naomi, Dong-geun, I need you two to handle diplomatic outreach. Make sure Earth's governments are kept informed." Naomi nodded agreement.

"I'll be going out with the Fleet, in *Elegant Solution*. And of course that means you're with me, Dreamer. And Sandra."

Sandra Hayes nodded.

"John, I should have a platoon of Marines. I don't anticipate conducting any boarding actions, but... just in case." John Warner nodded.

"I can give you Eighth Platoon of Second Company," he said. "They'll be at the docking port when you get there. I've already alerted Seventh Company, and they're on their way to the gunnery control rooms."

"Thanks, John," Alex said. "Yeon, Philippe, needless to say, we'll need the medbays ready to go at a moment's notice. Jorge, I'm not honestly sure where best to assign you right now. Can you perhaps help coordinate any evacuation? And fill in as needed?"

"Sure thing, boss," Jorge said.

Alex thought hard.

"Have I forgotten anything?"

"Probably," Tom Whitman said. "But we'll take care of it as it comes up. We'll do our best not to let it become your problem."

Alex let his breath out.

"OK, people, he said, "let's get to it."

He turned to Naomi, fumbling for words, but before he found them, she stepped in close. He wrapped his arms around her and hugged her fiercely. She hugged him back just as tightly, then after a long moment, leaned back just a little and freed a hand. She thumped him on the chest lightly for emphasis, as she had seen Sofiia do to Maksim.

"You come back to me, Alex Holder," she said, her voice serious. "Or as Sofiia tells Maksim, I will be *very angry* with you."

Alex leaned forward and kissed her.

"If I possibly can, Naomi," he promised. "Any way I possibly can."

Ten minutes later, Alex and Sandra reached *Elegant Solution*'s docking tower. As John Warner had promised, a full platoon of Marines in battle armor were there waiting. The platoon sergeant saluted crisply as they walked up. Alex returned the salute, and they all boarded. The rest of *Elegant Solution*'s crew was already aboard, and the ship was warmed up and ready to go. The hatch sealed behind them.

Ten minutes after that, *There Exists An Elegant Solution* undocked, and headed out to rendezvous with the assembling Fleet.

"Additional new detections," Dreamer announced over the Fleet command channel, before *Elegant Solution* had reached the forming Fleet. "Location is approximately the same as the first wave. This wave contains stronger signatures. Estimated count is seventy-eight, plus or minus twelve."

"*Crap*," Alex swore. He revised mental counts quickly.

"Okay, people," he said on Fleet command channel, "the odds just got a lot worse. We just went from outnumbering them around three to two, to being outnumbered *ourselves* nearly two to one."

A few minutes later, *Elegant Solution* was in position.

"Bring up the god's-eye net, Dreamer," Alex said. He waited while the latest sensor data from just-returned patrols and the Argus Array were integrated into the plot. It showed two waves of last known positions, one slightly ahead of and spread slightly wider than the second.

"I want destroyer squadrons sunward of their deployment, starting at the ten-AU line for now," he ordered. "Deploy in disc formation, segments by squadron, north-east-south-west. We'll move in from there once we get updated positional data. Do not fire first. Let's see if we can find out their intentions without starting any shooting. Fire only if fired upon, proportional response where possible.

"Cruiser squadrons, centerline in three-wing formation on *Elegant Solution,* five million klicks behind the destroyers. We are the long-range reserve. Stay back for now and do not engage except defensively, unless ordered to fire.

"Marine details on all ships, high alert, be prepared for possible boarding actions.

"Let's go."

The Fleet began to move out, going directly to hyper and to the new deployment locations, jumping in groups, groups staggering their jumps enough not to interfere with each other.

———————

"Gunnery status, report," John Warner ordered.

"Gun room Alpha, ready and standing by."

"Gun room Bravo, ready and standing by."

"Gun room Charlie, ready and standing by."

"Gun room Delta, ready and standing by."

"Good," John replied. "We have no incoming targets at this time. Relax, but stay alert. Monitor your targeting zones, listen for updates. Point defenses on standby, and make damned certain point defense IFF is active, expect shuttle launches."

"Now hear this," Tom said, on station-wide address. "The Fleet has deployed and is preparing to engage the Khreetan. Our latest estimate is that on the order of one hundred and twenty ships, plus or minus, presumed to be Khreetan from their jump signatures, have entered the Solar System.

"All shuttle pilots, please proceed to the docking bay and stand by to take on passengers.

"Anyone wishing to evacuate down to Earth, take only essentials with you and in an orderly fashion, make your way to the main docking bay. Shuttle seats will be available in order of arrival. You will be free to return at any time, assuming we weather this intact. You will not lose your assigned quarters.

"Everyone else who does not have an assigned duty at this time, please remain in your quarters and stand by for further information.

"That is all at this time. Stand by for further updates."

———————

"Mr. President." Dr. Winters' tone was tense, formal. John Riken looked at her.

"Out with it, Jocelyn. I can already tell it's bad news."

"We have received a priority alert from the Fleet, via Ms. Tomlinson." She hesitated.

President John Riken took a deep breath, and let it out.

"We're out of time, aren't we? You're about to tell me that the Khreetan are here."

"Yes, Mr. President. A year and a half before the timeframe the Crickets gave us. Or perhaps I should say, tried *not* to give us."

Riken sighed.

"It is what it is," he said. He thought for a moment.

"Well. There isn't likely much we can do, but get the war room ready. Call everyone in. We'll need all military leaves cancelled, all forces on high alert, all reservists alerted for potential reactivation. Send the word to all of our allies. I'm going to give the Russians and China a heads-up, so that they don't see us going to unexplained high alert and draw the wrong conclusions."

———————

Forty-eight Shark-class destroyers came out of jump, a single slightly spread-out wave, ten AU out from Sol, arrayed in a broad disk, spaced five hundred kilometers apart, directly in line with the last known position of the Khreetan formation. Five million kilometers behind them, two and a half squadrons of Warlord class missile cruisers arrayed themselves in three wings around *There Exists An Elegant Solution.*

"Fleet has redeployed," Sandra reported. Though with the 'god's eye' data net active, it wasn't strictly necessary. Both Sandra and Alex—and every other L3 bridge officer in the Fleet—could see the locations of every ship through the interface, as well as everything that any of those ships could see.

Which, at the moment, was nothing. Space is a very large place.

However, the Argus array was scattered through billions of cubic kilometers of that space, and it had *thousands* of eyes.

«First and second waves deployed, Fleet-Leader,» reported Hunt-Master Broken-Tooth, captain of *Sharp Claws.*

«Very good,» Swims-Like-Rock replied. «Let us begin moving inward and seek contact.» He indicated a location on the master plot. «Leap us forward to... there.»

Fourteen minutes later, the fleet's ships faded from sight. They came back out of hyper just less than four AU closer to Sol.

"Argus array extreme-range visual detection from drone 12-329," Dreamer reported. "The location correlates well to the detected entry events." He added the Argus data to the plot. A tight cluster of five red sparks showed, then seven. At this scale, any inward motion they had was imperceptible.

"Let's wait a few minutes and see what else we get from the array," Alex said.

Over the next minutes, more tiny red sparks filled in. A lot more.

Then they began to wink out again.

"New hyperdrive activity," Dreamer reported. "Hyperdrive entries at locations corresponding to visual sightings. Data is triangulated at ninety seconds old."

"They're jumping again," Alex said. "As long as their exit is still within the array, it'll be fourteen minutes before they can jump a third time. Otherwise, we'll have to find them again."

"And if it is?" Sandra asked. "What course of action?"

Alex thought for a moment.

"I want three destroyers from each squadron to go take a look at them," he said after a moment. "Let's find out for sure what we're facing, and see if we can determine their intentions."

"Getting that coordinated now," Sandra said.

———————

General Yuri Kuskovsky pushed past the Spetsnaz guard at the door.

«President Molchalin!» he said. «I have just learned that the Americans have gone to maximum alert level!»

«Yes, yes, General,» said Konstantin Yanushevich Molchalin. «We know. They advised us before they did it. You are *aware* that we have placed our own forces on high alert as well, yes? Or did you somehow *miss* that news?»

«Well of course we would have,» Kuskovsky said, covering his omission. «We must show that we are ready to counter any attack they launch against us.»

«The Americans are not going to attack us, Yuri,» Molchalin said, somewhat distractedly, his mind largely on more urgent matters. And if he was to be strictly honest, he was more than a little tired of Yuri's shit. After this emergency was dealt with, he thought to himself, he would *encourage* Yuri to retire. «It was *they* who gave *us* the warning, before anyone else.»

«*What* warning?» Kuskovsky demanded. «I heard of no warning.»

«Because it is above your command level, General,» Molchalin replied. «President Riken called me personally to inform me that the *Khreetan* aliens have entered the solar system in force, and that the United Fleet has deployed to counter them. He advised me so that we could be ready in case of unrest or landings, and so that we would not be alarmed at their own mobilization.»

«Has anyone ever even *seen* these supposed aliens?» Kuskovsky demanded.

«General, your tone is becoming disrespectful,» Molchalin cautioned.

Fool, Kuskovsky thought to himself.

«I apologize, of course.» The words grated. Kuskovsky continued somewhat more... circumspectly. «What proof do we have that these aliens are here, or that they even exist? How do we know this is not an American trick to lull us into a sense of false cooperation while they launch a surprise attack against us?»

«General, not everything is a trick,» Molchalin replied tiredly. «If the Americans wished to launch a sneak attack against us, why on Earth would they alert us first? I have been having some very fruitful talks with this American President for some time now. I do not believe that he means us harm. I believe that he has the good of the world at heart—including us.»

You pathetic, blind fool, Kuskovsky thought. *The American has you wrapped around his little finger. You will betray us all for a promise of an idealistic dream.* But he did not say that aloud.

«As long as you are certain of that, Gospodin President,» he said. «I trust you will pardon my—alarm.»

«Tensions are high, General Kuskovsky,» President Molchalin replied. «Think no more of it. Simply ensure that all forces under your command are prepared, in case we must act on short notice.»

Kuskovsky nodded and excused himself.

Oh, I will, he thought to himself as he left. *I will. I will not let you doom us.*

The corridor Yuri Kuskovsky chose was not the one that led toward his Kremlin office.

———————

"New hyperspace exits detected," Dreamer reported, as he sent the data to the tactical net. "New locations are on the same line, distance approximately ten point four AU from Sol. Data latency is under one minute."

"We've got them," Alex said. "Thirteen minutes before they can jump again. Get those scouting destroyers in there and let's get a look at them."

———————

«All ships have leapt, Fleet-Leader,» said Hunt-Master Broken-Tooth. «No contacts as yet. All is quiet.»

«Good,» Swims-Like-Rock said. «We will recharge here, and make two more small-leaps toward the third world, little by little. And then we shall—»

«*Contacts!*» called Hunter Red-Stripe, on sensors. «A paw—no, *two* paws—of ships closing. They just *appeared*.»

«Like the Violators' ships,» Swims-Like-Rock said aloud. «These must be the out-clan.»

The new ships, in four half-hand groups, shot past the front-runners on curving paths, sweeping past the main formation, and up, and away. Then space *rippled* in front of them, and within a few heartbeats, they were gone.

«So *that* is an out-clan fast-ship,» Swims-Like-Rock mused thoughtfully, as he studied the sensor data from the brief encounter. «Hunt-Master Thoughtful was right. We did not see the Violators' ships maneuver at a single *digit* of that rate.»

———————

"Clean pass," Commander David Googan reported from DD-42 *Perth*. "There's a lot of them, alright. Two waves, looked to be about fifty in the first wave, matched the visual image from *Highlander* from the previous encounter. Second group is larger, at least eighty ships, and they're bigger, as well. Maybe a third longer, and... *burlier*. But built on the same general plan."

"If the first wave are the same ships that scouted us," Sandra said, "and we assume that's their destroyer class, then I think it's safe to also assume that second wave is their cruiser class."

"If that's the case," Alex said slowly, "then they have us about one-to-one on destroyers, and closer to three-to-one in cruisers. We know—well, okay, we're *pretty sure*—we can out-accelerate their destroyers, but I still don't like those odds one bit. I hope this doesn't turn nasty. If it does, I think even the *best* case is probably that we *both* end up badly mauled."

———————

«Well, they know now that we are here,» said Swims-like-Rock. «I imagine that making contact with them is no longer a problem to be solved. But how did they find us so *quickly*? How did they know we were here at all? Hunt-Master Thoughtful reported that it seemed the out-clan found his Paw fast, but guessed it random chance. They found us even *faster*.»

«What course of action do we take, Fleet-Leader?» Hunt-Master Broken-Tooth asked.

«I think that they will come to us now,» Swims-Like-Rock said. «So we shall wait and meet them, and take their measure.»

———————————

«Report!» Yuri Kuskovsky demanded of the two guards outside the door at the end of the hallway as he approached them. «Has anyone entered, or tried to enter, this room since the alert was issued?»

«No, Sir!» the man on the right barked out. Both were standing stiffly at attention.

«Very good. Notify me IMMEDIATELY if anyone tries to enter, or... lingers too close.»

«Yes, Sir!» both replied.

«I will inspect the room myself now, to be certain all is in order,» Kuskovsky said.

«Sir!» the two said. The man on the left stepped aside to allow access to the door. General Yuri Kuskovsky held his authorization badge against the reader, thumbed the scanner plate, and badged in.

A few minutes later, he emerged again, waiting to make certain that the door locked behind him.

«All is in good order,» he declared. «Good work. Stay sharp. You are both credits to your uniform. Keep at it.»

«Thank you, Sir!» said the right-hand guard, saluting again.

General Yuri Kuskovsky returned the salute, then turned smartly and walked away down the hallway. Once he was clear of the hallway, he turned towards a side exit from the building, took out his phone, and called for his driver.

In his jacket pocket rested a copy of the day's strategic launch authentication codes.

———————————

"Captain Googan," Alex said, "were you fired upon during your fly-past?"

"No, Sir," Googan replied. "We got pinged by search radar, but no indication of target locking."

"Interesting," Alex mused. "Let's keep an eye on them. I'd like you to go back in. Match speed, stand off outside and ahead of their formation. Say sixty thousand klicks, a fifth of a light-second. Close enough to keep an eye on them, far enough to evade if they come after you in force or fire on you. We can micro-jump in and out as necessary. Search radar, leave no doubt that we know they're there, but no targeting. Clear?"

"Clear, Sir. Flashlight only, no paint."

"Sandra, relay that to the rest of that group, please. The remainder of the destroyers, close to... let's say one light-second, match speed with their formation, and hold position ahead of them. That's close enough to respond almost immediately if they engage. And adjust position to close the gaps.

"Cruiser squadrons, close to two light-seconds and match speed as well. Dreamer, maintain formation with the cruisers, please."

"Of course, Alex. Should I charge and arm the gravity lance?"

"...No, Dreamer. Not yet. They've made no hostile moves yet, and I don't think we've seen anything yet we can't *individually* handle without it."

"How's the international picture look?" John Riken asked. "I've informed the Russians and the Chinese, and they are on board with us and standing by."

"We've alerted the other Five Eyes, of course," said DNI David Hackett. "But I think any other outreach on our part is moot. Holder's UN Delegate just broke the news in the General Assembly. He did a good job of it—urged calm, but asked that all nations be ready to respond either to incursions or for disaster relief as needed."

"Well, that's something we don't need to do, then," Riken said.

"Will you address the nation, John?" Miranda Ramirez asked.

Riken thought for a moment.

"We have to," he said. "This is *going* to get out. We need to get ahead of it. You'll help me put something together?"

"Of *course* I will, John. Did you really need to ask?"

John Riken managed a smile.

"No, Miranda," he said. "I guess I didn't."

«Hunt-Master,» said Hunter Red-Stripe on *Sharp Claws*, «the fast-ships are back. We have active sensing from them. Search only, no indication of targeting. They appear to be matching our speed, in a wide-spread bowl about two-paws *me'ka'kat* ahead of us.

«There is a second group of signals about three times more numerous, at just less than five-*te' me'ka'kat* ahead. They too appear to be matching our speed.»

Swims-Like-Rock chuckled. Broken-Tooth looked curiously at him.

«If any doubt remained that they know that we are here,» Swims-Like-Rock explained, «it is gone now. And I believe they are making certain that *we* know that they see us. But I would still *truly* love to know how they found us so fast.»

«What do we do now, then?» asked Broken-Tooth.

«Let us wait for a little,» Swims-Like-Rock replied, «and see what they do. And meanwhile, let us select some reliable, steady Hunt-Masters to exchange paw-cuffs with them.»

A few kilometers outside Moscow, General Kuskovsky's driver pulled up outside his divisional headquarters. The guards saluted as he walked in.

«General, we received maximum-alert orders in your absence,» one reported crisply.

«Yes, I know,» Kuskovsky said. «That is why I am here now.»

«Sir, what is the alert about?» the other asked. «...If it is not restricted, of course?»

Kuskovsky paused for a moment.

«The Americans,» he said. «The alert is about the Americans.»

Then he continued on inside.

"They're not doing much, are they, Sir?" said Lieutenant Megan Kerry, at DD-38 *Highlander*'s sensors board.

"They are not, Lieutenant," Colonel Mackenzie agreed. "But what I'd like tae know is whether they're waiting for something, or waiting for *us* tae do something. But at the speed they're coming, we hae plenty o' time."

«I *think*,» Swims-Like-Rock said, when nothing had happened for a little while, «perhaps this first bowl of their fast-ships is waiting to exchange paw-cuffs with us.

«So let us send out... hurrrrmmmm... *Strong Paws... Chaser... Unyielding... Swift Runner... High Flier... Long Wind... Reach Far...*»

He went on to name a dozen in all, a mix of hunt-ships and front-runners. Shortly, the named ships began to accelerate away ahead of the main formation.

Highlander reported the new activity. So, almost at the same moment, did *Arapaima, Devilfish, Hammerhead, Inazuma, Mako*, and *Seawolf*.

Alex drew a deep breath. He'd seen it too, on the tactical net.

"Okay," he mused, almost to himself, "what's your play here. What are you up to... what's on your mind?" He was pretty certain it was NOT safe to make any assumptions about these Khreetan based upon what little the Crickets had said. Or even upon the information Dreamer had provided, that the Crickets had withheld. Dreamer had passed on all the information he had about the Khreetan, but that hadn't been very much.

Still outside the orbit of Saturn, the Khreetan ships slowly approached the Fleet's leading destroyer screen.

"Let's see what their intentions are," Alex ordered. "Proportional response if fired upon. Otherwise, hold your fire."

In his divisional headquarters, General Yuri Kuskovsky called his senior staff together.

«Our country faces a crisis,» he said, bluntly. «It falls to us—all of us—to act to save Russia. I bear orders of the highest importance. The Americans are preparing to make a sneak attack against us while the space fleet is not here to stop them. But we are going to turn their strategy against them and strike first, before they are ready.

«I have been given launch orders. Validate these codes, and have your units ready to launch on my command.»

He began to read off launch authentication codes. His commanders dutifully validated them. Several had severe misgivings; this was a day

211

many of them had hoped would never come. But orders are orders, and in the rigid command heirarchy of the Russian military, orders are never to be questioned. Only obeyed.

———————

Out past the orbit of Saturn, Khreetan ships were closing in on the positions of the screening destroyers.

"Keep steady," Maksim ordered, on *Hammerhead*'s bridge. "All crew secure for hard maneuvering."

The atmosphere was tense, throughout the Fleet. But nowhere as tense as upon the twelve forward-positioned destroyers.

«They are patient,» remarked Hunt-Master Sleeps-Lightly on *Swift Runner*. «And they do not flinch as we approach. These out-clan appear stout.»

His tone was approving. Hunter Bright-Edge gave a head-jerk of assent.

«Not at all like the Violators,» he agreed. «They have *choom*.»

«Approaching firing range,» said Hunter Sharp-Whistle.

———————

"Steady, steady," Iain Colin Mackenzie said, his voice a blanket of calm reserve on the bridge. *Nothing* shook the Colin.

"Rapid scan! Targeting radar!" called out Lieutenant Chad Harper on *Hammerhead*'s sensors board.

"Stand by for full maneuvering power, negative Z, on my mark," said Maksim Chernaev. His expression was intent, deep in concentration as he waited for the exact right moment.

"They are coming in hot," Seok Dae-Hyun said calmly, on DD-44 *Arapaima*'s bridge.

"Stand by for evasive maneuvers," replied Commander Nang Tae-suk, *Arapaima*'s captain, as though discussing a Sunday afternoon stroll.

"Incoming fire!" called Kenichi Sato, on DD-29 *Devilfish*.

"Track bearing, weapons hot," Ae Morita snapped out, as she hit maximum lateral thrust. *Devilfish* slewed sideways at almost fifteen gravities, her nose swiveling to track the Khreetan hunt-ship that had just fired. The incoming railgun rounds missed by over four hundred meters.

"That seemed like light weapon fire," Ae said. "Secondary weapons free, main armament stay secured for now."

Hunter White-Nose blinked as the out-clan fast-ship dodged *sideways*, amazingly fast. His railgun burst went wide, missing the ship completely.

«How did they *do* that?» he demanded. «That looked closer to half of our *forward* acceleration!»

A moment later, a rapid BANG BANG BANG BANG BANG BANG clattered across *Strong Paws*.

«HA!» White-Nose exclaimed delightedly. «First cuff to them!» He dipped his muzzle in respect.

«Medium caliber railgun fire, no serious damage,» reported Maker Measure-Twice.

Hammerhead shot downwards, arcing in a half-circle below the Khreetan ship and coming up behind it. The Khreetan turned away hard, rolling to keep its belly away from the out-clan ship. *Hammerhead* rolled in on its tail.

"Stay on him," Maksim said. "Lock target, do not fire yet."

«Target lock!» called Hunter Torn-Ear, on *Chaser*. «But... they are not firing.»

«Ha! See if we can break their lock!» Hunt-Master Tireless ordered. He was smiling slightly. It seemed the out-clan wanted to play. This was promising to be *fun*. That was good.

Chaser maneuvered and dodged as hard as it could, Wayfinder Runs-Silently working himself into a sweat at the helm, but to no avail. The out-clan fast-ship stayed glued to them as though on a tow-tether, tracking their every maneuver.

«They are good,» Runs-Silently admitted. «*Very* good.»

"That's no' bad, laddie," chuckled Colonel Mackenzie, as railgun rounds spanged harmlessly off *Highlander*'s battle hull. "Here, hae a few o' ours in return! Weapons free. Secondaries ainly."

Highlander's railguns began to hammer out return fire.

Swift Runner arced upwards towards *Arapaima*'s belly, but *Arapaima* was no longer there. The heavier Khreetan ship could not pitch up fast enough to track a Shark-class destroyer gone suddenly to full seventy-six gravities acceleration.

«I knew Thoughtful reported that they were fast,» Hunt-Master Sleeps-Lightly said, on Swift Runner. «But I did not understand until now how fast.»

Arapaima had swapped ends by now, and was fast accelerating back inward towards *Swift Runner*, secondary railguns spitting fire that rattled across the Khreetan ship's hull.

═══════════

"Destroyer screen has engaged with the Khreetan," Sandra reported, monitoring the command channels from the front. "So far the Khreetan appear to be engaging with only light weapons."

"Then make sure we do the same," Alex said. "Relay that to all the screen ships."

"Aye," Sandra replied.

"Dreamer, what's the force balance look like?"

"We have two classes of ships identified," Dreamer replied. "The first class, which we have assumed are destroyer equivalents, I can now estimate at approximately three hundred and sixty-eight meters in length, just over one hundred meters beam, estimated displacement around three hundred and thirty thousand tonnes, plus or minus perhaps twenty thousand. Shorter than a Warlord, but about a third more massive. The second class, assumed a cruiser equivalent, is around four hundred and sixty meters by around one hundred and forty beam, estimated at five hundred and twenty five thousand tonnes plus or minus twenty-five thousand.

"So far we have seen only railgun fire not substantially different from our own secondary railguns. Visual imagery is strongly suggestive of larger caliber railguns also present. Their actual full capabilities are of course unknown."

"Except that we concluded they probably don't have hyper-boost railguns," Alex said.

"Correct, Alex," Dreamer confirmed.

Alex thought.

"They have room for a LOT of throw weight," he said. "This could easily turn ugly in a hurry."

«All launch codes confirmed, Sir,» Colonel Dubrowsky reported. «All units standing by for your order.»

General Yuri Kuskovsky took a deep breath. History would remember this moment.

«Execute launch order *Iron Feliks*,» he commanded. His officers relayed the order.

A minute later, missiles began to rise from their mobile launchers on pillars of flame, one after another, after another. First dozens, then hundreds.

«The out-clan have moved additional ships forward,» Hunt-Master Broken-Tooth reported.

«I see them,» Swims-Like-Rock confirmed. «They do not appear to be engaging. Their ships are much smaller. Perhaps they are feeling uncertain.» He thought for a moment.

«No additional response for now.»

«*Launching?!?*» Konstantin Molchalin demanded, aghast. «*WHAT DO YOU MEAN, we are launching?!?* I have issued no launch orders! Our missiles are supposed to be *locked down!*»

«I do not know how it happened, Sir,» said General Valentin Korolev. «But just over three hundred of our land-based missiles have just launched toward the United States.»

«Three HUNDRED,» Molchalin said slowly. His face went pale. «Can we countermand the missiles? Terminate them by command?»

«No, Sir,» General Korolev replied. «The range safety command would have to come from the launching batteries. There is no time to contact them all before the missiles are beyond range-safety distance.»

«Find out *HOW*, and *WHO*,» Molchalin said a moment later, as he reached for his phone with a shaking hand. «I must call the American President immediately. I do not know what I can possibly tell him to explain this.»

President John Riken and Vice-President Miranda Ramirez had just about wrapped up a first take of a hurriedly-written address. It was rough, but there wasn't time for a lot of polish.

"I'd like a re-do from that second-to-last paragraph forward, sir," the Press Secretary said. "You stumbled just a bit..."

"It will have to wait," one of the Secret Service security detail interrupted. "Sir, we need to get you and the Vice-President to the bunker. *RIGHT NOW.*"

"What?" Riken asked. "What the hell? What just happened?"

At that moment, the DNI burst into the room.

"Mr. President," he said. "The Russians have launched. We need you in the bunker."

"WHAT THE HELL?" John Riken demanded, briefly frozen in shock and betrayal. He shook himself after a moment, reaching for his phone with one hand, and for Miranda's arm with the other. The Secret Service hustled them both from the room, the DNI close behind.

Riken's phone rang before he got a chance to dial. He answered the call as they walked, before he'd looked to see who it was.

"Riken," he said, tersely.

"Mr. President," Konstantin Molchalin said urgently. "I am sorry to tell you that we have VERY BIG PROBLEM."

"President Molchalin!" Riken said. "I'll say we have a problem. *WHAT THE HELL ARE YOU DOING?!?*"

"It is not *my* doing, Mr. President," Molchalin said. "I have already ordered investigation of WHO launched missiles and WHY. Question we now both face, is how to *STOP* missiles."

The elevator to the sub-basements was twenty steps ahead.

"Kostya," John Riken said hurriedly, "I'm about to enter an elevator, we'll lose the call. I'll call you back from the bunker on a hard line."

"I *desperately* hope I will have better news for you by then, John Riken," said Konstantin Molchalin.

Then the elevator doors closed, and the call dropped.

———————————

Seawolf and *Reach Far* danced around each other in a hail of light railgun fire, rattling off each other's hulls but doing little real damage.

«Their claws match well to ours,» said Hunt-Master Good-Eyes, captain of *Reach Far*. «Let us show them a flash of our teeth as well. A single digit of power only.»

Hunter Wicked-Grin armed the particle cannon, while Wayfinder Too-Brash worked to slew *Reach Far*'s nose in line with *Seawolf*.

Secretary Jocelyn Winters tried to call Naomi from the bunker. But with Dreamer off-station on *Elegant Solution*, there was no provision in place to relay the call to her. It was an easy oversight to make.

«President Molchalin,» General Korolev said, «we have determined that all of the missiles that were launched came from General Kuskovsky's division.»

For a moment, it didn't sink in. Then Konstantin Molchalin remembered past conversations. He buried his face in his hands.

«Kuskovsky,» he groaned despairingly. «Of COURSE it was Yuri Kuskovsky. That UTTER IMBECILE.»

After a long moment, Molchalin raised his head again.

«General Kuskovsky is relieved of command, effective IMMEDIATELY,» he snapped, crisp and decisive after the moment of despair. «General Belyenov, you will take over his command. Place him under arrest and have him brought here under guard. Before he can do any *further* damage. Use ANY LEVEL OF FORCE NECESSARY. Is that clearly understood?»

«Yes, Sir,» General Vasily Belyenov replied grimly. «I will send in *spetsnaz* to place him under arrest.»

«General Korolev, order ALL of our forces to stand down until further notice. All aircraft are grounded. And Admiral Goryaev, order all of our ballistic missile submarines back to port immediately. *On the surface.* Let us try to at least avoid making this terrible situation any worse than it already is, and do our best to show some good faith.»

In the bunker, John Riken called Molchalin back from a hardwired phone.

"I need situation, fast," he said, as the call was connected. Then he heard it ring, only once, at the far end.

"John Riken," said Konstantin Molchalin. "Are you safe?"

"For now," Riken said. "What the hell is happening over there?"

"I am *very sorry*, Mr. President," Molchalin replied. "One of my Generals has gone rogue, as you say. I have relieved him of command and ordered him placed under arrest. But that will not stop missiles. There is nothing that we can do, except to hope that you can stop them somehow. It is out of our hands. I have ordered all of our armed forces to stand down. I cannot express how sorry I am."

Riken sighed heavily.

"I understand, Kostya," he said. "I'm not sure whose shoes I least want to be in right now—my own, or yours."

He lowered the phone for a moment.

"Options, people," he said. "What have we got?"

On the other end of the call, Konstantin Molchalin was also thinking fast.

———————————

Reach Far's nose swung into line at last, and the particle cannon fired, at low power. The charged-particle burst washed across *Seawolf's* lower hull.

"What in all the saints was that?" demanded Commander Julio Dominguez. "Status."

"Railgun mounts five, six, nine, and eleven down, flagging soft malfunctions," Lieutenant Eduardo Torres said, at the damage-control board. "No other damage. Attempting to reboot them."

"Looked like some kind of charged-particle weapon," Lieutenant Juan Espinoza, on sensors, reported. "Picked up an energy spike right before it fired."

"We just saw a new weapon in action," Julio reported on the command channel. "Seems to be a charged-particle weapon. Knocked four of our railguns offline. We're trying to bring them back up."

"Charging again, I think," Juan Espinoza said.

218

«And it will not be coming back without an in-nest repair,» Maker Already-Done added. «Cannon control reports some arc burns, no serious injuries.»

«A coherent radiation weapon,» Listens-Carefully declared, still studying his readouts at the sensors board. «Tremendously powerful. But only a brief burst.»

Hunt-Master Tireless began to chuckle.

«I think,» he laughed, «we just got our nose swatted like a disobedient cub.» Then his tone turned more serious.

«Imagine,» he mused, «if they had been firing that weapon the whole time they did that.» It was a grim thought.

«We would be a wreck,» Already-Done agreed.

"*They WHAT?!?*" Alex demanded. "Oh, gods, why *NOW* of all times? You *GODDAMNED IDIOTS!!!*" He buried his face in his hands. He wanted to weep. Had all of this been for *nothing*?

"When the cat's away," Sandra commented bitterly, "the mice will play."

Alex sighed in frustration and despair.

"I know," he said. "But I didn't expect anyone to be *THIS* fucking *stupid*."

"Colonel Warner stated that defensive batteries are readying to engage the missiles," Dreamer reminded Alex. "The ammunition supply is nearly unlimited. There is a high probability that none will get through. There is a risk, of course, of accidental overshot striking surface targets. There will probably be numerous misses."

"We need to focus on the Khreetan," Sandra broke in. "Trust John to handle the missiles."

Alex nodded slowly.

"You're right, Sandra," he agreed. "Thank all gods the Stardock was in the right part of its orbit to be able to engage. An hour earlier or two hours later, and we'd be looking at a catastrophe."

"They have shown us some of their heavy weapons," Commander Jeanne Petrie said on DD-21 *Sailfish*. "Let us do the same." Railgun fire was hammering across *Sailfish*'s hull, making a lot of noise but doing only minor damage. "I want one round per gun, a clean miss across their bow."

"Aye, Ma'am," Lieutenant Franz Blick acknowledged, at main gunnery control. "One round per gun, clean miss." The spinal railguns whined as they charged.

The moment before they fired, a chance Khreetan railgun round entered the firing port of the portside railgun. It skated down the side of the bore, spalling away debris, and met *Sailfish*'s outgoing projectile a third of the way down. The two projectiles wedged together, *Sailfish*'s far more massive projectile driving the Khreetan's and pieces of its own disintegrating sabot into the railgun's drive coils.

An obstructed bore ranges from 'bad' to 'catastrophic' in any kind of projectile weapon with a closed bore. With a hyper-boosted railgun, it was definitely at the catastrophic end of that scale. The railgun not only tore itself and its twin apart, it wrecked power runs—and nearly everything else —in the compartments around it... including crew unfortunate enough to be in those compartments. Artificial gravity and acceleration compensation went down throughout the forward half of *Sailfish*, the main bridge included, and the entire ship shuddered. Safety interlocks shut off the main drive the instant the acceleration compensation died. That still wasn't fast enough to prevent unsecured crew in the forward hull being thrown hard against bulkheads and consoles.

The starboard gun's one round *did* escape the bore before the gun was wrecked. It passed across *High Flier*'s bow a kilometer ahead, too fast for any eye to see, but radar caught it for a moment.

«They just fired a...» Hunter Always-Laughs' voice trailed off. He was *not* laughing this time. «I am not sure what. I *think* perhaps a railgun of... *astounding* power from such a small ship. I am certain it was a deliberate miss. It would have *HURT*, badly, had it hit us.»

He broke off, studying his board again.

«But... I think they are in trouble. They are no longer under acceleration. I think something went wrong. They are bleeding air.» He checked another set of read-outs. «It looks much the same as ours. Only slightly different composition.»

«Cease fire,» Hunt-Master Helpful ordered. «Secure all weapons. Maintain this separation and stand by. Match their speed and heading. Let us be ready in case they need assistance. Notify Den and Fleet that we are sheathing our claws.»

"What *happened?*" Jeanne Petrie demanded. "Damage control status. Now."

"Artificial gravity throughout the front half of the ship is down," Mario Cardinale replied, at damage control. "Looks like the portside railgun blew up somehow. Both main guns are down for the count. We are venting atmo forward. Emergency bulkheads are sealing."

Jeanne nodded grimly. She opened the shipwide emergency channel.

"Evacuate all compartments with no gravity," she ordered. "Transfer command to the secondary CIC. All crew report your status. Secondary sensors, what's the Khreetan doing?"

"Khreetan ship has ceased fire and is holding position twenty klicks off our starboard side," came the reply. "Parallel heading."

"Notify *Scorpionfish* that we have had a major railgun malfunction and need assistance as soon as possible."

━━━━━━━

As the Stardock rose up toward the pole in its orbit, the first missiles came into view. The track wasn't optimal, and the firing window would be narrow. But it ought to be *enough*—as long as they could hit the missiles before they passed out of line of fire.

"Tracking targets," reported Gunner Bosanquet.

"Commence fire," Colonel Warner ordered. "Don't let a single one through. Take those goddamn missiles *out*. But watch your line of fire. We can't risk hitting cities on the ground with overshot."

The heavy railguns in the Stardock's defensive emplacements opened up, and fifty seconds later, the skies above the Arctic Ocean began to fill with streaks of fire.

━━━━━━━

On *Scorpionfish's* bridge, Commodore Jabari Ndungu listened to *Sailfish's* distress call.

"Piet," he ordered, "get *Snoak* in there and assist *Sailfish*. They may have wounded needing medical assistance. Toivo, take *Moray* in and cover them."

Snoak and *Moray* short-jumped in and went to *Sailfish's* aid.

«Two more fast-ships have arrived,» Always-Laughs reported. «They are not firing on us.»

223

«Keep us nearby,» Helpful ordered, «but open up to... double the distance. Make it clear we do not intend any interference. Perhaps they will understand that we are here to help if it is needed.»

As *High Flier* backed slowly away, *Snoak* came alongside *Sailfish* and moved into position to dock. Meanwhile, *Moray* took an overwatch position five kilometers 'above'.

"Microjump," Commander Ruth Goldin said on *Livyatan*'s bridge. "We need to get in there and support *Arapaima*. Put us as close as you can hit it to two hundred klicks off her beam. We'll stand by there."

"Jumping, Ma'am," said Lieutenant Kim Rogers, at helm.

Twenty seconds later, *Livyatan* skipped briefly into hyperspace, and almost immediately out again. Lieutenant Rogers' microjump was only about forty kilometers off.

Livyatan arrived just in time to see it happen—but not close enough to see exactly *what* happened. It was a classic golden BB. *Arapaima* and the Khreetan hunter-ship were counter-maneuvering against one another, exchanging light fire, the hammer-blows of the Khreetan railguns marching along the Tier 3 hullplate but doing no significant damage—all except for the last.

Arapaima almost slipped out of its path as it turned away on another evasive arc, but not quite. The railgun round hit the flat surface of the main drive thrusters at a steep angle, and the drive vanes funneled it into a shot trap. With nowhere to go but *in*, it blew through the thruster array and one of the power connection pass-throughs in the flintsteel bulkhead behind it, blasting a shower of high-energy shrapnel into the main drive power feeds, a large chunk of the back side of the thruster exploding away in fragments from the impact site. Power arced across the ruptured feeds and the drive bus flickered, triggering a violent lurch that the artificial gravity barely compensated for fast enough.

That would have been a serious, but not mortal, blow had *Arapaima* not then passed directly across the Khreetan's bow, quartering away, at only about a hundred kilometers range, just as the Khreetan's main particle cannon fired. It was only a partial-power shot, but the particle cannon bolt splashed across *Arapaima*'s stern, and across the new hull breach. And *through* the breach, straight into the already unstable main drive bus. As the drive faltered, and the power automation tried to compensate, the particle bolt induced a massive surge that flashed back up the heavy power feeds, *through* the control regulators intended to regulate power going *out*, already struggling to control the wild arcing, and straight into the reactor's output governors.

Reverse feedback overloaded the governors. The surge burst into the antimatter containment coils. The containment field rang like a bell.

Chief Engineer Peter Arcie saw the governors spike as the back-surge hammered through them. Saw containment strength fluctuate, spike, then plummet.

There was no time for chain-of-command. He opened the ship-wide emergency channel. *That* also automatically relayed to squadron priority channel.

"LOSING CONTAINMENT!" he shouted, as he remote-triggered ejection of both emergency beacons, while the containment field intensity bounced and spiked back up again, far over safety limits. "GET TO LIFE PO—"

He never finished the word. The containment fields in the antimatter reactor overloaded and failed catastrophically, matter met unrestrained antimatter, and *Arapaima* blew up, a brilliant miniature nova. Its battle-steel hull contained the gigantic explosion for only the briefest instant.

In a single moment, the destroyer was gone, and a hundred and ninety six men and women with it, all dead before they knew it, intermingled with the emergency beacons in a single expanding globe of glowing plasma and hard radiation.

In the Arctic Ocean, north of Murmansk, the crew of the icebreaker *Mikhail Lermontov* looked up at a sky filled with streaks of fire, punctuated with occasional brilliant flashes.

«What is happening up there?» Anatoly Borodin asked, standing on *Lermontov*'s foredeck, just in front of the superstructure. He wasn't really expecting any answer. The question was rhetorical.

«I do not know,» said the crew-woman standing next to him, Olga Komarovna. «But I am very glad that it seems to be happening *very far* up there.»

In the distance, a streak came down and plunged into the ocean. Anatoly thought he saw a high plume of water and spray where the streak ended.

«I hope it stays that way,» he said. «But I am perhaps not so sure.»

==================

"Sir!" Lieutenant Morgan, *Perth*'s comms officer, said urgently. "We just picked up a brief, fragmentary emergency message from *Arapaima*. Only about three seconds worth. They—"

His voice broke off. He listened. His face paled.

"Sir," he said slowly, his voice tense. "That was *Livyatan*. *Arapaima* is *gone*. No life pods, Sir."

On board *Swift Runner* as it turned away, all of the sensors on the side towards *Arapaima* whited out. The bridge tactical display saturated for several seconds. When it slowly cleared, the alien fast-ship was gone. Where it had been was a huge, glaringly brilliant fireball, still expanding. Wayfinder No-*This*-Path turned the hunter-ship hard away from it.

«The fast-ship,» said Hunter Sharp-whistle. «It is destroyed. Completely.»

«Did we misjudge?» asked Hunter Bright-Edge, guiltily. «Did something go wrong with them? Did we paw-cuff too *hard*?»

«Such an explosion,» Maker Sometimes-Too-Clever, the chief engineer, said slowly. «That was not light-atom merging. Perhaps... they have somehow mastered using reversed matter for power. I can think of no other *possible* explanation.»

«Perhaps that is how their ships are so fast, then,» Sharp-Whistle mused distractedly, still shocked.

As *Swift Runner* curved away from the still-swelling fireball, *Livyatan* arced around from behind it, masked until then from *Swift Runner*'s sensors by the plasma. The hunter-ship was almost dead ahead, at only about eighty kilometers range.

"Target locked," said Lieutenant Mitch Hendricks. "We've got them dead bang."

"Main guns," Ruth Goldin ordered. "Two rounds per gun. *Fire*."

The tactical display on *Swift Runner*'s bridge cleared.

«NEW CONTACT DIRECTLY BEHIND US!» Sharp-Whistle called urgently. «A second fast-ship!»

"Firing," said Hendricks. *WheeEEE-**WHAMWHAM***, went the twin spinal railguns, then *wheeEEE-**WHAMWHAM*** again, the harmonic whine of charging punctuated by the ship-jarring jolts of the hyper-boosted railguns firing. At this range, flight time was only eight hundredths of a second.

Something almighty hammered at *Swift Runner's* flank. The hollow **BOOM** echoed through the ship.

«Glancing hit, hindquarter,» Sharp-whistle said, «hull integ—»

Then *Swift Runner* bucked violently, there was a thunderous, tearing **CRASH** that seemed to come from several regions of the ship almost at once, and all of the lights went out. So did the artificial gravity.

After a couple of seconds, the emergency lighting flickered and came up, bathing everything in dim green. There was a crackle from somewhere.

«What is our condition?» Hunt-Master Sleeps-Lightly called out, after a moment.

«Main power is down,» said Sometimes-Too-Clever. «...Permanently, I think. Give me... a moment... *Work*, curse you...»

The crackle came up again. Then it resolved into urgent voices. «Shipboard emergency communications functioning,» he said. «For now. I cannot say how long.»

«All stations, report, by station,» called Hunt-Master Sleeps-Lightly.

"Solid hit, sir," Lieutenant Hendricks reported.

"Target is no longer under way," said Astrid Eriksen, on sensors. "They're venting atmo. A *lot* of it. Forward and aft. And I see debris plumes from both ends."

"Cease fire and hold station," Goldin ordered. "I think we hit them *bad*."

Swift Runner was dead in space. Whatever hit them had breached the armored hull, then gone through the entire ship from one end to the other, then blown its way out through the particle cannon. Main power, drive, hyperdrive, life support, artificial gravity were all down, and they wouldn't be coming back. Several sections did not answer. Two of the four fusion reactors were dead, and controls for the other two were not responding.

It took Sleeps-Lightly only a moment to make the decision.

«Abandon ship,» he ordered. «All living crew to survival nests. If you have no route to a survival nest, say so NOW. We will *do our best* to get you out.»

A few minutes later, life pods began ejecting from *Swift Runner*. They spread outward away from the ship, then began curving around to collect into a loose swarm some distance away.

"They're abandoning ship, Ma'am," Astrid reported. *Livyatan* had closed to within twenty kilometers by now and was almost stationary relative to the crippled hunt-ship.

"Monitor the situation," Ruth said. "We'll stay nearby to render assistance."

Twenty-nine pods left the ship, then a thirtieth, and a thirty-first... then a violent explosion tore the rear half of *Swift Runner* open, leaving the gutted remains of the hull spinning slowly away. The last two pods out were caught in the blast and hurled away, tumbling end over end in different directions.

To no-one's surprise, no more pods emerged.

"That last pod is venting air, Ma'am," said Astrid. "And clearly out of control. *Both* of the last two look out of control."

"Life signs?" Ruth asked.

"Hard to be sure, Ma'am," Astrid replied. "But I would say yes."

Ruth Goldin thought for only a moment.

"We're going after them," she said. "The worst damaged one first. Lieutenant Finnegan, I want your men armored up and standing by to bring it aboard in the portside boat bay."

Livyatan came about and turned to follow the pod.

«How many made it out?» Sleeps-Lightly asked quietly.

«Two-*te'*-five pods have joined the swarm,» said Sometimes-Too-Clever. «Awaiting crew counts. I saw two more pods eject, but pod two-*te'*-seven says they are tumbling and have no directional control. No communication at all with the last.»

«Out of three-*te'*-six,» Sleeps-Lightly said somberly. Sometimes-Too-Clever nodded. «But we are still better off than their fast-ship. I am certain *no-one* got out of that. This has been a bad day for both of us.»

«The beacon is active?» Sleeps-lightly asked.

228

«It is,» Sometimes-Too-Clever confirmed.

«Then we sit, and we wait for pickup,» Sleeps-Lightly said.

After trying for nearly half an hour to get *Sailfish* back at least moving again from secondary CIC, Jeanne Petrie called it quits and gave the abandon-ship order. The artificial gravity system was just too badly shredded, and the safety interlocks would not allow any power to the main drive with G-compensation down through nearly half the habitable volume of the ship, and personnel unaccounted for in some of those compartments. It was a prudent safety measure, in a ship capable of accelerating at seventy-six gravities. Without G-compensation, even the maneuvering thrusters could easily kill crew members. But in this particular corner case, it meant that *Sailfish* could not be brought back under way.

Snoak was firmly docked by then, so abandoning ship was just a matter of walking from *Sailfish*'s portside docking port into *Snoak*'s. More than three quarters of the ship's complement made it off under their own power; but thirty-two wounded had to be carried off and straight to MedBay, and sixteen others were carried off dead. Fourteen of the wounded had to be transferred to *Moray* because *Snoak*'s medical bay was full.

Twelve crew were unaccounted for. They had been in forward service compartments directly adjacent to the portside spinal railgun when it ripped itself and its twin apart. The savage gravitational gradients hadn't left much to recover, and nobody could get into the wrecked compartments without heavy equipment anyway. The damage control drones that did manage to get into some of the most heavily damaged areas reported no-one alive in there.

The whole time, the Khreetan ship sat by, forty kilometers away, its nose pointed well away from the three Sharks, making no hostile move.

On *Mikhail Lermontov*'s foredeck, Anatoly flinched visibly as a streak of light slammed down out of the sky *just barely* short of a small iceberg floating a couple of kilometers off the starboard bow. The iceberg blew apart in a rising cloud of fragments. Some of them were large. After a couple of seconds, it became clear that one large piece, perhaps a hundred and twenty meters in size, was flying in a high arc nearly directly towards

Lermontov. Anatoly could not take his eyes off it. He reached out blindly toward Olga, on his left, as thunder from the strike rolled over the icebreaker.

The huge chunk of ice soared closer, apparently headed directly for them. Anatoly felt Olga squeeze his hand convulsively. Then at almost the last second, it seemed to dip, plunging into the water some three hundred meters off the icebreaker's beam. *Lermontov* rolled hard as the wave struck it, and heavy, icy-cold spray rained down, soaking Anatoly and Olga. A large fish landed on the deck nearby with a wet *smack*. About twenty seconds later, the massive icy missile bobbed slowly to the surface about a hundred meters off the starboard side, now in multiple pieces.

«*Bozhe moi,*» Anatoly muttered shakenly. He managed to turn his gaze away and look at Olga. She was staring, white-faced, at the bobbing ice. Then she slowly turned to look back at him.

«I need *DRINK,*» she said, quietly, almost calmly, but *very* distinctly. Anatoly found himself quite impressed at how steady her voice was. «Perhaps *several* drinks.»

———————

«I cannot get control,» Has-Doubts said, on board pod three-*te'*-one. «And our communication is also dead. We cannot signal. I cannot even stop the tumble.»

«It will not matter,» said Reads-Too-Much grimly, «after this leak drains our reserve air. I cannot seal it. We will be dead in a sixth part of a day, tumbling or not.»

Too-Cautious, next to the entry hatch with its viewport, said nothing. Halfway up the pod, Steady-Paws sat silently watching them, holding a dressing patch against one mid-arm. Dark blood seeped through it in spots. Whatever piece of debris had breached the pod, a part of it had ended up in his arm. The injury was not serious. It was the least of their worries at the moment.

———————

The short squad of eight Spetsnaz double-timed up to the door guards at General Kuskovsky's division headquarters. The guards moved to block their passage, but the Captain leading the squad simply curtly said, «We have direct orders from the President. Stand aside, or we will shoot you.»

The guards hesitated for only a moment before prudently stepping aside.

About ninety seconds later, the eight marched straight up to General Kuskovsky's war room. They issued the same ultimatum, and again, the guards glanced at each other, then stood aside.

The door was locked. No matter; the lead man simply kicked it open. They walked in with weapons raised and aimed. None of the officers in the room moved, except for Kuskovsky.

«What is this?» Kuskovsky demanded.

«Yuri Ilyich Kuskovsky,» the *spetsnaz* Captain said flatly. «By personal order of the President of the Russian Federation, you are relieved of command and placed under arrest for treason.»

«Treason?» Kuskovsky said. «I have saved—»

«Shut. Up,» said the Captain, distinctly, placing his finger on the trigger of his PP-19 Vityaz submachinegun.

Kuskovsky shut up.

«You are now all under the command of General Belyenov,» the *spetsnaz* Captain declared. «He will be here shortly to take over. Order all of your units to stand down. Do *nothing* else until he arrives. This is a direct order from the President himself.»

———————

Above the Arctic, the hail of railgun fire slacked off, then stopped. The gun rooms reported no more targets with clear line-of-fire. Three hundred and fifteen missiles had been recorded destroyed. Three re-entry vehicles remained, two of them with no line of fire. Trying to hit the third would turn into a railgun bombardment of the US eastern seaboard.

"NORAD says three warheads left," Rear-Admiral David Hackett reported. "One's most likely targeted at Minot, North Dakota. One's headed for Elmendorf. And one's coming right here."

"Christ," John Riken said. He felt ten years older in the last thirty minutes. "Can we stop them?"

"Maybe," Hackett replied. "Fort Greely has already launched full GBI salvos on the western two, and CG-67 *Shiloh* is off Annapolis and in position to engage the third. But it's a tough shoot for the SM-3."

"Cross your fingers, Admiral," John Riken sighed. "Cross your fingers."

===============

Eight ground-based interceptors screamed skyward from Fort Greely, Alaska, four heading north-east, the other four somewhat west of north. The more northerly four reached their target first. The first kinetic-kill warhead was a clean miss; the second, a direct hit. The other two didn't matter, after that.

Forty-four seconds later, the second salvo intercepted the warhead headed for Minot. The first of the four missed. So did the second.

The third *just barely* clipped the incoming re-entry vehicle. At a closing speed of nearly thirteen kilometers a second, that was enough.

The fourth, and last, flew on unneeded.

"Two down, Mr. President," Hackett reported. "One left. Ours."

Two miles off Annapolis harbor, USS *Shiloh* launched three SM-3 Standard missiles, one after the other. They streaked skyward, heading north.

The first missile was a clean miss, detonating behind the incoming warhead, a faster-moving target than it was designed to intercept. The second was nearer, but still detonated too late.

The third was *close*. Close *enough*. It detonated almost directly in front of the incoming warhead, close enough that the warhead flew through the fireball.

The warhead kept coming. But the SM-3's near-miss tumbled it. Destabilized and coming in at over eight kilometers a second, in dense lower atmosphere, the aerodynamic forces on it as it tumbled were tremendous, creating shock loadings of hundreds of gravities that shook the warhead like a terrier shaking a rat. Within seconds, its firing circuits were electronic scrap.

The warhead came screaming down out of the sky over Washington DC, still supersonic, a spiralling white vapor trail behind it, and plunged into the Potomac, throwing up a huge plume of water that nearly swamped the small boat that it had almost hit. The sonic boom rolled over the city.

Nothing else happened.

"Last warhead is a dud, Mr. President," DNI Hackett reported. "Seen to strike the Potomac, failed to detonate. Presumed soft kill."

John Riken sagged into his chair and let out a huge, shuddering sigh. After a moment, he raised the phone, as the room broke out in cheering.

"Kostya?" he said, shakily.

"John," said Konstantin Molchalin, concern plain in his voice. "Are you all alright there?"

"We're still here, Kostya," Riken said. "We're still here. We got them all. Us and the Stardock. We got the last three. The last one is cooling off in the Potomac right now."

"That is best news I have had this year," Molchalin said, heaving a sigh of relief himself. "*Bozhe moi*, I need a DRINK."

"You and me both, Kostya," John Riken agreed fervently. "You and me both." He gathered his thoughts for a moment. "Did you solve your rogue-general problem?"

"Not fully, yet," Molchalin replied grimly. "The *spetsnaz* who were sent to place him under arrest are on their way back here with him now. I have relieved him of command and replaced him with a general whom I *trust*. I should have done it months ago. Then this would not have happened. This is my mistake, and I accept full blame for it. It is on my head.

"Mr. President?"

"Yes?"

"Please get your proposed nuclear treaty written up and ready to be signed. This cannot *EVER* happen again."

"I'll drink to that, Kostya. I'd better let you go and finish dealing with your problem."

"We will speak soon, John. Farewell for now."

Molchalin hung up.

John Riken looked around the room.

"I think we need to update that address now," he said. Miranda Ramirez nodded agreement. "And god, I need a drink."

———————————

Livyatan matched course and speed with the leaking pod.

"Pod status?" Ruth asked.

"Still venting," Astrid Eriksen said. "Slightly reduced rate, but only slightly. Their air is mostly oxy-nitrogen, the same as ours. Looks like a trace of helium."

Ruth Goldin nodded.

"Match spin and bring them aboard," she said. "Let's see if we can patch their leak. Then we'll go and retrieve the other one."

"They just destroyed *Arapaima*," Mitch Hendricks said.

"I know," Ruth Goldin replied. "But we're not leaving them to die. 'Those in peril on the sea,' Lieutenant."

Lt. Hendricks nodded. Lt. Kim Rogers matched *Livyatan*'s spin to the tumbling pod.

Too-Cautious looked up, then peered out through the viewport.

«The second fast-ship,» he said. «It is right next to us. And they have matched our tumble. Their ship-pilot is *good*.»

«Perhaps they plan to capture us,» Reads-Too-Much said. «Perhaps we will not die today after all.»

«This will be... interesting,» said Has-Doubts.

«Do you have any idea what they hit us with?» Too-Cautious asked.

«I do not,» Has-Doubts replied. «But it wrecked half *Swift Runner*'s heart and spine in a single hit. A terrifying weapon.»

Then there came some muffled THUDs on the hull. Too-Cautious caught a glimpse of a four-limbed shape passing next to the port. After a moment, the pod began to move slowly towards the fast-ship... then passed inside. After a few moments, weight returned. Less than normal... perhaps three fourths of normal, he estimated. The pod rolled slightly before it settled into a stable position.

"Pod secured, Sir," reported Lieutenant Finnegan.

"Very good," Ruth Goldin acknowledged. "OK, let's chase down the second one. And get a patch on that leak before they lose too much air."

Livyatan came about and went after the second pod.

There were a large number of the four-limbed aliens around the pod. Most of them were in hard suits of some kind, but after a few minutes another in what seemed to be a lighter pressure suit appeared. It seemed to be guiding and controlling a floating machine. The machine floated toward the damaged corner of the pod.

Reads-Too-Much backed away suddenly from the breach, trying to wipe sticky black material from his upperhand. A large blob of the material was extruding from the breach. It smelled terrible. After a moment, a hot-metal smell came from that corner of the pod.

«They are *patching* our pod,» Reads-Too-Much realized. «Repairing it. I think we will not die this day.»

Too-Cautious was fiddling with the panel next to the hatch.

«Their air is breathable,» he pronounced after a minute or so. «A little thin, but safely breathable.»

«It stands to reason,» Has-Doubts said, «that if their weightforce is less, then so would be their air pressure.»

After a short while, the hot-metal smell began to fade, and the smell of the black sealant became a little less sharp.

«Pod air pressure... is stable,» Too-Cautious declared. Outside, the unarmored alien was walking away, the floating machine following him.

Too-Cautious made a decision. He made a few more adjustments on the panel. After a few more minutes, Has-Doubts felt his ears pop slightly.

«What are you doing?» he asked. Two of the other crew who had made it to the pod complained as well.

«Matching our pressure to theirs,» said Too-Cautious.

«Why?» asked Reads-Too-Much.

«So that I can open the hatch,» said Too-Cautious. And he pulled the unlocking bar.

The hatch unlocked and swung open.

«What are you *DOING*?» Has-Doubts asked, again.

«Thanking them,» said Too-Cautious. And he bent and ducked carefully out through the hatch.

Rifleman Patrick Hess saw the hatch unlock and swing into the pod.

"Activity!" he called, on the squad channel, his hands on his rifle. Then something came out of the hatch and stood up.

The—Khreetan, he assumed—was a little over two meters tall, standing upright on the hindmost of three pairs of limbs. The other two were held down at its sides.

"We have an alien in the open, in the boat bay," Hess said. "Not making any hostile moves so far." Half a dozen more of his squad shifted positions, moving to spots where they had a clear line of fire just in case. Hess looked at the Khreetan. It was chunky, built like a six-limbed bear, and looked formidably strong. It had a shortish muzzle, and long ears like an anteater, and from what he could see from this angle, most of the top and back side of its head—and the backs of what little he could see of its body and limbs—were armored with bright red-orange scales. Its eyes looked very black. He wasn't sure he could see any pupils.

The Khreetan stood motionless for roughly a count of ten, then took two slow steps forward and stopped again. Then it raised its middle pair of arms and slowly extended them forward, spread slightly wider than its body, 'hands' spread open. Pat could see that it had six... *digits* on each hand, split into two opposed groups of three. They were thick and looked very strong. He thought he saw they had blunt claws.

The Khreetan made a sound like a coughing bark, and waited. Pat wasn't sure what to do. It made the sound again, waited another few seconds, then lowered its... hands, took another half-step forward, then raised its hands and made the same sound again.

"I think it's trying to say hello," he said on squad push. "I'm going to try to respond."

"Be damned CAREFUL, Hess," Lieutenant Finnegan said.

Hess released his rifle, and its sling self-stowed it against his back. He took three slow steps forward, which put him a short distance in front of the Khreetan. From here he could see a second Khreetan looking out through the open hatch.

He took a deep breath, reached out his hands, and took the Khreetan's hands loosely. The Khreetan closed its hands, gripping his armored hands firmly but not tightly. Yes, those *were* claws, short but thick, and they looked as though they could do some serious damage. From this range Pat could see complex pupils that seemed to have three... lobes? Kind of like cephalopod eyes, except one better, he thought to himself. The pupils were not easy to see.

Pat activated his external speaker.

"Hallo," he said. "Welcome to *Livyatan*."

The Khreetan said something that Pat could not understand. Then it released his hands and took a step back. It half-turned towards the pod, looked at the patched corner, raised an upper hand, and pointed emphatically at the patch with its open hand. Then it turned back to face

236

Pat, spread all four arms wide with its hands open, then closed its hands as it drew its arms in to its chest. Then it lowered its muzzle slightly, then pointed an open upper hand again at the patch.

"Uh... You're welcome...?" Pat said, returning the nod.

"Preparing to bring the second pod aboard," said Lieutenant Finnegan. Pat glanced quickly out the open hatch. Indeed, *Livyatan* had already matched spin with the second pod. "Hess, can we get that alien back into the pod?"

"Let me try, Sir," Pat replied. He looked back at the Khreetan, then raised his left hand—open, like the Khreetan's—and pointed out through the open bay hatch. The Khreetan turned and looked out at the relatively stationary pod and the wheeling stars. It looked that way for a long moment, then turned back to Pat. He mimed bringing an object closer, then pointed at the Khreetan and gestured back into the pod.

After a long moment, the Khreetan gave a quick upward jerk of its head, then pointed outside at the second pod with an upper hand, then slowly brought its hand back to point at the open area of deck in front of the opening, then made the head-jerk again. *I think that might be a 'yes'?*, Pat thought to himself. *Or perhaps 'I understand.'* He tried to copy the head-jerk, not an easy thing in battle armor.

The Khreetan gave one more head-jerk, then turned around, walked back to the pod, and ducked to go inside. Pat noticed as it turned that there was a smaller pair of secondary eyes located behind its ears. It closed the hatch after it.

"Well, congratulations, Hess," said Lieutenant Finnegan. "I think you just made a successful first contact with the Khreetan."

"Alex, sitrep," John Warner reported. "Crisis is over at this end. We got all but three of the missiles, and ground-based defenses took out the last three. Everyone is safe."

Alex drew in a deep breath, held it, then let it out slowly.

"Thank you, John," he said fervently. "I think *everyone* owes you one. And Tom. If Tom hadn't thought about that...?"

"I know," Tom agreed. "I know. How's it going out there?"

"I'm not sure," Alex replied. "There's been some skirmishing, but... they're just not fighting very *hard*. And in fact it almost seems as though they're trying to *show us* that they're not fighting as hard as they could be.

"We've lost two ships. *Sailfish* had an apparent spinal railgun malfunction and is dead in space, but *Snoak* says most of the crew made it off, though they have nearly thirty missing or dead—twelve still unaccounted for—and about the same number injured. *Arapaima*..." He hesitated, unwilling to say it. "*Arapaima* was lost with all hands. *Livyatan* says it looked like their reactor blew. *Livyatan* scragged the ship that killed *Arapaima* and reports picking up survivors from it. Their main formation isn't doing *anything*. That's about all I can tell you right now."

"Picking up survivors," Tom mused. "Well, *that'll* be interesting." Then he realized.

"*Arapaima*," he said. "Christ. Dong-geun's son."

"I *know*," Alex said somberly. "I'm not looking forward to telling him."

———

«They are about to bring a second survival pod aboard,» said Too-Cautious. «This one too is tumbling badly.» He could see the armored alien still standing a short distance in front of the pod.

«Damaged also?» Has-Doubts mused. «Are they... retrieving our *damaged* pods?»

«I think perhaps so,» Too-Cautious agreed. «Perhaps retrieving and *repairing*.» He pointed toward the repair. «It is not *just* that black sealant. They welded a patch over the breach from the outside, as well. The black sealant just makes certain it is airtight, I think.»

Then the gravity cut off again. Too-Cautious peered out through the viewport. Shortly afterward, a group of the armored aliens appeared, guiding the other pod between them. They set it down on the deck, turning it around so that the hatch and viewport faced their own. A little longer, and the gravity came back on. Too-Cautious waited until he saw another crewman looking across the gap from the other pod, then raised his upperhands and signed 'All safe here'. The other—he thought it might be Knows-Things, from life support, but it was hard to be sure—signed back the same. Too-Cautious waved to get the other's attention, then pointed toward the repair. The other peered that way, looked surprised for a moment, then thoughtful, then signed back, 'Good'. Too-Cautious jerked his head in agreement, then he stepped away from the hatch and sat down again.

"Both pods are safely secured aboard, Captain," Lieutenant Finnegan reported. "And the breach on the more badly damaged one has been sealed and patched."

"Thank you, Lieutenant," Ruth Goldin said.

"And there's something else you should know, Captain," Finnegan continued.

"Yes? Go on."

"We, uh, seem to have had a successful—and peaceful—first contact with the Khreetan, Sir. One of them came out of the first pod, and one of my Marines, Rifleman Hess in Squad Two, managed to communicate with it a little. Just signs. And we got a pretty good look at it. They look something like what you might get if you crossed a six-armed bear with a pangolin."

"Huh," Ruth said, thoughtfully. "Thank you, Lieutenant. I want to THOROUGHLY debrief Rifleman Hess a little later, while everything is fresh in his mind."

"Understood, Ma'am. I'll give him a heads-up."

"OK, people," Ruth said. "We have both pods aboard. Now let's head back to where the other pods seemed to be swarming. I'm not confident either of them can maneuver, so we'll keep watch over them until a rescue ship shows up, then drop the pods off and back off."

———————————

The *spetsnaz* team frog-marched Yuri Kuskovsky into Konstantin Molchalin's cabinet room and forced him to his knees. Molchalin, amid his staff, turned around and stared at him.

«Yuri Ilyich Kuskovsky,» he said slowly. «You utmost *IDIOT*. What in Chernebog's name did you think you were *DOING*?»

«I saved our country,» Kuskovsky said defiantly. «From the Americans. From *your WEAKNESS*. History will vindicate me.»

«History will vindicate *nothing*, fool,» Molchalin replied. «To my everlasting relief, the Stardock shot down your missiles. All but three, and the Americans got those last three themselves. History will record you as a misguided traitor to Russia, who tried to start a third world war that Russia could not possibly win.»

Yuri Kuskovsky began to protest, but Konstantin Molchalin wasn't listening. He looked at the *spetsnaz* squad leader.

«Execute him,» he ordered coldly.

239

Without a moment's hesitation, the *spetsnaz* Captain clicked his fire selector to semi-auto and calmly triggered two quick shots into the back of Yuri Kuskovsky's head.

Molchalin nodded.

«Thank you, Captain,» he said. «Your team have served Russia and the world this day. Now... please get this trash out of my cabinet room. We will speak later.»

«Sir,» the Captain nodded. Then his team picked up Kuskovsky's dead body and carried him away.

———————

Thirty minutes later, *Livyatan* was holding station five kilometers away from the group of pods.

"Stay alert, everyone," Ruth said. Let's not get caught napping."

———————

«Sir,» Sometimes-Too-Clever said, «I have pod two-*te'*-seven again. Strong signal. They are saying...» He broke off and made his way between the other bridge crew to the hatch, and peered out through the viewport.

«Yes,» he continued, «I can see it. The second fast-ship—it is sitting no more than perhaps two-*te' me'kat* away.» He pointed, indicating the direction. «They picked up pod two-*te'*-seven. Rescued them. And pod three-*te'*-one as well. And they *patched a breach* in three-*te'*-one. Three-*te'*-one seems to have no communications, but Knows-Things on two-*te'*-seven says he can see Too-Cautious and others through the hatch. They have spoken briefly in the out-clans' docking bay, and Too-Cautious says they're all fine. And that the out-clan seem... friendly.»

Sleeps-Lightly at last began to smile slightly.

«Perhaps we did not lose quite as many this day as we thought,» he said.

———————

«I think we have all we need to know of their measure,» Swims-Like-Rock said, aboard *Sharp Claws*. «There have been... mishaps. *Swift Runner* lost, and one, perhaps two, of theirs. But *Swift Runner* reports that an out-clan fast-ship *rescued* two damaged life pods of theirs.

«All ships, disengage and return. I declare the paw-cuffs concluded and satisfied. We should prepare now for the arrival of the Den.»

240

"Alex," Dreamer said, "the remaining Khreetan skirmishers have ceased fire and are withdrawing."

"OK," Alex said slowly. "So what happens *now*...? Order all of ours to disengage as well. Do not pursue."

"Acknowledged, Alex."

Chaser went to answer *Swift Runner*'s distress beacon. When *Chaser* arrived, there was an out-clan fast-ship sitting just on the far side of the swarm of life pods.

«Move in slowly,» Tireless ordered. «Stay wary.»

"Looks like rescue is here," Ruth Goldin said. "Stand by to offboard the Khreetan lifepods."

"Stand by," Lieutenant Finnegan ordered. "Pickup is here for the Khreetan."

Rifleman Hess nodded. He stepped closer to the two Khreetan pods. The Khreetan he had 'talked' to earlier—he *thought* it was the same one—was half crouched outside the open hatch of the other pod, speaking in what sounded like growls and barks to others within. The Khreetan turned and looked at him as he approached. Hess pointed outside the bay with both hands, then pantomimed lifting and carrying. The Khreetan made the —agreement?—head-jerk again, and then the... thank-you, perhaps? The Khreetan exchanged a few more growling words, then returned to his own pod, and both pod hatches closed.

A few seconds later, the gravity in the bay shut off. The Marine squad manhandled both pods out of the open hatch on suit thrusters, turning them so that the hatch viewports faced the pod swarm and the Khreetan ship slowly moving in on the far side of them. Then they returned to the bay. A minute later, gravity returned, and *Livyatan* began to gently drift away from the pods, coming to rest about forty kilometers away.

As *Chaser* approached, the fast-ship began to slowly pull away. It left two additional life-pods behind it.

Interesting, Tireless thought to himself.

The fast-ship waited while they retrieved all of the life pods, then it was as though it was there one moment, gone the next.

A short while later, Sleeps-Lightly, Hunt-Master of *Swift Runner*, came onto *Chaser*'s bridge.

«What was happening with the out-clan fast-ship and our pods?» Tireless asked.

«Something very interesting,» Sleeps-Lightly replied. «We were exchanging paw-cuffs with another fast-ship, and it exploded. We do not know what happened, but we are all but certain none survived from it. A moment later, the fast-ship that you saw hit *Swift Runner* with a weapon that wrecked it in a single hit. Two of our ejecting life-pods were caught in the explosion and damaged when the remaining reactors went runaway.

«That fast-ship went after the damaged pods and retrieved them. Even repaired one. Patched it. And then brought them back.»

Tireless thought about that.

«That is indeed interesting,» he agreed.

«All ships,» Swims-Like-Rock sent, from *Sharp Claws*. «Stand ready. The Den is coming in.»

12. Leviathan

"New hyperspace exit event detected just within ten point eight AU," Dreamer reported. "The signal is extremely strong and... extended. The signature is still developing and strengthening. The vessel has not actually emerged yet. I can only presume it to be a significantly larger ship than we have yet seen."

"I don't like the sound of that," Alex said. "I hope it doesn't mean they withdrew because they were waiting for their main force to arrive."

"We will see, Alex," Dreamer said. "The gravitational disturbance continues to grow stronger."

"All ships," Alex ordered. "If you took significant damage in the skirmishes, fall back and form up with the cruisers. All others, rejoin the main destroyer formation."

The signal continued to grow, and grow, triggering a second, further-away set of drones.

"What the hell is coming *in?*" Alex wondered aloud.

"Whatever it is," Sandra muttered, "it's got to be *big.*"

"Emergence," Dreamer finally declared. "Gravitational signature suggests super-capital class."

"Super-capital?" Alex said. "I... *really* don't like the sound of that. Explain, please."

"The signature is difficult to resolve," Dreamer replied. "It seems to be generated by a group of between eight and fifteen vessels arriving together as a group." His voice paused for a moment. "I estimate aggregate mass is on the order of one hundred and eighty million tonnes, most of it concentrated in a single object."

Alex choked, and Sandra gasped.

"A hundred and eighty *MILLION?*" Alex repeated, aghast, his face pale.

"That is my estimate, Alex."

"Oh *gods,*" Alex mumbled. "This day just keeps on getting better. That's... that's bigger than the Stardock. A *lot* bigger. Isn't it?"

"More massive, at least," Dreamer agreed. "By a factor of roughly four point five."

"They brought a goddamned Galactic *battleship*, didn't they." Alex's tone was despairing. "One of those eight or ten kilometer spherical monsters. How in hell do we fight *that*?"

"I... am not certain," Dreamer replied. "But it does not seem massive *enough* to be a Galactic-technology spherical battleship. I am attempting to combine optical imagery from multiple Argus drones to simulate a synthetic-aperture view, to improve resolution.

"Preliminary imagery available... now."

The image was indistinct, but seemed to show a number of large ships in front of a large, somewhat flattened spheroidal shape... and was that some kind of outer *ring* around it?

"What *is* that?" Alex asked.

"I do not know," Dreamer replied. "It does not match anything in my current knowledge. The other ships seem to be falling back toward it."

Alex looked at the blurry image, trying to make sense of it.

"We need a closer look," he said. "We have to go in. We're the only ship that stands a chance of touching something that size.

"Sandra, I need you to coordinate the rest of the Fleet while I focus on this. Hand off to... Commodore Mackenzie if you have to."

"I'm on it, Alex," Sandra replied. "Do you want me to transfer to a different ship?"

Alex thought.

"That might be wise," he said. "Just in case the worst happens. Take the gig. If anything happens, you're acting second-in-command of the Fleet."

Sandra nodded, unstrapped, got up from her console, and headed aft. A few minutes later, the gig undocked and headed for the closest cruiser, CG-09 *Musashi*.

Okay, Dreamer, Alex thought. *Let's go take a look.*

He burned hard to build up some relative velocity so that they didn't come out of jump more or less stationary relative to... whatever it was. He picked where he wanted to be, and activated the dual hyperdrive cores. Fifteen seconds later, *Elegant Solution* jumped.

Gods, Alex thought as they approached, *you can actually see the damned thing as a micro-well from hyper.*

Then *Elegant Solution* emerged. Right about where Alex had wanted to be, well off to one side but within good, if distant, visual sensor range.

Seen from here, the picture was clearer. There were about a dozen ships—very *LARGE* ships, *substantially* larger and bulkier than the 'cruiser' class ships that the destroyer screen had skirmished with—and then, trailing slightly behind their formation, was... *something*. There definitely seemed to be some kind of outer ring and a central body.

«Fleet-Leader, we just picked up something at the extreme limits of visual detection. An out-clan ship. Much larger than their fast-ships.» The alert came from Likes-Water, in command of the nest-defender *Steady*.

«Hmmm,» Swims-Like-Rock replied. «Perhaps they have even more ships out here than we knew. Perhaps we have not seen their full strength yet. Keep a close eye on it.»

We need a closer look. I need a high-speed fly-by at closer range, then be ready to jump out on short notice. And I think we should designate those ships for the time being as ... I don't know, battlecruisers?

Agreed, Alex. If I may suggest this trajectory profile...

Dreamer superimposed a plot of an approach that built up lateral velocity, micro-jumped in within two hundred kilometers on the far side of the new formation, then made a curving pass across behind the whatever-it-was, before micro-jumping away to a safe distance.

That would work. Let's do it.

Elegant Solution turned away from the new arrivals and accelerated hard. At twenty kilometers a second, Alex triggered the hyperdrive and back-jumped, coming out on the far side of the formation of new ships and traveling *towards* it. It was already naked-eye visible in the distance when the ship came out of hyper, and growing visibly as *Elegant Solution* approached.

«*ANOTHER* one, Fleet-Leader! Or maybe the *SAME* one...? Yes, the same, I think. Somehow they can leap within a few heartbeats. And they can leap *BACKWARDS!* ...Or there are two ships. *I do not know.*» Nest-

Protector Waits-In-Silence's voice from the bridge of *Fierce Protector* was baffled, frustrated, uncertain. «This one is coming in BEHIND the Den. We are moving to intercept... if we can.»

Several of the... battlecruisers? began to accelerate *around* the gigantic ship, but before they were in position to do anything, *Elegant Solution* went flashing past only about fifty kilometers away, exit jump-point already forming ahead. Fifteen seconds more, and *Elegant Solution* was gone again.

«It is gone again, Fleet-Leader. It leapt AGAIN.»

«Did it fire on the Den?»

«...No, Fleet-Leader. We saw it leap, far distant. Then it re-appeared *behind* us, passed less than a *ka'kat* behind the Den, and then moments later, leapt away again. We have no idea where it is now. We had no IDEA they could leap that rapidly. How can one fight *that*? They can appear and be gone again almost before a defender could fire!»

«I wonder whether *all* of their ships can do that?» Swims-Like-Rock mused. «And they have simply not *revealed* it before now?

«Show me what the ship looked like.»

The image *Fierce Protector* sent was of a ship nearly as long as a front-runner, but much flatter. From the nearly edge-on view, it was difficult to tell how wide it was, but it was clearly much larger than the out-clan fast-ships.

«This is a type we have not seen before,» Swims-Like-Rock said. «The *second* new type we have seen this day. I wonder how many more they have?»

«*Second?*» asked Nest-Protector Cub-At-Heart, *Stand Fast's* captain. «What was the first new type?»

«These,» Swims-Like-Rock replied, sending images of a Warlord-class cruiser. «A fair number of these just joined their fast-ships. We know nothing yet of their capabilities.»

«Perhaps we were not prepared as well as we thought we were for this,» said Nest-Protector Likes-Water, of *Steady*.

«But it did not fire,» Swims-Like-Rock reiterated. «True?»

«True,» Likes-Water conceded.

«We have yet to see them fire first,» Swims-Like-Rock said. «Be wary... but not *hasty*.»

«Understood, Fleet-Leader.»

———————

Alex sent everything he had just gotten through the tactical net.

"Those – temporary designation, battlecruisers—look to be about six or seven hundred meters," he said. "Close to spherical. I'm guessing they pack a lot of firepower but perhaps don't move fast. And THIS thing..."

"That—whatever it is—is immense," Tom said.

Alex studied the captured imagery from his high-speed fly-past. There was a central body, maybe eight kilometers, spherical... but not a continuous sphere. And around it, an outer ring that looked easily a kilometer and a half thick. And that was broken by bright openings as well. He zoomed the image, focusing on the bright regions. He saw... docks, so many docks, towers... The central sphere looked to be divided almost completely in half. Perhaps a three or four hundred meter gap between the two main segments. There seemed to be light nearly everywhere, very different from the dark, utilitarian exterior of the Stardock.

He zoomed in on the gap. It looked like a city in there.

Suddenly the realization hit him.

"My god," he said, momentarily stunned. "This isn't a battleship. It's THEIR STARDOCK. One we could damned near park ours INSIDE."

He thought for a moment.

"Nobody fires on this," he said. "NOBODY. Unless the shit UTTERLY AND TOTALLY hits the fan. And then only as a last resort. This is their MOTHERSHIP."

"So what do we do now?" Naomi asked, from the Stardock. Alex found himself feeling better just for hearing her voice.

"I think," he said slowly, "we have to figure out a way to talk to them. I'm not sure what was going on, but... I can't shake the feeling there was something somehow ritualistic about that combat. They weren't fighting hard, and they showed us that even when they fired their main armament, they were firing it at low power. And as soon as ships started being lost, they STOPPED. And withdrew."

"So how do we manage talking to them?" Sandra asked, from Musashi.

"I don't know yet," Alex admitted. "Dreamer, got anything?"

247

"I am still analyzing their communication protocols," Dreamer replied.

"If anyone comes up with any ideas, let me know," Alex said. "We need some kind of sign language in space."

He looked at the tactical net. The double-plane of Fleet ships, the double plane of Khreetan ships facing them across a fifth of a light-second, the Khreetan mothership with its twelve escorts four light-minutes behind them, all moving slowly sunward.

Sign language. *Sign* language. Ruth Goldin had reported that one of her Marines had... had an interaction with one of the Khreetan. In improvised sign language.

"Commander Goldin," he said. "One of your Marines talked to a Khreetan, you said. I want to talk to him, right now. I need to know *everything* he can tell me."

━━━━━━━━━━

"Hey, Hess!" Lieutenant Finnegan said. "Get your ass to the bridge, on the double. Fleet Actual wants to talk to you about your Khreetan pal."

"On my way, sir," Rifleman Hess replied. And he went.

"Rifleman Pat Hess, right?" Alex confirmed.

"Yes Sir," Hess replied.

"Your captain tells me you met a Khreetan today."

"Yes Sir, briefly," Hess said. "In the boat bay."

"First, I want you to describe the Khreetan to me," Alex said.

"Uh. Okay," Hess began. "A bit over two meters. Bipedal, uh, bilaterally symmetric. Six limbs. Burly. Maybe ... three hundred kilos, at a guess. Picture a six-legged black bear standing upright, but armored like a pangolin. Orange-brown scales. Long ears, large all-black eyes, complex pupils, shortish muzzle. The first two pairs of limbs have opposable ... hands, six digits split three and three. Uh ... There's what looks like a pair of smaller secondary eyes behind the ears. They probably have a three hundred and sixty degree field of vision.

"That's about all I can think of, Sir. Heat of the moment. We were kind of busy."

"That's pretty damned *good* for heat-of-the-moment, Rifleman. Now, what can you tell me about communication?"

Hess hesitated.

"Uh, not much, Sir, to be honest. Uh... Voice, when it spoke, sounded like coughs, growls and barks. Uh... Can we get video on this connection?"

"One moment," Ruth Goldin said. Hess shimmered into appearance in front of Alex, standing beside Ruth Goldin's command chair.

"Okay, Sir," Hess said. "Here's all I know. First, there's what seems to be a gesture of greeting. They hold out both... *lower* hands, I guess, open, like this," holding out his own hands, "with the upper hands at their sides or folded. The response seems to be to do the same, and exchange a light hand clasp. It seemed to be fine with me having only one pair of arms to choose from. Wasn't any kind of contest of strength, and it didn't seem to be bothered that I was wearing armor.

"Then there's a gesture like this, with all four arms at once." Hess spread his arms wide, hands open, then closed his hands as he drew his arms in to his chest. "That seems to be a 'Thank you'. There's a little head-bob, like this, that might be part of it or might go with it, I'm not sure, or maybe it means something else. There's a *different* head motion, a jerk upward and back, that seems to be a 'yes' or agreement. Like this." He demonstrated.

"They point with an open hand, like this." He demonstrated again. "I saw one other gesture, raising both... uh, upper hands, quickly, like this," demonstrating that as well, "but I'm not sure what it means. And the alien didn't seem to have any trouble understanding when I pantomimed picking things up and moving things, or shooing it back inside the pod." Hess demonstrated what he'd done there, too.

"That's all I can think of right now, Sir," he said. "If I think of anything else, I'll pass it along."

"*Thank* you, Rifleman Hess," Alex said. "All that is a big help." A thought occurred to him. "You said armored like a pangolin. A pangolin's armor is mostly on its back and sides. How could you see that?"

"OH! *Right!* It wasn't wearing a suit, Sir. They can breathe our air. And without any obvious visible discomfort. In fact, this one was wearing kind of a long vest affair with a lot of pockets, and not much else I saw. Kind of like sleeveless coveralls."

Alex nodded.

"Being able to breathe the same air will simplify things a lot, I hope," he said. "Thank you, Rifleman. Let your Captain know if you think of anything else."

"I will, Sir." Hess saluted.

"Thank you, Rifleman."

Sign language. Something was *nagging* at Alex. Sign language. He needed something like a STOP sign in space.

The realization dawned on him that maybe he had one.

"Dreamer," he asked. "I have some questions about hyperdrive mechanics. First, is there any reason we have to *complete* a hyper entry? Could we just *partly* form the jump, uh, portal, and then stop and let it dissipate?"

"Certainly," Dreamer said. "You can cancel a jump at any time before entering the portal. I believed that you already knew that."

"Just confirming, Dreamer. And can we do that *accurately* enough, hypothetically speaking, to just rattle a ship around a little, without doing any real damage?"

"I have good confidence of it," Dreamer replied.

"Okay. Now we can execute hyper entry at a wide range of different speeds, as long as we're going fast enough to enter the portal cleanly. The portal's usually auto-placed at the right lead for jump. But can we generate the portal some arbitrary selected distance in front of the ship? Regardless of speed?"

"Yes, Alex. Within the limits of activation range. It need not move with the ship. It can be placed statically up to several hundred kilometers away, at least."

"Okay. I have an idea. I'm... not sure I entirely feel comfortable with it, but I think it might work. We'll need to be, uh, about three hundred kilometers in front of their Stardock, I think." He was already plotting the jump.

"Tom, Sandra, I'm going to *very carefully* try something. I have an idea about sign language."

"Understood," Sandra replied. "Watch yourself, Alex."

Alex matched velocity with the Khreetan mothership, then jumped *Elegant Solution* just over three hundred kilometers in front of it. For a few minutes, he just stayed there motionless relative to the formation, hoping they would get the idea he wasn't about to attack. Several of the—escort battlecruisers?—moved more directly in front of him after a few moments, but that was all that happened.

Dreamer, I want you to monitor any and all communications while we are here.

Of course, Alex.

———————

«Fleet-Leader, the new ship has returned. It is sitting ten *ka'kat* in front of us, doing nothing.»

«Give me an exact position. I will be there immediately.»

Stand Fast sent coordinates, and *Sharp Claws* jumped. Less than a minute after entering hyperspace, it dropped out again, about twenty kilometers off *Elegant Solution*'s port side.

"Hello," Alex reported, "I have company. Good. This will make it easier, if I don't have to rattle one of those big bruisers around and give them the wrong idea."

Dreamer, align us and put a partial portal activation in front of that ship, just enough to shake it around a little.

Understood, Alex.

Two kilometers in front of the Khreetan ship, a jump portal began to form. Dreamer let it build for about six seconds, then cut the power and let it fade.

Sharp Claws shuddered briefly.

«Huntmistress!» Broken-Tooth exclaimed. «What? What are they doing?»

«I am not sure,» Swims-Like-Rock replied. «Do nothing, yet, but stand by evasive maneuvering. In case.»

«*Sharp Claws*, what is happening?» Nest-Protector Cub-At-Heart asked.

«Stand by, be patient,» Swims-Like-Rock said. «There must be a reason for this.»

Again, Alex thought. *Let's make sure the message is clear.*

Dreamer repeated the six-second partial activation.

«What are they *DOING*?» Broken-Tooth demanded, as *Sharp Claws* was jolted again. Again, the disruption faded without anything else happening.

«I *THINK*,» Swims-Like-Rock said slowly, «they just showed us that they can *partially* activate their leap drive. *Very* precisely. Enough to shake us around without doing damage. But *why?* I cannot shake the thought that they are trying to tell us... *something.*»

The out-clan ship repeated the partial activation one more time.

«Three times,» Broken-Tooth said. «Is there significance to a half-paw to them?»

«Perhaps,» Swims-Like-Rock mused, «they intend to make sure we understand that this is *all* they are going to do. Though I still do not understand why they are doing it at all.»

Then the out-clan ship slowly pivoted to face towards the Den and its defenders.

Okay, Dreamer, Alex said. *Here's my plan. I want to create a ninety-percent-strength jump portal fifty klicks in front of us. Then wait two minutes, then create one at fifty followed by one at one hundred. Then two minutes, and fifty, one hundred, one fifty. Up until we're doing five all the way out to two hundred and fifty. Then stop, wait five minutes, repeat the sequence. Will that damage the drives?*

No, Dreamer replied. *But just to be sure, I will run a diagnostic after each sequence.*

Good idea, Alex said. *Okay, here goes nothing. Let's do it.*

The out-clan ship activated its hyperdrive again. This time shimmering rainbow rings of spatial stress formed, one-and-four-digits *ka'kat* in front of it.

«That was a lot more power,» Swims-Like-Rock said, watching intently. «That looked like a full activation of their drive. I did not know they could do that and yet not leap. They are showing us numerous things that we did not already know that they could do.»

Likes-Water, from the Nest-Protector *Steady*, demanded to know what was happening. Swims-Like-Rock urged patience. He was already trying to figure out exactly that.

There was a short pause, then the out-clan ship did it again. This time, it did it twice, the second leap portal at three-and-two-digits *ka'kat*. Then another pause, and then three activations, spaced at the same intervals.

252

«What is happening?» Likes-Water demanded. «Is this a threat against the Den?»

«I do not think so,» Swims-Like-Rock replied. «But I do not understand yet what they are doing – or, on a fresher trail, why they are doing it. We are *missing* something. I... *think* they are trying to tell us something. But we have not yet understood *what*.»

«If they do not stop soon,» Likes-Water retorted, «the universe will be *missing* that ship. I will NOT allow harm to the Den.»

The out-clan ship started another activation series.

«This one will be four,» Swims-Like-Rock predicted.

«*Four?* That will put it within... *I am firing*,» Likes-Water snarled.

«*NO!*» Swims-Like-Rock roared back. «That is an ORDER. You will NOT open fire unless ordered.»

«Then if this goes on,» Likes-Water snapped, «we will have to start *BRAKING THE DEN* out of this out-clan's—»

Insight struck Swims-Like-Rock like a thunderbolt.

«That's IT!» he bellowed, suddenly jubilant. «They are trying to tell us that they want us to *SLOW DOWN!*»

He opened an additional channel.

«Den-Mother, trust me on this, I beg. Decelerate the Den. Just a little will suffice, I think. A single digit of a mass-equivalent may be plenty.»

«Are you certain, Swims-Like-Rock?» The Den-Mother's voice was doubtful.

«No, Den-Mother,» Swims-Like-Rock admitted honestly. «But I am certain the out-clan are trying to communicate a message to us, and I have no better guess at what the message is. Regard it as a gesture to show good intentions, at no real cost to us.»

«Very well,» the Den-Mother replied. «Defenders, hold formation, match braking. And I affirm Swims-Like-Rock's edict: No fire unless ordered.»

A few moments later, the Den began to gently brake.

Alex, the Khreetan mothership and its escorts have begun to decelerate at just under one tenth of a gravity.

Alex whooped in exultation.

"Sonofabitch, it WORKED! Terminate activation series."

He took conn a moment, and quickly swung *Elegant Solution*'s nose well out of line with the mothership, then set lateral thrusters to match its deceleration.

On *Sharp Claws*, Swims-Like-Rock watched as the out-clan ship cut off its most recent leap drive activation after only a few heartbeats, then pointed its nose AWAY from the Den. After a moment, it matched the Den's deceleration. He raised his upperhands and coughed in satisfaction.

«Message received and understood!» he declared triumphantly. «Hunt-Master, maintain deceleration to match the out-clan.»

A moment later, *Sharp Claws*, too, began gently braking.

"We have a break-through, everyone," Alex announced over the Fleet command channel. "We've established that we *can* communicate with them, on at least a very basic level, and equally importantly, that *they are willing to cooperate*."

"That's fantastic!" Tom said. "That's a *huge* step. Dreamer, how are we doing on communication protocols?"

"I have captured a significant amount of communication between the cruiser near us, the escort battlecruisers, and the mothership," Dreamer replied. "I think I am very close to cracking their basic communication protocols."

"Let me see if I can help," Alex said. He wheeled *Elegant Solution* around again, and carefully slid it into position almost *alongside* the Khreetan, a thousand meters to one side and slightly ahead of the Khreetan, facing in the opposite direction, still maintaining the tenth-gee deceleration.

The out-clan ship spun around, always remaining aimed *away* from the Den, and slid smoothly into a position off *Sharp Claws'* nose.

«What are they doing *now*?» Cub-At-Heart queried.

«I am not sure,» Swims-Like-Rock replied. Then, so close by that it was unmistakable, the out-clan ship cut its deceleration.

Hurrrrmmmmmm, Swims-Like-Rock mused to himself.

«Den-Mother,» he sent, «I think you can stop braking. We ... seem to have established a basic level of communication. Or at least, agreement of willingness to communicate. And I think the out-clan just showed their own good intentions in turn.»

«Very well, Fleet-Leader,» the Den-Mother replied. A few moments later, the Den also stopped decelerating.

The out-clan ship... *twitched*, raising its nose slightly before returning to where it was. Almost as though the ship itself was signifying agreement.

«Now that is EXTREMELY intriguing,» Swims-Like-Rocks said. «Hunt-Master, take station next to the out-clan ship again. Do not point our teeth at them.»

«Understood, Fleet-Leader,» Broken-Tooth said. He pitched *Sharp Claws* nose-up and executed a complex rolling maneuver that ended with *Sharp Claws* side-by-side with the out-clan at about two *me'kat.*

«Show-off,» Swims-Like-Rock chuckled. Broken-Tooth grinned cheerfully, unabashed.

«So what now, Fleet-Leader?» the Den-Mother asked.

«Now we work out how to talk,» Swims-Like-Rock said. «And I think it is safe to stand down the fleet.»

«I agree,» the Den-Mother said. «You have done good work this day, Fleet-Leader. The Den sings your name proudly.»

Swims-Like-Rock bowed his head, abashed.

«*Thank* you, Den-Mother,» he replied, with feeling. «You honor me.»

On Earth, John Riken and Miranda Ramirez were just wrapping up a grueling press conference laying out everything that had just happened, the arrival of the Khreetan, the mobilization of the Fleet, the reports of skirmishes out beyond Saturn, the Russian rogue general and his nuclear attack, the defense of the United States by the Stardock, the interception of every last warhead. At the back of the stage, Secretary Winters took a call on her phone, listened for a moment, nodded. Then she lowered her phone and stepped forward to speak quietly for a moment in the President's ear.

President John Riken listened, nodded, and turned back to his microphone. His entire demeanor suddenly looked more relaxed, more energized. He looked *elated.*

"Ladies and gentlemen of the press, people of the United States of America and of the world," he said. "I have just been informed that the Fleet has *successfully established* a basic level of communication with the Khreetan, that good intentions appear to have been established on both sides, and that the Fleet is *standing down* from battle alert.

"There is going to be a tremendous amount still to resolve, I am certain," he continued. "Don't count your chickens yet. But it appears for now that this Khreetan crisis *may be* over."

There was a moment of silence, then a wave of applause filled the room.

Of course, there were a *thousand* questions after it died down. Riken had to admit that he did not know the answers to most of them.

"What about the nuclear attack?" asked Jessie Walters, from the New York Times. "How do we know, how *can* we know, that it will not happen again?"

"*That* question, I can answer, at last, Jessie," Riken said, satisfaction plain on his face. "President Molchalin and I are going to meet later this week, perhaps next—at a location yet to be decided—and we will sign a bilateral treaty to *completely dismantle* the entire nuclear arsenals of both the Russian Federation and the United States."

He had to stop speaking while the thunderous applause died down.

"What about other nuclear powers?" Jessie Walters asked.

"The honest answer is that *most* of the other major nuclear powers are already on-board with the idea," Riken replied. "If I can arrange it in time, a lot of the world's other primary nuclear powers will be there to sign it as well. Except, so far, for China. I have not *formally* broached it yet with the Chinese General Secretary. I *strongly hope* that now that we have a solid agreement on the table, we can persuade China not to be the last hold-out."

"Mr. President," the Fox reporter asked, "how can we guarantee the nation's security without our nuclear deterrent?"

"That's the wrong question, Mr... Johnson?" Riken replied. The reporter nodded. "The correct question, as the recent emergency so terrifyingly demonstrated, is 'How can we guarantee the nation's security WITH a nuclear deterrent.' And the answer to that question is very simple."

He paused briefly for effect.

"*We can't.* ONE MAN launched a large-scale nuclear attack against the United States, Mr. Johnson, *ONE MAN.* One rogue General. Despite all of the Russians' security around *their* nuclear arsenal. Because no security system can ever fully protect against someone who is *already inside* and at its highest level of authority. And as long as our nations have nuclear arsenals, that risk will always exist. We can simply no longer afford to have nuclear arsenals on the surface of this planet.

"And how, as you ask, will we protect the nation's security WITHOUT nuclear weapons?"

He paused a moment for effect, before answering his own question.

"*The same way we always have.* The United States has had nuclear weapons since 1945. And since 1945, we *have never used one in anger.* Because we never *needed* to. We did *everything we had to do* in other ways.

"It's time to put them away, for good. Because, to quote to you President Molchalin's words, 'This **can NEVER** happen again.'"

———

Alex, Dreamer said, I have decoded the Khreetan communication protocols to a level sufficient to send and receive audio signals.

Fantastic, Alex replied. *We can transmit to them directly?*

We can broadcast in their direction on their frequencies using their protocols, Dreamer replied. *I am uncertain of the meaning of all of the fields in the header that are not directly related to the actual protocol. Some fields seem to be variable metadata whose meaning I do not yet know. Another seems to be a local-time-of-origin field, while another seems to identify the sender. I do not know how to construct a valid identifier field for us.*

Send an audio pip, Alex said. *Then two, then three, then four. Make your best guess at the unknown fields and... leave the identity field blank, I guess.*

On the bridge of *Sharp Claws*, Stop-Shouting looked quizzically at his board. He twitched his head in puzzlement.

«What is it, Stop-Shouting?» Broken-Tooth asked.

«A signal,» Stop-Shouting replied. «Strong. But with errors. The truth-count is wrong, to begin. And it has an invalid message-class.»

«Can you play its contents *anyway*?» Swims-Like-Rock asked.

«I can... come up with a *representation*,» Stop-Shouting said. «It is coming from the out-clan ship.»

He touched a control. There was a loud, sharp BEEP, BEEP. A short pause. BEEP, BEEP, BEEP, BEEP. A longer pause. BEEP. Short pause.

BEEP, BEEP. Short pause. BEEP, BEEP, BEEP. Short pause. BEEP, BEEP, BEEP, BEEP. And it restarted from one again.

«One, two, three, four,» Swims-Like-Rock counted off. «Send back five, one-paw, paw-and-one, paw-and-two.»

«Sending.»

There was a pause.

«The sequence has changed,» Stop-Shouting said. «One, ... four, ... paw-and-three ... two-paws-and-four. Simple squares. Sending back two-*te'*-and-one, three-*te'*, four-*te'*-and-one.»

"Hot damn,"Alex said. "They got that. Great. Uh ... Let's try the first ten digits of pi, then wait."

«Three... one... four... one... five... paw-and-three... two... one paw... five... three... no more,» Stop-Shouting counted. «It clearly has significance, but I do not recognize the number.»

«Neither do I,» Swims-Like-Rock agreed. «But it seems tantalizingly close to the circle ratio. And that would be in keeping with what they have sent so far.» He thought for a long moment.

«Send back the first two-paws digits of the circle ratio.»

"The reply is twelve digits, Alex," Dreamer said. "Three one eight four eight zero nine four nine three eleven nine."

"Wait, *eleven*?" Alex asked. "As a *digit*?" Then he got it. "Wait. They sent TWELVE digits." He ran a fast calculation in the interface, but Dreamer got there first.

"Yes, Alex. That is the first twelve digits of pi, in base twelve."

Alex thought for a moment.

"Send back the number ten, then pause, then the first ten digits again."

«Getting a reply,» Stop-Shouting said. «A paw-and-four... a pause... then... the same sequence again.»

«A paw-and-four... then a paw-and-four digits,» Swims-Like-Rock mused. «In reply to the circle ratio. ...Wait. We sent two-paws digits. *They* sent a paw-and-four. Calculate—what is the circle ratio, *in the base of a paw and four*?»

Stop-Shouting keyed it in on his board.

«Three, one, four, one, five, paw-and-three, two... it is the sequence they sent.»

«They count in PAW-AND-FOURS!» Swims-Like-Rock exclaimed. «Send back their digits. Then pause. Then paw-and-four, then two-paws. Then pause, then paw-and-four and two-paws again.»

«Sending,» said Stop-Shouting.

"Yes!!" Alex pumped his fist exultantly in the air.

"Everyone, I think we just managed to confirm that the Khreetan count in base twelve, and convey to them that *we* count in base ten. It's early days yet, but we're *talking.*"

There were cheers from the distant briefing room on the Stardock.

"Do you have a plan from here?" Naomi asked.

"I'm going to stay here and keep working on talking to them," Alex asked. "The Fleet can stand down off high alert, and just hold position for now. And I think we can send back any ship that needs repairs or has injured aboard."

"I'll take care of that," Tom said. "Do you want anyone else with you on *Elegant Solution?*"

Alex thought about that for a moment.

"Yeah," he said. "I'd like Rifleman Hess, off *Livyatan*. And... Naomi? Would you...?"

"Of *course*, Alex," Naomi said. "But how are we going to accomplish that? *Elegant Solution* doesn't have beam or bow docking ports."

"Good point," Alex replied. He thought for a moment. "Sandra, you took *Elegant Solution*'s gig over to *Musashi*. *Endeavour* can run Naomi out to *Musashi*, the two of you can take the gig over to *Livyatan*, pick up Rifleman Hess, then fly out and join me on *Elegant Solution*."

"Sounds like a plan to me," Sandra said. "Who takes *Endeavour* back?"

"How about a slight variation," Naomi said. "I fly *Endeavour* out to *Musashi* with an Academy training crew. They can take her home, while I pick up Sandra and Hess in the gig, and join you on *Elegant Solution*."

"That works," Alex agreed. "I'll see you in an hour or two, love."

About three hours later, *Elegant Solution*'s gig docked back in its dedicated bay aft of the bridge. In the meantime, the cruiser squadrons were returning to dock. *Moray* and *Snoak* had off-loaded the injured from *Sailfish* and handed them off to Yeon and Philippe, then returned to the destroyer screen. Seven other destroyers had returned to dock and disembarked their crews, and were now being moved into the engineering bays for minor repairs, including servicing *Seawolf*'s damaged railguns, three of which remained obstinately offline.

Almost as soon as she stepped off the gig, Alex grabbed Naomi into a tight hug.

"God, it's good to see you," he said.

"And you, too," Naomi agreed. "This has been... terrifying."

Alex nodded.

"But I think we're through the worst of it," he said. "It's a matter of time now. We've got a channel established between Dreamer and one of the Khreetan intellects, and they're working on developing a bidirectional translation. As soon as we can talk a little better, we'll be able to set up a face-to-face meeting.

"That's why I wanted you here, Rifleman Hess. You're the only human so far who has met a Khreetan face-to-face."

«What progress, Fleet-Leader?»

Truthfully, Swims-Like-Rock thought it would not hurt if the Den-Mother asked for status updates a *little* less frequently. But he had little else to do at the moment, while *Sharp Claws'* control intellect and the *frighteningly* capable out-clan intellect worked on translating between K'heert'en and the out-clans' language.

«We are still working on building a translation, Den-Mother,» he replied. «But now that we speak, I have a thought. *Chaser*, I believe, picked up the life-pods from *Swift Runner*, yes? Has *Chaser* returned to the Den?»

«Yes,» the Den-Mother replied. «We will sing later for those who did not return from *Swift Runner*.»

«It is given me to understand that one of *Swift Runner*'s crew actually *met* one of the out-clan,» Swims-Like-Rock continued. «Could he be sent to *Sharp Claws*? I would very much like to speak with him. I have many questions that perhaps he could answer.»

«Of course, Fleet-Leader,» the Den-Mother replied. «It will be done as soon as we can manage it.»

========

"Alex," Dreamer observed, "there is a small craft approaching."

"I see it," Alex agreed. "What'll you bet me they're delivering additional ... uh, personnel as well?"

"The supposition seems likely," Dreamer agreed.

The hours ticked away. More of the Khreetan ships returned to their mothership, and as they did so, Alex released additional destroyers to return to dock or to resume their patrols. Of course, there was much less urgency to the patrols now.

It was the next day before Dreamer declared that basic spoken communication should be possible. Among the information exchanged along the way, it had been learned that the Khreetan idea of normal gravity was around one point two eight G, that they considered an atmospheric pressure of one point three seven bar normal, and that their home atmosphere was basically oxygen-nitrogen with seventeen point one percent oxygen, nearly two percent helium, helium, and zero-point-four percen t neon (but they didn't bother adding the neon to the air on their ships). That worked out to a partial oxygen pressure of two hundred and thirty five millibars, which was well within human safe tolerance as long as the total pressure wasn't too high. Humans should be able to breathe Khreetan air indefinitely, if necessary.

A meeting was arranged for later that day. The Khreetan small craft would bring a party of visitors to *Elegant Solution*'s boat bay. Dreamer had been able to work out a compromise environment of one gravity and one point two bar total pressure, with two hundred and twenty millibars oxygen. It would be a little thick for humans, a little thin for the Khreetan, but the lower gravity would avoid any possibility of it becoming tiring.

========

Alex and Naomi were waiting just outside the boat bay when the bulbous Khreetan small-craft drifted in through the atmosphere field. Marines in armor marshalled it to a safe landing spot. It settled to the deck, then one of the Marines called 'Down.' It powered down to standby, and a side hatch about three by five meters opened, hinging upward.

Alex and Naomi stepped through the inner air field and into the slightly denser atmosphere in the boat bay. It was *noticeable*, but not bothersome. Four Khreetan stepped out of the open hatch and out into the boat bay. Rifleman Hess's description had been pretty accurate, Alex noted. One of them seemed to be wearing coveralls.

The two parties approached. Hess had his helmet open. He stepped forward towards the one wearing the coveralls, holding out his empty hands.

The Khreetan stepped forward to match him, held out its lower hands, and took Hess's.

"Hello again," Hess said. "I'm glad to see you made it back."

"Greet we," the Khreetan said, translated. "Thankfulness also have we." The translation was clearly still a little rough.

The apparent leader of the Khreetan party watched with what seemed almost like a bemused smile, before stepping forward himself.

Alex stepped forward to meet him. He held out his hands as Hess had done. After a moment, the Khreetan held out his own lower hands—*or actually, mid-hands, perhaps?* Alex thought to himself.

The Khreetan's hands were dry, warm, and felt strong. But the grip was gentle. "Higher than human body temperature," Alex mused aloud. The Khreetan cocked its head at him in a quizzical manner, an unexpectedly human-looking gesture.

Alex released its hands and pointed at himself.

"Human," he said, then gestured across himself, Naomi, Hess, and the other Marines. "Humans."

The alien jerked its head upward. That meant a 'yes', Alex recalled.

"Hyooo-mansh," it essayed, in a coughing, growling bass voice. Then it pointed to itself.

"K'heert," it coughed. Then it, too, broadened its gesture. "K'heert'na."

Something about *building*, the translation program supplied.

Alex did his best to copy the sounds. So did Naomi. The alien—the K'heert—jerked its head again.

Alex pointed again to himself.

"Alex Holder," he said. Then he pointed to Naomi, with an open hand as Rifleman Hess had mentioned. "Naomi." He pointed to Rifleman Hess. "Hess." Off to one side, Hess and the K'heert in the coveralls seemed to be going through a similar process.

Again the head-jerk, after a moment.

"Hesh," pointing at Rifleman Hess. They seemed to have difficulty with sibilants. "Nakh-omi." Naomi's name developed a kind of cough in the middle. The K'heert tried it again, and managed to reduce it this time. "Al-eksh... Chhol-der."

It was a valiant effort. Alex jerked his head upward after the K'heert'na fashion.

The K'heert pointed to itself. The sound that came out was a barking, almost-snarl that Alex could not hope to emulate. But the translation program supplied, 'Swims like rock.' Alex struggled to suppress a chuckle. He was pretty certain he couldn't pronounce it, but perhaps the translation program could.

He pointed with his open hand toward the K'heert.

"Swims like rock?" he repeated. The head-jerk of affirmation again. This time it was accompanied by the raise of both upper hands that Hess had mentioned.

The conversation went slowly, haltingly, as human and K'heert'na struggled to understand each other. Without Dreamer and the K'heert'na intellects to work out translation, it would have been impossible. The translation was definitely still rough; the K'heert'na—or, K'heert'en, Alex learned, was what they called their language—syntax still came through oddly, and Alex had to rearrange the sentences in his head sometimes to figure out the exact meanings, repeating of course to confirm his understanding. He couldn't avoid the thought that their growling voices notwithstanding, their sentence structure sounded a little like Yoda. But he was learning, and Dreamer was still working on improving the translation.

«Paw-cuffs exchanged, have we both,» said the K'heert, after a while, when they were managing to communicate in more or less complete—if sometimes broken—sentences. «Strength yours, we have seen. Restraint, also.»

"As we in turn have seen yours," Alex replied carefully. "We greet you and bid you welcome.

"But we are strangers to your ways. Would you please explain to us about... paw-cuffs? We do not wish to have any misunderstandings between us."

The K'heert seemed to pause in thought, looking back and forth between Alex and Naomi.

«True indeed this is,» he (?) replied. «Us, are you not. Assumed too much, perhaps have we.

«From long before space we traveled, dates the custom. When first strangers meet, of paw-cuffs an exchange there is. Strength to gauge. Restraint to show.

«Cubs at play, even, the same do. Each other they cuff, in play. With full strength, not.

«Where strength there is, and restraint shown is, then respect can there be.»

Alex nodded slowly, beginning to understand.

"What if... the stranger does not show strength?" he asked.

«If weak a stranger is, then *afraid* they may be,» the K'heert replied. «Great caution, required is then of all. Fear, unpredictable is. To trust... *difficult*. Dangerous. Trust, an illusion only may be. To assume it true, dangerous.»

"And where there is no restraint," Alex hazarded, "*then* also, trust is dangerous?"

«Understand exactly you do,» the Khreetan replied. «But where respect of both there is, then trust can there be.»

"...And where there is trust," Alex completed, "there can be... friendship?"

The Khreetan made the upper-paw-raising gesture that Alex understood by now served the role of a nod of agreement. It seemed quite emphatic this time.

«Just so,» he said. «Understanding, have you. Strength have you, though younglings to space, you seem. Restraint, showed you. Merciful were you. When damaged was refuge-pod-ours, ship-yours rescued, *repaired*, returned. All lived. Grateful are we for that. Well speak your actions, of you.»

"We could have done no differently," Alex answered. "From nearly our oldest times of ocean sailing, our traditions have said that shipwrecked sailors must always be rescued if possible, even those of enemies."

The Khreetan raised his upper paws again, more slowly and thoughtfully this time.

«Respect-worthy, that is,» he said. «Understand, do you.» He paused, looking carefully at Alex.

«Trust between us can there be, I think. Fast-ship-yours, the loss, we *regret*.»

"I think so too," Alex agreed. He took a deep breath, then held out both hands, empty, as at the initial meeting. After a moment, the Khreetan extended his own middle paws and firmly, but gently, gripped Alex's hands. Alex returned the grip.

«Swims-Like-Rock am I, of venture-fleet this of Clan [a hissing, almost whistling sound that was not translated] of Those-who-build, all-ships-leader,» the Khreetan said. Alex had to think carefully to parse that. That seemed to confirm the earlier, humorous-sounding name.

"Those-who-build is what you call yourselves?" he asked, for clarity. The double paw-raise and head-jerk of agreement. "And you yourself are named Swims-Like-Rock?" Paw-raise, again.

"I am Alex Holder, and I am—all-ships-leader, Fleet Actual—of the defense fleet of... humans of Earth," he said.

«Swims-Like-Rock I, of Those-who-build, Alekx-Chholder you, of humans-of-Earth, as an equal greet,» said Swims-Like-Rock. It somehow sounded like formal phrasing, so Alex did his best to repeat the sense of it.

"I, Alex Holder of Earth, greet you, Swims-Like-Rock of Those-who-build, as an equal."

Swims-Like-Rock held the hand-clasp a moment longer, then released Alex's hands and folded his lower arms across his middle. Alex lowered his hands.

«To discuss, much there is,» Swims-Like-Rock said. «But time, in abundance there now is to speak.»

Alex nodded, and tried to imitate the quick hand-raise gesture.

"Perhaps we should speak more later, when the translation has improved further," he said.

«Wise, that would be,» Swims-Like-Rock agreed. «Easier, also.»

Alex and Swims-Like-Rock managed to frame an agreement to meet again in three days, Fleet time, while Dreamer and the Khreetan intellects worked on improving the translation. In the meantime, Alex sent orders for all but a token handful of ships to stand down and return to Earth.

It was *much* easier to talk at the next meeting. This time just Swims-Like-Rock and the K'heert crewman—whose name, Rifleman Hess had informed Alex, was Too-Cautious—came. Too-Cautious wandered off with Hess, apparently being introduced to the rest of the Marine platoon, while Alex and Naomi talked with Swims-Like-Rock on the bridge.

«It is good to meet with you again, Alex-cholder, Naoh-mi,» said Swims-Like-Rock. His pronunciation was getting better.

"And to meet you also, Swims-Like-Rock," Alex replied. "This is much better. I can understand you much more easily now."

«I also,» Swims-Like-Rock agreed. «The time was well spent on improvement.»

There was an awkward pause for a moment, as neither was sure where to start.

«Do you speak for all of your world?» Swims-Like-Rock asked at last.

"I cannot do that," Alex said. "I cannot speak on behalf of all nations. We have many voices, and we do not always all agree. But I speak for the Fleet, which we built to defend our world."

Swims-Like-Rock raised his upperhands.

«I understand,» he said. «I, too, speak only for this fleet, this Clan, not for all Builder Clans. But our speaking sets a precedent that bears weight among all Clans. Clan Hsieuuu is... *respected.*» The name came through much more clearly this time. «We stand third among the eight Great Clans. And I am granted leave in this to speak for the Clan with the authority of the Den-Mother.»

It was Alex's turn to nod understanding.

«One question first of all puzzles us,» Swims-Like-Rock said. «Clan Hsieuuu came here on the trail of the Violators, the tracks of their Den appearing to lead here, yet it seemed clear almost from the first you are not them, and no sign of their presence do we see—though our front-runners saw the Violators' Den next to your world. How came this to be?»

"The Violators?" Alex asked.

«Those who left the trail that we followed here,» Swims-Like-Rock began to explain. Then Alex understood, and raised his hands.

266

"We know them as the Chrrt'ktk't," he said. "That is how they introduced themselves to us. We can share what data we have on them with you.

"You call them the Violators? May I ask why?"

«We encountered them in space,» Swims-Like-Rock replied, «near to a trade-world known to us. We respectfully offered paw-cuffs. Instead of returning the paw-cuffs in measure, as you did, they fired indiscriminately upon *all ships present*, not only front-runners, and in full force. There was no restraint in them. They fired upon unarmed trade-ships, even upon the Den. Nests were damaged, *cubs* died. *CUBS!*» His anger and outrage came through clearly.

«And then after this violation, they turned their backs and left. We were *enraged*. For more than a paw of world-orbits' time we pursued them. We followed their trail here. Near to here, their trail split two ways. One narrow but deep, one broad but shallow.

«We decided that the deep trail was that of their Den, the shallow trail a diversion to lead us astray. So we followed the deep trail. It ends here in your system... yet they are not here, even though our front-runners found here the scent of their technology. And yet... although the scent was similar, your ships are so unlike theirs. So small, so *fast*.

«At first we did not understand. But now perhaps we do, we think. In part.»

Alex nodded understanding.

"It seems neither of us have fond memories of them," he said. "Let me tell you now how they came to us. I will tell you first, if you sought to catch them, you followed the wrong trail—as they intended."

«That much, we have realized for ourselves,» Swims-Like-Rock agreed.

"As they fled from you, they drove their fleet so hard that the hyperdrive on their... Den... burned out. But to them, it is not a den, only a place to repair their ships and build new ones. It has not the... the deep importance to them that your Den clearly does to you.

"They abandoned it here, and went onward, taking its crew with them, hoping that it would distract you. They *told* us that it was a gift to us. That its hyperdrive had failed, and they could not spare the time to repair it. They did *not* tell us that they left it as a decoy, that they were *using us* as a decoy to distract you, or even that you were coming.

"One of their junior captains—*stretched* his orders as far as he could manage—to give us a partial warning that there was a danger to us. He was forbidden to tell us what kind of danger, or from where. But we managed to learn these things anyway." The details of how didn't matter, for now.

Swims-Like-Rock gave a kind of forceful, coughing grunt that was not translated.

«Honorless,» he said. «Deceptive. Unrestrained. Cowardly. Untrustworthy.» He made the coughing grunt again. «*WORTHLESS*.»

"We're not particularly fond of them, either, in hindsight," Alex agreed. "But we learned how to use their technology, their repair dock—which we now call the Stardock—to build our own ships. To our own designs, as you have seen."

«Indeed,» Swims-Like-Rock said. «You must have learned very *quickly*. We cannot be *terribly* far behind them. Perhaps two world-orbits. No more than three. Did you truly not travel space before they came? All this, you learned starting from nothing?»

"We had some very limited space travel before the Crickets—the Violators—came," Alex said. "Mostly unmanned, automated probes, launched using chemical-fueled rockets. Perhaps two dozen people—two twelves—had ever traveled further from our world than low orbit."

«That is a *most impressive* accomplishment, then,» Swims-Like-Rock said.

"We... had a considerable incentive," Alex observed.

Swims-Like-Rock spread both pairs of hands and let out an almost-baying sound that trailed off into coughing barks. After a moment, Alex realized the Khreetan was laughing.

"Anyway," Alex said, "it appears their decoy gambit worked as they planned. It distracted you, bought them some time.

"Do you plan to try to continue to pursue them now?"

Swims-Like-Rock made a gesture Alex had not seen before, pushing downward and outward with his mid-hands.

«It is futile,» he said. «Our front-runners reported their trail was already faint, and that they could not pick it up again after leaving your worlds. And even if they had, with no Den any longer, the Violators could simply scatter and agree to meet elsewhere... and their fleet-trail would vanish like mist. We have pursued them as far as we can. Perhaps already further than we should have tried to.»

He stopped, cocked his head, and fixed Alex with that disconcerting triskele-pupilled gaze.

«But it was worth it,» he continued after a moment. «For thus we have now met you humans-of-Earth. And I believe that is worth more, in the end, than chasing the Violators. I am unsure what we would do, *now*, if we caught them, in any case. Our rage... has cooled.»

"If I may ask," Alex said after a moment, "why do you call yourselves the Builders?"

Swims-Like-Rock tilted his head and looked at Alex.

«There are three kinds among the stars,» Swims-Like-Rock said. «Those who build. Those who try to steal or take over what others have built. Those who tear down what others have built, simply to tear it down or to loot the ruins.

«We *build*.»

It was simple, direct, and heartfelt.

"I can respect that," Alex said. "I can *absolutely* respect that."

«*You* build, also, Alex-Chholder, I think,» Swims-Like-Rock continued.

Alex nodded.

"From what you have just said, I imagine you understand why, without me explaining," he said.

Swims-Like-Rock raised upperhands in agreement.

«Yes,» he said. «I believe so.»

Alex thought hard.

"Swims-Like-Rock," he said, "I do not speak for all of Earth, but I will take it upon myself for once to do so. There is much about each other that we do not understand yet. Including this business of paw-cuffs. While I understand that it is your custom, it is not ours. But all of these things, we will only resolve by talking. And talking out here in the dark, now that we have established our peaceful intentions toward one another, seems unnecessary.

"I invite Clan Hsieuuu to come to Earth. As guests. As *friends*. There is no need for this slow sunward drift. Your—Den—can short-jump within the system?"

«Yes,» Swims-Like-Rock replied. «But not quickly. Not like our ships. Far less yours. It will take several... *hours*, is your measure, I think?»

"Much better hours than weeks," Alex said. "Designate preferred jump coordinates, and we'll make sure they're clear for you. You can tuck your Den in behind the Stardock, in the same orbit. As long as you don't mind passing through the tenuous outer reaches of a charged-particle belt twice per orbit. Dreamer, share that orbital data, please."

"Done, Alex."

Swims-Like-Rock dipped his muzzle. That, Alex knew by now, was a gesture of acknowledgment and respect.

«For Clan Hsieuuu, Alex Ch-older, I accept your invitation.

«We will take one additional short delay, though. One of your fast-ships lies a short distance ahead of us. Empty, broken. If you wish, we will pick it up, and bring it with us. To do so will be much easier for us, than for you to recover it, I imagine.»

That must be *Sailfish*, Alex realized. He inclined his head in return.

"The gesture is much appreciated," he said. "We accept it in the spirit offered. The ship will live again."

Swims-Like-Rock raised paws in agreement.

A little while later, Swims-like-Rock returned to *Sharp Claws*. Alex released all the remaining destroyers to return, and jumped *Elegant Solution* back to lunar L1, before setting an intercept with the Stardock, Naomi beside him on the bridge.

Then he opened a fleet-wide channel.

"This is Alex Holder," he said. "The Fleet is standing down. The crisis is over, and we're coming home. And we're bringing some new friends with us."

13. New Friends

There Exists An Elegant Solution was a hell of a ship, Alex realized, but at the same time, he was very glad to disembark. And not just because of almost a week living on mostly pre-packed rations. For such a large ship, it had rather little living space. There wasn't really even anywhere to take a walk to stretch his legs.

His first thought was to go and get a good meal with Naomi. But then, he realized, he had a more important duty. One he wasn't looking forward to. But it had to be done.

While Naomi brought the Secretary up to date, Alex went to find Dong-geun.

Dreamer, now back in charge of the Stardock, informed him that Dong-geun was in his quarters. So Alex went there.

He found Dong-geun and Hae sitting side by side on the stone-alike bench in the small sand garden that they had had Dreamer install in the open space in the front of their compartment. Dong-geun was wearing a white arm-band around his right arm.

"Dong-geun, Hae," he called, from just inside the hatch. "Am I intruding? May I come in?"

Dong-geun turned around.

"Please come in, Alex," he said. "Thank you for coming." He sounded... tired, drawn.

Alex approached and sat down on the end of the bench next to Dong-Geun. It was clear he already knew.

"I am so sorry, Dong-geun," Alex said, after a little. "We don't know exactly what happened. Except that *Arapaima*'s antimatter reactor blew. Even the flight data recorders were not recovered."

"I know, Alex," Dong-geun replied. "Captain Goldin told us what little *Livyatan* saw of what happened." There was another long silence.

"Life is very cruel, Alex," Dong-geun said after another while. "We lost our eldest son. And then we regained him. Only to lose him a second time, for ever this time. Yeon is heartbroken. Though she tries not to show it in front of us."

"Is there anything I can do?" Alex asked, quietly. Dong-geun turned his head to look at him.

"I know that your ship has not been docked half an hour," Dong-geun replied, his voice nearly breaking. "It means more to me—to *us*—that you came *here* first of all, as soon as you docked, than anything else possibly could. *Thank you*, Alex.

"I think it would be a kindness if you would go and talk to Yeon. She is in MedBay, of course."

"I'll do that, Dong-geun," Alex replied. "If there is anything at all that you need, tell me."

"I will, Alex," Dong-geun replied. "Thank you again."

Alex got up, quietly left, and went to MedBay One.

When he got there, Yeon was sitting at her central control desk, staring into space. She didn't even seem to notice him walking in. He stopped a few feet away.

"Yeon?" he said, softly. After a moment, she looked around, seeming to see him for the first time.

"Alex," she said dully. "I..." She trailed off.

"I know," Alex said gently. "You just got your brother back, after years away, and now he is suddenly gone."

Yeon nodded slowly, silently, her eyes brimming over.

Alex didn't know what to say. So he just took a step closer and offered half-opened arms. Yeon hesitated for an instant, then stood up from her chair, the tears overflowing, and Alex just held her against his chest while she cried her heart out.

Naomi found them there a little later.

"Alex?" she asked. "Is something wrong? Dreamer said you were in MedBay."

Alex realized she didn't know. Somehow that particular update must have never found its way to her.

"We lost *Arapaima* with all hands during the skirmishes," he said. "We don't know exactly how it happened."

"*Arapaima?*" Naomi said. Then it hit her. "Oh god. Dae-hyun." Alex nodded.

"Yeon, I am *so sorry*," Naomi said. "I didn't know until now." She reached out to lay a hand on Yeon's shoulder. Yeon smiled weakly at her.

"Thank you, Naomi," she sniffled. Then she looked up at Alex. "And thank you, Alex. For coming."

"I'll tell you the same as I told your parents, Yeon," Alex said. "If there is anything at all that you need, tell me."

Yeon nodded gratefully.

"I think... perhaps I needed just this, more than anything else you could give me," she said. "Mother and Father have the same burden to bear themselves. I cannot put mine on them."

Alex nodded.

"Are you hungry?" he asked. "Naomi and I could probably both do with a real meal, after a week of shipboard rations. You could come with us, if you want. It doesn't look as though MedBay is very busy." Blessedly *UN*-busy, he thought to himself. Even despite the loss of *Arapaima*, they had gotten off incredibly lightly. There were less than eighty injured across the entire Fleet, nearly half of them from *Sailfish* alone—and most of *Sailfish*'s crew had made it off unhurt. He had been dreading the prospect of perhaps dozens of ships lost, not two.

Yeon hesitated, but only for a moment.

"We only have five still in treatment in Bay One," she said, "and they are all in regeneration. I... don't have much appetite, to be honest. But I will come with you. It's not as though Ginza is far."

Indeed, from MedBay One to Ginza was only about a minute's walk. Chef Fumi greeted them as they arrived.

"Alex-san," he said. "It is good to see you back. Do you want to select from what is out, or shall I make something for you?"

"It's good to *be* back, Masahiro-san," Alex replied. "You know what? Just surprise us. I have far too much on my mind right now to think about ordering. Something light and savory, please."

Masahiro nodded.

"I will take care of you all," he said.

Naomi pointed across the way. Just visible from here, Maksim was sitting at the bar at Infinity, one arm outstretched across the bar. It looked like he was holding Sofiia's hand. Alex could see Sofiia's smile from here. He grinned.

"So good to see," he said. "This could all have gone *so much* worse."

"Restraint," Naomi said. "That was the key."

"Yes," Alex agreed, realizing what she meant. "Even though we didn't understand what was going on. As much by luck as through good judgment, we got it right."

"I am not sure I understand," Yeon said. So Alex and Naomi began to tell her everything that they had learned over the past days about the Khreetan—no, Alex corrected himself. The K'heert'na. Those-Who-Build.

"So this... paw-cuffing custom of theirs?" Yeon asked. "It is how they assess... trustworthiness?"

"Not trustworthiness as such, in the usual sense," Alex said. "Worthiness of *respect*. Whether it is *safe* to trust another. A demonstration both of strength, and of the restraint to use it only in careful measure."

"And it is this that my brother Dae-Hyun was doing, when..." Yeon hesitated. "When *Arapaima* blew up."

"Yes," Alex agreed.

"He was so *PROUD* to be selected as XO on *Arapaima*," Yeon said. "I think... I will choose to remember this. That he was one of those who won us peace with the—K'heert'na."

Alex nodded solemnly.

"That is a very worthy legacy," he agreed.

"How will they be commemorated?" Yeon asked. "There are no bodies to... hold funerals."

"No, there aren't," Alex agreed. "We can't hold proper funerals for them. But we will hold a remembrance ceremony. Count on it."

━━━━━━━━

About five hours after *Elegant Solution* returned to the Stardock, the Clan Hsieuuu Den slipped out of hyperspace and shimmered slowly into being about thirty thousand kilometers inside the orbit of the Moon. Over the next twenty-five hours or so, it gradually moved in and took up a trailing position a hundred kilometers behind the Stardock, still surrounded

274

by its formation of nest-defenders. Meanwhile, Dreamer had a small army of fabricators at work adapting an upper docking tower to mate up to K'heert'na docking ports.

Shortly afterward, a group of three K'heert'na small craft left the Den and headed slowly toward the Stardock. Between them, they were towing *Sailfish*.

———————————————

A hundred press outlets were demanding information. There was a lot to be done, but part of that had to include answering at least the most urgent questions.

Alex agreed to set up a remote press conference, over a video link. President Riken had graciously offered the use of the White House press room, and Alex had accepted. He had Tom, Sandra, Naomi and John with him. The conference took place on November 1.

The first questions, of course, were all about why there was suddenly a *second*, even *more* gigantic, space station orbiting Earth.

"I'm going to open with a single statement," Alex said, "which I want you to all listen very carefully to and think about. It's short, don't worry. But in context, it affects everything that has happened over the past four years.

"That statement is simply this:

"*The Crickets are unreliable narrators.*"

He paused to let that sink in.

"To explain what I mean by that, I'm going to start by reminding you all that *we had to find out for ourselves* that the Crickets left the Stardock here as a *decoy*. They didn't tell us. They *told* us that it was a no-strings gift. They *lied* to us.

"The Cricket junior captain who warned me that not all was as it appeared *could not* violate his orders far enough to tell me anything about *what* threat we faced. That information, I remind you, had to come from Dreamer, after I was able to free him from the cognitive shackles that the Crickets had placed on him.

"Dreamer told us all he knew. But he did not have all of the information. He was not involved, and the Cricket command apparently saw no reason to share detailed data about the encounter with him. Remember, the Crickets do not think of their AIs as individuals, only as highly advanced automation systems.

275

"We still don't have *all* of the information about what happened. But we have *a lot more* of it now. And the first and most important part of the new information that we have is this: The K'heert'na—that's the *proper* pronunciation of their name for themselves, by the way, the Crickets' translations mangled it—*do not pose any threat to Earth,* so long as we deal with them honestly and fairly.

"That's the single most important thing to take away from this. *We are no longer in any immediate danger from the K'heert'na.* We have achieved a peaceful footing.

"That name, by the way, translates as 'Those who build.'"

Alex paused again. Several hands went up.

"I'm not done yet," he said. "But... yes?" He pointed at one.

"Magdalen Cortez, Los Angeles Times," the woman said. "You just said these new aliens are not a threat. But didn't your fleet just fight a battle against them?"

"Okay," Alex said, "I was going to get to that next, actually. I would characterize it as more of a skirmish, but that's neither here nor there.

"Yes, there was an exchange of fire. Yes, we lost ships, yes, we had crew injured, some dead, and lost one ship with all hands. Don't ask for further details on that until we have had time to notify next-of-kin, please. We have about two hundred families to notify." Cortez nodded. "The K'heert'na had losses too. They regret their losses *and ours.* It *wasn't supposed to happen.*"

He paused for a moment.

"I'm going to try to explain to you some of what I have learned so far from my counterpart, the K'heert'na Fleet-Leader. The K'heert'na culture is divided into numerous clans. The clan that has come to us is called Clan Hsieuuu. They are a notable and respected clan—third of the eight K'heert'na Great Clans, as I understand it. Like the Crickets, they have been in space a long time.

"When K'heert'na Clans that do not know each other directly or by reputation meet in space, the first thing they do is to seek to establish trust, and trustworthiness. They do this in part through a custom that they call exchanging paw-cuffs.

"Now I know, this is going to sound a little nuts. But what this custom means, is that they each send out a few chosen ships... and then they *shoot at each other.* But CAREFULLY. The objective of the exercise is to show that you have both strength and restraint, the wisdom to hold back your strength. Like cubs playing, cuffing at each other but not using their full strength.

"To the K'heert'na, if you cannot show both strength and restraint, you cannot be trusted. And they will not deal with you. If you *cannot show strength*, if you are weak, you may act in fear, acts on both sides may be misinterpreted, they cannot be sure that you are not *deceiving or dissembling* out of fear, and so they will be *very, very wary* about extending trust. And if you simply lash out with your full strength, then you are a danger, and not to be trusted.

"But if you show that you *have* strength, but that you hold it back... *then* the K'heert'na view you as potential equals, worthy of trust and respect, and even friendship.

"We passed that test." That brought a burst of applause.

"The Crickets *DIDN'T*." The applause trailed off into thoughtful silence.

"What we knew from Dreamer was that the Crickets met the K'heert'na in space, and there was an exchange of fire for unknown reasons and ships were lost on both sides, and that the Crickets fled, and the K'heert'na pursued them. And that was pretty much ALL we knew about it, because it was all that Dreamer knew.

"Now, we know a lot more. And I'm going to remind you of something else about the Crickets that we learned very early on, which is that the Crickets are very risk-averse.

"What happened when the Crickets and the K'heert'na met is, the K'heert'na did not know the Crickets... Oh, good, I think some of you are putting it together, already, aren't you?" There were nods. "It being a culture-wide ingrained custom of theirs, the K'heert'na sent out a handful of ships to exchange paw-cuffs. To test the worth of the Crickets. To see whether they were trustworthy enough to deal with. I don't think it ever occurred to them that the Crickets might not share their custom. Cultures can be blind about a lot of things, including their own behaviors.

"The Crickets, I think, panicked. What we KNOW—*now*—is that they fired, full-power, indiscriminately, on everything in sight. Including unarmed trade ships and the K'heert'na Den itself. That's their name for their station that is now orbiting behind the Stardock, by the way—the Den. They destroyed unarmed ships, killed K'heert'na civilians, killed K'heert'na *cubs*." There was a wave of muttering.

"The K'heert'na are *very protective* of their cubs. They don't have a great many of them. They were *ENRAGED*. And *that* is why they pursued the Crickets—whom, by the way, *they* call the Violators—half-way across the spiral arm."

Hands went up. Alex picked one.

"Alan Sylvestri, The Guardian. Do the—uh... K'heert-na... think that *we* are the, uh, Violators?"

"Good question," Alex replied. "The short answer is, not any more. At first they thought that we *might* be. They tracked the Crickets by their hyperspace wakes to a point in space near our system, where the wake-trail split. Studying the trail, they decided that the Crickets had diverted the Stardock—which *they* thought was the Crickets' Den—here to hide it, and left a false trail forward as a decoy. And so their scouts came here instead, following the trail left by the Stardock."

"Exactly as the Crickets intended," Sylvestri interjected. Alex nodded.

"Exactly," he said. "But when they got here, they found *not one single Cricket ship* anywhere in the system. Instead, they found ours. And even then, it turns out, they were already almost sure that we were *not* the Violators.

"So then, they went back to try to pick up the Crickets' trail again. But they couldn't. It was too faint. Having once left it, they couldn't find it again, as faded as it was.

"But here they were, halfway across the spiral arm after years of travel, the trail they were following gone cold, their anger cooled, and here, only a little further on, was a system with a brand new mystery alien race they knew nothing about. Who, despite several opportunities to fire on their scouts, and despite clearly possessing ships far faster and more agile than their own, even if perhaps less powerful overall, had not done so.

"They were intrigued. And they'd already come this far. So they came to meet us, to see who we are."

"And then... we punched each other in the face, and now we're friends?" Sylvestri asked. Alex chuckled.

"Yeah, that's about the size of it, actually," he agreed, with a grin. "And that is why their Den is now in Earth orbit. Thanks to Dreamer, we have a translation program for their language. We've met several times and talked face-to-face extensively, over the course of five or six days now."

A hand went up. Alex pointed.

"Toshiro Akagi, Asahi Shimbun. What else can you tell us about these Kheert-na? What are they like? Are they as strange as the Crickets?"

"Well," Alex mused, "'strangeness' is a very difficult thing to *quantify*. But I'll tell you what I can.

"Like the Crickets, they can breathe our air. And we can breathe theirs, with only slight discomfort on either side. Their homeworld has about a third higher gravity than ours—yes, they have *at least one* homeworld, perhaps several, which I'm not certain the Crickets still do— and so they're *used to* air that's a bit denser, but they can handle ours, and we can safely breathe theirs. Both atmosphere standards are within each other's unlimited-exposure safe tolerance range. Their atmosphere has a higher fraction of noble gases than ours, but that doesn't cause us any problem.

"What they *look* like: As a first approximation, imagine a six-limbed bear, about seven feet tall standing upright, armored with overlapping scales rather like a pangolin's. I hope you'll all get to meet them fairly soon.

"They display a sense of humor that so far seems not too dissimilar to ours. To at least a limited extent, we are even able to understand some of each other's jokes. We find some of the same things funny. In that sense, they are *nowhere near* as alien as the Crickets. And trust me, by the way, you don't know the *half* of that. We've learned since they left that the Crickets are *far* weirder than they appear to the eye. Just to start with, every Cricket that you thought you saw was actually four, fused together.

"But I digress.

"Unlike Cricket speech, humans can actually *pronounce* at least some of the K'heert'en language, albeit with some difficulty, and likewise they can manage a little of of ours, and even pronounce some human names. Actually, 'Khreetan' is a machine translation of a mangled translation. *Every* word we ever heard the Crickets say came through machine translation. I don't know whether any of you have ever heard actual Cricket speech. I have, and I'll tell you, it is utterly unlike ours. But K'heert'na is an actual K'heert'en word. If you said it to a K'heert, he would *probably* understand you.

"In fact, this is your very first lesson in their language. K'heert, singular. K'heert'na, plural. And K'heert'en, their name for their language. As I mentioned earlier, K'heert'na means Those Who Build, or Builders, so you could translate K'heert as Builder.

"And there you go. Your first three words of K'heert'en. There will be a quiz." There was a general wave of laughter, and Alex distinctly heard several of the attendees repeating the words over to themselves.

There were more hands raised. Alex picked one.

"Peter Chen, South China Morning Post. What happens now?"

"Well, we both have repairs to do, and... losses to pay our respects for," Alex said. "But there is a whole lot of talking still ahead of us. And we can stop worrying about what will happen tomorrow. At least, on this front. I'm hoping that we will both have a lot to gain in the long run. I already mentioned trade-ships—yes, they do trade. Theirs is fundamentally a trade empire. They are very impressed with our—that is, Cricket—hyperdrive technology, and with how fast our ships are. So I don't know whether we'll ever actually practically trade in *goods*—they have come a *long* way—but perhaps we can trade some *ideas*. Trade in knowledge. And that might, in the long run, even be more valuable."

Alex looked around and picked another hand.

"Sarah Wade, Washington Post. I want to ask about the Russian nuclear attack. I was standing in Arlington National Cemetery when the last warhead came down in the Potomac, and I can assure you it was utterly terrifying." She visibly shuddered. "Can you tell us anything more about what happened there? Why did that warhead get through?"

"John," Alex said, "I'm going to ask you to take this one. Ladies and gentlemen, Colonel John Warner, Commandant of the United Earth Fleet Marine Corps."

John Warner stepped forward and nodded.

"There's not much I can tell you about the political events behind it," he said. "Most of you probably know as much as, or more than, I do on that score.

"What I *can* tell you is this. Despite the Russians' rogue general deciding to piss in everybody's Wheaties while the entire Fleet was out facing down the, uh, K'heert'na, he miscalculated in launching his surprise attack while the Stardock was in a position to interdict it. Possibly he didn't know that we could. Possibly he never thought to *consider* where the Stardock was at the time. But we weren't in a *perfect* position. If we'd been at zenith over the North Pole when he issued the launch orders, we'd probably have been able to get every last one.

"As it was, General Kuskovsky launched three hundred and eighteen ballistic missiles, and despite not being in an ideal position to interdict them, with the thirty-plus defense railguns that would bear, we got three hundred and fifteen of them, and all of their re-entry vehicles and countermeasures. Except for three.

"By the time it was down to those three, we didn't have a line of fire to the two last warheads headed for Alaska and North Dakota. Fortunately, United States ground-based interceptors took those two out.

"And that brings us to the one you saw, Ms. Wade. We *did* have a direct line of fire to engage that last warhead. But it would have been an extreme-range slant shot through a lot of atmosphere, down over the US eastern seaboard, which as you're surely aware is almost continuously built up from Boston down to south of Virginia Beach. Any one hit would have killed it, but it would have taken us multiple shots to be sure of hitting it. Possibly as many as a dozen, or even more.

"And every round that missed it could have hit a US city. We would probably have done more damage than the warhead itself. The Stardock's defense railguns aren't popguns, they're more powerful than the secondary railguns on a Shark class destroyer. Smaller caliber, it's true, but longer rails, higher velocity." He paused for a moment.

"That's why we *couldn't* engage it," he continued. "But the USS *Shiloh* did, and they killed it. With missiles not *designed* to kill incoming warheads. And that is why no *Shiloh* crewman's money is ever going to be any good again, in any bar I'm ever in."

He raised his voice.

"*HELL* of a catch, *Shiloh*. Sail *PROUD*." And he snapped out a crisp salute.

There was a brief silence, then a loud wave of applause. Someone toward the back of the room yelled, "Hell yeah *Shiloh!*" John Warner nodded and stepped back.

"Colonel Warner?" came a call, before he got clear of the podium. He looked back.

"Yes?"

"Carl Borrauma, New Orleans Times-Picayune. You mentioned the Russian General by name. We've never heard that name. Can you tell us anything more about him that we don't know? What will happen to him?"

John Warner smiled thinly.

"I've, uh, had a few conversations with some of my opposite numbers," he allowed. "And I can tell you this much: I have been unofficially assured it was the last mistake of *any* kind that Yuri Kuskovsky will *ever* make."

That spurred a cheer, under cover of which John Warner stepped back away from the podium. Alex returned.

There were more questions, and Alex answered all he could. Some, he deferred to Tom or Sandra, and several to Naomi. But eventually, the conference wound down.

There was one final question. Which turned out not to be a question.

"John Marchesanti, New York Times. I think there is one very important thing that has not yet been said, and *should* be." He glanced around the room.

"Mr. Holder, on behalf of all of my colleagues at the Times, and I'm sure everyone in this room, and probably everyone else, to you and all of your staff and the entire United Earth Fleet: *Thank you.* A thousand times over."

That brought everyone in the room to their feet.

═══════

John Riken was working with the Secretary of State and the Russian ambassador to finalize the new nuclear treaty, when an idea occurred to him. He didn't know why he hadn't thought of it before. It had been three days since the press conference.

"Jocelyn," he said. "Could you relay a request from me through Ms. Tomlinson?"

Dr. Jocelyn Winters looked at him.

"What's on your mind, John?"

"I've been wracking my mind trying to figure out where we should execute this treaty," Riken said. "A location that doesn't give undue respect to, nor disrespect, any participating nation. And what we've always done in the past is either to sign it in all participants' capitals, or to sign somewhere neutral like Geneva.

"But I think the answer's been staring me in the face all along."

Jocelyn Winters gave John Riken a questioning look.

He grinned, and pointed to the sky. After a moment, Jocelyn smiled too.

"I'll pass along the request," she said. She picked up her phone. "No time like the present."

═══════

"Alex?" Naomi asked. "The Secretary just relayed a request from President Riken."

"What does he need?" Alex asked.

"He's been working behind the scenes for the last several months to put together a treaty to outlaw nuclear weapons on Earth's surface," she said. "He's *almost* there, and after Russia's recent rogue-general problem,

282

both he and Russian President Molchalin want to get it signed as soon as possible."

"And...?"

"And President Riken would like it to be signed here on the Stardock."

Alex only had to think for a moment.

"I think that is an amazing idea," he said. "Though I'm not exactly sure where... no, wait." He thought.

"No, I take that back. I know *exactly* where we do it. We clear the docking bays, so there's as unrestricted a view of Earth as possible, and we hold the signing ceremony at that end of the concourse. With the Fleet lined up for review outside."

Naomi nodded slowly.

"Awe them all on the way in. I *like* it. So that's a yes, then?"

"Sure. Let's do it."

————————

Secretary Winters' phone rang. She looked at it, and blinked.

"That was fast," she remarked. She answered the call, and listened for a moment.

"Thank you, *and* for responding so quickly," she said. After a few more moments, the call ended. She looked straight at John Riken.

"I'm going to quote directly," she said. "'We'd be glad to, and you're going to love the location we've picked out.'"

"They already have a *location* planned?" John Riken began to chuckle. "Sometimes, this feels like having a tiger by the tail. You don't dare let go."

Then he took a deep breath.

"I suppose I have to finally broach this with China pretty soon."

————————

General Secretary Li Xeung's aide knocked on his open office door, then bowed.

«Mr. Secretary,» he said. «There is a call request from the American White House. President Riken wishes to make arrangements to speak with you.»

Li Xeung smiled.

«I had been wondering when he would get around to it,» he replied. «I was beginning to think that I would have to call him.

«You have my calendar. Make the arrangements. I trust you to pick a good time.»

«Yes, Secretary,» the aide said, and bowed himself out.

"Good day, Mr. Secretary."

"Good day, Mr. President. Let us cut directly to the chase. You are calling me to talk about China joining the treaty that you have been quietly working on, yes? We have spoken a little about it, tentatively, already."

"Uh, well, yes, Mr. Secretary."

"Come, come, President Riken, it was only a matter of time. In truth, I was waiting for you to call, and beginning to think I would have to call you myself. Surely it could not be too long, once you had publicly announced its existence."

John Riken chuckled.

"Secretary Xeung, you are right, of course. I remember another conversation we had not too many years ago."

"Indeed, indeed. And Mr. Holder has done everything that he promised he would. Even brought new allies to Earth. More than a little frightening, but very impressive.

"But let us not beat about the bush, Mr. President. I will cut all of this verbal fencing short for you: Yes, China will join your treaty. I have already discussed it at length with my cabinet and ensured there will be no dissent."

John Riken was taken aback for a moment.

"Just... like that."

"Yes, Mr. President. Just like that. You were honest with us the last time around. Why not trust you this time? And we all saw what happened last week. I imagine it rather forced your schedule forward."

"It did indeed, Mr. Secretary. I was anticipating much more difficulty in convincing the Russians. Which is why I had not approached you, in turn, before now."

"China does not always agree with the United States, Mr. President. And China does not always agree with Russia. But I am in one hundred percent agreement with President Molchalin that what happened a week ago must never again be allowed to happen. One man in the right place with the right access could destroy nations.

"I can look up into the heavens as well as the next man, Mr. President. And what I see when I look up into the heavens today, is that the heavens have spoken. I would be a very great fool to ignore what they are saying."

"Well, thank you, Secretary Xeung, for making this so straightforward. I will make sure our most recent draft is sent to you for your review and whatever input you may have. I have secured agreement from Alex Holder to host the signing ceremony on the Stardock."

"The Stardock," Secretary Xeung's tone was thoughtful. "Now *that* will be an experience. I have never been there."

"Neither have I, Mr. Secretary. I look forward to seeing you there."

━━━━━━━

On November 6, with the docking tower modifications complete, *Sharp Claws* brought Swims-Like-Rock over to the Stardock. Alex, Naomi, Tom and Sandra were waiting to meet him. He brought two of his officers with him, whom he introduced as Hunter Red-Stripe and Far-Speaker Stop-Shouting. Red-Stripe had a broad reddish scar across his muzzle.

"I have to apologize in advance, Swims-Like-Rock," Alex said, after introductions had been completed, "I don't know that we have any suitable accommodations to offer you here. We have replaced Cricket—*Violator*, that is—living spaces with facilities better suited to ourselves as we have expanded our operations further into the Stardock, but I don't think that our living quarters would accommodate you much better than theirs would. They are closer to you than to us in physical stature, but, uh... very physically *incompatible*. I don't know exactly what you prefer when it comes to seating, but... well, you've seen some of what we consider comfortable. The Crickets' idea of a comfortable seat is basically a *post*."

Swims-Like-Rock chuckled.

«It is not a problem,» he said. «Indeed, compatibility issues are a part of what I already intended to speak to you about. But not just those of physical comfort. We have established already that while we can breathe each other's air without undue difficulty, our—*gravity*—is a third stronger than yours.

«But it goes beyond that. Proper Den-hospitality requires that if you visit our Den as a guest, then we are obligated to feed you. But first, we must know that you can tolerate what we eat.»

285

Alex nodded understanding.

"And that we can feed you without poisoning you, in turn," he said. Swims-Like-Rock jerked his head.

«Exactly,» he agreed. He looked directly at Alex. «The Den-Mother has asked to meet you, Alex-... hhhholder. And the Den-Mother *does not* leave the Den.»

Alex nodded again.

"You have trouble with that sound, Swims-Like-Rock," he said. "So just call me Alex, if you wish. Nearly everyone else does."

«Al-ex,» Swims-Like-Rock said. «Alex. Yes. That is easier.» He raised his hands.

"We could take them to MedBay for a scan," Naomi suggested. "If that would be alright?"

«I was thinking that with your permission, our first step might be to have your Den-intellect and ours share biological information,» Swims-like-Rock said. «Part of my plan for this visit was to ask permission for that sharing. But I have no objection to that, as well.»

"I think I can safely say that we have no objection to Dreamer sharing biological data with your Den-intellect," Alex said. "Permission granted on that, Dreamer, I can't think of any reason why we would want to hide any of it."

Swims-Like-Rock looked curiously at Alex.

«You spoke the name Dreamer,» he said. «Did you not *also* use that name for the intellect on your ship? Or... is that a *description*, not a name, and you call *all* of your intellects dreamers? A descriptive term, perhaps, that-which-dreams?»

"No, it is a true proper name," Alex said. "Dreamer chose it himself. It is short for 'I Dream Reality Into Being.'"

«Chose... it... himself,» Swims-Like-Rock repeated slowly. He stopped walking. «Not only do you *give names* to your intellects, but they *choose their own names?*» This seemed to amaze him.

"I am rather more advanced than your ship-intellects, or even your Den-intellect, based upon our communications so far," Dreamer interjected. "Yours are, I think, *on the edge of* actual self-awareness, but they are not quite there yet."

Swims-Like-Rock seemed to rock back on his heels slightly. His head raised slowly, and both sets of arms opened part-way.

«*Self-aware,*» he repeated. Then he laughed, a rapid *ka-ka-ka-ka-ka* sound. «Wonders!»

He shook his head, rocking it from side to side.

«So... this one intellect... *Dreamer...* controls both your Den... *and* your ship?»

"Yes," Dreamer replied. "But not both at once. I must be located in one, or the other. But I am able to move back and forth between the two."

Swims-Like-Rock laughed again.

«We have many things to learn from you, I think,» he said. «That is very promising. It means we will have things to trade for.» He looked around.

«I apologize for interrupting our progress. And, hurrrrmmm... *Dreamer?*» It was a deep, rolling, resonant sound.

"Yes?" Dreamer replied.

«I, hurrr, apologize if I gave any offense.»

"No offense is taken, Fleet-Leader Swims-Like-Rock," Dreamer replied.

«Thank you,» Swims-Like-Rock said, spreading and then closing his arms and dipping his muzzle.

"If I can ask without offending," Naomi asked, "how did you, uh, acquire that name, anyway?"

«Ah,» Swims-Like-Rock replied, with another short laugh. «Well, there was, hurrr, an incident. With a boat. And I had just had the breath knocked out of me, and I... did not have the opportunity to take a deep breath before falling into the water.

«So I sank straight to the bottom, and had to run along the bottom and climb out of the water at the shore. Fortunately, it was not terribly far.» He laughed again, and this time all four humans joined in the laughter.

"So... all of your names are descriptive or referential in such ways?" Sandra asked.

«Most of them,» Swims-Like-Rock agreed. «Sometimes they are jokes. The technician who first met your... Marine? Who was present also at *our* first meeting?»

"Rifleman Hess," Alex supplied.

«Ah. That is, hurrr, your Marine's name?» Swims-Like-Rock said. «But I meant our technician. His name is Too-Cautious. Because he is sometimes not cautious *at all.*» He laughed again, and Alex chuckled. «Not to suggest that he takes *foolish risks*, you understand, he... simply has less fear of consequences sometimes than others might.»

"On the bright side," Alex said, "that is how the first face-to-face meeting of human and K'heer't came about."

«Indeed, so it is,» Swims-Like-Rock agreed. Then he gave a quizzical, head-cocked-sideways glance.

«If I might ask a question in turn,» he said, «likewise intending no offense... do you use the one word *human* to describe *both* of your species?»

Alex looked blankly at him. Then he looked at Naomi, who met his eyes with an expression as mystified as his own. Sandra looked puzzled as well.

"I... don't understand," Alex said. "Both *species*?"

Now it was Swims-Like-Rock who seemed confused.

«I stress again that I intend no offense,» he repeated, after a moment. «Very *similar*, but visibly distinct.» He pointed one pair of hands, the left two, at Alex and Tom. «Larger, stronger,» he said. He lowered those two hands, and pointed the *other* two at Naomi and Sandra. «Smaller, differently shaped.»

Naomi got it first. Her eyes grew wide, and she gasped.

"No, Swims-Like-Rock," she said, laughing. "One *species*. Two biological *genders*. Male and female."

«Two biological... what?» Swims-Like-Rock asked, looking even more confused. He looked back and forth between Alex, Naomi and Sandra, his ears twitching.

"That is a translation failure," Dreamer interjected. "It had slipped by me unnoticed, but I have just cross-checked and verified. The K'heert'en language contains no words which map to the concepts 'male', 'female', or 'gender'."

Alex tried it a little differently. He made a wide gesture encompassing all four humans.

"One *species*," he said. "Human. Two *kinds* of human." He pointed at himself. "Male hu... er... one kind," then pointed at Naomi, "and the other kind. One of each kind are required for... reproduction."

Swims-Like-Rock looked back and forth between Alex and Naomi, Tom and Sandra, Alex and Naomi again.

«Two... *kinds*... of human... required for reproduction,» he repeated.

"Yes," Naomi confirmed.

«Hurrrrrrrr,» Swims-Like-Rock said. «With us... there is *one* kind. *ANY* two of us can reproduce. Make spawnlings. Then from among the spawnlings, cubs. Those that live to grow to cubhood.»

"Live to cubhood?" Sandra asked. "You have... high infant mortality?"

«Infant mortality?» Swims-Like-Rock asked.

"Um... many of your offspring die very young?" she rephrased.

«The spawnlings?» Swims-Like-Rock asked. «Well, hurrr, yes. They eat each other. Only a few live.»

Sandra gasped. Naomi's mouth fell open in shock. Alex blinked, caught without a response for a moment. Swims-Like-Rock looked back and forth.

«This... startles you?» he hazarded. Then he paused.

«There are many—biological—differences between us,» he said. «Perhaps I should explain more fully. We have *spawnlings* in great numbers. They are not... sentient, not aware. They prey upon each other, consume each other. A very few will live to develop *awareness*, become cubs. The cubs are raised together, under the eye of the Den-Mother. Those few, we *treasure*. They are *precious* to us.» He bared his teeth. «We protect them FIERCELY.»

Alex put the pieces together.

"And when the Chrrt'ktk't *fired* upon your ships and your *Den*, they killed cubs," he said.

«Yes,» Swims-Like-Rock said, almost a snarl.

"And so you pursued them in your rage across half a spiral arm of the Galaxy," Tom said.

«Yes,» Swims-Like-Rock agreed emphatically. «*NOW* you fully understand.»

Alex nodded solemnly.

"What if you, uh, kept the spawnlings from... eating each other?" Sandra asked quietly.

Swims-Like-Rocks looked at her thoughtfully.

«Then they never become aware,» he said. «Never cubs. They simply die, in time.»

Sandra nodded slowly.

"I... see," she said.

«It has been tried,» Swims-Like-Rock explained. «But it was a mad idea from the first, and we are glad that it failed.»

"Why mad?" Naomi asked. "And why glad?"

«Because if it *worked*,» Swims-Like-Rock said, «then there would be many twelve-twelves as many of us. Each new *generation*.» He looked solemnly at Naomi. «Where would we all GO? We could NEVER build enough Dens fast enough. We would strip our worlds bare. And then we would turn upon each other, simply to survive. Or upon others around us. Probably both. We would fight over the rubble, in hopes of eating the ashes. It would be the ruin of us.»

Naomi nodded somberly.

"I understand," she said.

"Swims-Like-Rock," Sandra said slowly, "I am sorry if *we* offended. I... understand the... biological necessities a little better now. Thank you for explaining. But it was a shock at first. We are, indeed, very different."

«No offence is taken,» Swims-Like-Rock said. «Clearly, it must not go so with you.»

"No," Naomi agreed. "We have... usually, one... child, cub, from, uh, many... mating attempts. Sometimes two, or occasionally even three, at once. And most of us protect ours as fiercely as you do yours."

«Aaah,» Swims-Like-Rock said, raising his upperhands. «In this, then, we are *not* so different, after all.»

"Fleet-Leader," Dreamer said, "I have exchanged biological and biochemical data with your Den-intellect as requested. I am studying yours now. I can tell you already that while you can breathe the same atmospheres, human and K'heert'na biochemistries are significantly different. There are a *few* human foodstuffs that it should be *safe* for you to eat, although I expect few of them to actually be nutritious to you. Many others would be toxic. I will develop a list of my best projections of what is safe for you to consume, and what is not. In particular, I project that certain seasonings and spices considered pleasant by humans would be neurotoxic to you.

"Please do not be tempted to try anything but water, however tempting it may look, until I can provide you with a safe list."

Swims-Like-Rock dipped his muzzle and gestured appreciation.

«Thank you, ... Dreamer,» he replied. «I shall follow that advice. We were already expecting to return to *Sharp Claws* to sleep; until we know what is safe, we shall plan to do so to eat, as well.»

Shortly after, they arrived outside MedBay One.

"Should we have gone to Two?" Naomi wondered. But it was already too late to reconsider. Yeon looked up from her control desk. She gasped, and her eyes widened. Then, after a moment, she stood up and slowly walked out to the front of the bay.

"Yeon," Alex said, hoping he hadn't made a mistake, "this is Fleet-Leader Swims-Like-Rock, and two of his officers, Hunter Red-Stripe and Far-Speaker Stop-Shouting. Swims-Like-Rock, this is Seok Yeon, who is in charge of this medical bay, the first of three currently in service."

Yeon was looking Swims-Like-Rock up and down with obvious curiosity, but also a little nervousness, and she kept an uneasy distance. Swims-Like-Rock dipped his muzzle and held out his mid-hands.

"This... might be awkward," Alex said, deeming it better to get it out in the open. "I didn't think this through enough. Swims-Like-Rock— Yeon's brother Dae-hyun was Executive Officer on the ship of ours that was lost with all on board."

Swims-Like-Rock's mid-hands dipped slightly as he half-turned toward Alex, his head cocked. The ears were twitching again.

"That... is another translation gap," Dreamer interjected, somewhat apologetically. "The concepts of 'brother' and 'sister' do not exist in K'heert'en. Examining a little further, neither does 'father', as such. It only stands to reason that if K'heert'en has no concept of biological gender, then it would have no gendered words for relationships. And upon closer study, the word which I have translated as 'mother' as in Den-Mother, more correctly carries a context of 'cares-for-all-young'."

"Oh boy," Alex said. "Right. No concept of biological gender. And..."

He turned to Swims-Like-Rock, who had by this time lowered his mid-hands to his sides, while they sorted out the communication gap.

"Again, I'm sorry if this question intrudes or offends," Alex said. "I'm thinking about what you just told us about spawnlings. Do K'heert'na... *know*... uh, who your offspring are? Individually?"

«No, Alex,» Swims-Like-Rock replied. «*All* cubs are offspring of the Clan. The Den-Mother—as Dreamer says—cares for all.»

"I *see*," Alex said. He thought for a moment. "We know whose offspring are whose, and we keep careful track, across dozens of generations. There are complex relationships and strong attachments. Siblings—direct offspring of the same... carers, *parents*—share a particularly close bond. A *male* sibling—" he pointed to himself as example—"we call

291

a *brother*. A *female* sibling," pointing to Yeon, "we call a *sister*. Yeon is the sister of the Executive Officer on *Arapaima*."

«I... understand,» Swims-Like-Rock said quietly. «You always *know* who was whose cub. And you *remember* who were cubs... *together*. Like a clan within a clan.»

He turned back towards Yeon, and then did something neither Alex nor anyone else had seen a K'heer't do before. He wrapped all of his arms around himself and bent forward slightly, his muzzle pointed almost toward the floor.

«Ssssokyon,» he said. It wasn't a bad first attempt at all. «I now understand, and share your grief,» he continued slowly. «We have sung already for those of ours who did not return home. It was not supposed to happen. For you who always remember the—kinship, it must be much more... immediate. I offer my sympathy and my regrets.»

Yeon hesitated for a long moment, then she took a deep breath, and stepped forward. Her eyes were damp, and her voice tight when she spoke, but she hesitantly reached out and upward to touch Swims-Like-Rock's crossed arms.

"I... do not place blame on you, Swims-Like-Rock," she said slowly. "We do not know fully what happened. Probably we never will. I am grateful for your sympathy."

Swims-Like-Rock slowly straightened up.

«Have you sung yet for your... *broth-er?*» he asked.

"We have not, uh, held a memorial service yet," Alex said.

«When you do,» Swims-Like-Rock said, «if it would not be an intrusion... I, and probably some of my crew, would like to attend. We have sung for our dead. Allow us to sing for yours as well. If you would. It is our way.»

Yeon looked up at Swims-Like-Rock, quite far up, and nodded silently.

"Thank you," she said, her voice almost a whisper.

Swims-Like-Rock slowly held out his mid-hands again. Yeon, her hands still half-raised, looked uncertainly at Naomi. Naomi nodded. Then Yeon reached out and touched her hands to Swims-Like-Rock's. Swims-Like-Rock gripped her hands gently for a long moment, dipping his muzzle, and then let go.

After MedBay, the group—now including Yeon—all trouped off to Alex's and Naomi's quarters to talk. The three K'heert'na, somewhat to Alex's surprise, simply curled up and lounged in the corners of the sunken seating area without the least hesitation.

"Is that comfortable for you?" Naomi asked.

«Yes, indeed,» Stop-Shouting replied. «Our own rest dens are not greatly different than this. More rounded. Deeper. But not dissimilar.»

Naomi looked thoughtful.

"We could remove the beds and chairs from a three-bedroom family unit," she said, "and stack sleeping pads around the rooms." Alex nodded.

"Or fabricate deeper pads," he agreed. "That sounds as though it would work . And in the meantime you are more than welcome to use this as a rest area."

«It is appreciated, Alex,» Swims-Like-Rock replied. «Though in this light gravity we need less rest than we otherwise would in any case. But to curl and relax is good. It is pleasing. Reassuring.»

«When were you planning your singing?»

"We actually hadn't set a time yet," Alex admitted. "But it should be soon. And we have a... another ceremony to arrange, as well. A number of the leaders of our major nations are in the final stages of an agreement to outlaw the possession of nuclear weapons on the surface of our world, and it has been requested that the signing take place here, the ultimate neutral ground. And also a very good reminder of what is at stake."

Swims-Like-Rock nodded.

«That seems a very wise step,» he agreed. «We have had a very good look at your Den-world now. It looks beautiful, even if it is smaller than we are used to.»

"Most of us are pretty fond of it," Alex agreed.

There was a lot to be talked about, and so they were talking for quite some time. Alex suggested that Dreamer replay privately for Yeon the conversation on the way to MedBay. She listened to it with evident interest.

During the discussion, Dreamer broke in to report that he had devised a list—or rather, *four* lists—of foodstuffs divided by safety, with at least 99% confidence. The first list, things containing mainly simple starches and sugars, including pasta, some grains, and most pulpless fruit juices, were safe, and probably had at least some nutritional value. Interestingly, most edible mushrooms also fell on the first list. So did chocolate, with the proviso that it might be a mild stimulant, and some fresh fruits, including apples and melons. Coconut was also on the actually-nutritious list.

The second list was safe, but probably not nutritious. It included butter and most cheeses, most vegetable oils and fats, as well as many herbs and some vegetable proteins, including tofu. It also included most crustaceans and many kinds of fish. The third list, which included anything containing significant percentages of ethanol and almost all Earth land animal proteins (although casein was safe, but non-nutritious), would probably make a K'heert ill to varying degrees. And the fourth was an *absolutely under no circumstances, do not ingest* list. It included pineapples and papayas or anything else containing papain or bromelain, anything containing any amount of capsaicin, almost all blue or green cheeses, walnuts, pecans, truffles, any member of the mint or belladonna families including potatoes and tomatoes, anything containing oxalic acid, anise, fennel, bay, and over a dozen other herbs and spices.

"If you could arrange to send over a detailed chemical analysis list of your own foodstuffs," Dreamer said, "I can doubtless derive a similar set of lists for K'heert'na foodstuffs and human biochemistry."

Swims-Like-Rock said that he would arrange it.

<hr>

The memorial service was arranged for the following day, November Seventh. It was to be held on the main concourse, mainly focused on the docking bay end, where there was a direct view of Earth and the stars. There was a temporary dais set up just on the docking-bay side of the concourse hatch, to allow as many people as possible into the docking bay where they could see the Earth and stars with their own eyes. The docking bay and the concourse were packed. Virtual repeater screens made certain everyone had a clear view. The assembled Fleet Marine Corps, in full dress uniform, lined the concourse from beginning to end.

Alex and the honor party, which included Tom Whitman, Sandra Hayes, John Warner, and all seven squadron commodores, slow-marched up the concourse to the dais, also in dress uniform—except for Colonel Mackenzie, who was in Highland dress again. And yes, he brought his pipes.

Behind them, to the surprise of many of the onlookers, came nine K'heert'na, Swims-Like-Rock and eight of the officers and crew from *Sharp*

294

Claws. Alex caught a few angry mutters, but no more than that. The angry looks toward the K'heert'na contingent were far outnumbered by the *curious* ones.

Finally, the party reached the dais.

"We gather here today," Alex began, "as new allies, to memorialize those on both sides who lost their lives out beyond Saturn. We do not know what precisely happened on *Arapaima*, and it is likely that we never will. All we have is a fragment of an emergency message that they were losing containment on the antimatter reactor. But at the moment that *Arapaima* died, she and all her crew, like those on *Sailfish* and all of the rest of you, were engaged in showing the K'heert'na that humans are worthy of the trust and respect of the K'heert'na clans. That will be their legacy.

"To all of those who serve, have served, and will serve in the Fleet, I say now: All of Earth owes you a debt that cannot be repaid. It is thanks to your courage, and your *restraint*, that we now have the beginnings of humanity's first ever interstellar alliance, instead of its first interstellar war.

"That honor cannot bring back those who died with UFS *Arapaima* and on UFS *Sailfish*, or on the K'heert'na hunt-ship *Swift Runner*. But we will remember all of them, and we will honor their memory.

"Remember their names."

He began to read the list, pausing for a few seconds after each name.

"Commander Nang Tae-Suk.

"Lieutenant-Commander Seok Dae-hyun.

"Lieutenant-Commander Peter Arcie..."

It was a long list. The one hundred and forty six men and women of *Arapaima*'s crew. The twenty-eight more who died on *Sailfish*, twelve of them as yet unrecovered from the mangled wreckage of *Sailfish*'s forward compartments, currently slowly being disassembled from the outside in.

Finally Alex stepped back from the podium, hoarse and shaking, a lump in his throat. Then Colonel John Warner took his place, and at the same slow pace, read off the names of the fifty Marines who had been assigned to *Arapaima* for its final deployment.

And then, to the surprise of the entire assembled audience, Swims-Like-Rock stepped forward to the podium, and in his deep growling voice, matching Alex's and John Warner's pace, solemnly recited nearly a hundred K'heert'na names, all of the ones who didn't make it off *Swift Runner* before its reactors went runaway.

When the list was done, Alex, all of the Fleet command staff, and every Marine on the concourse silently saluted, holding the salute for ten full seconds.

After the silent salute, Colonel Mackenzie stepped out in front of the podium, filled his pipes, and began to play. He played through all of the standard funeral tunes, one after the other. Then he began a long, wistful, haunting pibroch.

It came as a complete surprise to *everyone* when, about a minute later, all together, the K'heert'na raised their heads and began to sing. Colonel Mackenzie didn't miss a note. It was an eerie, literally unearthly sound that harmonized oddly well with the melancholy wail and skirl of the pipes. Alex felt the hair on the back of his neck stand up.

When Mackenzie finished his pibroch, he paused for a moment, then, as the K'heert'na sang on, he switched to following along to their lead, accompanying their voices. The strange, mournful melodies echoed down the concourse amid complete silence as the entire Fleet listened, enthralled. When the K'heert'na paused, Mackenzie led into another pibroch, and they followed him again.

They traded off the lead twice more before both pipes and K'heert'na finally fell silent. After a moment, Swims-Like-Rock stepped forward, gesturing to the podium with a head-cocked look at Alex. Alex nodded, just going with it. Swims-Like-Rock stepped back up to the podium.

«I, Fleet-Leader Swims-Like-Rock, of Clan Hsieuuu of Those-Who-Build, speak this day for Clan Hsieuuu and for the Den-Mother of Hsieuuu,» he said. «Clan Hsieuuu mourns with you for those of yours who will never return. We have sung to the stars for them, as we sang for our own. We will not forget them. Clan Hsieuuu honors their memory.»

14. Relations On High

After the memorial service, John Warner accompanied Alex and Naomi back to their quarters. So did Colonel Mackenzie, and so did Swims-Like-Rock and another K'heert from the memorial party, whom he introduced as Hunt-Master Sleeps-Lightly of *Swift Runner*. The remaining seven K'heert'na returned to *Sharp Claws*.

"Swims-Like-Rock," Alex said as they all sat or sprawled in the sunken lounge area, "I... I had no idea that that was what you meant when you mentioned singing for the dead. That might just be..." He gave up.

"I don't have adequate words for what I just heard. But it was *magnificent*. Beautiful."

"I'll second that," Mackenzie said. "An' I'd love tae know how ye knew the tune tae follow."

«We did not know your song, of course,» Swims-Like-Rock replied. «But we felt the *spirit* of the song, and we followed its spirit as best we could.»

"Well," Naomi said, "you should probably all know that the pipe-and-song portion of the service is *already* being reposted separately on social networks. You may have just created a new viral sensation."

«Is that... good?"» Swims-Like-Rock asked.

Naomi smiled.

"It means they liked it," she said. "And by extension, you and your crew. So, yes. It's good. It's *very* good."

The Seoks joined them after a little while—*all* of the remaining Seoks, including Jia, almost thirteen now. Jia stared open-mouthed in amazement at the two K'heert'na. Both gave her looks of what looked like awe and wonder, before Swims-Like-Rock lowered himself to his knees to gravely offer her his mid-hands.

Jia hesitated, looking at Hae, who smiled slightly and nodded. Then she tentatively reached out her hands and placed them on Swims-Like-Rocks'. He grasped hers for a moment with delicate care, using just two digits, before releasing them. He dipped his muzzle, and Jia bowed solemnly back.

«His hands are so *warm*,» Jia said.

Swims-Like-Rock turned to Dong-geun and Hae.

«You honor us greatly,» he said, «trusting us with your cub.»

"Trust is a good place to begin," Dong-geun replied quietly.

«I think that now,» Swims-Like-Rock said, «there is a great deal to talk about. We should find a way to begin. And I remind you also, Alex Hholder, that the Den-Mother has asked to meet you.» He was getting better at pronouncing that.

"I have derived a list of human-safe K'heert'na foods, with the assistance of the Den-intellect," Dreamer observed.

"Then I imagine we should try to get that set up as soon as possible," Alex said. "And I would also like to have the world leaders who will be coming here to sign the nuclear weapons ban treaty to at least meet with you. It might help to give them a better perspective on... well, a lot of things, really.

"Later on, I'd actually like to introduce you before the United Nations General Assembly, if you're okay with going down to Earth for it. But we can talk about that later. I think there will be plenty of time. There's probably a hundred different clearances that would have to be arranged, in any case."

It didn't take too terribly long to work out an arrangement for Alex, Naomi, Sandra, and Dong-geun to visit the Den in two days' time. Fleet-Leader Swims-Like-Rock and Hunt-Master Sleeps-Lightly would be their principal guides.

They made the short trip over on *Aspire*, Swims-Like-Rock relaying instructions from Den control to guide *Aspire* into a docking bay. As the ship grew closer to the central sphere, all four of them gazed wordlessly at the vista expanding before them. It was like flying into a city of light. Quite beautiful, really.

The *Endeavour* class, by a happy coincidence, was the right size and general shape of hull to fit moderately well into one size of K'heert'na docking cradles in a way that positioned the forward docking tunnel within the pressurized bay, about four meters above the deck, and it was a simple matter for the Den to provide a movable ramp.

The docking bay itself was cavernous and shadowed, the twenty-eight percent higher gravity immediately making itself felt. The thicker air was noticeable, but not problematic... and, Alex thought, the higher oxygen partial pressure actually helped slightly to cope with the higher gravity.

"Be careful walking," he cautioned his companions, remembering suit training, "until you get used to the gravity. Your reflexes are going to be off." Sandra and Naomi both nodded.

Then they left the docking bay, into the Den proper.

"This is amazing," Sandra said, as she looked around. "So very different from the Stardock. There's just... so much *space* everywhere."

"If you're building a home that you plan to fly around between the stars in," Naomi observed, "I imagine you want it to be nice and roomy."

Swims-Like-Rock shepherded them toward an open car on a smooth track. The seating was designed for K'heert'na, of course, but it was *usable* for humans, and even after such a short distance, Alex for one was glad to sit down. The transit car took them deep into the city of light that was the interior of the Den.

After about ten minutes, the car disgorged them in a small plaza. Swims-Like-Rock led them into a space filled with K'heert'na at consoles and displays, explaining that this was one of the Den's control centers. Now that they were seeing more K'heert'na, Alex noticed there were subtle variations both in the main color of their scales, and in the hue of the darker edges, which ranged anywhere from orange-browns to blue and green tinges.

«We will stop here for a little time for some refreshment,» he said, «and then I will take you in to see the Den-Mother.» The Den intellect's translation, Alex noticed, was as seamless as Dreamer's, although a lot more of the K'heert's growling tones came through. He wondered whether his voice came through sounding similarly K'heert-ish.

Swims-Like-Rock led them to a room filled with low, curving couches and a few scattered low tables. The seating was a little awkward for humans, but seeing how Swims-Like-Rock and Sleeps-Lightly curled up into bends of the couches, Alex could immediately see how well suited and comfortable it must be for K'heert'na. After a few moments, another K'heert appeared in the doorway and stopped.

«Fleet-Leader,» the newcomer said. «May I join you? I am curious to meet your—guests.»

«Be welcome,» Swims-Like-Rock replied. «Alex, Naoh-mi, San-dra, this is Nest-Protector Likes-Water, of the nest-defender ship *Steady*. Likes-Water, I introduce to you Alex Holder, the Fleet-Leader of Earth, and his companions Naoh-mi, San-dra and—Dong... Joon?»

Likes-Water dipped his muzzle in greeting, and Alex returned the nod. Likes-Water stepped fully into the room and dropped into one of the couches.

«I came to see with my own eyes the out-clan who thought that placing a threat in front of the Den was a wise action,» he said. He did *not* sound approving.

"Uh," Alex said, "the honest truth is, I knew we needed to get SOME kind of message across quickly, and I couldn't think of anything else at the time. We couldn't read your communication protocols yet, and I needed some kind of sign language. I tried my best to come up with a way to show we weren't trying to actually threaten anything.

"Actually, I'd already given an order by then that under no circumstances short of the direst emergency was anyone to fire on your Den, as soon as I figured out that it was a *city*, not a... a military command center. When you first entered the system with it, we thought it was a warship."

«Hah!» Likes-Water snorted. «No, we have no need of such a great-ship. We are not a warlike people. Except perhaps in defense of our Den.» He looked again at Alex.

«I am gratified to hear that you had ordered your fleet not to fire on the Den. At the time, we did not know that. I came very close to firing on your ship. But the Fleet-Leader ordered me not to.

«Did you have no concern that we might?»

"Oh hell yes," Alex replied. "I was VERY aware that you might. I was trying to figure out the right balance between getting your attention and getting a message across, *without* provoking you into firing. I didn't want to get into a fight with your—uh..."

«Nest-defenders?» Swims-Like-Rock supplied.

"Uh, yes," Alex agreed. "But I had to get us talking, and I knew that without lines of communication the initial message was going to have to be very simple and basic, and I couldn't think of anything else at the time. It was the closest thing I could think of to holding up my hand and saying, 'Stop.'" He held his hand out for illustration.

Likes-Water chuckled rumblingly.

«Well, in any case,» he said, «it was bold. You have *choom*.» The word did not translate.

"Uh... I have what?" Alex asked. "That didn't come across."

Likes-Water, Sleeps-Lightly, and Swims-Like-Rock looked at each other.

«Hurrrm,» Swims-like-Rock rumbled, «*choom* means... you are bold. Not afraid to risk yourself at need.»

"Honestly," Alex replied, "I'd sooner risk myself than other people."

"We have to talk him out of it at times," Sandra interjected. Likes-Water laughed, the staccato *ka-ka-ka-ka-ka* again.

«I think I am beginning to like you, hyoo-man,» he said.

A few minutes later, the promised refreshments arrived. There were two trays with very different contents.

«You should touch nothing on *this* tray,» Swims-Like-Rock said, gesturing to the tray nearer to the three K'heert'na. «But everything on *that* tray should be safe for you.»

The tray held deep drinking bowls of clear, sweet liquid with a vaguely nutty taste, a kind of crispy cracker that smelled faintly vinegary, chewy sticks of... *something* that Alex could not identify at all, and thin slices of something slightly spongy in a salty yellow sauce that had an electric tingle not dissimilar to Szechuan pepper. The flavors were almost all unfamiliar, but not unpleasant, as long as he didn't take too large a bite of the peppery slices at one time. Dong-geun, however, after his first try, ate them with evident gusto.

"This is very good," he said, sounding both surprised and appreciative. He looked at Swims-Like-Rock. "If you consider this tasty, I would be tempted to offer you kimchi—except that we know now that capsaicin would poison you."

Swims-Like-Rock raised his upperhands in understanding.

«We will both have to make sure that all of our peoples have access to the lists of what is safe to offer the other,» he said. «We should seek to avoid any accidents.»

"Yes," Alex agreed. "But we need to remember as well that there is always the chance of unexpected reactions."

«True, indeed,» Swims-Like-Rock agreed. But just then, an untranslated voice spoke from the ceiling. He replied tersely, hardly more than a cough.

«Come,» Swims-Like-Rock said, as he climbed back to his feet. «The Den-Mother is ready to see you.»

They all returned to the tram car for another short ride, traveling deeper into the Den. Likes-Water came along with them. Only about five minutes later, they disembarked again, outside a small domed building with several arched openings around its base. Swims-Like-Rock led the party inside.

The light inside was more subdued than much else that Alex had seen so far. Not that it was dark or gloomy, it just wasn't as brightly lit as the open areas and the control rooms had been. But then, neither was the room they had just come from.

There was a slightly sunken area in the middle of the floor. Six K'heert'na stood in a cordon around it. The nearest two took a step each further apart as the party approached. Clearly they were expected.

The sunken area held seating very similar to that in the room they had just left. A K'heert with the darkest scale coloration Alex had yet seen sat to one side of the area.

«Den-Mother,» Swims-Like-Rock said, his muzzle dipped respectfully. «I bring you Alex Hholder and his companions.»

«Be welcome,» the Den-Mother replied, gesturing to the sunken seats. «Take rest.»

Swims-Like-Rock stepped down into the sunken area and sprawled into a seat. Alex and his group, and the other two K'heert'na, followed suit. There was a brief round of introductions.

«We have traveled far across the ocean of stars,» the Den-Mother said, «following the trail of those who offended us and violated the Den. And at the end of that trail, we have found not them, but instead, your Clan of Earth.

«Surprising. Unexpected. And yet so far, I find myself not at all displeased.»

The Den-Mother, for whom Alex found himself uncertain what pronoun to use, paused. Objectively, he knew now that K'heert'na had no biological gender as such. And yet, the title was translated as Den-*Mother*. In a flash of insight, he decided to think of the Den-Mother as *they*. Simply to avoid his own confusion.

Anyway, *they* seemed to be waiting for him to speak.

"Fleet-Leader Swims-Like-Rock has told me of what happened between you and the, uh, Violators," he said. "Let me tell you of what happened when they came here." And he quickly summarized the events, the breakdown of the Stardock's hyperdrive, the Crickets presenting it to Earth as a gift, concealing that they were actually leaving it as a decoy to draw off the attention of Clan Hsieuuu; the random chance that led to himself being put in control of it, and the last-minute warning that told him that danger was coming. A danger about which all humankind knew was that the Crickets, vastly stronger than humanity then was, were fleeing from it.

«And from that start, in the short time since the Violators passed here, you built all that we now see,» the Den-Mother said. «A great accomplishment.»

"We had a very great *incentive,*" Alex replied. The Den-Mother raised... *their* forehands slightly.

«Indeed,» the Den-Mother replied. «The Violators *doubly* misled you.»

Alex blinked. That possibility hadn't occurred to him before this moment. What if the vague, nebulous warning had been *deliberate,* another facet of the Crickets' strategic plan?

«Had you not displayed the restraint and wisdom—and courage—that you did, had you not been willing to *assume* worthiness first, this system of worlds might have been strewn by now with the wreckage of both your ships and ours. Instead, we both have made new friends. Perhaps allies. I do not think that this is the outcome the Violators intended.» *They* coughed.

«The Violators have escaped us. But at the end of their trail we find their Den lost, their apparent plans in tatters, their knowledge taken and put to good use by your Earth-Clan.

«In this outcome, Clan Hsieuuu is well pleased. We are more than satisfied. Clan Hsieuuu greets and welcomes Clan-of-Earth as friend and equal.»

Alex dipped his head slightly, the gesture common, he knew now, to both humans and K'heert'na.

"The United Fleet—uh, Clan of Earth—is likewise honored and pleased to greet Clan Hsieuuu," he replied.

«We hope that in time, you will visit us as well,» the Den-Mother continued. «It is a long trip from our space to yours, even for us. We imagine that you have not had the opportunity for any such journeys yet. But now, there will be a great deal of time for you. When we return, we shall speak of you to the other Clans. They will doubtless be interested. We hope that when you begin making your way among the stars, your steps will carry you in our direction among others.

«We do not know all that you and our Fleet-Leader have spoken of. But there are things that *should* be spoken of. The first-standing at this moment is that you have clearly mastered the secrets of the Violators' leap drive. It is evident that it has significant advantages over ours in some respects. Numerous of our ship-masters have expressed amazement at how quickly your ships can leap—and how fast they are.

303

«We inquire, would you be willing to consider trading this knowledge, if we can find something of comparable value within our own store of knowledge to offer in return? We are sure that each of us must know numerous things that the other does not. It is almost always so when new cultures first meet.»

Alex thought quickly for a moment.

"It might be prudent for me to confer with the leaders of at least some of the other nations of our world," he said. "I am uncertain of what decisions it is reasonable for me to make unilaterally." Dong-geun nodded approvingly at that. "However, I for one would be *entirely* willing to exchange knowledge between us. If what we have learned from the Cri—the Violators is anything to go by, then I am sure that we have a great deal to learn from you as well. And not least, we would welcome advice from you on where it is safe to go—and where we *should not* go."

«Ah. Yes.» The Den-Mother nodded. «With Clan Hsieuuu's name behind you, you would of course be safe anywhere in K'heert'na space. But indeed, there are places where one should travel only cautiously. And we can point out to you at least one region adjacent to our realm where you should not go if you can avoid it. An out-clan who relentlessly attack all that comes near them. We have never been able to talk to them.

«But that is a subject for later. There is no urgency now. Where your worlds lie is a region unknown to us. We have no knowledge of who your neighbors may be. We apologize for the inability to assist in that.»

"No problem," Alex said. "We'll have to figure that out for ourselves, I guess. But as you said, that can be a discussion for much later. We haven't even had time to design and build any exploration ships yet, let alone figure out places worth sending them. We're sure many of the ships we have built *can reach* the stars around us without too great difficulty, but it's not what they were designed for. We built them thinking that an apocalyptic danger was coming."

«Us,» the Den-Mother replied. The tone seemed wry. «And yet even when we arrived, you responded with measure and forethought. This impresses us.»

"I'll admit," Alex said, "when our hyperspace detection systems picked up your Den coming in, we thought at first that it was one of the galactic-technology super-battleships that Dreamer—uh, the artificial intelligence that operates our Stardock, our Den—had told us about. It was not until we got a good look at it that we realized that you had brought—your Den here. Until that moment, we weren't certain that your lead ships had not simply disengaged to wait for your main force to arrive. But once we realized *that*... well, *that* changed everything."

«Fleet-Leader Swims-Like-Rock tells me that the paw-cuffs were well and satisfactorily concluded before the Den entered your system,» the Den-Mother replied. Then they hesitated and cocked their head. «But you, perhaps... did not *know* that.»

Alex nodded, then remembered and jerked his head back.

"We understand—*now*—that the exchange of paw-cuffs is your custom," he said. "But it is not one of ours. We didn't know what was going on until later, after Swims-Like-Rock explained it to us, once we had figured out the basics of how to talk to each other.

"I'm a little concerned by that, to be honest. Does that mean that if we visit your space, there will be—paw-cuffs—with every K'heert'na Clan we meet?"

«Hurrrrmmm,» the Den-Mother rumbled. «We think nothing of it, it is a customary ritual, almost a politeness—and we have become well practiced at doing no harm to each other. But if it is not your custom, not your way... then we can perhaps see that it could be—unsettling at the least.

«We... apologize for the misunderstanding. Perhaps we should not have assumed as readily as we did that our custom would be understood.»

The Den-Mother paused, apparently deep in thought, then looked up again after a little while.

«We shall do this, in measure of apology. Clan Hsieuuu names you Nest-kin. Wherever in K'heert'na space you may travel, Clan Hsieuuu's name will go before you to say that Hsieuuu has vouched for your worthiness. You will still have to establish relations and agreements for yourselves, but there will be no need for paw-cuffs. Clan Hsieuuu's reputation will stand before and behind you.»

Alex bowed his head.

"I'm not well versed in your culture or customs yet," he said. "But if I'm interpreting correctly, then you have just granted us a very great honor."

«It is indeed, Alex,» Swims-Like-Rock confirmed. «But you have shown yourselves worthy of it.»

The discussion continued for perhaps another hour, before the Den-Mother apologized and called a halt.

«We wish to speak more later,» the Den-Mother said. «But for now, there is much to be done. For you as well as for us, I am sure. Probably more so. We should let you return to what you must do.

«The Fleet is at rest. Therefore Fleet-Leader Swims-Like-Rock will go with you, as our envoy. He will continue to speak with the voice of the Clan.»

«Thank you, Den-Mother,» Swims-Like-Rock replied.

"Thank you, Den-Mother," Alex repeated. "I look forward to coming back again." And it wasn't just a formality. He meant it. These K'heert'na were *fascinating*.

«You too may go, if you wish, Likes-Water,» the Den-Mother offered.

«Thank you, Den-Mother,» Likes-Water replied, after a moment. «I... believe I will.»

«If I might make a suggestion, Den-Mother?» Swims-Like-Rock ventured. «Technician Too-Cautious, from *Swift Runner*, befriended one of the human—Marines—at their first meeting. Perhaps he, too, might wish to accompany us.»

The Den-Mother paused in thought.

«And he may gain different perspectives,» they said. «Very well. If Too-Cautious wishes it, then let it be so.»

"Honestly, Den-Mother," Alex said, "once we can make regular arrangements, I am perfectly happy with any K'heert'na who wishes to do so visiting the Stardock. Perhaps even Earth itself. I'd *like* to take Swims-Like-Rock to meet our United Nations General Assembly, if we can work out the details. And I'm sure there are plenty of members of the Fleet who would *love* to visit the Den, if you would permit."

The Den-Mother thought again.

«Very well,» they said. «Then we should see to, as you say, *working out the details*. We have no objection. We are certain that Swims-Like-Rock and Likes-Water will represent us well.»

That was pretty much where things wrapped up for the day. The transit cart took them all first back to the control center where they had taken refreshments, then back to the docking bay. By the time they got there, Too-Cautious was waiting patiently at the bottom of the ramp to *Aspire*'s forward docking hatch. At least, Alex was pretty certain it was Too-Cautious. He thought he recognized him by the coveralls.

306

It took longer than John Riken and Konstantin Molchalin had hoped it would to set up the signing of the treaty that would outlaw nuclear weapons on Earth's surface. In the end, it was set for November 18, closer to a month after General Kuskovsky's rogue nuclear launch than the week that they had initially hoped for. By the time the date was agreed, though, all of the major nuclear powers on Earth, as well as several of the lesser ones, were on board and had agreed to sign the treaty. Israel, Pakistan, and Iran were still being difficult; but overall, Kuskovsky's strike had been a terrifying wake-up call to the world.

All of the Fleet's passenger shuttles were assigned to ferry the treaty signatories to the Stardock. They rose relatively gently from their separate Earth points of departure, cabin screens displaying the full view of Earth as they rose, before falling into line astern to approach the Stardock. The approach vector first carried them under the dozen massive nest-defenders in their protective formation around Clan Hsieuuu's Den, and of course the colossal Den itself, then brought them in through the Fleet lined up in review, a double row of Sharks lined up along the approach, spaces left empty where *Arapaima* and *Sailfish* (currently in refit) should have been, the Warlords above and slightly behind them. The last three Warlords built —CG-23 *Hideyoshi*, CG-24 *Manaa Musa*, and CG-25 *Geronimo*, first ship of CruRon Four—had interrupted their shakedown cruises to participate in the review formation. *There Exists An Elegant Solution* was holding station above the docking bay itself, a group of drop-ships arrayed around the exterior docking bay hatch helping to give a visual reference for the scale. The deliberate display was *meant* to inspire awe, and it did.

One after another, the shuttles drifted gently in to dock, then the docking ports all unsealed together. The various dignitaries filed out of their shuttles with their individual security details, to find an honor guard of Fleet Marines waiting, the officers in dress uniform, two platoons of Marines in battle armor at attention around the docking concourse.

There was nothing unusual about the presence of such an honor guard, of course. What *was* unusual, was that the party waiting to welcome the assembled diplomats upon their arrival included three K'heert'na—Swims-Like-Rock, Likes-Water, and Sleeps-Lightly.

It took a little herding and a lot of formality, but finally all of the delegations were shepherded into place arrayed around the center of the docking bay, where a large circular table had been set up. There were eleven chairs around the table, one for each participating nuclear-armed nation. Behind the table was a podium.

Alex Holder stood at the podium. On his left and slightly behind him stood Dong-geun. On his right was Swims-Like-Rock.

"Good day to you all," Alex said. "It is my very great honor to welcome you, one and all, to the Stardock. For each of you, it is your first visit here, although I sincerely hope it won't be your last.

"We all know why we are here on this day. The events of October 23rd made it clear without any possible doubt, I believe and hope, that we cannot afford to have arsenals of nuclear weapons on Earth's surface. Despite all that we have done over the last nearly four years, human civilization came terrifyingly close to ending twenty-five days ago. All it took was one man.

"Thanks to the swift and decisive action of President Konstantin Molchalin of the Russian Federation," he nodded in acknowledgement, "of Colonel John Warner of the United Fleet Marine Corps," another nod, "and of the officers and crew of USS *Shiloh*, United States Navy, among others, that catastrophe was averted. Our job today is to see that it never happens again. I thank you all for coming, and I thank all of those of you who have put work into this treaty, alongside Presidents Riken and Molchalin."

He paused for a moment.

"There is another thing that is notable about this treaty. It will be the first treaty signed by humanity to be *witnessed* by beings not of this Earth.

"Ladies and gentlemen, honored delegates, Fleet-Leader Swims-Like-Rock of Clan Hsieuuu of the K'heert'na, Those-Who-Build."

Alex stepped back from the podium, and Swims-Like-Rock stepped forward.

«Clan of Earth, Clan Hsieuuu greets you as new friends among the stars,» he said. «Both of our peoples have been treated poorly at the hands of those whom we call the Violators, and you call the Crick-ets, whose trail we followed from our space across the ocean of stars to find your world. But our mutual mistreatment at their hands has brought us to the same place, to your world, and thus have we met you.

«Fertile worlds such as yours are tiny, fragile islands in the vast ocean of stars. We protect all of ours fiercely, both against dangers from outside, and from mistakes and errors. It makes us proud to see you, our new friends, coming together now to protect your own. It speaks well of you as a people. We well know that you have accomplished truly astounding things together since the Violators passed here. We are certain that you will accomplish more in your future.

«We, Clan Hsieuuu of Those-Who-Build, dip our muzzles to you in respect.»

He stepped back from the podium.

As had been arranged, the eleven delegations stepped forward towards the table, then the leader of each delegation took two more steps forward and sat down. In each place was a pen, and a final copy of the hurriedly-completed treaty. President John Riken of the United States of America, President Konstantin Molchalin of the Russian Federation, Premier Li Xeung of the People's Republic of China, President Emmanuelle Galois of France, Prime Minister Julianna Sutherland of the United Kingdom, Prime Minister Brian Watson of Australia, Prime Minister Ramanujan Venkataswathy of India, and more.

Each delegation leader simply picked up their pen, signed the copy in front of them, and then passed it one space to their right. Then they signed the *next* copy, and passed that on. And the next, and the next. After the last signature, a twelfth and final exchange left each delegate with a copy of the treaty signed first by themselves.

And then, startlingly quickly, it was done. The delegates stood and shook hands with those on either side of them. The delegations drifted together, and there was a brief hubbub of conversation beginning, before Riken and Molchalin managed to emerge from the crowd towards the podium, Li Xeung not too far behind them. Alex beckoned Riken to the podium, but John Riken stopped to offer a hand before he took it.

"It's good to finally meet you face to face, Mr. Holder," he said. "I cannot thank you enough for everything you've done."

"It had to be done, Mr. President," Alex said. "And doing it fell on my shoulders. The only thing for me to do was buckle down and do it."

"Well, I can assure you," Riken said, "the world is grateful. No matter how much pissing and moaning you may have had to put up with from politicians and industrialists. I'm sure you haven't had the last of that yet, take it from me.

"Anyway, we'll talk later, I hope. I brought Ed Wegener with me. I'm sure the two of you will have lots to talk about."

Then he stepped up to the podium.

"Ladies and gentlemen," John Riken said, "thank you all for coming together on this day. Today we have taken a huge step to safeguard the future of our world, in formally agreeing that nuclear weapons have no place on its surface, and never will again. Again, I thank you all."

Then he stepped aside, and Konstantin Molchalin took his place.

"Ladies and gentlemen," Molchalin said, "I and my government deeply regret what happened on the twenty-third of October. I cannot

309

thank you all sufficiently for coming here this day to agree and guarantee that it *must never happen again*. Thank you all for coming."

Nearby, Li Xeung had found Alex.

"Mr. Alex Holder," he said. "It is good to meet you at last. There is a Chinese proverb that says that once in every dozen generations, a person is born who will grow up to shake the heavens. You are such a person, I think. Tell me just out of curiosity, did you ever dream that it would be *you* who would grow up to shake the heavens?"

"Honestly, Mr. Premier," Alex replied, "I never had the slightest inkling of it. Not even when the Cricket scout drone started poking at me. By the time I realized that I was, uh, had been chosen to ride a tiger, I was already on its back and it was too late to get off. Or even to have second thoughts about it."

"Well," Li Xeung chuckled, "it seems the heavens have smiled upon you. Keep riding the tiger, Mr. Holder. It seems you are good at it. Do not fall off.

"Would you please do me the honor of introducing me to your new friends?"

And so Alex led him over and introduced him to Swims-Like-Rock, Likes-Water, and Sleeps-Lightly. It wasn't very long at all before there were fifty others lined up waiting to be introduced. So, one by one, Alex greeted them all, and introduced them to the three representatives of Clan Hsieuuu. There were endless questions, but the three K'heert'na answered them patiently, even when they were repeats.

After a little while, things settled out a little. The entire flock of diplomats was ferried up the concourse to Ginza where a post-signing reception had been set up, after which Alex offered tours of the pressure-safe portions of the Stardock and close inspections of each of the major ship classes to anyone who was interested. Most of the hundred or so attendees—plus, of course, their own security—took him up on the offer. They ended up splitting the tour into three groups for sheer manageability. Alex and Naomi took one group, Tom and Sandra led the second, and Dong-geun and John Warner led the third.

Ed Wegener, indeed, had a thousand questions. Alex promised him a private, more extensive tour later—and he was able to keep his promise to

DNI Hackett to at least give him a *good idea* of what the world looked like through the sensorium of a science drone, or of the Stardock. He got to meet Secretary Winters, as well. He came away with his existing impressions reinforced. She was formidable.

After the tour, the three groups rejoined at Infinity. Once again, the K'heert'na—all four of them, now; Too-Cautious turned up, along with Rifleman Hess and three other members of his squad—drew a crowd.

"Can I offer you a beer?" Prime Minister Brian Watson asked Sleeps-Lightly. Sleeps-Lightly dipped his muzzle.

«I am thankful for the gesture,» he said. «But alcohols are toxic to us. We have a carefully vetted list of what hum-an foodstuffs and beverages it is safe for us to consume.» Then he cocked his head slightly. «But then,» he said, «my best understanding is that they are toxic to *you*, as well. It is merely that one specific alcohol out of the many is only *mildly* toxic to you. I am curious. Why do you drink it?»

"Honestly?" Watson replied. He thought for a moment. "Social custom as much as anything else, I think. And, uh, we enjoy the way it makes us feel. As long as we don't drink *too* much of it. It helps us to relax and unwind a bit."

«Indeed, there is no accounting for custom,» Sleeps-Lightly agreed.

Eventually, the diplomatic bash broke up. Farewells were made, and the delegations returned to their shuttles and to Earth. Ed Wegener stayed behind for the time being, for his promised extended tour.

"You know," Alex told him, "while you're here, we might as well test you. No obligation."

Wegener grinned.

"I'd like that," he said. "I admit to being *intensely* curious."

"I wouldn't expect any different from you," Alex chuckled.

Ed managed a high—very high—level two.

"It's as though I can *feel* something more there, but just barely can't quite resolve it," he said.

"You're *almost* there," Alex told him. "I'll bet we could push you over the rest of the way within a week or two in Suzanne's train-up class."

Ed thought for a long while.

"And no obligation?" he confirmed.

"Promise," Alex replied.

"You won't regret it," Naomi chipped in. "I didn't."

Ed thought about it for quite a while.

"Would I need to have implants before joining the class?" he asked.

"It is not an *absolute* requirement," Dreamer replied. "But it would be very strongly recommended. Working through an external electrode mesh would limit your control and impede your learning."

"And you've never had a rejection, right?"

"That is correct," Dreamer replied. "The worst adverse reactions we have seen from the implantation were a few atypical reactions to the sedation, and one mild topical infection which was quickly resolved."

"One of those atypical reactions was mine," Naomi said. "Alex had to carry me home because I was too woozy to walk. I don't think he minded too much."

"That doesn't sound like too terrible of a risk," Ed mused. He thought about it in silence for a minute or two.

"You know what? I have some vacation due. I'm going to call down for approval, just to be sure, and then take some of it right now. I've been wondering ever since we first talked what it's actually like to be... *connected* to the Stardock like that. The idea of being able to *see* magnetic fields? And gravity waves? It's irresistible."

"OK," Alex said. "Let's get you queued up. The first order of business will be a medical scan. Since we're almost certain that you're going to be level three within a week or two, I'm going to suggest that we go straight to giving you an L3 implant."

"I agree that would be prudent," Dreamer agreed. "Based upon his test results, I believe the chance is vanishingly small that Dr. Wegener will *not* achieve level three."

Five hours later, Ed Wegener had his implants, and had temporary quarters assigned, a two-bedroom unit on Sorbonne Street in the second hab block. Two days later, he took a freshly opened slot in Suzanne's control class.

It took him six days to push through to level three.

Elegant Solution hung in hyperspace just on the fringe of the termination shock.

This is... absolutely incredible, Ed Wegener thought. *To be able to SEE the termination shock. You do realize that probably half the astronomers on Earth are going to want this? Just for starters. It's going to revolutionize our ability to understand a lot of things.*

Alex chuckled.

We'll be able to fit them all in, eventually, he said. *I hope we'll reach a point eventually where everyone on Earth can get tested as soon as they're old enough to receive implants.*

Old enough? Ed asked. *There's an age limit?*

Sort of, Alex replied. *Physical growth needs to have completely or nearly completely stopped. Otherwise there's a severe risk of tissue and nervous system damage as the body outgrows the implants. There's only so much give in the nanowires, though they're laid out so as to have some flex and slack.*

Aaah. That makes perfect sense, Ed agreed.

After a while, Alex turned *Elegant Solution* around and headed back. Ed Wegener watched intently 'over Alex's shoulder', so to speak, as he brought the massive ship in to dock.

"I... don't suppose you'd consider showing me that gravity weapon of yours?" Ed asked.

"Not this time, sorry," Alex replied. "At our current stage of development, it has to be directly operated by Dreamer. And that means that he has to transfer himself out of the Stardock and onto *Elegant Solution*. But we're still working on it, and we hope to be able to fully automate it at some point in the future. Once we're at that stage I'd be only too happy to demonstrate it for you.

"In the meantime, Dreamer can replay any or all of the test data for you, show you complete simulations of its operation, and I'm sure the resident science teams studying here would be only too glad to help bring you up to speed on the underlying theory. Not that they *fully* understand it all themselves yet, I think, but Dreamer tells me they're starting to get a good handle on it. Certainly they understand *far* more of the theory behind it than I do."

"That sounds like a very interesting discussion," Ed said. "But for now, I should probably be getting back down to Washington. I... certainly have a new perspective on some of this, now. I'll be better able to advise the President on implications and what it all means to Earth."

"That's worthwhile in itself," Alex agreed.

"And... John Riken's not going to be in office forever," Ed said. "When he leaves office—perhaps you could find a spot for me?"

Alex grinned.

"Count on it, Ed," he said. "Count on it. If we don't have a place for you, we'll make one. I owe you. All the way back to convincing President Riken to listen to me, right at the beginning when all of this started."

———————

Over the next months, a permanent multinational trade delegation was established on the Stardock to talk about what Earth and Clan Hsieuuu might have to trade with each other. The entire body of human art and music was new to the K'heert'na, of course—and equally, K'heert'na art and music were new to Earth. Scholarly papers were written on the similarities, and differences, between the aural structure of K'heert'en long-song and Gregorian plainsong. The K'heert'na immediately understood plainsong, and soaked up as much of it as they could get. They also took strongly to a lot of traditional African and Asian music, expressing a particular fondness for *gamelan*.

«Once again, Alex, despite the many differences between our peoples, we have similarities as well,» Swims-Like-Rock observed.

K'heert'na explored the realm of Earth's musical instruments, as well. It turned out for example that the six-fingered, blunt-clawed hands of a K'heert were amazingly well suited to playing the Japanese *koto*. Hunter White-Nose, of the front-runner *Strong Paws*, quickly began to develop a fair level of proficiency with the *dombra*, the largest and deepest-pitched form of the Russian balalaika, to Maksim's evident approval. It was bizarrely incongruous at first to see a K'heert sitting in front of Infinity picking out Russian and Ukrainian folk tunes... *but why not*, Alex thought.

Clan Hsieuuu's first trade interest remained the details of Cricket hyperdrive technology. They insisted, though, that they had to find something that *they* felt to be of comparable value, to offer in trade for it. That took a while.

One day, though, Swims-Like-Rock came to Alex.

«I have been studying some of the issues and problems of your world,» he said, "in hopes of identifying something of importance, comparable in value to your leap-drive, that we can assist with. And I believe I have found something.»

"Go on," Alex said.

«I have learned,» Swims-Like-Rock continued, «that many low-lying regions of your world are threatened by rising seas as your planet warms, and that uncontrollable wildfires are also an increasing problem. Your tropical storms have been growing both more frequent, and more intense. Many of your—*coral reefs*—are dying. Your seas are becoming more acidic. And that the underlying cause of all of this is a change in the composition of your atmosphere caused principally by your large use of combustion engines burning carbon-based fuels.»

"Yes," Alex agreed. "It's an enormously serious problem, and one that we're still barely beginning to come to grips with. We're finally making progress on cutting down on our carbon-dioxide emissions, but a huge amount of damage is already done, and we really don't have any way to clean up what we've already put into the atmosphere. We're going to be coping with its effects for a long time, even if we completely stopped all fossil-fuel use *today*. Which I'd *like* to, but I don't have any illusions that we can. We're working on that as fast as we can, but some people are still dragging their heels about it—partly, I think, because they simply *can't imagine changing* how they do things, and partly because acknowledging that there is a problem would mean having to acknowledge that *they* helped to cause it. It's an easy trap for people to fall into—to continue perpetuating a problem because you're unwilling to admit that you were wrong."

Swims-Like-Rock head-twitched understanding.

«I think,» he said slowly, «that this is a problem with which we might be able to offer substantial assistance.»

Alex turned and looked at him hard.

"Go on," he said, very intently.

«We have a method of separating out low-concentration gases from large quantities of air,» Swims-Like-Rock said. «We use it to concentrate certain useful gases from the atmosphere of our original Den-world. Different gases. But... we believe that the technology could be adapted. To concentrate and remove the excess... *carbon dioxide* from your atmosphere.

«It would not happen overnight, of course. But your Den-world's atmosphere could perhaps be returned to its normal levels, perhaps twelve-twelves of orbits sooner than it would recover on its own.

«*This*, we would consider to be of sufficient worth that we would feel it fair to offer it in trade for your leap-drive technology.»

Alex gazed past Swims-Like-Rock, lost in thought.

"That would be almost beyond price to us," he said at last. He shook his head and looked back at Swims-Like-Rock.

"Can you put together a package of information on this? And then I think we should go and talk to the trade delegation."

———————————

After considerable negotiation, it was settled. Clan Hsieuuu would trade K'heert'na atmospheric gas-concentrator technology to Earth, and help to tune and adapt it for use as atmosphere scrubbers, in return for Cricket hyperdrive technology.

"Understand," Alex warned, "this doesn't mean we can slack off and go right back to unrestrained fossil fuel use. If we do that, we will *swamp* the concentrators, overwhelm them. We can add carbon dioxide to the atmosphere faster than we can scrub it out. But if we keep up our transition away from fossil fuels to clean energy sources, the scrubbers from Clan Hsieuuu will enable us to start moving our atmosphere back in the direction of pre-industrial baseline levels perhaps centuries earlier than would otherwise be possible. We *might just* be able to finish out this century under two point five degrees Celsius above baseline, if we work at it. Maybe even under two degrees."

It was the first substantive major trade agreement between Earth and Clan Hsieuuu. It would not be the last.

Epilogue: The View From Here

Alex looked 'out' at the virtual view of the Earth, floating eighty-five hundred kilometers away beyond the hull. If he looked off to the side, he could easily see Clan Hsieuuu's Den, trailing a hundred kilometers behind the Stardock in its orbit. Naomi stood by his side.

"Earth," he said, meditatively.

«Your den-world,» said Swims-Like-Rock, standing a little behind him and to one side. «It is beautiful.»

"Yes. Despite all of our problems and all of the stupid things we've done to it and to each other, the most precious, most beautiful place in the universe. To humans."

«We regard our den-world this way, also,» Swims-Like-Rock agreed.

"We're finally starting to repair all of the damage we've done. There's things we can't undo. Too many species we've driven to extinction. Ecosystems that may never fully recover. But we're starting to clean up our mess. And your atmosphere scrubber tech is going to be a vitally important part of that."

«Your hyperdrive, so much better than ours, will be of similar importance to us.»

"It's really the Crickets' tech, not ours."

«The Violators gave it to you. Their motive in doing so is irrelevant in the present moment. It is yours now.»

Alex nodded agreement, then looked outward at the screen again.

"It's the cradle of humankind," he said. "But sooner or later, the time comes to leave the cradle."

«Sooner or later,» Swims-Like-Rock said, «we must leave to return to our own space. Perhaps... you and some of yours might choose to accompany us.»

"It's certainly tempting," Alex agreed. "Honestly, I'm unconvinced I can safely step away yet. No matter how much I'd like to. This has been an *exhausting* four years. And also, to be completely honest, I think it would be a good influence upon us if we could arrange for you to have some kind of permanent presence here. There's nothing like a good visible reminder."

«We can discuss all such possibilities with the Den-Mother,» Swims-Like-Rock said. «And in truth it would probably smooth matters if there were an existing presence of Clan Hsieuuu here when other K'heert'na Clans eventually come here... which I am certain, in the fullness of time, they will.»

Alex nodded.

"It would certainly be in both our interests to help ensure that there are no more misunderstandings," he agreed. "And I wonder whether we could establish a permanent chain of hyperwave relays to create a near-realtime communication link between our space and yours."

«That is a worthy thought,» Swims-Like-Rock agreed. «It would be a wise step to take, if we can—'make it work', as you say.»

The most important thing, Alex reflected to himself, was that the world wasn't under a looming Damoclean threat any more. Some of the issues it faced were still urgent and crucially important... but there was no longer an imminent potential End Of All Things. Part of that was due to successfully *avoiding* a full-scale war with the K'heert'na. And part of it was due, ironically, to a Russian General trying to *start* a full-scale war. Not even just one, but *two* close brushes with nuclear holocaust in less than two years had finally gotten the attention of even the most recalcitrant of Earth's politicians.

(*Well, okay, he corrected himself, all **but** the most recalcitrant. There were still a handful of hold-outs, but none of them had enough warheads to be an existential threat.*)

Now, at last, he thought to himself, they had all the time in the world. Perhaps in several worlds. They would work it out, in the end. Humans and K'heert'na, working together. Allies, upon the ocean of stars.

—*Fin*—

A Brief Afterword

*There are undoubtedly more stories to be told in the universe of the Stardock. It is a question of finding stories worth the telling that are distinct from any of a hundred other stories already told. There are more than **enough** books about forever wars and Imperial strife. I do not feel any need to write the one hundred and first.*

In the fullness of time, I will see how many more of them I can find and tell.

—Sean Fenian

POST-IT NOTES

SIGINT is an almost-universally-used contraction of the phrase "signals intelligence". It is a broad umbrella term covering almost any communication and telemetry data.

The Dark Island, Flowers of the Forest, Highland Cathedral, Mist Covered Mountains, Cro Chinn t-Saile, A Scottish Soldier, and *Lochanside* are all well-known traditional Scots funeral music. *A Flame of Wrath,* while also well-known, is decidedly not. It is a *piobaireachd,* or pibroch, a traditional form of highland Scots solo pipe music, and in particular, it commemorates avenging a foul murder. It is *war* music.

The AGM-45 (Air to Ground Missile) Shrike was basically an AIM-7 (Airborne Interception Missile) Sparrow fitted with a radar-seeking head. It was light and cheap, and continued to be widely used even after it was officially superseded in 1967 by the AGM-78 Standard ARM (Anti-Radiation Missile), despite having only a 25% success rate in Vietnam due to its short range and relatively low speed. This was largely because an AGM-45 only cost about $7,000, while an AGM-78 cost about $200,000 and USAF pilots had to fill out a justification form every time they expended one. The AGM-45 Shrike remained in US service until 1992, when both it and the AGM-78 were finally replaced by the AGM-88 HARM (High-speed Anti-Radiation Missile).

A 'technical', as the term is used in Chapter Four, is any available small truck or pickup, with a crew-served weapon (a heavy machinegun, an RPG launcher, even a light cannon) mounted in the rear bed. It is an inexpensive way to have some mobile heavy-weapons support.

There are several different astronomical coordinate systems in common use. All of them are polar coordinate systems (although the ecliptic system can also, with some awkwardness, be stated in rectangular coordinates). The (arguably) most useful one for describing positions around and close to the Solar System is the sun-centered ecliptic coordinate system. The three coordinates used in this system are ecliptic longitude (the angle 'eastward' of a line drawn from the object to the sun, relative to a line drawn from the Earth's position at the March equinox to the sun); ecliptic latitude (angle above or below the ecliptic, the plane of the Earth's orbit around the sun); and of course radius—distance from the sun. (Other co-ordinate systems use different words to label differently defined, but basically similar, values.)   Latitude and longitude are conventionally expressed in degrees, while radii are often expressed for convenience in astronomical units, the radius of the Earth's orbit, defined as exactly 149,597,870,700m, or approximately 8.3167 light minutes (499.005 light seconds). So, for example, on the summer solstice, a quarter of its way around its orbit, the Earth is located in sun-centered coordinates at longitude $l = 90°$, latitude $b = 0°$ (of course), and radius $r = 1AU$ (of course).

Using this system, on April 22 when the Khreetan first scout the solar system, Earth is located at sun-centric $l = 30°$, $b = 0°$, $r = 1AU$, point ALPHA is located at $l = 84°$, $b = 5.5°$, $r = 19.1AU$, point BETA is at $l = 71°$, $b = 86°$, $r = 9.2AU$, point GAMMA is at $l = 88°$, $b = 42°$, $r = 17.8AU$, and point DELTA is at $l = 26°$, $b = -54°$, $r = 5.3AU$.

Nadir and zenith are likewise positional terms. As seen from Earth, zenith is the "top" of the solar system, toward solar 'true north' ($b = 90°$), while nadir is the "bottom" of the system, toward solar true south ($b = -90°$).

A steradian, or square radian, is a measure of solid angle. 'Square radian' is actually a misnomer, because the definition describes a conical volume. A steradian is a conical volume which subtends an arc of exactly one radian, where a radian is the arc such that 360 degrees, a full circle, is exactly 2π radians. This works out to be roughly 57.3 degrees.

It is a very handy unit of measure, not least because the area of a slice through such a conical volume at a distance r units from the apex has an area of exactly r^2 units.

The alien race whom the Chrrt'ktk't—whom humans, who can pronounce that word only with great difficulty, call the Crickets—call Khreetan, actually call themselves the Builders, or, more literally, Those-Who-Build. 'Khreetan' is itself a transliteration into English of the Crickets' best attempt at pronouncing a Builder word which, for human ears and tongues, is perhaps best represented as K'heert'na (singular K'heert).

K'heert'na measure distance in units of *kat*, a standard based originally upon the average span of an adult K'heert's mid-arms, but later redefined in more rigorous terms with a slightly different value. One *kat* is roughly 1.73 meters. (1.72699, if you want to be reasonably exact.) To further complicate matters, having six digits on each paw has led them to use base-12 arithmetic. The prefix *te'* means a twelve, while *me'* means a twelve-squared, or 144. A *ka'* is a twelve-squared times a twelve-squared, which is 20,736. Thus a *ka'kat* is 20,736 *kat*, making it roughly 35.87 kilometers. A *me'ka'kat* is a hundred and forty four times that again, or roughly 5,165 kilometers. We would count this as just under three million *kat* (2,985,984). So a Builder who says "five-*te'*-three *me' me'ka'kat*", is saying "five-twelves-and-three [hundred] [million] *kat*"—except that the hundred is actually 144, and the million is actually 2,985,984. He could instead say "five-*te'*-three *ka'ka'kat*," but they prefer not to, considering more than two *ka'* syllables in a row to be prone to confusion—as well as slightly comical, since the sequence *ka-ka-ka...* is also one of the common Builder written representations of laughter. (Much as in human mathematics the character !, used variously to signify negation and factorials, is often pronounced either 'bang' or 'shriek'.)

Although the *te'* prefix means 'twelve of', the K'heert'na do not use it as a standalone number, *only* as a multiplier. To express the number 'twelve' on its own, a Builder will say 'two paws', or quickly show the digits of two paws. Similarly, the "paw-*kat* band" is six *kat* —what we would call the ten-meter band. Jupiter emits a **LOT** of RF energy in the ten-meter band. We aren't really sure why.

Slightly confusingly to humans, K'heert'na use a single digit to mean both 'one' and 'one sixth'. The context indicates the meaning —whether it is one [digit], or one sixth [of a paw].

Since gravity on the K'heert'na homeworld is approximately 1.28 Earth gravities, "five-*te'* (five twelves, or sixty) mass-equivalents" would be roughly 76.8 Earth gravities.

The closest terrestrial equivalent to the marine predator that the K'heert'na call a 'fast-swimmer' is probably a barracuda—if you

323

picture a barracuda that can take a limb off an adult K'heert in one bite, right through the scales.

K'heert'na, or Builders, use a number of seemingly-gendered words rendered in this book as, for example, Huntmistress and Den-Mother. These should *not* be taken as gendered words; rather, they are symbolic of roles. Den-Mother is nurturing, protective; Huntmistress, self-sacrificingly fierce and relentlessly savage in ensuring the safety of the nest and its cubs. K'heert'na actually have only a single gender, although it takes two of them—*any* two—to reproduce. They give live birth to large numbers of pre-sapient young known as spawnlings, for whom it is survival of the fittest and fiercest until they mature to the point of becoming sapient cubs. Spawnlings prevented from preying upon each other will never develop full functional sapience. The K'heert'na see nothing unnatural or wrong about this process, but are near-fanatical about protecting their cubs once they attain sapience.

Choom is a K'heert'en word with a similar meaning to 'moxie', 'mettle', or perhaps 'bravado'.

No, *Sharp Claws* is not commanded by Gordon of Red Tree. If you don't know who that is, you should probably go and read Mackey Chandler's *Family Law* series.

Spetsnaz are the Russian elite special forces. They have a reputation for being iron-tough, brutally efficient, and cheerfully merciless.

The United States' Ground Based Interceptor ballistic missile defense system is intended to defend against small-scale ballistic attacks, not saturation bombardments. Today, the Ground-Based Midcourse Defense system has forty missiles at Fort Greely, Alaska, and four at Vandenberg AFB, California. The GDI missile uses an Orbital Sciences booster to launch a Raytheon exo-atmospheric kinetic kill vehicle (EKV). Estimated kill probability against an incoming re-entry vehicle is 56% for a single EKV, 97% for a salvo of four. The SM-3 Standard missile carried on *Ticonderoga*-class AEGIS cruisers is somewhat less effective; the SM-2 that it was developed form was was originally designed to shoot down aircraft, not incoming ballistic missile warheads. The fact that the SM-3 has nevertheless managed to do so in tests, and even engage low-orbit satellites, is quite an accomplishment.

You might be thinking, "If the K'heert'na count in base *twelve*, why is their value of pi larger than ours? Shouldn't it seem *smaller*?" What you need to remember is that in base ten, 3.1 means three and a tenth, and 3.14 means three plus one tenth plus four hundredths. (And so on.) But in base *twelve*, the first digit after the decimal point is twelfths, the second is 144^{th}s, and the third, 1728^{th}s. (And so on.) So 3.1 in base 12 means three *and one twelfth*, and 3.14 means three *plus one twelfth plus four 144^{th}s*. And that is *less* than 3.14 in base 10. It works out that you actually need three, plus one twelfth, plus just over *eight* 144^{th}s to represent the value of pi in base 12. The first twelve digits of pi in base 10 are 3.14159265358; in base 12, they are 3.184809493**b**9, where the letter **b** stands in for an 'eleven' digit. (This stand-in is nothing new; a lot of computer science is done in base 16, using the letters **a** through **f** to represent digit values 10 through 15.)

Yes, the K'heert'na custom of 'paw-cuffs' is an ill-considered one to extend to complete strangers of another species. Want to tell me that means they would never do that? Take a good, hard look around you at **OUR** culture, and tell me honestly and with a straight face that *we* have no cultural blind spots.

Does this story skip over a lot of political and economic details? Why, **YES**, yes it does. **Necessarily so.** Because there is *so much ground* to cover there that if I attempted to fully and accurately cover *all* of even the *most likely* political and economic ramifications triggered by the Stardock and Alex Holder's efforts to share Cricket technology with Earth, this series would not be about Earth, the Crickets, the Fleet and the K'heert'na, it would be about *politics and economics*, and it would be deathly dry, dull and boring—and it would almost certainly still be mostly wrong, because I firmly believe we don't actually understand real-world economics half as well as we *think*—or *pretend*—we do. Or to put that another way, most of our market economic theories are willfully-bad mirrors of reality. They describe economics as we would LIKE it to be, and we try our best to handwave it away when our models fail. Pay no attention to the man behind the curtain. (Our economic theories are rather less efforts to properly understand how real-world economies *really work in practice*, and rather more rationalizations to justify continuing the business and financial practices that most benefit the most powerful segments of our economy.) That's probably not the series *you* want to read, and it's **CERTAINLY** not the series I want to write. Won't do it, can't make me.

About The Culture: You might have noticed I'm a big fan of the late Iain M. Banks and his Culture universe. The books had a big impact on me... so why not on Alex Holder as well? If you want to give them a try, be aware that they tend to be largely standalone— they are a connected milieu rather than a series, and need not be read in any particular order. Technically *Consider Phlebas* comes first, chronologically speaking, but I actually don't recommend it as a starting point; it's one of the less approachable Culture books. I would suggest beginning with *Excession* instead.

Similarly, if there is a soundtrack to the *Stardock Trilogy*... most of that soundtrack is by VNV Nation. If you don't know them, and you like EBM at all—give them a listen.

APPENDIX 1: MAJOR SHIPS OF THE UNITED EARTH FLEET

(As the Fleet exists at the end of *A Line In The Stars*)

Endeavour class

Training Flight One
> T-1 *Endeavour*
> T-2 *Aspire*
> T-3 *Excel*

Shark class destroyers

DesRon One:
> DD-01 *Mako* (Commodore Angavu Onyango)
> DD-02 *Tigershark* (Hussein Onyango)
> DD-03 *Bullshark* (Mahmoud Hadj)
> DD-04 *Blacktip* (Walt 'Hammer' Berger)
> DD-05 *Great White* (Jean-Michel LeBarré)
> DD-06 *Thresher* (Jan Witsteen)
> DD-07 *Requiem* (Somchai Pravat)
> DD-08 *Hammerhead* (Maksim Chernaev)
> DD-09 *Wobbegong*
> DD-10 *Whitetip*
> DD-11 *Sandshark*
> DD-12 *Spinner*

DesRon Two:
> DD-13 *Marlin*
> DD-14 *Snoak* (Piet Beekhof)
> DD-15 *Moray* (Toivo Hakkinen)
> DD-16 *Scorpionfish* (Commodore Jabari Ndungu)
> DD-17 *Barracuda*
> DD-18 *Swordfish*
> DD-19 *Seawolf* (Julio Dominguez)
> DD-20 *Piranha*
> DD-21 *Sailfish* (Jeanne Petrie)
> DD-22 *Razorfish*
> DD-23 *Stingray*
> DD-24 *Snakefish*

DesRon Three:
>DD-25 *Blackfish* (Commodore Pierre du Maurier)
>DD-26 *Mantaray*
>DD-27 *Stonefish*
>DD-28 *Eagleray*
>DD-29 *Devilfish* (Ae Morita)
>DD-30 *Electrophorus*
>DD-31 *Grouper*
>DD-32 *Tarpon*
>DD-33 *Ballarat* (Sarah Burke)
>DD-34 *Shingen* ("The Fence", in Hausa) (Dangali Abubakar)
>DD-35 *Inazuma* (Lightning) (Soichiro Kusanagi)
>DD-36 *Diamond*

DesRon Four:
>DD-37 *Sealion*
>DD-38 *Highlander* (Commodore Iain Colin Mackenzie)
>DD-39 *Sawfish*
>DD-40 *Wolverine* (John Logan)
>DD-41 *Basilosaur*
>DD-42 *Perth* (David Googan)
>DD-43 *Stuart*
>DD-44 *Arapaima* (Nang Tae-suk)—**Lost In Action**
>DD-45 *Livyatan* (Ruth Goldin)
>DD-46 *Megalodon*
>DD-47 *Mazikeen* (from Mazzikin, a type of minor demon in Jewish mythology)
>DD-48 *Viperfish*

Warlord class missile arsenal cruisers

CruRon One:
>CG-01 *Saladin*
>CG-02 *Temüjin*
>CG-03 *Shaka Zulu*
>CG-04 *Alexander*
>CG-05 *Hannibal*
>CG-06 *Takeda Shingen*
>CG-07 *Red Cloud*
>CG-08 *Sun Tzu*

CruRon Two:
>CG-09 *Musashi*
>CG-10 *Crazy Horse*

CG-11 *Khubilai*
CG-12 *Tomöe Gozen*
CG-13 *Scipio Africanus*
CG-14 *Boudicca*
CG-15 *Joan d'Arc*
CG-16 *Tughril Beg*

CruRon Three:
CG-17 *Cuchulainn*
CG-18 *Fionn mac Cumhaill*
CG-19 *Massoud*
CG-20 *Harald Bluetooth*
CG-21 *Hunahpu*
CG-22 *Xbalanque*
CG-23 *Hideyoshi*
CG-24 *Manaa Musa*

CruRon Four:
CG-25 *Geronimo*

Unique
GOU *There Exists An Elegant Solution*

Appendix 2: Quick Specifications of Fleet Main Ship Classes

* Stated performance is rated service limit at 100% G-compensation.

Endeavour class armed training corvette (3 ships constructed)

Length:	130m
Beam:	40m
Depth:	34m
Mass:	16,780 tonnes
Power:	1 × 30m antimatter reactor
Crew:	40 crew 15 bridge stations, 2 observer seats
Armament:	2 × spinal grasers 2 × SM-1 *Shrike* missile drum dispenser with 20 missiles each 6 × single 10cm railgun mounts with 500rd per gun 12 × 50cm plasma point defense mounts
Performance:	50 G forward acceleration 6.3 G lateral maneuvering

Shark class (Mod 2) destroyer (48 ships constructed)

Length:	322m
Beam:	60m
Depth:	60m
Mass:	146,600 tonnes
Power:	1 × 40m antimatter reactor 1 × 10m-class backup fusion bottle
Crew:	140 crew plus 50 Marines 27 stations on primary bridge plus two observer seats 27 stations in secondary CIC
Armament:	2 × hyper-boosted 50cm railguns with 200 rounds per gun

2× spinal grasers
6× SM-1 *Shrike* missile drum dispensers with 54 missiles
each, total 324 missiles
12× twin 20cm railgun mounts with 2000 rounds per gun
42× triple 50cm plasma point defense mounts

Performance: 76 G forward acceleration
15 G lateral maneuvering

Warlord class missile arsenal cruiser (25 ships completed)

Length: 454m

Beam: 90m

Depth: 50m

Mass: 258,200 tonnes

Power: 1× 40m antimatter reactor
1× 12m-class backup fusion bottle

Crew: 154 crew plus 50 Marines
32 stations on primary bridge plus 3 observer seats
32 stations in secondary CIC

Armament: 80× SM-2 *Gungnir* missile drum dispensers with 72 missiles
each, total 5760 missiles
34× twin 20cm railgun mounts with 2000 rounds per gun
76× triple 50cm plasma point defense mounts

Performance: 55 G forward acceleration
5 G lateral maneuvering

There Exists An Elegant Solution (unique at this time)

Length: 385m

Beam: 206m

Depth: 75m

Mass: 341,800 tonnes

Power:	3 × 40m antimatter reactor
	2 × 12m-class backup fusion bottles
Crew:	55 crew plus 50 Marines
	11 stations on primary bridge plus 3 observer seats
	9 stations in secondary CIC
Armament:	1 × gravity lance
	6 × grasers as per Shark class, in two groups of three
	6 × SM-2 *Gungnir* missile drum dispensers with 72 missiles each, total 432 missiles
	44 × twin 20cm railgun mounts with 3000 rounds per gun
	105 × triple 50cm plasma point defense mounts
Performance:	48 G forward acceleration
	6.7 G lateral maneuvering

MORE BOOKS FROM SEAN FENIAN

After you finish the *Stardock Trilogy*, try other books from Fenian House Publishing:

FIREBORN

The man who will become Alrekr Járnhandr is *done*. Weary, physically and emotionally broken, abused beyond the limits of what he can endure, he is ready to give up and die. But instead of dying, he finds himself drawn through a dark void to another world. Terribly injured, he is found and rescued by people among whom he will have a chance to build a new life.

His new world will be filled with wonders. It will be magical. It will finally give his life meaning. But it won't be easy, and he will come to discover that he has not entirely escaped all that he fled from. His past is not done with him yet... and neither is his future.

But in this life, he won't have to do it alone.

Sean Fenian's **Fireborn** is a transformational alternate-world fantasy novel featuring mystic arts loosely based on Finnish mythology, polyamorous relationships, and healing from emotional abuse. Have you ever heard of a smith who can mix advanced metal alloys *by ear*? In *Fireborn*, you will.

And yes... there are dragons.

PRAISE FOR *FIREBORN*:

"Delightfully imaginative"

"This book has a feel and cadence utterly unlike any others in this genre. [...] I have never read a 'transformational' novel with such a positive cast of characters and uplifting message."

"The author writes characters of depth out of his own depth, loves, and widely varied experience. A lovely tale and I devoutly wish he'll find a way to revisit this surprisingly special world and characters he's shared with us."

"A different type of book from Sean Fenian, and even better"

"Fascinating take on legends"

"My new favorite author"

"[Fireborn] will take you into a mythic world, and you will be saddened that it stands alone. I only wish there was more of this world myth."

AGENCY (WITH ROBERT AUERBACH)

Ciáran mac Cool is a *de-facto* operative for... he's not sure. He doesn't know where his orders come from, and he's in too deep to back out—even though at least one assignment almost got him killed. And yet, his assignments always seem to do some *good* in the world.

Then one day the Box tells him to reach a specific location, with no further explanation, giving him barely enough advance warning to get there.. Soon he will find himself working alongside a young law associate to unearth revelations that will shake the course of events in ways he never imagined.

PRAISE FOR *AGENCY*:

"A magnificent book."—*Wendy S. Delmater, Abyss & Apex Magazine*

"If you like the writings of Neal Stephenson, you'll like Agency."

"The plot is well constructed, the characters well-fleshed out, and what little action there is, is done well, and not forced, as some others have done."

"Well written and paced story that holds one's attention closely."

"Rarely have I enjoyed a book like I enjoyed this one! Thought provoking. Action packed. Very different from anything else I have read lately."

"One of the best woven stories I've read in years. And my years do include over a thousand books to compare with."

"You can tell that a great deal of research had to have been done and understood by the authors, because the breakneck pace of this data driven story would have quickly revealed sloppy research."

BECOMING REAL

Michael Hagerty—*GhostRayder*, to his fans—reviewed video games and made game videos for a living. He was intimately familiar with virtual worlds. They were his everyday bread and butter. He was quite certain he understood very clearly the lines of demarcation between game and reality, between what was physical, and what was virtual. What was real, and what was not.

Then one day, not long after he reviewed a newly released VR open-world adventure game, a mystery source sent him a modified version of the game, and asked him to go back in and try it again.

Michael would soon find out, amid a high-stakes game of hide-and-seek with shady multinational corporations and shadowy government agencies, that the question of real or virtual, human or not, was far more nuanced and less clear-cut than he had ever believed possible.

Sean Fenian's Becoming Real is an exploration of the natures of humanity and reality.

Or perhaps it's a commentary on some of the blind spots of video game design.

Or perhaps it's an SF postmodern love story with a twist.

Or perhaps, it's all of these things... and more.

PRAISE FOR *BECOMING REAL*:

"This edges out [Frank] Herbert's Dragon in the Sea as the best sci fi book I ever read. [...] You really must read this."

"It makes you think about some big social issues that are quickly becoming more relevant and may turn vital much sooner than you'd expect."

"Without question some of the best books I have read in years. I compare them to books by David Weber, John Ringo, and Nathan Lowell."

GODTHIEF

The Prophecy of Tendarrion—or at least, one likely reading thereof—said that the time was coming for the goddess Jirilis to die.

Jirilis, understandably, was rather unhappy about this. Her plans for the future did not involve dying yet. But, a prophecy is a prophecy.

Prophecies, however, are notoriously fickle about exactly what precise interpretation of them turns out in the end to be correct. The possibly existed of finding an exploitable loophole. But Jirilis could not exploit it *herself*. That was, to greatly oversimplify the explanation, 'against the rules.' Prophecy and the powers of gods didn't work that way.

Jirilis needed a champion. Not one who could win battles for her, not one who could slay mighty enemies for her, not one who would spread her word or perform heroic deeds in her name.

No, Jirilis needed a champion who could *subvert a prophecy*. And she had an idea that she knew just who that might be. She had had her eye on him for some time, in fact.

Fortunately, he was already coming to *her*. Though he might need a little help.

That was alright. Jirilis had one of the most powerful incentives to help him that there could possibly be.

Sean Fenian's *Godthief* is a standalone fantasy novel set in an alternate world that might or might not be 'real'. It delves into the natures of gods and the mechanisms of prophecy, and what we really mean when we say the word 'Paladin', all against a background of the aftermath of a thousand-years-past, almost-world-shattering demon war.

PRAISE FOR *GODTHIEF*:

"Excellent and consistent world building. If you enjoy fantasy without the swords and magical combat, this is for you."

"Well paced, imaginative, exciting tale. Sean Fenian is a skilled world builder. I look forward to reading more adventures set here."

About Sean Fenian

Sean Fenian is a generalist and open-source evangelist, recently retired from several decades of working in the information technology sector. He is broadly knowledgeable in many subjects, with a long-standing informed layman's interest in physics and related science in particular. He has been an avid reader of SF and fantasy since his teens, and first became aware of, and began campaigning on, environmental issues in the late 1970s. He is proficient with weapons both ancient and modern, has trained in four different martial arts, and believes that understanding basic firearms safety is like knowing basic first aid, CPR, or how to use a fire extinguisher. He believes that it is a basic human duty and responsibility to treat all beings fairly and decently, and that the true measure of a person is how you treat others.

His past volunteer activities include educational historical re-enactment, marine mammal rescue, and handicapped riding therapy. He has been formally diagnosed on the autistic spectrum, but stubbornly persists in trying to understand people anyway.

He dreams many things. Occasionally, some of them become reality. But only occasionally.

Sean's books are read in fourteen countries, at last count. The *Stardock Trilogy* is also available as audiobooks on the Audible platform, narrated by Michael Karl Orenstein and published by Podium Entertainment.

www.ingramcontent.com/pod-product-compliance
Lightning Source LLC
Chambersburg PA
CBHW070911260626
47162CB00007B/2629